ANOTHER
FLESH

Also by Philip Callow and published by Allison & Busby

THE PAINTER'S CONFESSIONS
YOURS

ANOTHER FLESH

Philip Callow

Allison & Busby
Published by W. H. Allen & Co. Plc

An Allison & Busby Book
Published in 1989 by
W.H. Allen & Co. Plc
Sekforde House
175/9 St John St
London EC1V 4LL

This omnibus edition first published 1989

GOING TO THE MOON copyright © 1968 Philip Callow
THE BLISS BODY copyright © 1969 Philip Callow
FLESH OF MORNING copyright © 1971 Philip Callow

Printed and bound in Great Britain by
Courier International Ltd, Tiptree, Essex

ISBN 085031 915 3 (Hardback edition)
ISBN 0 74900 005 8 (Paperback edition)

Going to the Moon

We are going to the moon . . .
                          ANAIS NIN

THAT'S life : we must get going. Can't wait. Century on century, pressing out of the mothers. Sex is a necessary crime.

Before I left school my mother gave me a piece of paper with the 'facts of life' scribbled on, and told me to read it out in the lavatory and then flush it away, quick. Mystified, slightly sick in advance, I went into the backyard, shut myself in the reading room and read the scrap of paper. It said something like—'The man puts his thing into the woman's thing, and makes babies.' Immediately I felt dirty, contaminated by this horrible shithouse secret. I dropped the paper hastily, watched it flutter into the pan and float. I dragged on the chain in a panic, came out and didn't go back in the house. I burned with shame at the thought of facing my mother, burned with her shame as well as my own.

Not long after this the war started. I was nearly fifteen, in four months I'd be at work. With my brother, younger than me, I was evacuated to some indifferent relatives who had a caravan in the country. Being sensitive kids we knew we weren't wanted, which made our homesickness worse. Before on holidays it had been a marvellous spot, the river down below your feet, at the end of the day the fields and thistles and flickering rabbits all still, and you swam and floated in the strange evening peace, wanting to stand still, wanting to whisper. Now I hated it all, lying in the bunk in the mornings listening to Tommy Handley on the battery radio up on the shelf, waiting to be called, and told, while they made the breakfast. We howled to come home as soon as our mother visited us. Alan had put his legs into a sleeping bag and it was full of dead wasps. He was stung all over. So an uncle came, Geoff the factory worker, he worked in a car factory and he took us back in his car to the factory town we were suddenly passionate to see again, which was in a hollow anyway and the Germans wouldn't find it.

They found it and they found my father: nearly dropping a land mine on him. He was a warden, the ARP post was at the corner of Ernaldlhay Street, in St Stephen's School. I used to go and play table tennis with him in the very classroom I'd known as a schoolboy. It was a weird sensation, standing on the old uneven boards and trying to visualise how it had been—and then trying to stop it coming back, trying not to remember: this was all wrong, a joke, it had to mean more than this, surely? I stared round at the shrunken room, flaking cream distemper on the walls, the map of the world spattered with red bits, the iron stove that used to be the very core of the room, the heart of my life, it glowed, it burned, it was alive, a mess of coke dust around the base inside the wire cage—and look at it now, dead as a drainpipe, shorn of beauty. An electric fire plugged in by the side of it, where the scuttle of coke used to be. I kept struggling in spite of myself to recreate everything. The desks had all been cleared out, men in rubber boots and greatcoats sat round drinking tea, playing cards, smoking fags—nothing was left of my world. This was like a dream, I walked in and out of it, played ping pong against my Dad who was different, bluff and slightly impersonal among the others, who danced about youthfully, all arms and legs at the other end of the table shouting 'Wake up, dreamy! You've got a hole in yer bat, son!' I was dreamy because it was a dream: one day I'd wake up.

Then the land mine floated down, while I was in the shelter with my mother, brother, and two or three people from across the street. The floor moved, and the bunks, as if we were riding a wave that bulged through the ground and went on and on until there was no more earth. Someone started to whimper, then a tinkle of water in the dark. One of the girls from over the street was pissing in our enamel pot.

Afterwards my mother went looking for my father, found the school smashed and asked a policeman. 'If he's diseased'—meaning deceased—'he'll be at London Road'. This was a joke we repeated grimly for a long time after, when things were in one piece again. It was a kind of shorthand, perfect for getting across to people at one stroke how horrible and daft and *the same* things were during the bombing. As a joke though it was lousy—you had to explain what was meant. Nobody got it the first time.

When we found the right hospital and got in to see my father, he'd been cleaned up. Still it scared me stiff, seeing him there with his head smothered in bandages, his face naked and helpless without glasses, his voice quavery as the thread of life. I wanted to sob, I wanted to leave. I stood and stared. The school wall had collapsed on him, buried him, filled his mouth with rubble and smashed his false teeth. The dirt blinded him. His jaw was splintered and fractured, nothing else. Only it was. The old life was smashed to bits that night, and for good. Fatherless, we shifted to Lillington and lived there throughout the war. After several months at a special hospital at Bromsgrove my father joined us again—we had some rooms in a basement—and the night of the blitz came. Next morning I was pedalling hard to work as usual and got turned back at a roadblock. The centre was a shambles, fires still blazed, the whole shopping district had been gutted, they were still digging out the bodies. Nothing of this affected me, except vaguely as an excitement. Funny thing this is: it was my home town and yet the raid had missed me and I couldn't feel it. The final, terrible thing had happened already, now I was broken away; I belonged somewhere else.

And that was what they were telling me at the roadblock. Go back—and I thought I heard the word corpses. I'd never seen a corpse in my life. I showed my identity card. 'You can't come through here this morning, nobody can,' the man said, important with it. I didn't need telling twice: wheeled round, the tyres sang hooray, long live the blitz, my legs pushed harder than ever, and willingly. Going in the opposite direction I opened my eyes and marvelled, and saw what a wonderful road it was. Freedom—the same road, only in the opposite direction. What beauty it had now, how it invited, opened, led on. The same road: I couldn't get over that.

Those war years, all that period in the basement, shuttling across the fields through the lands and old hamlets to the brand-new factory on Hammer Lane, opposite Ferguson's, acres of that, with Geoff in there somewhere—to and fro between factory and basement, then the daylight on Saturday, half day, falling asleep in broad daylight on the bus going home, tired out. Yet when I think of it now it was a sort of trance-like waiting time, snug really. The sirens wailing before six at night and the guns around the city letting off crumps sometimes before I'd even got over the bridge across the river and up Warmeleigh Hill alongside the park, pushing my bike and with my back to it all, never looking back. Too scared. But snug because I was on the way home, I knew where I belonged, I had no girls, no personal problems. Getting the taste for solitude early, my beam slicing the night in front of my wheel as the search-lights sliced at sky behind me, over the city: turning the bike into a companion, listening to noises of complaints, tell-tale rattles, liking it for carrying me, wanting to coax it like an animal.

Later on, when the raids got worse, you could see long queues at the bus station every night waiting for the Midland Red to take them out of it. There was talk of the anti-aircraft guns running out of shells, fighters clustered around London and Buckingham Palace and none left for the Midlands, none in the air over the provinces—there was a lot of dull bitterness and the queues were growing. They carried bundles of blankets like refugees, plenty of them: the story goes that they knocked on doors up and down Lillington and the sods wouldn't let them stay. I don't know, I was in a trance, I kept pedalling.

Towards the end of the war I was more restive, finding out things from books in queer accidents, with nobody to guide, advise or warn me. In the warm months I wandered in the fields and felt how lonely the summer was, and sat down by spinneys reading a soft warm weepy writer, Saroyan, for the first time, weeping inside like him and choking back love for every damn thing. It was a funny time. I got to know an apprentice in the factory, Barry Joy, an excitable, pop-eyed, superior lad, excited by the idea of young Ustinov in his white shirt, audacious as Orson Welles, and Barry talked very fast and rolled his eyes, watching for the

foreman and keeping his machine working as he poured
out this heady stuff about plays he was trying to write—
plays!—and, very polite, would I have a glance at this
article on Ustinov he'd ripped from a *Picture Post*. He kept
harking back to his own efforts, modelled on those of his
idol Ibsen, and to the symbolism of those great plays—
'great, Colin!'—with his tongue feverishly licking, the sly
smile of conceit and ambition twitching up his lips. Then
the foreman sails round the corner. 'Here the bastard
comes—see you later.'

I was pure, in a trance. I never even masturbated. Once
I was wandering up and down longingly outside a cinema
and a G.I. took me in, paid for me and even bought me
chocolate. Nothing else. All I said to him was 'Thank you'
and 'Cheerio'. That was to see Danny Kaye's first film *Up
In Arms*. Another time I queued up in a Lillington side
street to get into a fleapit where they were showing a forbidden picture—I think Japanese. Remember nothing of it
now, no details whatsoever, only the sensation of mystery,
languor, filtered light, bamboo screens. Secrecy. More
trance, drugging me. And now I was making the first
feeble efforts to wake up, break out. I stood forlornly on a
street corner one vacant Saturday afternoon, longing for
something to happen to me.

Nearly every night I sat in the front bedroom of
that basement working at a correspondence course for
A.M.I.Mech.E. 'Success or No Fee' and 'Let Me Be
Your Father' the advert had said. I slaved at it for a
whole year, held my head and fought it, the solitary hero
again, then abruptly threw in my hand and changed to a
writers' school. I lasted four lessons, until my tutor told me
I couldn't repeat myself in the same sentence, there was
a rule. And other rules, about beginnings, middles and ends
—rules for this and that. Good-bye, good-bye. Back with
Saroyan in the grass, crying inside. Then in pure contrast
to this I had a sudden burning passion for a motorbike. I
belonged to a firewatching party, and I remember sitting
up in a room at the top of the building where we lived,
aching in every bone, nauseous, it was three in the morning
and I was on duty: reading a textbook on the two-stroke

motorbike, studying details of carburettor, plugs, the simple fundamentals. My father took me one Sunday to see a Velocette; fifteen pounds the man wanted. He wheeled it out of the shed, gave it a kick and the machine burst into life, deafening. I knew then I didn't like the reality at all, only the *idea* of a motorbike. The reality scared me. But it was too late now and anyway how could I explain it? Try it, have a run, the man was saying. I climbed on behind him, hugging the pillion with my legs to avoid having to clutch his mac too tightly; we went blasting through the streets in great style. I detested the fuss it made, the attention I felt sure we were getting. Then it was my father's turn for a trial run, squatting on the pillion rather than sitting because of his long legs. Off he went on the back, strangely wild-eyed, hair blowing, knees stuck out and the ends of his mac flapping. He came back excited, like a boy. I was the boy and I just stood there. What a fool. We hung about, hesitating, my father pretending to examine this and that, twitching at the sides of his trousers—I knew it took a long time for him to make a decision, these were the signs of him kneading one, forming words, but the man took it differently. ' Go on then, twelve quid—how about that?' We paid up and wheeled it away. The idea of having it, the practical side, fell through because when we enquired I was too young to be insured. So to make use of it as transport I rode pillion, my father taking me in each morning, dropping me off and then doubling back to reach his place. Long before it was time for me to take out a provisional licence and learn, I'd managed to drop hints about my lack of interest in motorbikes now. In the end somebody bought the Velocette for eight pounds.

I had a month off work with cardiac debility, exhausted by twenty-mile-a-day bike rides, and I lay in bed studying the stains and flaking plaster round the meter boxes, letting my mother dote on me. I read *Oliver Twist* in bed, I remember. Hot warm juicy tears rolled out, real ones. The doctor who examined me was a woman, Miss Laverty. She did her stuff with the stethoscope, then sent me out of the room while she talked to my mother. I liked her, she was human, not a bit like doctors I could remember as a child, who stormed in like whirlwinds without knocking, barking 'Good morning' if you were lucky—and you were expected to leave the door off the catch for them. Hell, you could no more think of them standing there on the doorstep banging than you could God Almighty. And, naturally, they were always late. The tension would be terrific; it was like expecting royalty. My mother wasn't cowed or overawed, even then, but she was clenched tight in readiness—the strain showed on her face. It wasn't difficult though to imagine the effect on some poor devils with less independence. Christ knows what we had to be independent about, we were poor enough. Yet we were, we all had a touch of it, all thought something of ourselves—it was in the family, a trait running right through. Those were the days of the 'Panel' and the 'Box', words you didn't need to understand or be told about, they were dinned into you while you were in the pram near enough. And clubs for this and that, Foresters, Hearts of Oak, Oddfellows, friendly societies, tiny insurances. Clubs were your only real safeguard. My grandfather belonged to about six, for sickness, death, old age, Christmas, holidays . . . there was no end to it. But doctors . . . the first one I remember was Dr Lamb. I didn't find him autocratic, I pitied him, even at that age. His huge balding forehead used to wrinkle convulsively all of a sudden, and the whole of his scalp jerked helplessly, while his eyes screwed tight. It was shell-shock, according to my mother. Of course, I was fascinated to see it, this mixed in naturally at my age with the pity. You used to wait for the next seizure, impatient for it to happen. His great ugly hole of a waiting-room, that was a place, gloomy as a free clinic. It echoed with feet and nervous coughs. When you tip-toed in you had to whisper up and down the rows of hard chairs furtively, 'Who am I next to, please?' My mother took me to Dr Lamb one day for him to look at my cock, to see if it needed circumcising or not. He pulled at it, let it lie in the palm of his hand, dragged the skin back fastidiously, gave me a brief radiant smile I've never forgotten and then he twitched, the foul wince convulsed his face and buckled the skin of his skull again. He still had hold of me. I felt terribly sorry for him.

I imagined his head bursting, ticking with too much brain.

'What d'you think, Doctor?' my mother was asking, red in the face with anxiety.

There was some discussion, more convulsions, but no, he didn't think it was necessary.

Out we came into the ugly street. Round the corner was a pill factory, stinking of chemicals, steam wafting out of the top windows. Courtaulds was another permanent stink, right across the other side of the town at Molesdale, towards the gasworks. If the wind was in your direction you caught the blended whiff of it, anywhere in the town.

When Dr Laverty called me back in, she strode up to me on her short thick legs and told me I had nothing to worry about (I wasn't worried because I was too young, and never stopped to think about funerals, death, heart failure applying to me), if I didn't do anything silly like running cross country races or swimming the Channel I'd live to a ripe old age. It was a matter of simple common sense. After all, she wouldn't dream of entering a beauty contest —'See what I mean?'—and with me on one side of her and my mother the other she put her arms round us, roughly, like a man. She was Irish, my mother said afterwards, as if that explained something.

2

IN paradise I was, if I'd only realised it, being at home and not sick, no pain, nothing the matter with me except that I was supposed to rest and eat butter and eggs and drink milk, build myself up. You must rest, my mother kept saying, and I sighed and muttered all right, as if it was something that went against the grain but I'd have a try. I was vaguely guilty, which added to the pleasure, and in a dim blurry way I knew I was in paradise, but I didn't seize it or say to myself how good if it only lasts. Very quickly I learned how to be slothful, how to take things easy. It was easy! Life was simple, no problems, not a worry in sight, and never, before or since, have I got on so well with my mother, never been so yielding, tender, so ready to agree, so eager to make her happy. Those lovely tranquil spells in the afternoons of a mellow September, still, smoky weather, leaves falling easily and rustling, keeping the peace, what did we do with ourselves except read, and wander out for walks down to the river, through the park, or go to the pictures and see something like *Mrs Miniver*. One afternoon I painted the shutters with cream paint in the living-room—indoor shutters they were, and it was cream she wanted, not white—while she sat reading her library book, and it would be a title so typical of her, so characteristic, say *One Pair of Hands* or *My Turn to Make the Tea*. Or we would go out shopping, me carrying the basket and walking on the outside in a proper manner. As we walked we passed comments, gossiped, made little jokes, and I saw how my mother glowed like the leaves, how vivid she was when she was happy, how alike we were in so many small ways. Truly we were in accord. All we needed was time, with the pressure blissfully off. It was good and it was beautiful while it lasted.

A year or so later I was off again, but only for a few days—the machine oil had given me a rash on the hands and arms. Instead of winning me some time, it got me transferred to another job, that's all. For some reason I can't remember we had changed doctors, perhaps because the new one was nearer to where we lived. So I sat in the tomb-like silence of this strange waiting-room one evening with dermatitis fingers itching, vile, bandaged—then up three stairs and in to his room when it came to my turn. A great difference, a revelation. A big expanse of thick carpet and then the huge desk across one dimmed corner, the table lamp softly shedding gold light, plummy velvet curtains to the left covering the french windows, brushing the floor. Nothing humane and jolly like Dr Laverty; this was different altogether. But very impressive. I had a feeling of grand proportions, authority, dignity, absolute calm and complete mastery over all our woes. And I'd brought my itchy fingers! The doctor was foreign, a sharp kindly man who preferred I think to maintain a professional distance between him and his patients. That was what the desk was there for. Strangely enough, I didn't resent it, and I liked him. I liked him very much. He had an instinctive grasp of character I felt, as his eyes watched me, as he examined me. I felt taken into account as a human being, and that's rare.

One day at the factory the sirens sang out in broad daylight, before dinner-time. Men straightened up from their machines, looking puzzled. Then the machines cut dead, over our heads the shafts stopped twirling, the belts slowed, flapped and hung quiet, there was the moment of portentous silence this killing of the power always created, and suddenly everybody was running like mad, crouching against the blast wall built against the stores pen. They must have heard a plane; I didn't. There was a crash, over in a far corner of the main shop, glass dropping, somebody shouting ' All right, don't panic, he's gone now—walk out to the shelters.' This was a good distance, out through the yards past the cycle racks, the cyanide and sandblasting sheds, through the gates where the works police lived in their concrete pillbox stinking of tobacco, sweat, bad breath, with the slits for windows, and across to a brick surface shelter in a bit of waste ground. We trooped out in the wintry light, staring round like convicts being taken for exercise, blinking up at the sky.

' There the bugger is!' a bloke yelled. We bent double and ran the last few yards, diving for the shelter doorway. I heard some ragged machine-gun fire, *tock-tock*, *tock-tock*, from the Home Guard on the top of Ferguson's roof—they'd let fly at a Whitley or a Wellington by mistake the week before, it was a great joke—out of the corner of my eye I saw it, lots of us did, circling slowly and banking, so casual; fascinated, I saw the black markings clearly as it made off. It seemed in no hurry. ' See the cheeky sod? See 'im?' everybody was saying, full of wonder and admiration.

3

SUBMERGED, it floats up, refracted. Faces, hundreds of faces, a buzzing hive of lives. Fragments, nothing permanent or ever likely to be, and you accepted it that way and lived it. What else was there? Nobody stopped to question, there was a ration even on questions. You kept dodging, living. War or no war, you hung on for the Saturdays and the holidays and the pension. Roll on the daylight.

Robust, ugly, close, describes the life around me as a kid and in youth, but my life in it fluttered like a candle, tremulous, delicate and supple in the draughts. The bomb blasts, incendiary raids, sirens shrieking, flames roaring— none of it toughened me. I seemed queerly immune. I stayed the same skinned rabbit. Funny thing was, the bombs didn't frighten me half as much as school did—the one I played truant from—where they got their hooks in you and made you tremble by looking at you in a certain way, even if they didn't do anything much. They had absolute power, that was what their look meant when they unmasked it, which they did, cruelly and cunningly and without any betraying words, for you and nobody else. And it followed you home, this dreaded blazing look of power, it waited for you at night, in dark corners of your bedroom, especially Sunday night lying in bed. You could feel them then, waiting, with that terrible power they had which you never hoped to explain, which nobody else suspected or would ever believe in. So you wept, hard and bitter into the pillow. You were lost. You knew there was no hope because that was what it meant, being lost. Perhaps by the time the Germans came, with that heavy pulsed engine sound we used to identify, lying under it in the Anderson, listening intently with our whole bodies— perhaps then I'd used up my terror. But I was born frightened. Pushing my bike out, climbing the cellar steps with it and getting on, feeling the balancing thinness of it under me in the dark, seven in the morning, earlier, pointing it at the city in the freezing fog I rode along in a quiver of fear and excitement. I was more alive than others because more afraid. Afraid of ice on the road, afraid of being late, afraid of shapes, noise, birds, cattle, vivid with fear and expectation. I chewed the rime of frost on the mouth-opening of my balaclava, made it warm and moist, listened for the knock in the bottom bearing as my pedals drove round, as the faulty dynamo hummed me along and the dark opened for me and swished shut again behind my saddlebag, friendly at the front and venomous in the rear, the hedges menacing and wet and fog-rotten, hanging over.

4

It was really a cellar, a dugout, our home during the war: once the servants' quarters to the big house up above which was now split into flats. In the buttressed passage was a board on the wall with a row of bells for calling whoever they needed—now disused, rusty, covered in a film of dirty cobwebs. The relatives nearby who had found us the place, they were snug and snotty as ever in a well-upholstered flat. How it must have been rubbed in to my mother, arriving there with a van-load of trashy, worn-out possessions, two boys and no husband—no wonder she looked round once in that draughty, damp hole in the ground and burst into tears. Up above—that was the thing!—in the next street, the rich relatives and their thick carpets, ivory paint, revolving bookcases, standard lamps, and—the thing that made a big impression on me—a row of gay tins on a shelf in the kitchen, labelled ' Sugar ', ' Coffee ', ' Flour ' and so on. All so gay and orderly and undisturbed, war or no war. They were up there so they had to look down. To be poor had been meaningless to me until then. I moved from house to house, street to street in the early days and it was the same element I swam in. No shame, no strain. Kids accept whatever they find anyhow—and we'd been on visits to these prosperous relatives at Lillington now and then, even slept in the richery once or twice, and I played with my cousins, two girls, holding them down on the bed, pinning their arms and feeling a strange excitement because they were girls, they smelled different, laughed different, and their father came in at night when we were having tea, immaculate at cuffs and collar, his suit a subtle shade of brown. He made his entrance rubbing his hands and chuckling in a peculiar way, as if he was telling a dirty joke to himself. His top lip fascinated me, it looked so sore around his Ronald Colman moustache, it was bright red on a white puffy face. He was a store manager with a flair for window dressing. The reps called in droves, especially around Christmas time, showered him with gifts and plied him with drinks. That was no doubt why his lip looked sore, he had a habit of sucking it after it had soaked well in the whisky. His firm, a big one with branches everywhere, sent him in a firm's car to conferences in London and the south. He was a big man, with bull-frog eyes trained on you coldly. He could deliver an opinion on any subject and sound authoritative, he could fix a car, an electrical gadget, a radio, he was organised and tuned in. A mixer, a man of the world. At home we called him Chief, he was such a big-head.

My mother burst into tears that first night in the cellar. I got it then in a flash, the bitter caste system, the up there and down here and half-ways, and Christ knows how many graduations in between. My mother felt the weight of it, I could see: I was terribly depressed. Yet what a cosy place she made of that hole, and when my Dad came out of hospital he was soon painting doors, walls, boarding over the great iron range the servants had cooked on for the upstairs people, getting a slow combustion stove installed—*The Otto*—and it was all different; transformed. No more inferiority. He just wasn't aware of it himself, he was too unworldly. So a clean feeling came in with him. When the bombers were going over in droves to Coventry they didn't feel too happy upstairs either, the flat owners and poodle fanciers, and on one occasion when the shit was falling a bit close—probably jettisoned by a stray plane— they were soon down banging on the door at the bottom of the area steps. My mother rushed to let them in. I'd have been hard of hearing for a while if it was me.

Coombe Park. I liked it very much, it was just the people. The whole town was like that, it had a reputation in the Midlands. We soon saw that it was the top end where we lived that was like it, not down the bottom past the theatre, under the arch and on the other side of the railway bridge. That was where the gasometer and coal yard and factories and working people had been shoved, in a stink of gas and glue. It was in two distinct halves, this

19

town, amazingly. Up at the top were wide streets planted with trees, chestnuts mostly. No rough kids, no parks: instead there were gardens and tennis courts, railed off, and a key for residents. I liked it though. It had a spacious feeling.

I began to buy a book now and then, getting them direct from publishers. Brand new—send me so-and-so. I wasn't doing anything with my money, no girls, drinks, records, and although it was a pittance, my apprentice pay, after I gave my mother some I still seemed to have plenty. Without knowing it hardly, in that same trance state, I was building up a little nucleus of a new world, different, dangerous, explosive, called a library. I bought Saroyan, Ethel Mannin, I bought Arturo Barea's trilogy—the lot in one go. That was exciting when the parcel came, the Faber label on the brown paper, and inside the cocoon, tightly pressed together, mint, the three books—*The Root*, *The Forge*, *The Track*. I think that was it. I can remember the smell of the new print better than the titles or the contents, the crisp paper, uncut pages ragged in the middle. It was wartime, the paper was terrible utility stuff, greyish lavatory paper. But it still looked good.

It could have been about this time that my parents started to worry about the way I was going, my isolation, solitary habits, avid reading and all that. Nothing was said, but one Saturday afternoon my father turned up with a friend, a workmate from his office, who brought his young daughter along, a girl of roughly my own age. She was shy, tall, a reader like me, and she wrote poems, apparently— wasn't that a coincidence! I could see she was a lonely bird and all she wanted was to stay that way; I think she realised too as soon as she set eyes on me that we were in the same boat. What did parents know about it? Blushing, she held out a collection of Chinese short stories she had brought along for me to borrow, that is if I'd like to borrow them. Sorry for her, I went to the bookshelf and got down the Ethel Mannin, *No More Mimosa*—could I lend her that? Yes, thank you ever so much. A murmur, scarcely moving her lips. So we sat there in frozen silence, such a farce, a fiasco, and waited to be left alone again, for them to all clear off and leave me alone, my father yapping happy and oblivious, my mother rattling cups and plates in the kitchen—my mother who loved her solitude as much as I did. She understood me through and through, I was certain of it, but she daren't approve, and it wasn't natural. But I knew damn well she was in there putting up with it, praying for the time to go, like I was. Another shy violet, another deep one.

At the factory I had mates among the apprentices, a few, but when I reached Lillington at nights and week-ends there was absolutely nobody. And it was the truth, mostly I liked it better on my own. The library, the Reference, a bookshop in the High Street, going to the pictures down by the river, or by the station, sitting in the dark wrapped in fantasies. Coming out was grisly, reality was always worse afterwards, drearier and more ugly because for that couple of hours you had really escaped, slipped the leash, as surely as if you'd been to an opium den. And like any other habit-forming drug it kept dragging you back in, magnetic. I felt remorse sometimes when I came out, grudging the waste of time, of life. It was beginning to grow in me, the necessity to do something, make something, use my life. Still I couldn't break the habit, it had started far too early, when I was eight or nine and the Prince of Wales was at the bottom of our street, Ernaldlhay Street, the gilt and plush fleapit where I went Saturday afternoons for the tuppenny rushes. Orange peel and silver paper flicking through the magic beam, deafening cheers in the serial, the Yankee cavalry thundering to the rescue in a majesty of pennants and uniforms and flashing hooves.

Later on it would be other palaces, the Globe, Scala, Gaumont, Palladium, Crown, Astoria, Regent—there must have been a couple of dozen nearly and I visited each one in turn, ringing the changes, even coming out half-way through a programme and changing to another cinema if I was very restless or just couldn't stick it. And kept this up every week, year in and year out, two or three times a week, tramping out to trim suburbs, slum districts, factory areas, waste lands, winter and summer—a real addict. (One of the first stories I ever wrote was on the subject of

21

this pernicious habit—called 'Twice a Week or Three Times'.) An avalanche of films, comedy, drama, news—most of it trash, utterly forgotten now. The influence on me and kids like me at this tender, impressionable age must be incalculable. I had constantly changing heroes and heroines, and some steadfast ones, like Henry Fonda, who still cast a spell now, though not strongly enough to drag me inside. Some films, like *The Al Jolson Story*, I'd see again and again. If it had an idol in it then I'd go anywhere, whatever it was—the very thought of a Fonda, a Gary Cooper, their aura, would be enough to force me out there, sometimes dragging my feet. It was worship, I was worshipping, adoring; these tatty temples where I attended to my devotions and begrudged the time bitterly afterwards, they enslaved me more than factories and offices ever did, and I poured some of the best of myself out there, in the cosy dark smelling of Flit. All my ardent desires, rebellion, rejection, all the fervour of youth, need for Something, idealism, the longing to enshrine and dedicate, all the marvellous love I was aching to give somebody.

5

OFTEN I'd be lonelier with pals than on my own. It was being forced home slowly, slow and steady, and I knew it but wasn't ready to admit it yet, that I couldn't hit it off with anybody; though most people I found seemed to like me. But I would find out soon enough, it had to be special pals, and there weren't many.

I was in the middle of the war, had seen the red glow in the sky from Lillington, firewatching at the top of the building, heard the dull thunder of guns, bombs, mines and heard them say 'They've had it.' It was blitzed, obliterated, but I was still going there every weekday, working, and I came in along the big new highway that went cutting across the main road towards Alvington, bypassing the city; so there was no reason for me to go into the city centre. I never did, until after the war. The city was blitzed; that meant the centre mainly, all the shops gone. People were still living there in their thousands, the factory filled up with them just the same. What did they mean, blitzed? I seemed devoid of curiosity: no interest in the smoking ruins, rubble and slag of shops, the gutted Council House. I kept coming in along the raw swooping bypass that was like a landing strip, rudimentary; past the barrage balloon and the Pioneer Corps, the derelict farm next to the cardboard box factory, the Highwayman, up and down on the last lap with aching legs, over that sod of a hill over the canal, the hump of the bridge, then the spread of factories before me and I could lean back sighing luxuriously and freewheel, sailing to the bottom; then sharp left at the chip shop for the gates, the bike sheds.

Dinner-times I mooched around the side streets with a little knot of apprentices, killing time and digesting the canteen dinner, or we stayed on in the canteen pulling faces at the screeches of some luckless soprano in the ENSA concert, grinning and feeling embarrassed when the blokes lost patience and banged their plates on the table, yelling insults, or just turned their backs and played cards, refusing to clap the acts. The regimental bands were something else, they had a fierce blaze of noise and power and that dominated, compelled attention. They were smart, disciplined, uniformed, they went into action like machine parts, the bandmaster jerking them along inhumanly, working the controls. It was beautifully co-ordinated, a precision job, and it was fiery and martial, conquering the din and forcing respect. Everybody liked the excitement and glamour and the fact that it was depersonalised; nobody making any personal appeals, nobody making themselves look cheap and daft, soliciting for claps. This was professional so you didn't have to worry.

I went on holiday with four apprentices, just as if it was peacetime. Somebody had the idea of hiring a boat, a yacht, where you could live on board, sleep and cook your food without any interference from adults. It sounded great. So that summer we went off to Leicester, changed buses for Nottingham, then out to Radcliffe in a taxi, in grand style. I was the only one with any experience of sailing—one or two holidays on the Broads as a boy with

23

Geoff, my uncle—but the others were falling over themselves to have a bash, drag on the ropes, hold the tiller, shout Help; anything. In a few hours on the wide brown river, amazing, we'd got the hang of it roughly; enough to set sail immediately for Nottingham, winding about through the flat meadows, semi-industrial and derelict-looking as we drew nearer, navigating two locks and nearly crashing the top of the mast against an iron bridge we thought looked high enough to float under. I was at the tiller, asking Johnny and Bob if we were clear as we slid closer; ten yards, nine, eight, seven—then they saw it wouldn't clear, no go, we were at least a foot too tall. No brakes. Stop—turn it round! they were squealing, running for the long pole, while I pushed desperately on the tiller and watched us spin, inches from the bridge.

Before we reached Nottingham Johnny had managed to cut his arm on the glass globe of the butane lamp in the cabin—he was trying to change the charred mantle.

'How in Christ's name did you do it?' Bob kept asking.

'I keep telling you—the glass was cracking—a big crack down the side of the bastard thing! It came to bits in my hand, I tell you!'

'How did you cut your bleeding stupid arm, then?'

'Oh Christ, listen to him. I done it, that's all I know— I done it!'

He looked so white-faced as we moored up at the concrete steps that we were scared: somebody ran off in a panic and called an ambulance while Johnny sat on the pavement outside a tobacconist's, feeling groggy. The woman inside brought out a little hard chair and got him on that. Soon the ambulance rushed up and we were all sitting in it, clanging through the streets of this unknown city. At the hospital Johnny was fine again, laughing round, but they made him go in and have the gash washed and dressed. Then we sauntered back all free and curious through the streets in the vague direction of the river, plenty of time, staring round and gaping at things. Our legs felt queer, from being several hours afloat. By the time we found the boat the feeling had worn off. I was sorry. I had felt unique like that, and it sent us into fits of laughter, the way we rolled and swayed like drunks. We did get drunk at a riverside village later, me for the first time. I drank five or six half-pints and lost control of my legs; I could think and see all right. We wandered back to the boat, testing each other on white lines, balancing on the edges of kerbs, and I seemed to be wading fatuously in the air, which was a thick substance. Lying in our bunks we kept roaring with laughter for no reason. I was happy, I felt at one with everybody.

Moored to the steps that first night at Bridgeford, near to where they played the tests, we decided to stay at Nottingham another night because the lads wanted to go to a dance at the Palais. I sat watching them getting ready; shoes being blacked and polished, Brylcreem rubbed in, combs flashing, clean shirts whipping out of the rucksacks like magic. Lou pranced around, enveloped in a snowy shirt that looked sizes too big for him until he folded back the cuffs, fastened them nattily with his chrome and mother-of-pearl links, slipped on his watch with the expanding chrome strap—all this before the crisp tails of his shirt disappeared into his pants. Tucking in his shirt he dug his hands down boisterously, right to the elbows, reaching under his crotch and grabbing the back flap. Then he buttoned up his flies and at the same time did a capering dance. Feeling the fresh shirt on his shoulders he crowed like a cock.

' Right, now then me cockers!'

He crouched like a boxer, leaned, punched the air, ducked, feinted. ' Where's the women!'

His black hair was flat on his head, slick with grease. It fitted him like a cap.

' Come on, come on,' Lou urged, on his toes now, punching.

' Ah belt up,' Johnny said from the mirror. He was studying a blackhead on his jaw and a fat pimple between his eyebrows that was festering. He touched the juicy yellow head of the pimple tenderly. ' You bastard,' he said softly, with respect.

' Who's ready then?' Eddie said, waiting to go, knocking

the dandruff off his shoulders for something to do. He had the middle button of his sports coat fastened and he looked a real dandy, his face sore and pink.

I wasn't going, I couldn't dance. The real reason was a crippling shyness and the fact that I was a late developer. Girls were a problem, another element entirely. I had no language I could talk to them in, it would be torment trying, so I kept right away. Instead I went to the pictures, to the Mechanics opposite Victoria Station. We'd arranged a taxi from there at eleven. When I came out there was still half an hour to wait before the lads turned up. It was dark, drizzling. To pass the time I headed up Mansfield Road in the warm rain, walking emptily in the strange dark into nowhere. I was nowhere, nothing. Clouds of a luxuriant loneliness drifting through me. Went past shops, alleys. Chemist on a corner. Church. Big hoarding at a junction. Avenue of trees and grass and a path up the middle, cutting through to the left, rising up a slope and going on, this swathe of green disappearing into the distance. Fantastic—seen nothing like it in the centre of a city. Went past, suddenly it was eerie. I was nowhere, nothing. I didn't belong here, I had nothing to do with these buildings, no connection with any of it. I stopped at another junction, peering this way and that. Where now? Straight on, that was safest. Felt lost already. So this was Nottingham. I would meet people here, vital things would happen, but I wasn't to know that. Peering up Mansfield Road I couldn't see anything; the street lights made a hole and the street went on and on, enormous, tunnelling northwards into nothing. I swung back and walked quickly downhill again to the pick-up place. Traffic, people had an air of menace, it was like being stranded on another planet. I saw the clock lit up on the station tower, still a long way off. Bleak, I made for that.

They turned up with a girl; she was having a lift in the taxi as far as the Bridges. Flushed with triumph, they were. I was glad to see them. We piled in the back, jammed tight, the driver saying something in his broad Nottingham. We bashed through the town, skirting the empty square; shooting down the narrow streets made the speed seem hectic. I was lost again. The girl was giggling, pressed up against me, hip bones grinding together. 'Hello, hand-some,' she cooed, and she put her hand to my chin and stroked it, to feel the bristles. I hadn't started to shave, I was eighteen. 'Rough,' the girl said softly. I was struck dumb. No girl had ever touched me before. I smiled like a loony, smiled and smiled, blissful and foolish, smiling. I was in a tumult.

6

THE summer holidays. Still innocent, but the days of real innocence are over now, the camps by the river with the family, my mother and father, brother, sometimes the old man as well. My mother's father, a short, dark, deaf, smouldery man, a cinder of a man : a labourer, a diabetic. The Old Sweat, they called him; it didn't matter, he was deaf. He worked at any kind of labou ing job, over acid vats in a plating shop, as a dustman, an ice-cream seller, Stop Me and Buy One. Ringing his bell, he swung round the corner, slow and steady, his short legs going at it, push-ing his burden fixed in front, that heavy white box. Push-ing and pushing for dear life, uphill and against head winds, when he would be forced to dismount and nearly crouch, get his shoulder to it. Pushing, pushing, as if he was building the Pyramids. On commission. He stopped at the end of our entry, we'd rush out and grab his offerings, frozen fruits. On he went slower than ever in his funny get-up, peaked cap and white coat, struggling to get it moving, overcome the inertia. He hitched about on the saddle like a boy to keep his feet on the pedals.

Sometimes he came with us on holidays. Usually though, at camps, it was just the four of us. Orford, and Strat-ford, and once to the Isle of Man. Orford was the one shining idyllic place. The whole area is effulgent now like a Blake engraving, the village, the road, the bridge, the ford, the baker's shop, the meadows and oaks and chest-nuts, willows, the river with its weeds, currents, shallows, pebbles, rapids, rushes, mud, minnows. Even the haulage depot just outside the village on the way to the ford, where the heavy lorries were parked, and cattle trucks. And the farmyard and dairy, the lovely country stink, carts and animals and gateposts sunk in stillness those hot drowsing summer afternoons, when a creaking peace descended and you walked scuffing your feet, in old canvas plimsolls, feeling wholesome and in paradise as only a town boy can. Orford was the one absolute paradise place. Others had fragments, there it was complete, a world. Once we stopped going there it was lost, it never came again. Stratford we had to share with hundreds, it was a bit like the banks of the Ganges. Half the Black Country seemed to pack in there. Still it was fine, lovely. The idyll even came back in snatches there, early in the morning with the mist lifting on the brown water, when you smelled the bacon and heard it sizzle, heard them pump at the primuses. ' This is the life!' my father would say, wolfing his breakfast in the open air, his eyes gleaming, head turning as he scanned the multitude. An army of peaceful townies, more than half Brummies, under canvas : all shapes and sizes of tents, some elaborate constructions with flysheets and porches—with just enough space between each to stretch the guy ropes. They were all stirring, up making breakfast, on the way to fetch water, milk, to the camp store, some arriving in old limping cars loaded with equipment, springs groaning as they edged round in search of a space. It was a temporary township, and it had an itinerant, circus atmosphere I liked. It was organised in a loose, free-and-easy way, there was a camp shop, brick lavatories, you could hire a float and paddle up the river as far as you wanted, dragging it through the shallows. It was good, but not the same. Orford was real country, empty flat fields and nobody there but us. Paradisal. You were aware of insects, birds, particles of dust, fissures in the ground. A goat, that came up and ate anything, wisp of beard and crafty yellow eyes like a farmer. We made a mascot of him, half frightened at first, sat on his back and clung to his curved horns. He stood there, submissive as a donkey. Only at twilight he went mad when the devil seemed to get into him. He caught my father fishing down at the river bank, and once he lowered his head like a bull and came belting after my mother as she crossed the farmyard coming back from the shops. She yelled for help and ran for it—I forget how it ended. The farmer was friendly, always stopping to pass the time of day, and his 'Windy betimes' joined the stock phrases of our household. Back home we repeated it as a joke, but it was more than that. Talismanic. Whenever we said it, in our attempt at a country accent, we were back there. For a short time. The life of the street blunted it soon enough. The welter of days and the racket drowned it. School hammered it into the ground.

7

OTHER holidays are obscure, the details foggy, the journey mysterious. It was nearly always camping, the only holiday we could afford in those days, but once it was to a Co-op camp outside Rhyl, in a big wooden hut that got roasting hot, in a flat dusty field, flat as a billiard table at the edge of the sand. The place was a sort of primitive Butlin's—no amusements. If there was any organisation I was too young to remember. The heat I remember—everything got burning hot. Sand, field, hut. The camp was a cluster of chalets in a wide square, open at one side. You went out through the opening in the grass bank and carried back your water from the standpipe by the fence, sometimes queuing for it. Queuing happily, smiling and chatting and letting another take your turn if they were in a hurry, because it didn't matter, you were benign and your whole personality changed when you were on holiday.

My father's back was burnt badly before we had been there a couple of days; my mother oiled it, dabbing the blistered skin, but it was too late, I heard him tossing and groaning in the middle of the night. Before that happened, he waded into the sea with my brother on his back. The sea glistened, almost oily with heat, swelled and pulled gently, creamed and frothed around your toes. It was white sand, a tropical holiday. My brother screamed, being carried into the water, screamed so loud it reached my mother sitting far back on the beach, but my father plodded on just the same, until my mother screamed as well.

'Don't be a fool,' she kept saying to him afterwards. 'He's only four, couldn't you *see* he was frightened?'

'How could I,' shouting, 'he was on me back!'

'Hear then—couldn't you hear him? Were you deaf or what?'

'And daft,' he said bitterly.

'Well then, don't be so stupid.'

'It wasn't hurting him,' Dad muttered. 'I had him, he wasn't even wet.'

'Don't do it again, don't do it!' my mother yelled, red with heat, exasperation, worries.

She was a prime worrier, like her own mother, who died in her fifties, cancer of the throat, before I could have any memories of her. There was a story about her I kept hearing, of when she was at Rhyl herself once for a holiday with her husband—with the family. Getting off the coach and making wearily for the boarding house, she saw a banknote on the ground and picked it up: a fiver. A terrible, terrifying discovery, because it haunted her, she carried it around in her purse for several days, afraid of her very shadow. They were poor. Five pounds in those days was a small fortune, must have been. Should she give it up? Should they keep it? God knows, they could do with it. The misery of this crisis of conscience, this conflict between need and what was right and proper, it ruined their holiday, even after she'd gone to the police station and handed it over. She was a decent woman, she went to All Souls Church, she'd worried endlessly all her life. Imagine the predicament. My mother often repeated this pitiful tale, trotting it out grimly with obvious fondness. It illustrated for her with simple force the terrible fact of Money, the need for it, the lack of it, how it could dominate and destroy. And there was no need for an example, she was a living one herself. A beautiful text-book illustration. Apt. Look no further. Not my father, her. My father had the far-off looks, he dreamed up one scheme after another in his early manhood, while the spirit was still strong and defiant in him. His whole character veered towards independence, something a little different. He wanted to take the initiative, invent, start a business. But he had no ruthlessness or egocentricity, he was astonishingly naïve about the world, and trusting, when it came to people. He had no insight into character whatsoever. And there was my mother, acutely aware of dangers, of snares and snags and pitfalls, rats and twisters, a worrier, a dogged fighter when it came to a roof over our heads and food in our mouths; otherwise she went in fear and trembling of any straying from the known path. My mother with her bitterly apt and crushing examples. So the dreamer stayed buried in my father. It gave him a boyishness, a childlike quality.

There was also another side to him, or, now I know myself better I'm inclined to think it another symptom of his thwarted, baffled state: a growing irritability. As a father he could be stern, severe, but for a long time I had sensed the cause of it and took no notice. He was wiry, thin, with a caved-in chest, ribs showing, deep salt-cellars, but bigboned. Tall, well over six feet—when he came out of the Tanks after the war he nearly joined the Special Police with his army pal Jim Brennan—nearly went to Ireland with the Black and Tans. It's just as well he didn't, he'd soon have been in trouble there—his instincts kept him out of it. But irritable—bursts of wild, violent irritability as long as I can remember. Later, in my teens, I kicked and rebelled and he came to control it. But it was always there. Sitting at the table having a meal, one hand dangling in your lap, suddenly he'd lash out savagely with his foot under the table. 'Both hands!' he'd yell, eyes popping. The shock of it used to unnerve me, then I'd sit there hating him, nearly shaking with hate. I'd vow this and that, store it up with venom, one more injustice to be brought to account, but it was soon forgotten. How could I keep it going, when he had clearly forgotten it in a matter of seconds? It was how he'd been treated as a kid himself, most likely. This wasn't punishment or cold discipline, it was a hot flash of unpredictable rage. If he did dish out punishment he had to be goaded—I might be talking upstairs in bed with my brother, or having mad fits of giggles.

'Go to sleep—this is the last time! Hear me?' he'd roar. 'Yes,' we chorused, heard the stairs door crash for the fifth, sixth time; and although we knew the dangers it was irresistibly hilarious, singing out in harmony like that and then the door, the howl of rage, the crash. Five minutes later we were at it again, couldn't stop. All at once a thunderbolt up the stairs, the bedroom door flung open and Dad towering there, a slipper in one hand. He burst in on us in dead silence, pure retribution, too awful to gaze upon. Paralysed, we writhed in terror under his great bony hand as the arm with the slipper rose and fell, merciless. ' John, that's enough, stop it, oh God,' my mother screamed up the stairs. She had lost control at last, it was a force of vengeance now up there, so she played her last desperate card —hysterics. Much later, as we sobbed and recovered, each one hearing the other bitterly crying, the noise of it changing gradually to a gulping, convulsive sob that had lost its meaning—it had gone on so long it was an end in itself— my mother would creep up the stairs with a bit of supper and a glass of milk. More ghastly even than these disasters was one time when she tried to stop him getting up the stairs to us. Barring his way, that was an awful mistake. I heard them struggling, banging against the boards, my mother sobbing ' Don't ' and ' You're hurting me ' and his ugly, unrecognisable voice yelling ' Gerrout—gerrout '. My mother won though, I could hear her crying brokenly ' Oh God ' and it was worse than if she'd let him come up and give us the slipper. I never once saw them come to blows, but in that scuffle at the bottom of the stairs he dragged her by the hair apparently in his struggle to get at us. Did my mother tell me that detail herself? I can't remember. How else would I know a thing like that?

As the oldest in his brood—three brothers and a sister— he had that firm, decisive, responsible air about him whenever they were gathered together, say at Christmas reunions, or if one of them called at the house, or was with us on some trip or other. Uncle Mike, Uncle Geoff, Auntie Caroline, John (Jack as he was called at work, and by his pal Jim Brennan)—all dreamy types in a way, but all very different. Of the three brothers I liked Geoff the best—

though this isn't fair, I can't separate my old man from his strict-father, slipper-wielding, ankle-kicking moods, and he could be so different, holding us at arm's length with his long arm, huge hand splayed out on our chest while we swung impotently at him in mock fights. Taking us fishing. Bike rides. But he was so distant most of the time, abstracted, silent behind the paper, or dropping off to sleep, tired out. A presence only. And this tendency increased, he grew shadowy with age.

Uncle Mike I admired—not that we saw a lot of him. Bright and breezy, sharp humorous eyes, buck teeth which increased his attractiveness for me—his mouth always seemed to be splitting in a grin. Shock of curly black hair brushed straight back. He'd bang on the front door with such a characteristic jaunty knock you'd know without opening it who it was—'It's our Mike'—and my mother would bustle through the house wiping her hands on her apron, muttering 'What does he want?' or 'Why doesn't he go round the back like everybody else?' or something equally complimentary. She muttered and moaned about him, his very name spelled selfishness to her, his knock meant 'I'm after something', so she resented him on sight. But for all that she was no match for him face to face; he was too breezy, confident, too sure of his charms. 'Hallo Nell!' he'd twinkle, grinning shrewdly yet frankly—it was his frank egotism that got you—and before long she'd be offering a cup of tea. 'If there is one Nell' he'd say, and the flash of charm, the wink, but not really listening, talking to John about something, the object of his visit—some tool he wanted to borrow. Of course my mother was right again, he never made social calls, his visits had an object, he was on the scrounge. She would rush in and out—'I'm busy, you'll have to excuse me'—hot in the face with trying to register her resentment. I didn't care, I liked him. 'How's life?' he'd ask me, or Alan, dragging off those massive gauntlets like funnels, leaving his cycle clips on because he wasn't staying, and if it was winter his thin vigorous body would be bundled in a thick tweed overcoat with a belt, the collar a bit yellowish. He had a green van, a three-wheeler without doors, and instead of a steering wheel the handlebars and controls of a motorbike. In this he delivered his fruit and vegetables—he was in business out at Ashmoor in a harum-scarum sort of fashion—and once I went the rounds with him. Not helping, I must have been too young; just sitting there. The way he leapt out like a spring at each call and went bounding up to the house, round to the back of the van dragging boxes about, thumping back into the cockpit and spluttering off down the road again—I remember the hectic quality, nothing much else. And the antiquated motor horn, the way he squeezed at that black rubber bulb with great aplomb, grabbing at it and squeezing for all he was worth, as if he had hold of his wife's breast; mouthing a curse, his front teeth sticking out. His drive, impatience. And a touch of ruthlessness.

Going to his house one evening, on my first visit—I was on an errand—my Aunt Olive let me in, and in the living-room there was my Uncle Mike stretched out full length on the sofa, hands behind his head, wide awake. Apparently he did that, every night. I was astonished and very impressed. There was something oriental about it. To be able to relax completely in your own house like that was wonder and mystery enough, without anything else. One thing I knew for certain, it would never have been possible in our household. Never. My mother was such an ill-sitting hen, the very atmosphere she generated was against it. What's the matter, don't you feel well? she'd have wanted to know. No good pretending you were under the weather either. Go to bed then, that's the place. You're taking up too much room—I don't care if nobody else is in or not—somebody might want to come in and sit down. I want to clean round there—your legs are in the way! A shower of reasons, answers. To have somebody sprawled in the living-room, *her* living-room, would have been no good at all, simply unthinkable. Whoever it was, she'd have soon tidied them up. Relaxation in our house meant my father slipping off to sleep in front of the fire, stupefied by heat and fatigue, his paper crumpled, his head sagging, and it meant the Old Sweat on the other side of the fire, in his own armchair—remnant of his own household, on his own squashed, stinking cushion, encased in deafness, glasses

mended with cotton, reading his library books, his Edgar
Wallace. My mother in the kitchen, naturally, working at
the washing-up or ironing or making supper—any damn
thing. The gospel of work, the guilt of idleness. Relaxation,
what's that? Never, not in my vocabulary. I have to keep
working, what would happen if I didn't? Who'd do all the
work? Would your father do it? The Old Sweat, would he
do it? What about the dinner, the dirt, the fire, the mess,
the holes? What about your torn vests, your frayed collars,
your pyjamas that need patching? How can I stop? Tell
me, go on. You talk daft, daft. What about the beds, the
crocks, the slops, the cobwebs? The song, flinty and self-
righteous and unanswerable, hangs over the sink and never
gets washed away. I bite my lip, sink my head lower over
my homework, in the workhouse.

It all changes when Uncle Geoff wanders in, on his way
to Ferguson's—he's on nights. Half awake, dopey, he
brings a new atmosphere. If I'm out of the room, out of
the house, I see his uncared-for bedstead of a bike first of
all, propped against the bricks in the entry—and my
spirit lifts. Coming in I can smell the aroma of the machine
oil his arms and hands are soaked with, even before I'm
through the door.

The very opposite of a work fiend, he sits in the first
chair he comes to, against the door, and waits slothfully
for a cup of tea.

' Where's Jack?'

' At work, where d'you think he is?'

' Oh ah.'

This is mechanical, his exchanges give no idea of his
intelligence. He is no fool, but sluggish. He drifts, and lets
everything drift. Perhaps spoiled—the only son who stays
at home, hangs on, the last one, and gets waited on, his
mother fetching and carrying for him as if he's still a boy,
when he's in his thirties. His mother dies, his father, in the
end he is reluctantly on his own. Still people look after
him, somebody turns up. His whole life runs on like that,
least line of resistance. He is shy, in a shell, and there he
stays, peering out sleepily, more and more fixed in his
bachelor habits. Something about him warns you off, says

Don't touch me. So you don't. That's all. It's just a peculiarity, something you accept, that makes him what he is. Nobody knows what he really feels, what goes on inside him. He never lets on. Nobody dreams of asking. In a sense a mystery man, yet transparent, helpless; not so much furtive as veiled. His eyes are like that, sleepy, hooded, and a surprising flick to them now and then. Never a straight gaze—always flick, flick, and away; timorous, veiled. Whatever secrets he has are locked away for life, unless a woman unlocks them one day. Which seems doubtful. He sits in our house for an hour or so nearly every day, on his way to Ferguson's—or comes in Saturday nights occasionally for a fish and chip supper. Pickles? Yes please. Vinegar? Yes please. Doesn't lift a finger, waits, yet the curious thing is it doesn't bother my mother, though sometimes she puts on an irritated act with him. She's fond of him basically. He's been coming so long he's almost part of the furniture. Passive, he puts up no resistance, gives in to her and to everybody. But all the while he is going his own way in his own style, own time, with the least possible effort. He sits there sweetly spooning his tea in a queer spinsterish fashion, as if guarding his cup; still young-looking, scratching his short hair and leaning forward drowsily to read a newspaper hung over a chair against the table, just out of reach. Pasty-faced, Stan Laurel-ish.

'You're the limit, you are—here,' and she snatches at the paper and half throws it at him.

'Ta,' and he's gone, utterly absorbed, lips puckered absently at the hot tea, sucking it in gingerly.

What a contrast to this brother is my father, who does everything thoroughly and looks after his things, takes care of them—if it's a pair of shoes, for instance, he talks of the need to 'feed the leather'. His bike is oiled and clean, so are his tools. When the bike isn't in use for a long period he slings it up carefully in the shed, on two hooks, to keep the weight off the tyres. The army training keeps coming out, and when the two of them are together in some activity my dad turns into a ratty, overbearing sod from sheer irritation, taking charge because he is the one with method and a sense of purpose. 'How long's our Geoff going to be

—what the devil's he playing at?' And Geoff arrives, sloth-fully late as usual, rubbing the sleep out of his eyes, the camping gear or whatever it is gets lashed on securely, and my father is in charge.

'The boss is doing it,' says Geoff to my mother, out of hearing. Then in strides my father, waving his exasperated hands at us. Uncouth, officious, in this mood everybody dislikes him. He mouths: 'Come on if you're comin'!' and my mother strikes back—'Who d'you think you're talking to?' We climb in, the journey begins, Geoff drives, Dad sullen and stiff-necked at the delay. From the very start the trip is tainted.

8

JIM BRENNAN and his brothers had set themselves up in business—car sales and contract repair work, a few deliveries—and finally my father joined them as manager at their garage in Teddington Court, a little cobbled back alley off the Birmingham Road at the top of Malpas Hill. I used to take up his sandwiches now and then during the school holidays. He'd be peering into the innards of a car, engrossed, strictly in an amateur capacity: he looked after the books, the queries, drivers' problems, wages, orders, in a wood and glass pen tucked inside the garage itself but lifted up on stilts, part of the petrol and oil smell. The booth where he worked was a mess, spilling with paper, overripe files, spikes loaded with invoices, bulldog clips hanging on nails hammered into the framework. Jim Brennan, managing director, would come in and lounge in the doorway, smoking; a big-faced, square-jawed, heavy man with no fat, sure of himself. His nerves, if he had any, were certainly not on the surface, like my father's—though it's strange, I thought of Dad at the time as a strong man, not nervy at all. At home he gave an impression of strength because he had a touch of the Victorian parent—'Your father is asleep!'—but as soon as I contrast him with others I see how nervy and twitchy he was. Jim Brennan didn't have a grain of that kind of nerve: on the surface he seemed barely alive, just breathing. His pale eyes glanced over the storm of papers in a bored way, and he was soon on the way out to his real interest, cars, engine parts. He'd nod at me and at my father and say 'Okay, Jack'. Sometimes they'd be in conference outside, in the alley of back-to-backs. My father would be talking away rapidly, concerned, agitated, and Jim Brennan nodding vaguely as if the problem was featherlight on his husky sloping shoulders, saying 'Okay, Jack, okay, we'll do that, yeh.' They had been close pals in the army; there was a sepia photo at home showing them both in uniform, soft caps, my father in steel-rimmed glasses, sitting down, and Jim Brennan standing beside him with his hand on his shoulder, a beefy hand to match those hulking shoulders, that great jaw like a boxer's. Now he had prospered and had a big new house behind Stanley Park that we were invited to visit 'any time'. 'Don't wait to be asked, come round any time, Jack.' My father, though, wanted to give us all a treat: he was as proud of this fairy palace as Jim was, and too naïve to see how the splendours of a detached, beautifully kept residence with central heating and God knows what else would upset my mother, how the space and furnishings would crucify her with embarrassment. He kept at her, determined to have his way for once, and she would fend him off with reasons, fears, excuses. 'He's only being polite,' she'd tell him. 'He doesn't really want us to come —it's just you that wants to go, poking your nose in . . . Well I don't, thank you.' Later on, weakening, she wailed plaintively, 'What can I wear?'

'Don't be so daft,' my father laughed, 'it's not royalty, it's Jim Brennan!'

'And his wife,' said my mother grimly.

One Saturday evening we went, me and my brother dressed to kill, my father leading the way up to the oak door, which was lit, as if he'd been there hundreds of times and this was merely one more visit. 'Don't stare,' my mother hissed at us in a final warning as we entered the blaze of electricity inside, 'it's rude!' We were there for an evening meal and to inspect and sample the wonders of the central heating, my father going down to see the boiler in the basement, as well as other marvels we had heard rumoured, such as parquet floors, fitted carpets, bathrooms. And apart from all this, the sudden transformation of a detached house, the kind of thing I'd only seen before from the outside, into a warm, spacious, elegant interior where people sat and ate and went to bed, people we actually knew—that was almost too much for me. So was the terrific dazing strain of that visit, the relief when we were outside again, trooping meekly down the gravel like visitors at the zoo, my father shouting out too loudly altogether in that superior residential district, ' Good-bye, good-bye—so long, Jim!' And the roughneck himself on the threshold with his wife, smiling, subtly transformed by his wealth and power out of all recognition.

It was while he was manager at Teddington Court— exalted title, poor pay—that we went to the Isle of Man one summer holiday, for a camping fortnight. The stuff had gone in advance in a tea chest, carefully packed and lashed and addressed, to the unknown site. We followed a week later, jammed in a small car from the garage, being delivered to Liverpool by Joe Brennan, one of the brothers. Joe driving. A cordial, phlegmatic man, beefy like all his tribe, wedged behind the wheel like a fixture and driving steady as a rock through the black night, up north through the Potteries, no mistakes, no faltering anywhere. He said with a laugh to my grandmother, when she asked him how on earth he didn't get lost with all the twists and turns in the dark, ' I could do it in me sleep just about—been up and down this road so many times.' They stopped once for me to clamber out stiff-legged and be sick on the grass verge, then it was dawn and strange country spreading out, mill chimneys, the bleak raw muck of the north, charred slums, miles of black terraces, a furnace pounding and belching flame, drop hammers smashing. We pulled up outside a door in the middle of all this, Joe's mother lived here, she'd have breakfast on the go for us, knowing we were coming. In we piled, and a little woman made a fuss of us at that hour, worn and haggard, in the eternal pina- fore: plates of sausage and egg, great heaps of beans, bread, thick cups nearly as big as jam jars full of hot tea, and I couldn't eat anything but I drank some tea, shakily, shivering with cold and strangeness.

It was good going over on the huge boat, amazing, climbing up into it from the quayside, then exploring it gradually, feeling it move, an utterly new sensation. But a terrible cloud descended when we found the field, three miles out of Douglas on the mountain road to Snaefell, right against the T.T. course. The field was as rough and inhospitable as a common, lumpy, with poor coarse grass thick with thistles. My father looked at it and said nothing, my mother tightened her mouth and went to find the farmhouse and see about milk and bread. She met a slobbering imbecile at the door of a filthy kitchen, her left arm withered and useless, hair in rats' tails, broken slippers falling off her feet. She came back to the thistle field, to my father and his lovely old mother, to the Old Sweat, me and my brother. She took one look at the tea chest that was half unpacked, tents and pans and blankets strewn around it pathetically, as if scattered by the wind. She clenched her fists, moaned and burst into tears. My heart broke in me with pity, I felt sick and utterly defeated, bone-poor, and in some awful way homeless and motherless. The only other time I ever felt that way was in the cellar, moving in with our miserable possessions.

A snap of the family on this occasion shows us posed in a Douglas glen, parents staring pensively down at the water in the gloomy light. Standing behind are the sons, both in grey flannel suits, Alan with a plastic camera from Woolworths dangled over his shoulder—against us the white X of the little bridge leaps out. I look tough, one elbow shoved akimbo, arm around Alan's shoulder in an elder brother stance, my mouth full and sulky. Alan looks rounder, cherubic, his nose shorter than mine, but already the face has the in-growing signs, the locked-away life—soon we'll be strangers. My Dad's bespectacled head is dark with thought, he sits brooding in his cheap striped sports shirt, his sports coat and flannels, preoccupied. As well as being on holiday he goes around Douglas during weekdays making mysterious calls on garages, forging business links for his firm, or trying. I never believe, never feel he is making much impression on the business world—even at that age I can sense it. The cannibalistic, fast-thinking, shifty-eyed businessmen are dealing in one currency and him another —and he can't see it. I'm a child, I can see it. He will never, never see it. Not through lack of ability; but he is some kind of misfit. Instead of loving him for it, I want to walk away and leave him, disown him. I feel unsafe. Where he should cut short a conversation he keeps on, and his approach isn't cold and efficient like theirs, machine-like; he halts in the middle of sentences, reminisces, changes direction, meanders, or else rattles on too eagerly. If he is listening, he is sympathetic, curious, ready to stand there all day, full of respect—fatally interested. He can't fake like them, he's no match for them. He thinks he can combine business with being a human being: no, he doesn't think it, he just can't act in any other way. Disastrous. In the photo my mother sits beside this ridiculously human being, her black hair scraped back, forehead puckered, her bony, handsome, gypsyish face gaunt with worry as usual. Perhaps his goodness makes her nervous, even terrifies her at times, as it does me. She stares into the shadows. Under her left arm a handbag, inside which is bound to be her purse. Unrelaxed, she clutches the handbag, hangs on to her worries and responsibilities, holiday or no holiday.

I came to hate and even despise the goodness of my father. It made him weak and comic, it got us trampled on. I had a ruthless period, a young pride and power, a hatred of weakness. Mine most of all. Now the only abiding impression I can give of my old man resurrects this despised goodness. I don't gloss him over, he was no saint. But too good and decent and straightforward in his dealings ever to get on in this world. So he stayed a clerk. An awkward customer for the bosses, the managements, I can imagine— in spite of his eager friendliness and adaptability. Not a rebel, just too honest for his own good. What a fool, stupid, a fool to himself, they must often have said in contempt behind his back. More than once he got sacked because of principles, conscience. There was the Humber story: with lockouts, strikes, pickets on their hands they tried to swear in office staff as works police, even issuing them with guns.

41

My father refused—and got his notice soon after: a neat little letter arrived while he was on holiday, informing him that his services were no longer required. As a labour exchange clerk in the thirties I can imagine him dealing fair, no little Hitler act, no doling it out grudgingly like a man with no arms. Again, he got nowhere. The whole of his working life it's been the same story.

Those names and faces connected with holidays, the snaps, the snatches of talk and incident, they are woven and interwoven into the very fabric of those times; names like Dennis Kingsbury, Caroline, Harry Bussell, Wal Leavins and Dora . . . faces of paradise. Benign, beaming, oiled with the sun of leisure, laughing. All connected in some way with Geoff, who opened out almost sunnily among them. Open for him, that is. For he belonged to our shy tribe, he always kept something back. Not like his old mate Wal Leavins, or Wal's wife Dora, both of them lovable, wide-open people, unbelievable, too good to be true. I watched them and listened to them and hung on to their words because they were so warm and happy, so wholesome. They fascinated me. And it was true, they really were like that. They glowed with simple happiness, or contentment. I saw them in the best possible circumstances, I know—but holidays or workdays or gloomy Sundays, they always seemed in that state of euphoria. Wal was ginger, fuzzy, a broad honest face covered in a mask of freckles, his voice cracking delightfully as he spoke—you could imagine it breaking down with the sheer weight of heart it carried —and he spoke slowly, quietly, in simple homely accents, screwing up his eyes and laughing every few minutes. He was a town yokel. Listening to his queer croak and looking fearlessly into his face I used to be stirred by an almost voluptuous sensation of happiness myself, and excited too, as if on the verge of a wonderful discovery. There was a tang sometimes in what he said—he was a skilled mechanic at Ferguson's—and he'd glance at Dora in silence while she was holding forth, give her salty, amused, indulgent glances. They were a lovely couple. She was plump, gasping out laughs, had a high excited voice and seemed permanently hot and flustered, and as if embarrassed by her own life, her health and joy. She overflowed with it, for no reason—how did it happen, why should she feel like it? It astonished her, plainly. She went red as a tomato with embarrassment, and Wal would look at her, shake his head, laugh, wrinkle his eyes, rub his freckled cheeks. His big mouth would crack open in a grin. 'Don't ask me,' was a thing he was always saying. 'Don't ask me, Geoff.' 'Don't ask me, Jack.' The talk was often about engine innards, either cars or motorbikes, the breakdowns and accidents and mishaps they'd had, which gave spice and adventure to their journeys: the smooth running performances were prideful, pleasant, but they weren't a patch on misfortunes when it came to holding the interest. This was in the days when to be on the road with your vehicle, coaxing and nursing it, was an adventure, an act of independence, a new freedom. Suddenly you owned land, you swooped over England from town to town and it intoxicated you, the freedom of the open road: you swung round the coasts and found out where you were living and this was real geography, on next to no money. Wal Leavins rode his Norton combination as if he was made of the same material—stamped it heavily into pulsing life and sat back, settling himself like an old aristocrat, or a groom. He'd sit there inert letting it throb under him, stationary, while he listened, a queer stoical abstraction now, his Dora wedged into the sidecar and silenced by the roar, doused by the hood, the celluloid screens. They'd thunder away, powerful rather than fast, bumping and rolling away from us and our camp, over the dry hard field. They'd never stay long: have a look at us for a few hours one afternoon, on their way to relatives or coming back from somewhere. Once or twice they stopped long enough for a swim. They had two kids, little girls, chips off the same laughing contentment, darting through the brown water like minnows. The bike thundered, then chugged and it was them, an amiable vehicle of life, going again. The Leavins'. *Ta-ra! Ta-ra!* We'd watch them until they disappeared.

9

IT occurs to me that a log of the writing of this book could
be stitched into it as it grows, just as those names I mentioned are sewn into the very cloth of my boy's heaven.
That's how a book should be, spilling its secrets as it goes.
Blabbing, giving the game away. Who believes in a book
cut away from its writer with surgical scissors? I don't, I
never did. I don't believe in fact and fiction, I don't believe in autobiography, poetry, philosophy, I don't believe
in chapters, in a story. Words tell their own story and not
the one you intended, ever. The power of words. You can
tell the tale of the flesh and waste your time, it's the scar
tissue you should have concentrated on. In the end you
find out what a prison a book is, no matter how you go at
it. If you're opposed to books as prisons, as I used to be—
still am, sometimes—you batter against the brick and never
get out. That's the queer thing. Once you give up hope,
give up external desires, your life turns inward and feeds
on what is there. Dreams fill out, expand, bulge through
the walls. When they ask you what it's like being locked
away for life, you want to laugh. The intensity of your
dreams has begun to dominate your existence; the word
freedom fades. It belonged with the hard look and the
surly mouth of youth, the insolent Rimbaud face, giving
the V-sign, blowing a dirty fat raspberry on the back of
your hand, showing authority your arse. Before long the
word will have misted over and then dropped out of your
vocabulary : soon you'll have a struggle to remember what
it means. That's the idyllic state and I'm a long way off.
What I do, I give myself instructions, orders of the day. As
a young clerk working out wages, I used to make entries
in red ink with a steel pen. The red ink stained my fingers;
I'd wash and scrub at them, and look—it was still there,
a faint stain like clerk's blood. I want to write a book like
that, in my clerk's blood. In the heart's blood. In a father's
blood, a lover's, in a boy's blood. Bull's blood. My mother's
blood. A dream in red ink. Blood from the cut artery,

straight into the red ledger.

My life so far falls clearly into three sections, each one a prison, the sentences running more or less concurrently, with time out on short paroles. School. Factory. Office. No, not quite as simple as that—nothing is ever that simple. Other conditions, prisons, half prisons, cut in and out of these three; all kinds of shadings, cross-hatchings. Parents. Marriage. Obscurity, and the journey out. The Midlands, then the complete break, the shift to the south of all of us: parents, brother, friend, wife. I seem to be concentrating on the first two sections now, and some paroles. The prison of sex closes in during the office section, which I am still i.., and when I've served my sentence there and come out I intend to deal with that. It may prove the richest in terms of points of departure, turning points, seeing a pattern emerge. Then the war should be coming to an end, fires banked: time to marry the whole thing together and see what issues, what kind of human family. Who's got piles, who belches and suffers from heartburn, who needs an operation for gallstones. Count the casualties and add up the winnings. Or maybe not like that at all—it's all too far away. When I think of the wounds and how they open without warning, the terrible sudden rages, exasperation, melancholia, choking fits—no, I can't imagine how it will end, not yet. So many unforeseen developments, surprises —that's life.

Who'd have dreamt, for instance, that I'd be so thick with a young blood twenty years younger than me—a car fiend? He's solid, stocky, blond curls, good-looking in a pug-nosed, pouting way: a real-life child of this age. A comedy fan, and that's what redeems him for me, that and his young kicking trapped life, his dirtied-up innocence. This century produced him and he jeers at everything in it, because he feels the phoney and the flash on his veins. The only thing worse than the cheating present is the dead hand of the past. He picks up an old glass inkwell, grips it in his hand like a grenade, grits his teeth and says, ' Christ, look at it—I hate anything like this. I do, I want to smash it—gives me the creeps.' He feels the same way about Dickens, about old anything. It traps him, chokes and drags, holds him back. I'm attracted to him by his goon humour, and by his contempt for guff, regulation and discipline—like most of his generation he's already left traditional England behind. When the boss gave him a playful cuff on the head for cheek, only a fortnight after Tommy had started, I heard ' Keep your hands off !' and looked up to see a bunched fist, the boss jerking back as if stung. I shivered with delight, hoping for more ferocity. Nothing doing : he's afraid his temper will expose him to ridicule. Now, if he's reprimanded like a schoolboy, he gets up with his face dark and goes out, slamming the door. The boss loathes him with the full force of his scrat-and-save soul, the whole span of his skin-and-grief years. Can't accept the inevitable, can't hear the death rattle of his day and age : he still expects respect. Doesn't he know the Time of the Hooligans is upon us? Tommy gives him the rasp-berry, loud and clear. It's mutual. The job is a means to an end for Tommy, with no pretence of worry or conscien-tiousness. He couldn't care less how a member of the staff is supposed to behave; at knocking-off time he makes for the door in one bound like a Ford worker. He's restless, empty, itching about for something to kill time. I cultivate his comic side as hard as I can go because then he flowers : we join forces, mimic, take the piss, and all anybody can complain of is our giggling. I know that basically he's sterile, deprived, wasted, and nobody is ever going to make use of his heroic qualities. The way he hurls himself around, leaps down staircases, lets his hair grow until it curls over his collar, then crops it off short angrily—these are point-less, beautiful gestures like his car driving. His projectile-like nature longs for a target : all he can find is marriage, and how it makes him writhe, the thought of it. He orders a suit for the day, decorates a flat, meets his girl every day, every night, every week-end. He's bored. Marriage won't fit him, he suspects—not his style. He'll be in the clutches then like all the others. What is his style? Ask him and he'll shrug, grin, pull down his cruel little mouth, hunch over the wheel and drive faster. He doesn't care for those direct questions. ' Jesus, I'm depressed !' he'll howl, too savage for laughs.

The open exhaust sounds like a plane dive-bombing the town centre. He drives too fast, with marvellous sham indifference. A power kid, born to it. Starting off, he drops into position as if into a cockpit. Slams the door, reaches immediately for the car radio under the dashboard. Distorted music crackles out, a jangly beat: the Light. The Mini tears off, the exhaust adds its yell to the singer's, the wheels contribute a separate, more dangerous rhythm. Tommy's eyes take on a drugged, sent, wall-eyed look. The change is physical, as the power runs into him, and it can happen a thousand times and I'll still find it uncanny. Belting down the straight, driving with the soles of his feet and just one hand that he lets droop on the vibrating wheel as if by accident, he lolls sideways against the offside door. Moodily he watches the road, lunges up savagely to rub at the smeared windscreen with the sleeve of his flying jacket, slumps back, swings in behind the tail of a lorry, suddenly snarls out violently, ' Come arn!' It's strange, all his attractive humour submerges when he gets in the car. His gravity, arrogance, masterful firmness join to explode him through the traffic in male assertion. When his girl gets in she is meek, submissive, and if he bothers to speak at all it's curtly, even brutally. King of the road, this is his kingdom. And she doesn't object to this neglect; her turn comes later. Ramming up through a side street he sees a hairy beatnik on the pavement. He yanks furiously at the window handle to wind down the glass, then bawls out ' Scruff!' as he rips past. Canada attracts him—his sister lives at Toronto—but his roots are his parents, his girl, her parents, the pub: he senses this resentfully. He is still after all English and rooted, not the world projectile he favours. Give him time, he could be, but he hasn't been anywhere yet. He's temporary: job, flat, car, country, everything is for the time being. I hope he doesn't leave yet or go abroad, I like him more and more. It's only in the car that I lose contact with him, when he ceases to be human. He's a killer then, I feel. His negative attitudes are sound enough. Routines, forms, politics, they're just ' cokernuts '. He drinks at the Embassy Club, the Astoria, the London Inn, and when he goes to bed he throws off his clothes and sleeps 'horny'. The class line cuts at him, same as everywhere in little England, and he reacts bitterly: jeers, sets his head uglily, but soon recovers his good humour. If he says a word wrong, or misspells, he blushes and loses his fine youthful swagger. Then I loathe England, good and proper. It seems crawling with shits. Ashamed, I bend over backwards to put him at his ease again. Nothing confuses him easier than class. He lives in a prefab and insults the tabloids, takes an occasional *Times*, then Sunday finds him with the *News of the World*. Girlie magazines are jammed in his car pockets. He's fine, he suits me. I steer us both through the day as cutely as he steers me through the town, only my driving is sly, unimpressive, and for different reasons. I drive to keep us travelling. If he leaves I shall be back in the graveyard with my thoughts. I work like a jester to keep him bobbing like a cork.

He doesn't even remember the war, though of course it's been dinned into him, and he grew up seeing the ruins, bomb sites, having the scars pointed out to him. That and war films, pulp stories, TV documentaries. Inside his car it's sluttish, like his desk, but he has no time for poverty. Hire purchase is second nature to him. The only way he can keep money is by handing it over to his girl or his mother. If a thing's dilapidated his instinct is to chuck it in the dustbin. He was driving his own Consul at seventeen, paying back the loan by instalments. If I could take him back to my childhood in Ernaldlhay Street, decent and respectable slum, I bet he'd turn up his nose.

Ernaldlhay Street—how did it get a name like that? If anybody asked you where you lived, you had to say it and then you were forced to spell it. Always.

And the other names, key names of the Street: Albey's, Miss Eames, the Macadams, the Shuters, Waterhouse's shop, Black's shop. The Eagle, St Stephen's School, the Parochial Rooms. Miller's newspaper shop on the Hyson Road corner—real name Müller, he changed it at the beginning of the first world war because of the hostility towards Germans. On the opposite corner to him, a garage, Scanlon's, then up that direction, towards the park, was another paper shop and a barber's, all belonging to Mr

Miller, who seemed to use the shop next to the barber's as his headquarters. Though it may have been that he was there so much because once in he couldn't get out again without a lot of trouble. The shopkeeper was short, bullet-headed, and the counter came up to his chin, so that he looked embedded in papers, magazines, boxes of chocolates and cartons of cigarettes, as well as a mass of miscellaneous junk such as stationery, doilys, serviettes, trashy pens and pencils.

At the back of the house, down the entry, the huge sinister block of the old Humber factory filled the sky, its grim red brick covered in zigzagging black fire escapes. As a boy I accepted without question this hideous backdrop —and now I come to think of it there *was* something theatrical and cardboard-like about it—just as I would have taken for granted a rolling landscape of lush fields and leafy trees. Between this gruesome vision and the slimy greenish wood of the entry fence was a dairy, steaming and rattling day and night. The cardboard tops of the used milk bottles were dumped against the fence, their undersides encrusted with sour milk. These mouldy discs were great for spinning, so we used to squeeze through gaps in the boards and grab handfuls. If you couldn't see any mounds, you just made for the smell.

The street was a link between two arteries, Hyson Road and Whatford Street. Taken on its own it was absolutely nondescript, just a slot between two rows of identical ter-raced houses with the front doors flush to the pavement; all exactly alike at first glance, even to the paintwork. You had to belong to the street to notice the differences. Mrs Stanley's net curtains sagged, and they got blacker and blacker, a disgrace to the street, hanging there shamelessly like tatters of dirty bandage: Mrs McCollam's was the one that had a whiff of coal gas clinging to it; the smell seeped under the front door, and if you had to knock and go in for shillings for the meter it nearly gassed you, in her kitchen. That gash in the wall under Slater's front window was where a van skidded and ran off the road.

Whatford Street was where the blood poured, especially Saturdays, because it went straight uphill to the Town, the shops, the market. And it was a street of shops in itself : shops, pubs, pictures, chapel, the great gloomy cliff of the Humber flanking it near the bottom of the hill. Hyson Hill had none of this character, nothing to gawp at—just a road for getting somewhere. It climbed up past the hospital and at the top where the workhouse stood on the corner it joined the main London road. We were always being warned about that, to watch out for the lorries. Heard grisly tales of accidents, a man on a bike dragged a hundred yards under a heavy lorry up there one winter's night, and when they got him out he had no legs, one arm . . . It was the way out to the big world, a vague meaningless place at the other end. We only knew it as the route to the Common, to Warmeleigh, to Sutton Aerodrome and Alvington and the Abbey. There was another link I came to know between these two arteries, really an alleyway between high factory walls and warehouses, no more than a slit, called Shut Lane. It filled me with a creepy feeling, half dread and half fascination. I used to start walking through it and end up by running madly in a panic. At the Hyson Road entrance was a stadium they used for all-in wrestling, and it came out in Whatford Street by the high railings of a monumental mason. It ought to have been called Shit Lane—there was dog shit everywhere. The bricks were decorated with chalk drawings of cocks and tits, there was the odd splash of vomit and the puddles of piss left by drunks turned out of pubs the night before.

Amazing how you kept to your own district as if you lived in a village; clung to it like a mother, hurried back to it fearfully when you were in trouble. And if you penetrated other districts, say in the company of your Grandpa, how the strangeness made you blink, how it chilled you, made you suffer. The Ford Street, Alma Road area was adjacent to ours, but subtly different, dominated by the B.T.H. factory as ours was overshadowed by the Humber building. East Street, Waterloo Street, Wellington Street, Broad Street, Springfield Road, Vernon Street and all the slums making Greenfields were different in another, more oppressive and menacing way—the entries tunnel-like, often cobbled, with common taps in the backs and lavatories in blocks of four, and ashy bits of dirt like poultry runs for gardens. Our streets were jammed tight with the same pinched and meagre dwellings, the people in them shared the same kind of life and hard times, but somehow the bricks didn't seem to have that harsh, north-bitten industrial look: not quite, not to the same extent. Yet they bordered on it, one side, while the other side trailed off into a pattern of streets with bits of trim front garden, and further on still the bay windows, till you were amongst the semis and garages and wrought-iron gates of Acacia Avenue and Harper Road. The thick walls of privet, the cropped lawns, glossy woodwork. Going through this clean, dead and snotty world was one way of getting to the Common—past the cemetery and the Stilbrook tucked away behind, down the London Road where the lorries batted, under the bridge, and suddenly it opened out, a scrubby no-man's land, with its gorse bushes and crab-apples and paths where the grass had worn bald, the clayey hummocks and pits free to anybody, no fences, no signs, no park keeper. You wanted to run and roll about and lie down, it was so exciting. There were secret hideouts in the jungle of thickets, among the stunted oaks and alder bushes—that was where Roy Turnbull took us one Saturday morning, unfastened his belt and showed us his hard bent prick—bent like a bow. It was thin and shiny and mean-looking, but the ugliest thing about it was the way it curved. I took an instant dislike to it.

Long before that, a gang of us took a girl up the concrete sewer which tunnelled into the bank of the Willey— at the edge of the cindery waste-piece where the fair came every Bank Holiday. Somebody had a candle. We didn't go far down the pipe, it looked black as hell and we got frightened, even though we could still see the rim of daylight. She had her knickers off, ready. ' Let's see then,' our leader said, the oldest. She started to whimper, frightened of the dark. Somebody lit the stump of candle. She lifted up her dress round her grubby belly just long enough for us to stare in disbelief at her little cunt. ' I want to go home,' she whimpered. We all scrambled out, split up. I got a good hiding for getting my feet wet.

10

THE story of my playmates has to begin with Desmond Brockway, the boy with the round felt hat like a girl's, the only boy who was ever frightened of me. First I chased him, then I befriended him on that first day of school. I chased him because of his hat, that's all; because it was a grey colour, and round, unusual, and I felt an urge to touch it. He cowered in a corner, panting, and I smiled at him, reached out and touched his hat. It dawned on him that I wasn't going to hurt him. I can see him even now, his soft spoiled mouth and those brown, not quite sincere eyes. Staring and pouting, fraternising, ready to run, make a bolt for it if I changed my mind and turned nasty. He was like that, expedient, even at the age of five. Maybe he's a successful politician now. His father had a furniture shop, he was well off by our standards. You only had to look at Desmond's clothes. He was an only child. He took me home to play a few times, up in the big room over the shop where they lived. It was warm, luxurious, spacious, a soft-carpeted world stocked with expensive toys, anything Desmond wanted. He lolled on the floor, heaps of toys and books strewn about, bored and spoiled. Over the road, nearly opposite, was the hovel where Doris Platt lived, a snot-nosed ragged kid in our class. Her father had a tiny greengrocer's shop right under the shadow of the Humber, and it was like a cave, the rough walls running with damp. It stank of mildew and poverty in there. The low ceiling bulged down ominously over the window, and on the blotchy walls he'd nailed square paintings he'd done himself on the lids of cardboard boxes. They were lurid pictures, a lopsided child's vision of the world, but with the innocence gone rancid and sickly, like the smell in his shop. Portraits there were, big swollen noses and heavy jaws, and several versions of a swan on a stagnant, acid-green pool. He had the same pockmarked, bulbous nose as his painted heads, and he came shuffling in from the back in his brown cow-gown, peering through his round steel glasses.

Well, no, he didn't exactly peer—he didn't anything. He was extinct, dead on his feet. His dirty yellowy-white hair looked unhealthy, and it was plastered down over the bald patches. He was pitiful, and he was a meek loony, so you weren't sorry so much as scared. He was queer, he belonged to another species, and you didn't waste pity on him because he was beyond pity, beyond hope, beyond everything. It was so obvious that he was out of reach, in another world. All the kids were scared of his blank look and his seized-up Frankenstein neck; they found him creepy, though it's true he didn't do anything. And that was what vaguely terrified; his silence, which nobody made any attempt to bridge. It was like a foreigner—nobody knew the language or bothered to learn it, or imagined they were capable of the same feelings as other people; they were on a different circuit. Old Platt was so far off he might have been on another planet—an extinct one. He'd shamble out of his hole from the living quarters in the back and stand at his counter—it was more like a fence. He stood there, dumb, cut off at the waist, legless, his face fixed in a permanent faint smile of weary hopelessness. It wasn't really an expression, it was eaten into his face, encrusted. The glasses magnified his eyes, blurring and distorting the iris into a huge grey oval swimming in sadness, so that he looked blind, waiting and listening for something to happen. No please or thank you—when you were served he turned like a sheep and trundled back through the hole in the wall again, an opening hardly big enough for him to push through. Perhaps he was engrossed in some picture he was painting and wanted to get back to it. Perhaps . . . but he had this sinister quality.

Poor Doris Platt stank, the stink reminded you of Platt's fetid little shop, and she was simple in the head. She sat in the classroom liking everybody, smiling round at everything, a gentle thing like a saint, as idiots are sometimes in this world. There was a woman I used to see who lived tucked away in a back street somewhere in the district who was half blind, and half off her rocker, fumbling round the corner at the same hour each day, taking her mongrel for a walk, and she'd catch sight of you dimly through her

glasses and the smile would break on her face spontaneously, welling up from deep inside and reaching her face
and flowering. Dorothy might have ended like that. She
wore round steel glasses, like her old man. She must have
been six or seven, no more; a lovely age. Completely oblivious of her ripped clothes and broken shoes.

It's true I didn't see any of it like this, I couldn't have
done—how could I? I was living it, breathing it in and
out, and on Saturdays in bustling Whatford Street I
dodged prams, shoppers, mingling with the parade. The
whole ugly shitheap was my homely romping ground: no
judgements were being passed on any of it, I had no values
or standards. Wherever it marked me, wounded me, it left
scars of paradise. I know I'll never get back there, though
I dream of it. I nearly described it once as a time of piercing sweetness, but that's wrong; it's only now when it's too
late that it pierces, and I suppose that's the purity. Then
it was simply wonderful, a wonderful enveloping sweetness,
a delicious terror. As a boy of five I sat in the strange room
called a classroom, quivering at the separation, torn away
from home, from my mother—she was only at the other
end of the street but it could have been the other side of
the world. I gazed in wonder at the teacher, Miss Warren,
behind her a slide of pale yellow wood to be used on wet
days, and I noticed the boy to the left of me, his bare knees
scratched and scabby. I saw the posies of wild flowers
arranged in jam jars on the windowsills, limp fountains of
wilting bluebells, the crayon pictures tacked up on the
walls. We sang *Away in a Manger*, we made marks on
squared paper, I chased the boy in the felt hat with the
brim to it, and ran home at twelve to tell my mother.

The boy on my left was Steve Mallard: the name is
heroic. I kept my pencils and rubber in a cardboard box
that had been used for Woodbines—it was still pungent
with the smell of tobacco. Tiny grains were lodged in the
corners. I may have asked for the box at the tobacconist's
across the street—' Please can I have an empty box, Mister '
—or they may have given it to me at home, or perhaps
the teacher did, I can't remember. Later on, older and
tougher already, we'd race round the corner to the cake

shop before nine, asking for stale cakes and broken biscuits. For tuppence you could get a bagful of buns and rock cakes a day or two old, if you were lucky. A little queue of kids would be bundled in there most mornings, panting from the run after hurling themselves at the door to get in first, a smoke of breath coming out of their mouths if it was frosty.

If I had the power and could relive it again, one tiny occasion would be sufficient to recapture the joy and bliss, the thrilling tenderness of those days, when nothing more than a sensation of wonder made you so happy, so rapt. We were in the Parochial Rooms, a rambling building of dusty bare rooms which belonged to the church, used by the school for concerts, and by other groups who organised lantern lectures, cinematograph shows—I saw the Charlie Chaplin silents there, itching about painfully on the hard wooden seats, craning my neck, groaning in anguish when the film snapped. But the moment of bliss, longed for ever since—maybe it's a dream—came one December morning in a top room of this building. It was a rehearsal for our Christmas concert. There was the wonder and mystery of being there at all during school time, and smelling the dust, and the paper chains were up, hanging over the lights, draping the doorway. One of my classmates was on the stage, piping up in his fresh beautiful voice, and it might have been 'Little Old Lady' or something atrocious like that he was singing. I had nothing to do, no part, no worry, it was a beautiful song to me and I loved him, loved the scene, the quality of the daylight, so grey it hardly entered the window, the time of the morning, the nearness to Christmas and the marvellous signs of it, tokens of delight, the paper chains, the red crêpe paper pinned along the front edge of the platform. I was so fused and in harmony with it all, I even loved the creak of the bare boards as the singer moved his feet nervously, and the way our high voices echoed in the big cold space.

True bliss. Like the Friday afternoons on the eve of breaking-up time, and they allowed you to bring your own books, even games, and as long as you kept quiet it was all right to change seats and go and sit beside your best friend, reading the same page of the same book with heads together, whispering 'Have you finished? Read it yet? Can I turn over now?' Like being given a special job outside, quite suddenly out of the blue, a pure gift from heaven—'Go and weed in front of the Headmaster's office.' Going out quietly with heart pounding, actually out in the open street, to the narrow strip of cobbles under His Window—you could even hear him rustling papers in there, hear his chair scrape as you stooped down under the windowsill, crouched on your heels and tugged at the grass tufts, dug with a stick or your fingernails at the ribs of soft moss. Like the journey through the streets with the wicker linen basket full of fresh eggs which the whole school had collected to give to the hospital—yours among them somewhere, wheedled out of your mother's pantry—and a white cloth over the eggs, you on one handle and a boy you didn't like much on the other, to help carry this cargo dangerous as dynamite, walking very gingerly so as not to stumble, feeling happier with every step and soon liking the boy better. 'Want to change sides?' And you liked the thought of the hospital drawing nearer, the journey more pleasurable and less terrifying as you dwelt on that and on the return trip with nothing, absolutely nothing to worry about, just an empty basket you could swing and let drop and even wear like a huge hat if there was a shower of rain.

11

WE tore up the roots and left the city, as if for good. We lived through the war, chained to the city by jobs, relatives. I didn't visit the old district once, it was submerged and lost, gone for ever as far as I was concerned. But there was no place for us in Lillington, no real home I suppose. We were like refugees, visitors, and though it didn't matter to me in the least, infected with the truly modern rootlessness, it did matter to my mother, born in St John Street with the church spires on her horizon. It may have mattered to my father too, but he was adaptable, he welcomed change.

It would be my mother, sensitive to atmospheres, feeling unwanted, homesick for the familiar, timid and stubborn and morose, she would be the driving force to get back to the old ground. I was too young to be in on the move, but my father always gave an impression of contentment, compared to my mother, who presented a suffering face : she struggled, put up with it, made the best of a bad job. Of the two, my father was undoubtedly the brightest, the one who shed light. He was blithe, abstracted. If he was suffering and making sacrifices, you weren't made aware of the fact. My mother had gone without food for us in the twenties, pushing the pram through the park in Leicester—where they lived in rooms for a while—feeling sick and faint, and long before I was told this I felt it. She was dark with sacrifice, burdened with love for us. We piled burdens on her willingly, remorseful now and then : if she didn't want us to, why didn't she stop us? Because she loved us too much. Because it all helped to bind us to her. When the weight of this love began to make us heavy with guilt, being sons we were soon kicking and longing to leave, yet afraid. Weak with love as we were, attenuated like that, the world frightened us half to death. The old, old story of sons in England, coddled and comforted by the mother who yearns over them like a lover, all sacrificial, till the spunk's sucked out of them. It nearly happened, nearly.

Back in the city after the war, in a nice clean modern district of semi-detached, gravel, front gates, the groves and avenues of suburbia, I went once deliberately down into town, plunging downhill on my bike past the Odeon into the dirty old district of those days, in a deliberate, vaguely desperate attempt to retrace my lost steps. I found the Street horribly shrunken and commonplace, not a shred of the glamour I'd dreamed of, and the Parochial Rooms, that hall of radiance, I almost passed it without noticing it, it was so tatty and inconspicuous and small. Small, everything small. No majesty. I even walked by the house itself, peered up the entry, and it was meaningless, utterly dead. I haven't been back there since. The only way I can go back, richly, truly, is in imagination. I had to learn, I wasn't to know that then. That was why, soon afterwards when I started to write about it in the first book I ever attempted, at the tender age of twenty-one, it was such a howling disaster. The war was over, we were back and installed in a bombed and rebuilt semi-detached at Bloomfield Grove—not streets, they were sunk in the past—and it was the quiet bottle-end of a short cul-de-sac, very new and suburban, near the Birmingham Road. I had a box-room to myself and a typewriter, an old office machine, table under the window—perfect conditions. I wanted to build something up, mine, to set against the factory, against school, against destruction, against my own inadequacy most of all. My father downstairs under my feet—I was screaming at him now inside and he got the message. Once or twice I blurted out my raging intolerance of the whole works, and, of course, it implicated him as an Elder, included him, because he was of it and took it for granted.

' You silly twerp,' he jeered.

' Open the prisons,' I yelled, my face on fire. ' What's everybody afraid of?' I fell into incoherence, I was easy meat. Even my mother joined in the game, chopping me to pieces with the same dull logic my father used, and she laughed indulgently. So I sat in my cell nursing this terrible desire to build, build something, for God's sake. Get me out of this. Build out of nothing, no experience, build by wanting to build urgently enough. Tear down their lies and hypocrisy, set fire to their churches and treadmills and sheep-pens and slaughterhouses. A clean start. Let them keep away from me—their very talk stinks up the place. Let them fight their own dirty wars, I was on my way out, on my own. Then I was face to face with the awful question : What are you going to build? What with? I'd made stories and poems, but they weren't nearly solid and substantial enough. A book was. It was a complete thing like a building, with its own foundations and plumbing. You used words like bricks, steadily and methodically like a bricklayer, one on top of the other : long straight lines, and the building rose, it was yours.

So I sat at the rickety table with a pile of crisp clean paper beside me, lovely. They thought I was all set to be harnessed to a lifetime of honest grafting, did they, just like them? Hard graft was the banner of their religion. Work was their God, I knew that, it had been hammered into me by example, and into them by their parents, and so on—right back to Carlyle. You could tell them God was a fairy tale, Jesus wasn't important like electricity, and they'd smile or go deaf. They weren't upset, or not deeply, and it certainly didn't worry them. My mother was ' religious ', but not if it interfered with the *important* duties, such as housework. She was too busy to go to church anyway—and as a child she was conscripted into bible classes, Sunday school, church services three times a day on the Sabbath, evangelist tent meetings, mission work, Sunshine Leagues—enough to last her for the rest of her life, you'd think. No wonder she was ' religious ' and felt she could afford to smile away my foolishness. My father had nothing whatever to say on the subject of religion. I think he kept quiet, hoping it would go away. But if you blasphemed against work, a great wail went up from your mother. Your father went for you viciously, pulverised you with contempt —' You little twerp, wipe your chin it's dribbling!' Or he gave you the blah blah about learning by experience, like an old goat. ' We had to fight for it, son, the right to work. Yes you can laugh—you'll find out.'

I did. But then I hadn't, and I wasn't going to, either. I chewed my lips, gulped, swallowed down my pride. I was about to go off like a lightning flash—what were they talking such drivel to me for? Did they know what was happening inside me, like a feast of blossom opening on a bush in the night? Well, perhaps they were being a little hasty. He's young, he's hot-headed, he hasn't even got the cradle marks off his behind yet, give him time and he'll find out and calm down, all by himself. We all go through the same phase. Let him paint and write and listen to records and act funny, mooning around in the front room every week-end, jabbing at the piano—it's nice to have hobbies. He'll come round : let it dribble off his chin for a while. I suppose he gets his daft ideas out of books : still never mind, you can't stop him reading. Education's a wonderful thing, gets you a good job. They used to try so hard to be understanding, it was pitiful sometimes—until I stuck my foot in it again, that great arsehole of creation they called Work and Money. You've got to have money, son, in this world. I'd try to stop it but no good, it'd jerk out, boiling hot: Why have you? Then they went nuts. Their platitudes caught alight, real passion at last; it was guaranteed. In the end they did their best to ignore me, let me go my own way, so that instead of having the luxury of hating them I felt nauseated by my own selfishness and stiff-necked pride. They'd been good to me and they were still good; that's where they always had you. You hated them for that most of all, like a man hates his creditors.

I sat up there in awful isolation, in a labyrinth of quiet avenues like the cemetery along the Birmingham Road. I was sickly with mother-love, a lovekin, even though I'd been blooded at the big school and the factory. I still trembled on the threshold. Why didn't they understand, when I dashed their hopes and rejected their beliefs, stamped on their fears, that the most savage revolt wasn't against them but going on inside me? They couldn't understand, no matter how deep their understanding, because I was on my own plot of land, my own kingdom, tearing down and dreaming and longing to build, and I was the only one with the key.

I wrote the book, sweated blood over its lousy pages, squeezed it out agonisingly, sentence by sentence, word by word. What I had in the end was terrible judgement on me: a heap of waste paper, dead feeling; an abortion. What killed it more than anything was my timidity. A voice inside me was demanding real facts, real names, even then. I didn't have the guts to listen, but even at this early stage I had an instinctive distrust of made-up stuff, fiction. I should have taken a pride in the place, made the people say ta and oh ah and our kid and any road, filled it with place names like Lob End and Cannon Street and White-lake. Instead I took refuge in the notion that you needed a style for writing, and if you didn't have one you had to find one from somewhere; graft it on. English writers hardly existed in my world, they were a class apart, right out of it with their noses in the air. I turned over Faulkner, Hemingway—at least they had a living, warm quality. But

I ended up with their styles and that was fatal. I needed something native to nourish me. The whole clue to me and what I wanted to say was in my Englishness. I was for ever peering at other books, seeing how other writers put things —I was like an art student trying to discover the secrets of perspective, light and shade, how to convey the illusion of a third dimension. How to make a nose stick out so that you can almost grab hold of it, how to make an eyeball look round and solid like a marble. And basically, bitterly, I had nothing to say anyway; no real impetus to carry me through a book. I wanted to build something, so why not a book? It was purely symbolic, a crutch to lean on and lash out with. Not surprisingly I did a thoroughly pastiche job, a patchwork quilt of my admirations. It grew so painfully, forcing, forcing, that I used to go to the library and stand there pulling out novel after novel in desperation, looking for the least number of pages I needed to be able to call my thing a book. Somehow I finished it—a testament to the very donkey work I despised—that and the ferocity of my will. Long before it was made I loathed it; it was so obviously hybrid and wrong. I was too ashamed to show it to anybody. It got buried at the back of a drawer, a miscarriage. Wrap it in newspaper quick, flush it down the lav. I know now that years of life have to roll through you, and then perhaps you can hit the right note. The tone is everything, the style nothing. If a sentence ever comes out stylish, my instinct is to straightway put kinks in it, make it angular, or anyway a little bent. Then it comes alive. It's queer. If you want to draw the sun, Renoir or somebody said, throw away your compasses. Perfection deadens. I struggled and failed, and struggled again. Nothing there. Empty. A nonentity. Nobody could have helped me, and what sort of advice would it have been if they had, telling me to wait and live a bit? I fairly seethed with impatience. Now I've learned to be tolerant and I tell myself I don't have to hurry: I'm alive, I've survived, they haven't dropped the Bomb yet, it's suspended or stuck up there— but I hurry just the same. That's the age we live in. I'm hurrying now.

So I wrote at another book and put the pages in a file

marked 'London', and this was going to convey the meagre three weeks of the London experience. I made it strong out of weakness, using the raw, naïve, sawn-off sentences of the iconoclast. And called it 'The Dream' because of how it developed, hypnotic, sweated-out, livid as a bad dream . . . 'He unfastened the suitcase and began to get things out. He felt pleased with himself. He was making a new start. He had taken a giant stride. Now he was in a different stream. He would drift along for a bit and see what happened. So this was London! He could hardly believe it. It could be anywhere, there must be rooms like this all over the world, he thought. London! Anything could happen, anything. It was such a vast place, teeming with people of all nationalities. He was very pleased with himself. He had done it. Won. He felt as though he wanted to give a shout of triumph. Instead he slammed his right fist into the pillow, to release the great force within him. He struck it again with all his strength. He didn't see a pillow but a face he had hated all his life . . .' Further on with it, I deleted 'Dream' and wrote 'Vortex', and the story opened with a train, ruthless engine of decision, hurling me into the capital punishment, the vortex—life. I was the bound and gagged neurotic : this was my last chance. I was off to the whirl, the wheel, the centre, hub and arsehole of civilisation, in a natty Weaver to Wearer blue serge suit, a trench coat with plastic-leather buttons, military epaulettes, and a cardboard case full of underwear and socks, held together by tin clasps, locks and hinges. Timid, quaking, loveless little man, stepping off the train and sniffing it : Euston, that huge porch over the threshold of London. Stepping out fearfully under the soot and zoom of those lacy iron arches, under fluttering pigeons, gloomy light, in a medley of yells, whistles, taxi hoots. The barber's half-way down the steps to the underground lavatories; sidestepping the man with the mop and bucket. The past bearing down on my shoulders in that clanging, echoing great shed. Dizzy, drunk, stupefied already at the thought of it, the enormous scurrying life waiting outside—what that meant in terms of freedom for an absolute nonentity like me.

62

I thought you had to have a theme. I thought you had to sit there grimly, deadly serious, and hammer through to a conclusion. Nobody told me there are no conclusions, it continues, nothing matters, it's just you and nobody else, and if you can't write then write about not being able to . . . Write about something fantastic like throwing money in the fire, like Dostoevsky. I read him in those fat editions in red and cream jackets, the Constance Garnett translations, and they were a bit antiquated and out of focus, as translations often are, but it doesn't matter a damn with Dostoevsky. He gave me splitting headaches, neuralgia, my eyes seemed to be popping out of my skull, I felt like a bedbug and I was dizzy and sick. When I got up and walked out of the room my knees sagged. I had a pal who was reading him at the same time, we'd exchange books and compare notes, or, to be more exact, look at each other and laugh. Because it was so daft and funny and fantastic, being plunged at such an early age into this world of furious suffering and love, our minds pushing out and expanding like mad, coming out of each book in a daze, shell-shocked, and not budging from the streets we lived in and nobody knowing but us.

' How d'you feel after that one?'

' Shattered!'

He didn't affect my writing in the slightest, this Dostoevsky, that was the strange thing. What I was writing, quiet, simple and restrained, a book based on my childhood, wasn't touched by his crazy characters jumping about and flapping their hands, falling down in fits and all the rest of it in those agitated pages. It left me feverish, yes, but where was the connection with my little English life? I couldn't see any. Yet my models were out of touch, utterly, compared with this mad Russian. He was the modern I should have imitated, and I wouldn't have been infected with a false style either, because he hasn't got one. He's slovenly, prolix, a talker more than a writer, littering everywhere with clichés. Still it gets across, factual and fantastic in one breath, the way we are and the way we're going. The raw Slavic force of the Russian is what puts you off and deludes you into thinking it can't apply here—that kind of blind creativity has been left far behind now. Well, it's coming round again: jump on and ride.

I wasn't far enough away from childhood either to describe it. For one thing I was still living at home, joined on. But I'd read *Stephen Hero* and it had done for me. Now I wanted to write mine as if looking through the eyes of a child. That's fake, fiction. Nobody ever returns to that state, they only long for it. The earliest days of my childhood were so serene, harmonious, untroubled, it was like Mozart only better—the only pure happiness I can remember. As soon as passion began, passionate longings, pain and loneliness became the order of the day. Then it was paradise lost: even the bursts of happiness would be bitter-sweet reminders of how it used to be always, in that unbroken morning of life.

12

PAIN and loneliness, heartaching confusion, enemies who love you. It had a funny side too, if you weren't too intense. Only you were always intense. You crackled with intensity, fears, worries. Knee joints seizing up—Christ, no, not chronic rheumatism at my age, I haven't lived yet. Don't say haven't shagged a woman yet, because it would have made me wince in those days. I was longing to simply put my arms round a girl and pour out love. My chest throbbed with loving tenderness. One day I couldn't stand the pain any longer. Driven to it, I sent in my name and address to a Lonely Hearts club I'd spotted in a woman's magazine—probably my mother's. That would have been appropriate. Such a relief and excitement when the letters came through the front door. I walked in from work as usual one night and my mother handed the packet to me without a word; perhaps a little barely perceptible tightening of the lips, a sign I knew so well. It meant: You have wounded me deeply but I shall never tell. You will never know how you made me suffer. Poor mute mother. I want to snatch the letters and run off, out of her sight. Or shout—'This is it, I'm in touch with the outer world!' I do neither, just walk off quietly as though nothing has happened, letting the packet dangle in my fingers. No importance. Stuff them in my pocket as soon as I'm up the stairs and make a dive for the toilet, the one truly private place in the house. Shove the bolt across in a quiver of exultation and open the first envelope with shaking fingers.

The first one was from a young fellow—how did I come to get that?—who lived in Liverpool and was suffering from a kind of creeping paralysis. He wanted a pen friend, he'd be more than glad to hear from me and he promised to keep writing faithfully as long as he could hold a pen, until his disease reached his fingers . . . I sat down on the lavatory seat, all the stuffing knocked out of me. He sounded so chirpy, God knows why. I stared at his childish, painfully-wobbling scrawl—the last sentence nose-dived into a corner, righted itself, fell backwards, stumbled on again to sign off in a name I couldn't decipher. Yours sincerely. I shut it away, slid it back in the envelope. I didn't want to know. Knock again, nobody at home here, try next door. No thanks—not today. Feeling sick and sad and frightened I opened the next one—a girl, an art student living outside Leeds. All right, but nothing, just how d'you do and would you like to correspond with me. I'd be delighted if you would—but not sounding it. Cool and firm, strapped in tight, a real nice English handshake, frosty. The last thing I wanted. The third letter, warm and sentimental and a bit simple, was from a lonely girl who lived with her widowed mother, worked in an office, comptometer operator, liked to read books and poetry and go for long walks in the country with a dog—it was the only one left and I clutched at it. Desperation works wonders, blinds you even better than love. It was half-witted I suppose, no need to read it twice—it was wet as a scrubber. I seized on it. Humble, good—I pressed virtues into its meek and sloppy sentiments. Who the hell wanted brains, some icy clever-dick? I rushed into the box-room and scribbled a reply there and then to Edwina—that was her name, believe it or not. Her address was Holmanthorpe, Huddersfield, Yorks. Meant nothing to me. I wrote back innocently and brightly, with a touch of fervour, just a touch, and a sort of brotherly warmth, so as not to scare her off. Kept everything out of it except the simple need to alleviate the pain of loneliness which hers betrayed. Only hers was her own, and I was terrified of being myself. I copied her style, cunningly insinuated myself into those half-baked phrases and trotted them out again, like an echo. Next day I wrote to the art student—may as well see if there was anything doing, get a photo at least—and that was different altogether. Jaunty, smart, provocative, the kind of thing I felt she was expecting. Entertainment. The one from the poor crippled bloke got ripped up small and dropped on the fire when nobody was looking. Hell, I was crippled myself, wasn't I?

And I went around the same as before as though nothing had happened, nursing the little secret, the female contact I couldn't possibly tell anybody about. The seed of hope. Breathing on it, magnifying it, working on it already in a thousand ways, this wonderful and vital illusion we need so much. The second letter when it came made me smile like a child—I could actually feel it happening, the germination. The illusion had taken root, it was real, more real than reality. How happy she was to get my letter: she'd read it twice, three times, unable to believe how very lucky she was. Please write again, but only if you feel you want to in your heart. ' In your heart '—what a thing to say. She ended by saying that it would be dreadful stopping now or being disappointed when her heart *sang with hope* —she really did use those phrases—but perhaps it would be better to go no further, less cruel . . . Did I mean what I said? Was I sure, could it be true I genuinely needed her letters? That's what she was yearning to know. Oh yes, and would I tell her more about myself, my likes and dislikes. Her favourite book was *Sorrel and Son*. A p.s.— dare she ask me for a photograph of myself? I didn't dare read her letters twice as she did mine, I read them once, very fast, then shoved them away out of sight quick, so that her ghastly old-maidish way of putting things didn't interfere with the sincerity, heartbreaking, and so that my imagination could get to work. The correspondence with Edwina blossomed as rapidly as the one with the art student wilted. Almost overnight I mastered the art of reassurance. The event I dreaded, yet waited for daily, was the arrival of her own photo, promised in exchange for mine. Love, we ended each time, and much later it was Your Loving . . . Still no photo. Then, ever so gently one time she reproached me for not calling her Dearest. Coy as a maiden aunt she promised her photo as a reward: I was being bribed. So I gave her full measure, My Dearest One, and the wishing and wanting had gone so far I didn't care any more. Christ, I half meant it, I'm sure I did. More than half. Who else was there apart from her, who did I have to confess to, open my heart to? You are the one, my daft drippy one, you know me now, my dearest one, I am at your mercy, in your care. Oh it was easy, nice and easy. When I wrote it there was nothing wrong, it flowed off my pen truly, for that instant, the stroke of the heart coincided with the stroke of the pen. I was close to tears. Writing My Dearest One affected me so much that the letter I wrote under it was the most loving she ever had from me. Her letter came speeding back in the next post, straight as an arrow of desire.

I opened the envelope in the secrecy of the lav, but sat on the seat first because of the gravity, the solemnity of the occasion. Grabbed it tremblingly and stared at it with my whole face—a bit of blurred card, a snapshot of her in a deckchair on some grass, under an arch of trellis plaited with rose briars, it looked like. Roses! And the floppy white hat she wore, her face out of focus, pale, shrinking back into the shadow of the brim—how gentle and modest it was, how quaint, and so typical. Like a letter from her, exactly. My eyes bored ruthlessly at it—to hell with illusions—trying to ferret out the truth. No good, I could stare at it all day and I'd never really see anything. This pathetic little snap told me one thing though, something I'd known right away and refused to admit. Her gentility. She was genteel and nice and romantic, in an absolutely inoffensive, pitiful way. Here was the proof of it, staring at me. So what? She loved me, didn't she? And I remembered her letter, forgotten in the excitement, took it out and read it and yes oh yes she loves me, more than ever now because she's got my photo, it's in her handbag and it goes everywhere she goes, and she's glad, she's terribly happy, the birds are singing and am I happy now that I have her photo too? Am I glad? It went on and on, clean daft, nine pages of it. And I was under the spell of it, for the first time, genuinely moved by *her* words, not mine.

Very carefully I stuffed the letter back into the envelope. Gently slipped in the blurry snap. Got up and yanked the chain, because after all I'd been in there for a hell of a time, and shuffled out, taking care not to look in the mirror because if I saw my face I should see the truth and I'd want to howl. Downstairs my mother breaking her heart quietly over me for having secrets, punishing me with silence. And it would get worse, not better. I was dying by inches, I had to get out : home was a prison, every comfort to keep you warm and safe and happy and all you want to do is break out. But I was shit-scared already of what I'd tasted of the outside—six years of factory life, a fair slice, the whole country littered with prisons like that, from one end to the other. Wander through the town on a weekday and it was uncanny how doglike you felt, how lost without a leash and collar, wandering along the pavements through the crowd of women and old men, schoolboys zigzagging up and down and the feeling of rush and purpose, everybody belonging to a prison of some kind, either just leaving it or running back there again. To be on your own in the middle of that lot was like roaming around in space, cut off from human kind, shut out of a closed community. The loneliness was terrible, the tide of traffic pulsing and flooding, a grey flood of faces rushing for hearth and home every night, lovers wrapped around each other—where could you take your love before it curdled, who wanted it? The world is a prison, the men with ashes tipped over their ugly cropped heads stand in long rows, speechless, not even grunting, drowning there without a word in din and stink, minding the machines that drill and stamp and hammer and cut into their days, and their eyes are cold snake eyes, their cheeks venomous, the hide of their necks loose and scored and pock-marked with dead boils, and their mouths drag down at the corners, the vinegary bastards. The nightmare is to end up like them—but outside you wander through space, on and on, utterly lost and separate, and come crawling back begging for the leash and collar.

The blurred face in the distance which simply asks for love, your love, is precious after all. Keep it out of sight, hide the truth, don't falter, don't ask questions—aren't you lonely enough yet? And the letters are posted and delivered, and you know the day is drawing nearer when you'll have to get on a train and go there, meet, and the thought fills you with dread. But nothing is worse than nothing. Make something happen—it might be worse than before or it might be better: who cares? Just something happening to prove to yourself that it's not too late. I'm still one of the living, me, half dead at twenty-one. I can function; try me. I can suffer as well as the next man, I can laugh and cry, bleed, drink tea. It's the nothingness that terrifies. The terror of being stranded on the bank in the prime of life, helpless to move a muscle, watching the blood gush freely. Waiting, waiting for a call. The thought gnawing that maybe you are deficient in some vital part, like a brand-new machine that's been tested and found dud. Standing at the bench with your head bowed over a tricky job, worrying at it, you pray between your teeth: Push me in, I can't stand this much longer. Christ, what's wrong with me? I want to swim with the others!

Ashes and rubies. It's like that at twenty-one. Ashes in the mouth, cold rain, fist banging on the stone, unable to speak, find words, choking with it one minute, the black night like a hole, life full of holes, smashed light bulbs, rotten teeth, red rust, and the next minute glowing all over like a ruby and laughing like a saint, in love with the loony jigsaw.

I sat in the train jogging over the points on the outskirts, in a muck sweat. Could have been in one of Hitler's cattle-trucks rolling towards the ovens, the way I felt. Why? What was the matter with me? I was licking my lips feverishly, sick with tension, heart thudding like a drum. For the fourth or fifth time I wiped the sweat off my palms. Would I recognise her on the platform? Bound to—it was only a one-eyed place, not much more than a halt. Condemned, I looked out bleakly at the grime and dirt, ripped ground, then raw new roads and blank concrete, new council houses, wire and concrete fences, compounds for the knobbly sprouts and grimy cabbages to stand to attention in, ragged flapping stumps. Here it comes, yards and sidings, a pile of cable drums, a junk heap like a tank where they emptied scrap iron, bashed-in car bodies, dead boilers, stove pipes, gas cookers. Rolling into the station, and it slid up to meet us, deathly quiet and inexorable.

No sign of her anywhere. I got off the train. Suddenly she was there beside me—where had she come from, out of the clouds?—fluttering, agitated, breathless, flushed. So close, her face only a few inches from me, that at first the shock didn't register. She was old! Much older than me—I was no good at guessing ages and it may have been her round-shouldered figure—she was shrunken, bent, musty, her bones looked frail and brittle. The soft, thin hair clung to her cheeks, she seemed to be hiding in it like a little old lady. I walked along with her, stunned. I went slowly, because she walked with difficult, hobbling steps like an invalid. The nightmarish quality of it all stopped me from speaking; I just gulped and struggled with my face, letting her chatter in a babyish breathless voice, calling me by my first name as if she owned me, was on intimate terms—this crone! I wanted to turn round and jump on the train and shout through the window : I'll be back, I'm sorry, there's been a terrible mistake. I could still feel the handshake, the tiny bundle of rheumatic bones she offered me, coyly cringing and squeaking and smiling 'Hello, Colin—you've come! You're right on time !'

A little speech of welcome came gushing out of her mouth as we went those few yards to the ticket collector. She used it up in a matter of seconds, and then there was nothing, absolutely nothing. The thing was killed stone dead before we even got off the platform. I suppose she could see the whole story on my face, unless she was half blind like me. We went through the barrier and into the street and then, from then on, it was the funeral march up to her place, a pre-war council estate, the straight rows bisecting each other at regular intervals, and dead flat and tight and orderly, so that you longed to see something with a twist in it. Square little faded brick homes with wooden bays, or flat-fronted, every one from the same mould, same wire fences of square mesh. As soon as the station disappeared from sight I was lost, no bearings. It was Saturday afternoon and I saw one old bloke with crutches and a dog on a lead crossing the road ahead of us, and that's all. We were going past a pillar box on the flat damp pavement in this waste of silence when Edwina blurted out:

' That's where I put my letters!'

It was a gruesome last attempt to resurrect the romance. I followed the direction of her pointing finger as if that was the only way I could see it, nodded as I stared dumbly at the sleek red sides, the square-cut corners of its Fo-dog mouth, loathing its greedy fat belly for aiding and abetting. I kept staring, not having the guts to look at her. The forced note of gaiety cut into me like a shriek. I went limp with relief when she stopped at her gate. A bungalow.

Her mother, a big, blunt-spoken woman, came out of the kitchen and shook hands with me, then went blundering round in the tiny living-room of this doll's house rearranging things, as nervous as her daughter but putting a defensive attack into her movements. She would rest her beefy fists on her hips and ask a question suddenly, brutally direct. Edwina scurried about, twittery and grotesque, patting her hair and running for the family album—blotted out completely by her mother. I saw in a flash what it was, how she'd lived in the shadow of this woman ever since her father had died, ever since her sister had left home to go nursing, ever since her brother had pushed off abroad—there he was with his colleagues, in his white shirt and shorts, swart frowning face like his mother, framed and deathless on top of the piano. India. A missionary, he was. Somebody smoothed and patted the settee and I sat there, family history was poured at me, the females hard at it, Edwina almost relaxed now on her own ground. There were even some spiteful-sounding rejoinders now and then, masked by her cracked spinsterish laugh, a running battle that continued between the two of them, I imagined—though I didn't have any clues so it was lost on me—and

71

it couldn't be stopped now, with a gentleman caller in the house, any more than they could stop the tap dripping. Edwina would glance at me after one of these spiteful jabs, and she'd duck her head and blush apologetically, smiling her ghostly photograph-smile. It made me shudder, but apart from those moments I was struggling to live with the horror of the situation, make the best of it—it was bearable with her mother there between us.

Somehow the farce came to an end—the longest, most painful week-end I ever spent. Saturday night we went back through the ruled streets to a cinema, queued for three-quarters of an hour in grim silence, sat through it side by side in the dark like two liners that pass in the night, never touching, ablaze with trapped life, engines thumping madly. Letting ourselves back into the place again we found the light on in the living-room, sandwiches under a plate on the table and, planted bang in the middle like a vase, a bottle of stout specially for me. For me—the man of the house! And on the sideboard the current issue of the church magazine.

I stuck it out till Sunday afternoon, the time I was supposed to leave anyway—couldn't think of an excuse for leaving earlier. Long before that, though, it had sunk in: she didn't come to say good-bye at the station. And she didn't get another word from me. The ground swallowed me up. Cruel, despicable—but it didn't matter by then what a bastard I was, my one desire was to get rid of her. No more lies on paper—my lies had caught and choked me, I'd paid. I took it all back home, the self-disgust, the shame, like an unspeakable bag of dirty washing I wasn't going to let anybody see, ever. If I'd pretended, put on an act and then slowly, bit by bit, from a distance . . . but my stomach wouldn't take it. Anyway, I was sure she knew. That last glance of reproach or resignation or whatever it was, before she ducked back inside and closed the door— I can still see it. It disintegrated me. No, it needn't have happened but it did and it wasn't her fault, it wasn't mine either, or anybody's—just life playing a dirty trick on us both. The worst part of the lot was the silence and the mute acceptance, not being insulted, accused, spat at, having to imagine it and then do it yourself, a thousand times.

I bet they pushed her about at work, made a drudge of her. 'Edwina, come on, *move*!' How did she cope with things like phone calls? 'Edwina, always ask who it is at the other end.' 'I did, I did.' 'Well, who was it?' 'I couldn't hear what they said.' 'That's because you listen too hard—and you're a bag of nerves to begin with.' And she'd hang her head, go back to her corner and sit quietly. I could imagine it. I bet that big healthy sod of a brother kicked her around when he lived at home. I bet she let him. Even her catty little jabs at her mother aren't really meant to hurt, they're spoken innocently; no claws out, no idea of the score. Her mother could send her flying with one swipe, anyway. And if she did, I bet Edwina would scramble up and say *she* was sorry, her soft brown eyes bright with forgiveness.

She looked wizened, old, antiquated, older than her mother sometimes, but it was her childishness that made me aware quite soon that she was cracked. This defenceless child in her struck terror into me and it shamed me: every action of mine seemed brutal and calculated. I don't mean she was right round the twist—not like a navvy I used to see when I was a kid, bouncing down our street with springy animal strides, great floury boots and short legs in a trance, his cap set dead level and under it those huge watery eyes of his, bright with amazement or terror, I could never decide. The Mole, they called him. On site he worked nonstop all day, so I heard, sweat pouring off him; would go through his dinner-break if his mates let him. At knocking-off time they had to stop him again and hang his knapsack round his neck and push him through the stockade gate into the road and he was all right if he faced in the right direction, off he went home, his tragic Van Gogh boots slamming up and down, cap screwed tight on his grey cropped head which he held well lowered, arms and shoulders working, working. Human Mole. Donkey. Carthorse. Mule. I saw him break into a gallop once, leaping over the uncharted macadam from one pavement to the other like a hunted kangaroo.

There was a girl during the war—a Lillington girl—and

I had just the same impulse then, to get right away. I suppose that's the reaction of any healthy organism. I didn't know she was off her nut at first, and she was, this one: I mean completely. I saw her several times on the bus—she'd get off at Kenilworth—and thought she looked a bit odd, that's all. England's crammed full of odd-looking people. Pale puffy face, nut-crackery. How old was she? It was that part again which was wrong, the age thing. Then once when the bus happened to be jammed tight she was standing up near me hanging on to the strap, swaying slightly more than normal. I may have started watching her more closely all of a sudden for this reason. Soon my nerves tingled, I was riveted on her. She hadn't done anything but now I knew something was wrong. There was an awful tension, something terribly cock-eyed was happening right under my nose. She twisted her head this way and that. It was hot and close, a rattletrap of a bus, men smoking, not a window open.

'I've got to get out,' she said suddenly, calmly and loudly.

It was a public announcement, peremptory. I shivered, it struck me as so grisly, and I found myself longing for her stop to come.

'I can't breathe,' came a second announcement, louder.

My teeth were grinding together. Any minute now she'll throw a fit or dive headlong through the glass, I thought. Everybody deliberately not hearing, not looking, in that sickening manner we have, either from decency or hypocrisy—you can never tell with an Englishman. That isn't surprising, because they don't know themselves, and they don't want to know. And if the truth were known it's probably a bit of each. They'd rather die than acknowledge a sneaky fart to be theirs, partly out of shame and partly because they can't bear to embarrass the other fellow. Better ignore it completely—pretend it never happened, like Nelson. Like him they were all equipped, man, woman and child, with a blind eye. I was the same only different; I was looking, only with me it was sheer fright. Bunched up tight as a watch spring, ready for anything. Nothing happened, she got off at the right place, stepped down like a normal person and walked off, and I relaxed, shakily off the hook.

Another time she seemed to be in conversation with a couple of older girls who knew her. More people got on, the three girls were pushed up the gangway nearer to me. I got a ringside seat. They were baiting her with a few questions for a giggle. One was saying, ' I like fruit gums, Hazel, don't you?'

' Yes, I like fruit gums. I like pastilles too. I like cashews as well. Cashews remind me of birdseed.'

Giggles and big-eyed glances. ' They do?'

' I mean ants' eggs.'

' Really?'

' I don't know what you mean.'

' Anyway you like them.'

' What?'

' Cashews—you just said so.'

' Well I can't remember things. I can't remember, can't remember.'

Then a lull, so they had another prod and a stir. You little lousebound bastards, I said to myself, sitting there against them with my listening ear not far off the belly-button of this smart piece. They were off again:

' Do you like birdseed then, Hazel?'

' Oh no, horrible. I don't like dog food either.'

Wonderful, but there was better to come, and without any prompting. The public announcement voice again:

' There's a peculiar smell in here.'

Shrieks of mirth over my head, the two bright little bitches half collapsing on each other.

' Is there? Perhaps it's your feet.'

Shocked at this, she cried out in what I guessed must have been a pure echo of her mother:

' You mustn't say things like that!'

' Why not?'

' It's rude.'

There came a spell of chatter which would have seemed perfectly normal to a casual listener. I wasn't casually listening though, I was half straining my tabhole off. ' I'm going to do Christmas shopping today,' she said, and that was fine, nobody could swop sly looks. But she had to go and tag on, 'to get Christmas stuff.' Towards the end of the trip she came out with really preposterous things, like 'Why is it raining?' and 'We should stay indoors when it's bad weather like this. Why don't we?'

I was always glad when she got out, she scared me, caught on my nerves, and though I couldn't care less what she came out with, personally, the world of others who did, sitting all around in judgement, made it a big strain; so I didn't like it. I wanted her to shut up. The word for this feeling is embarrassment. Yes, I was glad to see the back of her. Then afterwards like a hypocrite I was sorry for her and thought how much better she was than those sly cagey bitches who kept doubling up with attacks of the giggles. They were only passing the time, it's true, and I suppose she was oblivious anyway. I was a fool, getting worked up for nothing. Merry Christmas! Happy New Year! She was at least sixteen, black-haired, dressed like a little girl, pallid straight legs in ankle socks, bull-nosed shoes, a kid's woollen bonnet on her head. Clambering down from the bus she was terribly stiff-legged and cautious, no suppleness at all: more like an old girl of eighty.

13

AFTER Edwina I made sure of the body first. I wasn't exactly callous—I mean I didn't go deliberately shopping for it or anything like that. I was a hard innocent. I saw this girl Kay, playing tennis with her pal, another teenager. Kay, the pouter pigeon. She had a peaches-and-cream complexion, she bulged fore and aft and she was only nineteen, still growing. Could have been puppy fat but it was still real, her plump titties bounced up and down inside her cream blouse in a generous, jolly sort of motion. I studied them more than the ball as she charged around red in the face, whooping, socking the ball back ineffectually. Her partner was short, and much more purposeful. I wasn't struck on her.

Like all my forced friendships it was abortive, doomed

to frustration, this one. I joined the tennis club so that I didn't have to keep staring through the mesh. The biggest obstacle was her friend, who stuck like glue—they were both training to be librarians. When I got a date with Kay we had to take Valerie with us the first evening. I suppose Kay must have had a little chat with her between then and the next occasion, because when I asked where Valerie was, out came an unlikely story about a sick aunt she'd had to rush off and see all of a sudden.

Kay was bespoke, she was a frozen virgin, her father had died earlier that year and her mother was in bed suffering from shock. Things were under a cloud, to say the least. Kay was sexless with tragedy, devotion, self-sacrifice, and various morbid thoughts and preoccupations concerning death. Her breasts bounced in a jolly way and no mistake, but independently of her, with a perverse life of their own. She was a kind of mirage. We went for gloomy walks across the fields behind Orley. Once she had to clip the grass on her father's new grave, so I trailed with her up the freshly raked and weeded gravel paths one Saturday afternoon, in a cool breeze. Then we got on our bikes and cycled over to the bloody fields again, for more silent walking. You idiot, I kept telling myself. That afternoon I bought her a peach and she ate it soundlessly, curled in the grass, without spilling a drop. Her large moony eyes with their vaguely reproachful expression avoided me, and the only time she ever spoke warmly was when she got on to the subject of Chris, a fellow student at the librarians' training college.

'I can't stop thinking about him,' she told me. 'What do *you* think I ought to do? Should I tell him how I feel about him or not? He probably isn't even aware of my existence. What would you do in my place?'

She took me in to see her mother once, while I was hanging around waiting for her to get herself ready. She led me into the boxy bedroom on the ground floor at the front of the house and left me to make conversation as best as I could. There was her mother, yellowish, black marks under her eyes, propped up on the pillows and smiling weakly. The resemblance to her daughter was amazing— even to the reproach in her eyes. It was life they were accusing mutely, both of them, in a fundamental complaint they had no words for. How cruel and heartless, their eyes said. I stood there at the foot of the bed, racking my brains for something to say. I took off my cycle clips as a sign of respect.

'Hello, young man,' she said. 'What a lovely day!'

If it wasn't her mother, or her father's grave, it would be this Chris—I loathed him already—she was mooning over. I didn't touch her once—not even a goodnight kiss. If she wanted to freeze me out, I kept saying to myself, then why does she let me go trailing round with her like this? It was unreal. All that flesh, and you had the feeling that if you poked a finger at her you'd go right through. Nothing there. Absent. In any case she was untouchable. I'd no more have wanted to slip my hand up her dress than fart at Sunday School; it was just unthinkable. Long before I admitted it to myself, my tool realised what a fiasco it all was. Even lying in bed thinking about her I never once got an erection; not even first thing in the morning.

I was ripe for the pros. Yet with years of instruction in the factory, the street, hanging around at street corners, I was still a novice in the art of being tough. Still a skinned rabbit. Two features, eyes and lips, betrayed me every time I came face to face with a 'situation'. I couldn't stare people in the face like my pals did without flinching, I had no hard fixed gaze to dish out, I couldn't flick those razor-sharp glances, or tell somebody flatly to 'fuck off'. Yet I was getting more like them, the cyanide was case-hardening me, it was only a matter of time. In the dinner hour there was a small gang of us apprentices, four or five. We'd queue up for the canteen dinner—you went to one tin counter and bought tickets first, main meal, pudding, tea—and sit together at the long unpainted trestles, then get to work. Abusing it, naturally, that was the thing:

'Where's the bleedin' meat then?'

'There it is, you cunt, under them carrots.'

'Christ I thought it was a shadow.'

You spread your elbows, kept your head down over the plate like a dog sticking its snout in the dish, and chewing away it didn't matter if your mouth was open or shut, or how much noise you made. Afterwards it was the grunt, sigh, plate shoved away as if with contempt, and a ripe belch or two if you felt like it :

' Ah, that's better—excuse a pig.'

There was a feeling of rancour. If you spoke to your mates it had to be jeering, violent. Insults were spat out freely, as a matter of course, in a joyless kind of humour, and you retaliated in the same way, loud-mouthed, hard, or kept quiet. There was no freedom, nobody relaxed or spoke in confidence; none of that stuff to do with homes and girls, mothers, the female. The bitter taste was on our tongues, the iron hook dug in cruelly. We were men, in a man's world, but with one terrible disadvantage : we were virgins. Not knowing how to cope we kept spitting words, aiming blows, lashing out at friends if they came too close or noticed too much, saw what a green kid you were :

' Fuck off, you cunt.'

It was a howling travesty of how we really were inside, under the masks, and there was no breaking the rigid pattern of behaviour laid down for us, as clear and fixed as the white lines of the gangways.

My eyes were no good, a soft brown, soft and yielding, but much worse were my lips. The lips of my mouth. I had no more control over them than a man with no teeth. At times of stress my mouth just collapsed, the lips wobbled like a baby's, horribly out of control. Again and again it disgraced me. I choked with eloquence, burned with desperate locked fire, I was tender as a lamb, stiff with young pride; I'd show a woman, she'd be wild with gratitude when she unlocked me—my hands glowed with the knowledge of what I was, hands of power. And there was this lady's mouth caving in, pouting, drooping piteously at the corners as if it was going to cry.

After the grub, we'd either play pontoon or go for a stroll and a breath of air in the side streets. Walk out past the closed serving hatches with our backs to the stage. If there was a soprano screeching for dear life up there then Lou would probably give her the V-sign, keeping his fingers close to his head as a precaution, in case she twisted round at the crucial moment in his direction. Then he'd be giving his scalp a scratch, his face deadpan. He was our comic. I'd be a mixture of pity and hatred for these third-rate performers who were supposed to be keeping up our morale and helping the war effort. Didn't they have a clue about working men, what they were like? Why couldn't somebody tell them the score? We slouched along, legs too far apart like young colts, down the canteen steps and out : then it was either the back way, trailing through the factory outbuildings, or straight on to the highway, the big trunk connection with the outside. We went out raggedly, no direction in particular, as if our feet were taking us for a walk. We were killing time. It was unreal, being let out at this time of day. Nothing had released us, we were merely out for exercise. On the trunk, but not travelling, not using it to go anywhere. Hands stuck in our pockets, we swaggered, dragged our feet, kicked a fag packet along with us, dribbling, passing—all with a studied lack of interest. We cultivated the air of louts; this was the act fixed for us, a ritual of long standing, till we reached manhood and got married, loaded with responsibilities. This was the uneasy interim. If anything female and young enough tripped by, the instinct was to degrade it, drag it down :

' Jesus, she's pale—I bet she's got the jam rags on.'

If it looked rough, a vicious chorus of insults rose up.

' I bet her fanny's like a horse's collar.'

' She's rough enough for any dog to tackle.'

' If you fucked her, bugger me—it'd be like stirring a bucket of whitewash.'

The best at it was Ray, who shaved morning and night and had a real man's jowl, already bristly and black by dinnertime. He had an endless stream of foul remarks, uttered calmly, harsh and firm and intractable. His gait was angry, caged, explosive. He tried to dawdle like the rest of us, but after a bit he'd burst out in a seizure of rage at the one lagging behind :

' Come on, man, for fuck's sake !'

He gave the most brutal impression of a man without any forcing, he was all ready to enter the world, yet like us he hadn't been anywhere or done anything, except get drunk. There was that chin of his, rough as emery cloth.

Yet he wasn't a thug: far from it. His clouded, defensive eyes were gentle, with long curly lashes, and now and then he stuttered. You sensed that his violence was directed inwards.

We went haunting the streets, shackled invisibly, drifting round corners like shadows, and in the winter especially we stayed away from the main arteries where the traffic rammed through indifferent to us, long-distance heavies, big stuff. These were rancid, poor days. We hated the vacuity but it caught us, and our arrogance took on an edge like an east wind. Outside we really felt poverty-stricken, directionless, we watched the free purposeful lorries and it made us worse. The contrast dehumanised us. Inside the beehive it was work, din, stink, chat, real solitude, the cup of tea and the fag, a sly visit to a mate on another section right out of sight, trips to the shithouses—and you had a good selection. It was better inside, living and breathing, human; it was where you belonged. Nobody was free, nobody could get out. It was equal and all right.

Nine years. Imagine thirty, forty years in a single span. Who'd stick a sentence like that in their right mind if they knew it was definite, a fact? Nobody knows how long they've actually got. It's day to day. Add it up later, reckon the score, and try to feel shocked but don't really, because it's history now. Used up. Tomorrow's knocking on the door—hang on, I'm coming. Answer the door, quick, you might have won the pools. Millions to one but it could be you; somebody wins it every week. It could be you. Nobody admits they're under sentence. Who could bear it?

Nine years. Gone in one snap, gobbled up by Mr Purlham, white-haired, stiff-backed, rosy-cheeked self-made industrialist, with his pop-eyed glare of a fanatic, his canteen speeches and his sleek nephew at his right hand. The crazy empire-builder, Adam's apple gulping in his stringy old throat like a danger signal. Choking on his own will power, drive, ambition. Towards the end his nephew, fresh from the army, starts appearing by his side on the canteen platform. Blond, plump and glossy like an otter, with none of the fiery monomania of the old man, who makes an effort to control himself and speak calmly but still storms at the eyeballs, still stiffens his old neck at the sound of jeers from the back; tyrannical as ever, forcing the men into sullen silence and obedience by his old master's trick of just standing there in a smoulder of disgust, refusing to speak. Then the withering contempt as he opened, and you knew what came after, the trampling and bending and dismissing of the hostility in a pep talk that opened and closed with a threat:

'Don't think I can't deal with people who are too rowdy to let me speak . . .'

A whole world, remember—even its own barber. This was to cut down on absenteeism during the war, when the six-day weeks were being worked by everybody, and a man would have to take a day off to get his hair cut. Own barber, own surgery, canteen, social club, police, fire brigade, big and small outbuildings and still growing, sheds, stores, boiler houses, pill-boxes, shelters, dug-outs, all with roads between. A complex. The dispatch and packing came first, as you entered through the main doors over the wood-block floor soaked in machine oil, studded with lathe cuttings, milling chips, capstan swarf, drill curls, iron filings, steel, brass, copper, aluminium. Gangways marked out in white lines, fading here and there, freshened up for Royal visits. Punch clocks and racks of clock cards and notice boards carrying warnings, dotted about strategically. The Ordnance Department, Aviation Department, Dispatch, Millwrights, Horizontal Millers, Vertical Millers, Borers, Turning Shop. Paint Shop, Test Bay, Inspectors, Press Tools, Injection, Teleprinters, Machine Tool, Progress Chasers, Time and Motion, Surface Grinders, Internal Grinders, External Grinders, Screwcutters. Capstan Section, Shapers, Fitters, Precision Tool, Hardening Shop, Sandblasting, Apprentice School, Experimental, Auto, Design Department, Projection, Stores. Vertical Planers, Horizontal Planers, Radial, Broach, Testers.

And shithouses. Dotted about strategically like the boards and punch clocks, but every one built against an outer wall. Some with urinals, the porcelain trough clogged with fag ends, matches, fag packets, the water squirting and farting out of the brass sprinklers to dilute the rivers of piss, swill-

ing round the garbage and draining off somehow. Some
with no urinal but a filthy encrusted wash basin. Some
without either wash basin or urinal—just a row of bogs like
horse boxes. Each shithouse reeking of poison gas first
thing, with all the booths occupied and going full blast, but
otherwise each one different from the next, with a character of its own. It's funny but I can't recall now what we
used for paper in those places, whether a roll supplied by
the firm, bearing their name, or newspaper, or what. They
didn't give anything away, that firm, and if toilet rolls had
been provided they'd have been lifted the same day for
certain, name or no name. In the shithouses nearest to the
main gates there were no doors on the booths, and for a
long time I wondered if they'd been pinched, or unscrewed
by the management so as to make our stay as short as possible. Then one morning I looked closer at the door jamb,
there were no screw holes, so it looked as if the bastards
had put the things up without doors to begin with. For a
bit of privacy you sat on the throne with the morning
paper spread out in front of you. Wandering down the line
of pans looking for a vacancy first thing that's all you'd
see: rows of newspapers, boots, fingers, dangling braces,
concertina trousers. So there was no lingering, no chance
for graphic art either on the walls or door. But they made
up for it in the others. Every inch of space seemed to be
decorated, some of it with crabbed, tiny scrawl, sloping
down steeper and steeper, till you were nearly standing on
your head to read it, and sometimes the whole back of a
door occupied by a lavish sketch of a pair of tits. Swelling,
rampant images were attempted, and when the artist
couldn't get the proportions right or the realism convincing
he got desperate and drew on a bigger scale. Pricks hung
their bloated heads and dripped spunk in thick gobbets;
cunts yawned, as if on the point of giving birth, and one
or two were carnivorous, equipped with a set of teeth by
wits. ' It makes you think with all this wit that Shakespeare
has been here to shit.' One of the longest stories was on the
brickwork where the downpipe from the cistern was fastened. It had been gouged out with a steel scriber, by the
look of it, then the grooves inked in crudely with indelible

pencil. Maybe several hands had a go at it. Because it had to find space where it could it wound down in a spiral to the left of the pan, then petered out; a characteristic fantasy about a man who puts up for the night at his brother's flat. 'One night I got stranded in the town where my brother lived so I called and asked if he would put me up for the night he said yes I could sleep in his bed with him if I liked and his wife would sleep on the living-room sofa which is what I did Well next morning he left early to go to work and I was flaked out asleep dead tired when suddenly I felt a hand on my thigh creeping round softly so I did nothing anyway I was too drowsy then I felt the same hand taking a handful of my balls then my cock which was soft as shit I just lay there lovely and warm wondering what the game was not that I cared would you And suddenly she was rubbing her tits up and down on my back then her leg wrapped round me I knew then who it was my brother's wife the randy little bitch Oh Tom she moaned I'm dying for it can't you get a hard-on and she no sooner said that than I started to I was stiff as a ramrod in no time where the strength came from I'll never know She was delighted I kept telling her it was no good I was too tired to fuck her oh never mind she said I'll fuck you and she did what a hot bitch she was . . .'

Well, it was here my good father delivered me in all innocence, on January 1st, at the tender age of fifteen. Innocent as babes, both of us. He had gone through it with the rest, that legendary Slump everybody in our family referred to—it was one long slump between the wars as far as I could make out—and though living in Brum and the El Dorado had saved him to some extent, the experience was branded on him like an injury, an attribute. He'd sunk low enough at one point to tramp the streets doing door-to-door canvassing for the *Express*. He was never out, even in the worst times, more than a few months. That was not long after they were married, and it broke up the marriage for a while; they had to separate and go back to living with their parents while he tried his luck in another town. Anyway it was bitter, it marked them, now it was over and done with, and when they brought it out it was to adorn themselves with it as an attribute, and put the fear of God into the kids. The factory was bound to be the place to take me. Live, humming, desirable—it would drag him there by instinct, it was deeply in him from his young struggling days as a family man, along with Labour and the Slump and the war to end wars. The idea was stuck in his head that I ought to have a trade: he was for ever telling my mother in front of me that if he'd had one he'd have been kicked around a lot less. I was passive and victim-like, I waited in the concrete pill-box just inside the gates, sniffing with vague dread like an animal smelling the blood. They were fetching the Apprentice Supervisor. In he bustled, not a minute to lose, his white butcher's smock stained at the pockets with industry, the grime of iron in his fingernails. He frowned, then smiled just with the edges of his lips, leaving his eyes dead. Saying something he showed his tobacco-stained, spaced-out fangs, and that was a slight improvement. He stuck out a long skinny hand for my father to shake. I stared at his knobbly wrist thick with black hairs, until his horse jaw, working about sideways in a laborious chewing motion, started to fascinate me. Lugubrious Bristolian speech was being manufactured, leaden with phoney gravity. His eyes glinted grimly, flicking over me, the new brat. 'Quite frankly, your son will receive the best engineering training it's possible to have in this town. I can assure you of that. If he's keen and industrious, you understand, I can be perfectly honest and say that you won't have cause to regret bringing him to us. I can assure you on that point.' Turning to me:

' Are you keen, son?'

' Yessir.'

' Not afraid of work?'

' No, sir.'

It was settled. He rubbed his dry hands together like a workhouse master, then started washing them with invisible soap to keep the circulation going—it was cold where we stood, we were bundled in overcoats and I could see him shivering. He hung there, slack at the knees, his chest caved in, the top pocket of his white coat bristling with rules, pencils, gauges. He was all of a twitch because he was freezing, but also because he couldn't bear to be idle. Skin and grief. Another twitch, fangs again, and he was gone.

When I really got to know him though he wasn't all that bad. Funereal was the word for him. The other lads referred to him as Father to convey the episcopal voice and his habit of winding his fingers together and holding his hands while he walked. What I liked best about him was his preoccupation: he was too absorbed in problems to bother much with mere apprentices—he left that to his chargehands. He had a glassed-in box and he sat in there hatching schemes, having little secret conferences with his staff or sitting hunched over his desk in solitary state holding his head in his hands. Seeing him like that we used to say, 'Father's crying again' because it was exactly the attitude. It was easy to keep out of his way; you soon learned how to merge, be inconspicuous.

We were in a compound called the School, a corner of one of the main sheds, and it was charming if you could see it that way, like a model village, perfectly scaled, but with the reality of a real village sucked out of it. On the other side of the fence—and we could see it through the mesh, hear it and smell it, even if we couldn't touch it— was the throbbing world of men. Massive broaching machines out there groaned and shrieked, with queer lulls in between, and then blokes could be heard calling across to each other, letting out jeers, catcalls, guffaws, and if a chorus of wolf whistles rose up you could bet it was a woman going down the main aisle, haughty and statuesque or loose and jaunty or doing the rhumba, red-cheeked or indifferent or yelling back a mouthful, according to how seasoned she was. Our nursemaids the chargehands, who belonged out there and were only wet-nursing us because it was a soft number and paid a bit better, would exchange knowing looks and gaze through the mesh at the haze of blue smoke over the big howling machines as if yearningly. It was like being in a monastery for them. Swearing was against the rules, so were dirty stories; they swore and swapped filth just the same, but on the sly, and you could see how they resented that. They'd straddle their legs and have a quick smoke—that wasn't encouraged either—with their eyes sliding restlessly over their toy domain. Everything was in miniature in that place. We had our own stores, a boy storekeeper in charge. If he wouldn't cough up with more than one sheet of emery cloth there'd be scuffles over the low fence with somebody keeping an eye on the glass booth. The chargehands obligingly looked the other way. Unless it was serious, they were glad of any distraction. They had a secret language of derisive smiles which they exchanged across the compound, and they twitched their noses, raised eyebrows, worked in all kinds of refinements to express mockery and boredom. One, who had become a master of irony, used to shrug with marvellous eloquence as a sort of last word. How they loathed it, their little kingdom! The lathes, grinders, millers, shapers, bandsaw, benches were exactly the same as in the real factory, only smaller and cleaner altogether. Naturally there were no piece rates and no inspectors—we were playing at work.

There was a tall gawky youth they called Karl, a German refugee, whose English was stiff and formal like a public speech, and his black crinkly hair was cropped short and his neck was long, and stiff like his speech. He bent short-sightedly over his lathe, the most modern and gleaming, the biggest machine in the School, and the chargehands were deferential to him because his work was skilful and he was a favourite—his father had business connections with the firm. I didn't know any names or anything about the set-up, but in a day or two I could pick out the favourites by the way they stood and talked and strolled around. They had a proprietary air, like prefects at school, and they were haughty and so casual. These were the élite of our rarified little world. They lounged insolently against the best machines and spoke to the chargehands with their hands stuck in their pockets, as equals. When they went to the store and hung over the top of the barrier—they were all tall, naturally—the boy didn't argue the point as he did with the others. They got the best. The most intricate jobs were entrusted to them, jobs that would have made me tremble all over with fear and apprehension, terribly conscious of the precision, the fine tolerances, the critically sharp lines of the blueprint *and its silence*, icily blue like a map of hell. I was beaten before I began. But not these boys. They twirled the handles and cut finely and surely, calm as surgeons. I admired them, and I marvelled at their cruel radiance. They were always the tallest and handsomest, we were runts in comparison, the rest of us. We loathed and worshipped, kept clear and would never have dreamed of approaching them, or marching up boldly to them, direct, to borrow a tool.

The boy who fascinated me at the very beginning in that model farmyard—a boy so useless at manual work that his father must have been dippy to put him to a trade—had a strange surname. I remember it as Xerri, and you pronounced it to sound like sherry. He was there three months and then disappeared : I think his parents left the district. Or it may have been that his old man came to his senses and found him a more suitable occupation. I didn't pal up with Don Xerri, it was only that I couldn't help watching him all the time. I gathered he was well off, compared to us. He had a boarding school voice, and his face, soft and pink and beautiful, was—I realise now—like the face of a very young Scott Fitzgerald. Perhaps it was because he seemed so incongruous dirtying the pale baby skin of his hands in a factory that I couldn't take my eyes off him. The languor of his gestures belonged to another world entirely : seeing him at work, or what he meant to pass for work, pretending to be industrious and trying to stifle his giggles, you saw that he'd never be any use if he stood there for ever. When he paused—which he did every other minute—and straightened his back there was such luxury in the movement that you couldn't help grinning your head off. Filing along a template, the simplest exercise for beginners, he held his file like a banana and still hadn't mastered this fundamental skill after three months. I was ignorant of the very word homosexual in those days, but to say he was one tells me no more now than it would have done then. There was something soft and very corruptible about him, and there was a glamorous sweetness. I imagined him nestling seductively against the breasts of his elegant mother, his smile glistening, his shapely head tousled, milky and soft and beautiful. He wasn't elegant himself, he was too small and approachable. Mostly he had this subtle and secretive smile, or he was giggling with some close pal like a lover. If he did burst out laughing, it was a soft explosion of sensuousness, opening his mouth and stretching his throat, showing his hard white teeth, abandoning his whole body to it.

One corner of the compound was glassed-in and had a ceiling, instead of sharing the roof trusses and dirty skylights of the main shop, and this room was actually a classroom, with rows of seats and a blackboard like a proper school. Once a week a teacher used to arrive, a plump dynamic little Russian, middle-aged, a bald dome pushing through his thinning locks, which were black and well-greased, and hung over his ears in wings like a musician's. He was a professor or doctor, anyway important, who ran a private school for girls. His passion was mathematics. He spoke about it so ardently that I used to actually look forward to him coming, his fire inspired me, and you could relax and listen and not make any headway, nobody bothered, there were no exams to worry about at the end of it. My maths didn't improve but for the first time I was on the point of tasting its raptures and appreciating its almost mystical satisfactions. At the heart of it was power, the power men feel in a clean orderly room with the sounds of life sealed off—ours was like that, muffled, faintly humming on the other side of the glass—and the white-ruled paper, the pen as sharp as a scalpel, cutting methodically at the problem, proving Euclid, setting out abstract perfections according to the gospels of Calculus, Differential, Integral, Infinitesimal. It was a universe of supreme order impervious to change and accident, fire and storm, pestilence, night sweat. Above life. The rigorous, passionate little foreigner taught us to ignore the world surging soundlessly at the windows. He was trying to raise us up, purify us, and it affected me like a religion. His other subject, practical engineering, was concerned with tools, cutting edges, varying angles of drill points for different materials. It was useful to us, had an obvious application, and for that reason his heart wasn't in it, you could tell. He lacked fire, and I got bored and longed for the pure maths again, even though I knew I'd never master it.

Most of the week the lecture room was empty. Once I came back early from dinner and went in there to look for a pencil I'd lost. Over in a far corner, giggling softly, was Don Xerri with his chief pal, a bruiser with carroty hair and a red bull neck named Dawson, who was pushing him against the wall and mauling him, pawing at him with his ham fists. He turned his head and laughed, and I went out again quickly, confused, unable to look at Xerri's pale face, his sweet mouth and long-lashed eyes. I couldn't figure it out, what they were up to—that was how ignorant I was. Not long afterwards somebody passed on a pulp magazine for me to read—it was going the rounds like a chain letter, as these things did—and I slipped down the alleyway between the fences to the shithouse shared by apprentices and men. Locked in there, I read the stories by instalments during the day. It was a book for perverts—another world utterly foreign to me. Yet I read the incomprehensible details feeling hot and guilty, and my fingers shook as they turned the pages. Women in tiny frilled aprons that exposed their naked arses—' buttocks ' was a greatly favoured word, a key to the endless ritual—and other women with broad leather belts so tight they were gasping for breath, and others struggling to drag on boots as tight as gloves, so long they reached up to their crotches. Or they were being laced into corsets until their eyes bulged like Pekinese, while somebody joyfully beat those bared and offered buttocks. The theme was always the same : humiliation, flagellation, constriction. Pain and pleasure and punishment were inextricably mixed. Sickened and fascinated and lost, I passed it on, a dog-eared and ownerless manual. It burned in me for hours and then died of lack of fuel. My imagination couldn't function on no experience, so I suppose that saved me. While it lived I licked my lips and felt famished, I wanted more details, and at the same time the skin of my mind crawled in a kind of terror, as if I was contaminated with a disease.

The whole period was famished, pinched, hemmed around with fears and not knowing and the menace of beyond, where it was real and dirty and waiting. After six months or so you were automatically expelled and out-posted to whichever section had a free machine or a spare bench, and later you might go back in the School again for another spell, but not for long. By accident I use the word spell and it's true that the word goes with that place; but the spell only worked the first time. Going back in again afterwards you were on a different level, you saw it with different eyes, through a fog of nostalgia, dispossessed, it was sadly irrelevant and midget and laughable and you walked carefully and gently like a Gulliver, your ears full of shrill cries. I never went back again to stay but I should have liked to, just to experience the Gulliver feeling.

I moved around, I was with turners one year, fitters the next. The richest time and the most unhealthy was on the machine grinders. I liked it because it was self-contained, and easy, nobody bothered you too much or stopped your daydreams, there was no machine oil flooding about, making your clothes stink and giving you the itch on the forearms and fingers. It was small enough to secrete your-self in, a section of say half a dozen blokes, including the chargehand, yet in the middle of the main shop indis-tinguishable from the rest with all its lanes, belts and motors, hundreds of men intent on their own tasks; then as the minute hand on those punch clocks crept up to six the furtive edging and drifting would begin—a secret coalesc-ence. Two minutes to go and the boldest would walk up openly and plant themselves there, a *fait accompli*, tight against the racks of cards in a cheeky little queue. The most audacious would be the first one to make the move and arrive there, and as soon as he felt others begin to form up behind him—he didn't need to look—his hand would sneak up for his card from the rack. This would be a signal, the queue grew out faster behind his back, a long snake, while he watched that minute hand and waited tense as a sprinter for the gun. *Bang!* it jumped, the minute hand. His card moved that same instant and was in the slot and *bang!* he hit the punch lever, ripped out his card, found a home for it in the rack again, streaked off. *Bang! bang!* the clock was going. *Bang! bang!* and the stampede was away. That was the night, when old Purlham suddenly arose down the bottom end of the gangway, planted himself in the middle of the road to freedom, pop eyes blazing, his hand up like Canute as the flood bore down on him four abreast. 'Stop running!' he yelled. 'At once! I forbid it absolutely!' I wasn't there when it happened, I imagined it. Just the kind of thing the old fanatic would do. It nearly worked, too, but the faltering runners at the front couldn't put the brakes on quick enough, and even if they had their mates were in a trampling herd behind and they'd never have heard the old bastard, there was too much din, too many war cries, too much neighing of chargers, yells of delight, crazy hoots of laughter, girls whinnying and shrieking. He got knocked on one side and sat down with a thump. It was a wonder they didn't smash his arms or legs, trample all over him. I detested him, like the others, I wouldn't have shed a tear, but when they told me how he stood his ground, waving his arms and yelling like a lunatic, I had to admire his guts. Next day the warnings flowered on all the notice boards: instant dismissal for the next man caught running down the main gangways. So in future they walked, so fast it was the nearest thing to running I'd ever seen. They did it stiff-legged, clockwork fashion, legs working like mad scissors. After a week of that they were running naturally again, but not quite with the same joyous certitude: then it was only a matter of days till they were back to normal.

Outside, they funnelled through the gates and rushed in hunting packs for the buses, panting and victorious if they got themselves seats. If I was after a bus I didn't waste time either; it was a matter of keeping yourself upright in the torrent. But I was never first at the clocks, or one of the leading runners: that wasn't my way. It was my instinct to get overlooked, make myself anonymous. My check number suited me down to the ground—I preferred it to my name. Secrecy was second nature to me; either this or the most naked exposure. Anything competitive, like the survival-of-the-fittest race for the buses, and I was ready to drop out at the slightest excuse. I was solo. This flaw had to be protected, so I took elaborate precautions as a matter of instinct. If I was speaking to somebody and they spoke in a rough lingo, dropping aitches and so on, I did likewise. I liked to blend, please, agree, observe, listen sympathetically, if possible without having to contribute. I longed to contribute, pour myself happily without a thought, but I was beginning to sense treachery every-where. And I was still speechless. That was why I had to keep quiet—I was growing a tongue. I took to it even as a kid, this merging: now I could do it with ease. It was the next best thing to being invisible. A woman said once to a friend of mine, ' Isn't he quiet—like a girl!'

14

I was solo, yet little by little over the years I was making contact with the odd pal here and there; nothing deep, but the ones I did make clung, for some reason. Nobody seemed to be trying, no effort, and most of these contacts belonged in the factory, that's all. I preferred it that way, took care to cultivate them in such a way that they wouldn't con-tinue outside. Living at Lillington cut me off clean from them as soon as I jumped on my bike and bent over the handlebars. Back in the city again I tried, without being unfriendly, to keep my free hours solitary. That wasn't so easy. I was saved by their girls, mostly. Al Fillimore had a girl, he was a young apprentice fitter working nearby when I was on the lathes, and I often found myself biking home with him through the streets : he lived in my direction. He had hard red curls that seemed to cling to his forehead, and he clung to me in the same way, like a hard growth that was nothing to do with him personally. He was bright, younger than me, nervy and alert, charming with a touch of moodi-ness, and he affected an indifference that was either jeering or bored, bored like a boy walking in puddles, or the nearest he could get to the casual look he adored in his heroes. These were all singers, famous names, Americans. His face was freckled. He walked slightly hunched because he had one arm shorter than the other. A jellybaby, he did a tough guy act. You only had to fumble, search

for words and he'd let you have it: ' If you've got nothing to say, shut up!' I liked him, liked his nutty humour,
his plump bouncy body, but after a while he unnerved
me, made me restless. He was easier to be with, more
relaxed, when he was with his girl Francie, a young blonde
he was courting, who acted the tomboy and played his
stooge, wisecrack for wisecrack, but under the fun and
games meant business. And under his fooling and oh so
casual air, he was a bit wary. I saw them rowing once in
the street—she'd been kept waiting a few minutes. ' You're
late,' she said, and before he could open his mouth, off she
flounced up the street, white-faced, furious. He put on the
indifferent act for my benefit, but I saw the score.

So there was him, mad on the big bands, rolling his eyes
and saying ' Jesus!' and giving his imitation through the
hole in his fist, using it as a trumpet for those frenzied last
riffs, when the brass riots. And his Judy Garland, Sinatra,
Ella. Naturally it had to be Yank, the English were wet
as a can of piss. He'd sit listening to records he'd brought
round, and there was no point in him listening, he had
every note off by heart, every inflexion. Come to think of
it, he only half listened, grinning and twitching his hips,
having a boyish nibble at his girl's neck, saying in a stage
whisper with a wink in my direction, ' Let's go snogging
tonight,' and she'd say, ' Don't say that word, it's horrible!'

There were others, more stodgy, scattered about in
different departments, and they might hail me if I was
wandering past, say to the stores, or I'd walk over to their
position deliberately for a quick chat. Mostly they'd be fellow apprentices, but there was one older bloke—old enough
to be my father—I'd got to know years before, when I was
on the lathes. He was a veteran, a skilled turner. In idle
moments when I worked on his gang I used to watch him,
the great hoops of cast iron he had to manhandle into his
chuck, his face tense with effort, yanking over the wooden
crossbar to start his old machine, winding up the saddle
with one hand and to save a couple of seconds giving the
turret a final yank with the wrench as it slid in to the
attack. From morning to night he seemed like that, in a
mad rush. I worked on an even older machine, a real

wreck, right behind him. For some reason I never understood he befriended me, if you could call it that, and years later I couldn't go down his gangway without him calling me over to ask how I was. He couldn't stop working to have a yarn, even for a couple of minutes, and his moan was always the same: the time allowed on the job he was doing, whatever it happened to be, was too short. They'd undercut him, the only way he could make it pay was by flogging himself to death. 'I'd be stupid to do that, wouldn't I? What do you think?' He thrashed about in a fury, twisting his head at me to make sure I hadn't escaped, his face charred and contorted, now and then a ghastly smile lighting it up like a neon sign: on, off.

'The bleeders,' he'd pant, 'look at the time they've given me on this lot; I've got to do so-and-so '—and he'd reel off a string of processes 'and how much time for each? Eh? Eh? Have a guess, go on. The fuckers!'

He put the fear of God into me for some reason. I'd stand by the side of him, my will paralysed, wanting desperately to shove off and racking my brains for an excuse. He had a disconcerting habit of shooting out a personal, direct question, and his eyes bored into you and there was no escape. Once he rasped out, wiping his hands on a wad of cotton waste:

'Know how old I am? Have a guess.'

He dug his forefinger into the mess of Russian fat and daubed the bright points of his centres. I made some attempt, but what he was working round to was how old *my* old man was. He had a nasty buttonholing approach if he wanted information. All the years I knew him, he didn't once use my name.

'Hey,' he'd call out, as you went slipping by hopefully, 'come here.'

'Okay?' I said, pausing, trying to look friendly and harassed at the same time.

'What you got to tell me, then?'

'Nothing really . . .'

'What's the rush?'

'No rush.'

And he'd keep smiling, his bitter burning eyes fixed on

me, the smile like a rat-trap, gleaming, ferocious. 'What's the rush?' he'd repeat, eager and demanding, seeing me itching to be off. And the next move I knew by heart: his hand went up and grabbed the bar, tugged it violently and the machine stopped. He kept going, though, wiping the bed of his lathe, stripping down the turret, retooling, while he cross-examined me. This was his idea of a friendly chat. He kept it up for ten minutes, then all at once lost interest, the tempo of work increased, he had the chuck spinning and it was obvious he couldn't wait for you to push off. But if you went before he was ready, it was as if he was suffering pangs of jealousy.

'What's new then? What you got to tell me?'

'Oh, nothing . . . nothing much.'

'Must be something. Eh?'

'Can't think what.'

'Dad okay? Your mother?'

Or he might want an errand running. He begged, and pushed his face close, and his abjectness was so aggressive and resentful, jerked out, it made him uglier than ever. He hated me for doing him a good turn, even before I'd agreed to it. He'd rattle out harshly, like an accusation:

'Do me a favour?'

'Yes, sure.'

'Now hang on—not so fast—you don't know what it is yet.'

'No, alright . . .'

'Eh—eh?'

'Listen, it's nothing, nothing much, I'd do it myself, you know that, but this bastard job—up to the bleedin' eyes in it I am—you understand? You can see for yourself can't you how I'm fixed. Anybody can if they ain't blind. Working my balls off, I am.'

'That's alright, I'll go.'

'If it's any trouble, tell me. Don't want to put you out.'

'No trouble.'

I'd set off, and he'd bawl down the gangway after me, 'Hang on—what about my check number? Know it by heart?'

Usually it was a trip to the stores, say to take a drill

back. Hand it over the top of the fence to the storekeeper, who dropped it in the bin and looked for the check number stamped on the brass checks hanging on the row of cup hooks. The check I could return any time I was passing, 'don't come back specially this way, understand,' but I took it straight back and dropped it on his tin workstand while the visit was still fresh. That way I avoided the risk of another long session, later. If we had a chat, he had to nab me on the trot past, and most weeks I was lucky, his head was well down. His hands grubbed and clawed, nails split, clogged with muck and oil, he was driven by time, the bastards in the office kept undercutting him and he went faster and still made the price pay. He'd show the bastards! They wouldn't grind him down. Nil desper-andum illegitimo carborundum. He was more miserly than they were, and tougher. Case-hard. He lowered his cindery hard head, his ravaged face, sore eyes. Bitter, chippy. What did we have in common? Yet he had a soft spot for me.

The checks—I thought I'd forgotten those yellow discs stamped with my number, tokens of myself, perforated with the little hole near the edge so that they hung, mute and waiting, on the rows of cup hooks. They shine out now like suns! They're medallions round my neck, glorified by the years. The grey, tetchy old men stood at the wire fence waiting their turn irritably, a clock ticking away in their heads, the price of the job burning on their lined foreheads, and these brass bits would be between their fingers. They clutched them like misers, and the grim, purposeful middle-aged skilled men, the aristocrats, jingled them in their hands like easy money, the kids spun them up, tossed them, dropped them on the floor—the raw kids who, according to legend, were sent on those phoney errands to ask for rubber hammers, left-handed screwdrivers, bubbles for spirit levels, boxes of half-inch holes, tins of elbow grease.

I have no mastery, no cold skill, no deliberate craftsman-ship and never will have; more and more I trust in the song. They had a saying, those skilled men, to register their contempt for fumblers like me: they said 'He couldn't fit my arse to a bucket.' Now I am able to handle tools in a dull common-sense manner, out of necessity. When it comes to writing I'm at the mercy of moods. Then it's pure song senselessly cut off from my fellows; nothing in between. or nothing, joy or painful, futile and dragging labour, When it moves it pours and flashes, gallops, and all I do is name and name, convey a long-buried feeling, capture the truth, yet not for the truth's sake—truth goes by the board —but racing to keep up with the song. Who cares if somebody's waiting for a letter, if your socks stink, if your piles are bleeding? You sing. The singing becomes an end in itself (Listen to him, he thinks he can sing!). The joy of creation is the sudden haemorrhage. The Venus vein bursts, a blue stain appears on the back of the hand, a terrifying lump as long as an egg. You're so numb with shock you can't write. Instead you rush round to the doctor, bang on his door, interrupt his surgery: this is an emergency— might be a thrombosis. Push it under his nose, frantic— 'What is it?' All he does is glance at it in the half light through a crack in the door—the patients in his surgery craning their necks, flapping their ears—and snaps 'It's nothing, control yourself! Drink the medicine, it'll go away.' Go back to naming, staring at the stain. Tattoo-mark of creation—heaven emptied, draining away. Naming. Trust in that. ('When I write potatoes, I mean potatoes'.) The fading stain accuses all your struggles and toe-holds.

I was with the surface grinders when I sent Marion the note. She was a stocky little typist who worked somewhere in the offices at the front. I hadn't spotted her in there, it was her jaunty promenades every two or three days though the shop I'd seen, watching her through the thickets of machines and flapping belts with frightened eyes. I wasn't frightened of *her*, it was the action I contemplated, the web of circumstances I'd begun to spin, the fearful shyness of a youth who was all arrogance underneath, sickened by the sight of myself being rebuffed—I imagined it in detail, like a suicide about to jump who looks down and sees his shattered limbs down there on the pavement. She wore a white shirt-blouse, high lacy collar, a springy bubble-cut hair-do, her eyes were bright and mischievous, kept rigidly downcast most of the time on account of the wolf whistles.

Her fresh cheeks were flushed and childish. But it was her walk that got me, jaunty and eager for life. She bounced through the machine shop, gay and resilient as a rubber ball. I didn't have a crush on her—it was a matter of seizing the opportunity. There was a woman somewhere waiting for me, and who knows, it might be this one; if you didn't ask, how did you find out? The very thought of making a date with a girl vanquished me, but my mates did it all the time. And I'd reached such a pitch now, it was either her or prostitutes. I was on the point of going to London, just getting on a train and travelling there, solitary, waiting till it was dark and then standing there in one of those canyons behind Piccadilly till I was picked up. I'd mapped it out in my head a hundred times, how to turn myself into a he-man. But it wasn't sex I thought of when I saw Marion bouncing through, it was a breeze, a fresh breeze I felt. Her name ought to have been Jackie—something crisp and boyish. I saw her romantically as a bundle of life. And she issued from wonderland, crisp as a carol, clean and bright and shining. As a green apprentice, queuing in the spotless corridor at the front on Thursdays outside the Wages window, peering in at the purity of desks and dazzle of paper, the slick dandified staff, I felt a queer dizzy sensation—something like Alice in Wonderland. My brother was a clerk himself, but I never connected him with this Thursday vision. I was utterly in awe of her world.

Getting to know her cured that. The smiling face and nothing behind it—this was my first experience. The great thing was, I'd made the date, screwed myself up tight and gone up sweating, guts churning, and kept the appointment: an initiation ceremony. Meeting a girl. Girl. The very word was enough to make me stutter. You can always tell the ones who never have to struggle. They have a bored air, they never know the depths and the heights. I came away from that meeting dazed with marvels—and to think that I'd created such a moment by my own initiative! Everything had been against me—a non-mixer, non-dancer, working in a community of one sex just like a prison or a monastery. I'd overcome all that, and it's true that I had to wait years to get desperate for such effrontery. That's what it seemed, effrontery. Who passed in the note? I can't remember. It must have been someone I knew well and could trust, someone who knew her name so I could write 'Dear Marion'—flaming, fateful words—and could get it passed in to her without any trouble. 'Dear Marion, you won't know me. Would you like to meet me outside the main gate at ten to two this dinnertime?' Hardly inviting, and how could she see it was written in blood? Somehow it got passed back to me, with a smile of secrecy and a wink, and it was my own note back again, with one word scrawled across it. YES.

Close up she wasn't so hot, ignorant and a hint of a cast in one eye. She came up smiling, with that bouncy little walk which had freshened me, gave me a false impression of innocence. Close up she was more vacant than innocent, but sizing things up quick enough for all that.

'Hallo!' she said. 'How did you know my name?'

On the defensive already, I muttered: 'Somebody told me.'

'Somebody I know?'

We were getting near the gates, coming in. Forcing every breath, I asked her for a date.

'When?'

'Say Thursday night.'

Her eyes shining with triumph, she pretended to think.

'I can't Thursday. I wash my hair Thursdays.'

'Friday then.'

Again the hesitation, the little catlike smile. 'What time?' she said cautiously, because she'd only just met me and I might be anybody and if she said yes too quick, people would think she was loose.

Inside, nobody said anything, no one was aware of my transformation. Perhaps after all it wasn't visible. My head was whirling with impressions, and that afternoon went like a dream, as they say. I'd made a fool of myself, my voice had wavered at the crucial moment, and I re-enacted the idiotic little scene again and again, and all the time, gradually, I was beginning to let the truth about her register, enter through the cracks, a fragment at a time maybe, but the truth. Her voice, for instance, doing that coy dolly act. The cat-and-mouse game she played with me, and the look of cunning that flitted across her face at the mention of Thursday. Still, none of that mattered because I'd done it, I'd won, I was out—and I bowed my head lower, feeling the smile spreading and shining on my face like something indecent.

15

I WAS out, I sparkled. The thought of what I'd done shocked me, and if the daring hadn't been suspect, if I hadn't known how I'd been driven, it would have delighted me too. Being out meant I had to go on; I'd started something. To hell with that, for the moment I was out and free, standing there unsuspected, my boat pitching happily as it saw the open sea. I'd show those lover boys! It was like coming away from the dentist, no appointments, wandering down the pavement so blithe, head full of gibberish. A cloud in trousers. Only cowards know what paradise is. I got in a funk and it drove me to act and the anguish was worse. Suddenly you came out of the tunnel of fear into the pastures of heaven. Or you did it in reverse, tore yourself out of the buttercup field and went in. Like Dolphin Road School, grim as a reformatory, tramping up the stone stairs in a bunch, nameless, one of the damned, to the great barn of a room stinking of gas from the leaking taps where we coupled up the rubber tubes and lit the bunsen burners: home the other side of the world, my mother waving goodbye as I climbed on my bike and rode blindly, hopelessly away, sickened by the sight of the homely, crumbling infant and elementary school I had to pass at the bottom of our street, horrified by the rigour of the buildings, faces, crossings, all intent on delivering me to the hated place. And you thought as it closed round you, over and round, sucking, as you stepped into the prison yard for the first time and older kids ran up to try and flog you their old atlases, you thought you hated your parents for making you come to this place, you felt the pain and grief of their dreadful betrayal. A line of kids were playing that game where one boy ducked over double, his back horizontal and his hands braced against the brick wall, and another boy ran up and landed on his back. Then a rush of bodies, heads ducking like mad, backs bending, legs set apart and the one behind with his head wedged in your crotch and kids leap-frogging and landing every other minute on this long living horse of groaning backs. A blast of the whistle and the horse shuddered, then broke in the middle. Everybody scrambling off and running to form queues. Another whistle blast and we went shuffling in over the worn stone doorstep. The master was waiting for us at the top of the stairs. A giant in baggy trousers, with a fierce head of hair, bad teeth and black horn-rimmed glasses. He rolled the whites of his eyes, waited calmly for dead silence and then told us what would happen to us if we acted the fool instead of paying attention. He called the register. The strange names flowed, mine among them, and when he reaches the name Shelley, this boy, John Shelley, answers 'Here sir' with such lazy confidence or indifference that I can't believe I've heard right. The master doesn't pay any attention. I stared at this boy's head, at the back of his neck, in a kind of wonder and adoration. It was all right, I was going to get out of here, I'd go flying home through the streets tonight, nobody was going to touch me, nothing was going to happen while John Shelley was here. He was my first hero at this terrible stealthy place. I didn't pal up with him. I loved him from afar; I trembled for him, held my breath over him. Right from the beginning he seemed to attract wrath, without even trying : it was just his nature. He stuck up in the air and glittered with unconscious opposition, inviting the storm like a lightning conductor. He got warned repeatedly, hauled out and caned again and again, then he'd be absent for long sessions. We thought he was playing truant but he wasn't, he was ill of some obscure disease. In the end his parents took him away from that school.

That was when the dread reality gripped me, as we trooped in, a teacher herding us from the rear, and I put my feet on the bottom flight of those bare stone steps and saw how *hollowed-out* they were. I choked, something died

102

inside me at the sight of that wear and permanence. I was being abandoned. Abandon hope all ye who enter here. Infant school was nothing, sweet piping songs like 'Away in a Manger', those cosy ramshackle rooms with the crayon drawings tacked up, a big framed picture of Jesus behind glass bidding the little children to come unto Him, and there they were sitting in a circle at His feet, warm and close, all races, and He was in the middle, an effulgent, gentle, feminine figure, His head bathed in rosy light and His hands resting on the heads of the two nearest children and it was plain to see they trusted Him, loved Him . . . Miss Warren it could have been, teaching us to sing D'ye Ken John Peel, every now and then stoking up the round pot-bellied stove with more coke, rattling the bucket and tilting it and ramming the shovel under the stubborn coke energetically till she had a shovelful. I used to love the wintry sound of it. Then she'd pick up the steel hook and catch hold of the glowing lid and flip it open, we saw the red flames licking and leaping, in flew the coke and that was that. Maybe she'd give the ashes a shake through the grille at the bottom, jabbing a long poker through the bars. It was winter, the air sparkled outside the windows. You could see the adverts being changed on the wall of Fredman's sports shop, the billposter's ladder waving about and then the bloke climbing up in full view, a bag of posters slung round his neck, the bucket of paste in one hand and wide, long-handled brush in the other. Once he waved to us, the ones who saw him waved back excitedly and the teacher said if it happened again she'd draw the curtains. That was crabby old Miss Vercoe who took handicrafts, she was deaf and chalky, veins like fat worms on the backs of her hands, she shouted and lost her temper, but what was that now? I longed for her so much it was like a pain, I wanted her and the long whiskers growing out of her chin and Jesus on the wall and the filthy washhouse where we washed the inkwells and milk bottles, I wanted Joe Buckley coming at me in the playground with his shaved head down on his shitty jumper, his arms flailing like windmills, I wanted the shithouse where the same yellow porcelain trough ran under all the seats and boys at one end made paper boats and set fire to them and tried to make them sail along under your innocent little arse shining so white and moony. And dancing round the maypole, spiralling the white tapes, skipping round joyous as lambs, boys and girls together. No bitter gulf between school and home. You played with fag cards against the school wall, out in the street, you sat on the pavement skimming the cards and feeling sharp pangs of loss if you got beaten, and it was the same pavement outside your own house, just down the street. Everything was joined on, continuous. You played marbles in the gutter, going nearly all the way home like that, measuring and aiming and rolling the magic striped glass, eyes glued to the cobbles, and the gutter ended at the drain under the lamp-post opposite the entry which sliced down the side of your house. Now it was changed, it was strange and terrible. Dolphin Road ran parallel with Albert Road—a slow hill ending at a common. Dinnertimes I went slinking up to the common with my sandwiches, and sat in a crab-apple tree right over near the far edge, nearest the factories. I perched there morbidly, a pale ninny, a painted bird, and the weak sunlight pecked at me, or the drizzle, and it was all the same to me in my misery. I was lost in the void.

To begin with it was only the emptiness, the strangeness, the bigness, and of course the distance—travelling right into and through the town, along Ford Street, Corporation Street, glancing at the out-of-date film posters outside the Rex on a Monday and being stabbed and sickened by the reminder of that lost week-end. Lob End, Butchers' Row, Broomfield. It was a different town that side from the one you thought you knew. The emptiness didn't have a name so how could you tell your parents, how could you beg them to stop it? If you could have found words for it you'd have said *worn steps, worn steps*! They'd have said don't be silly, it's because you're new there and don't know anybody, don't be so daft making such a fuss, what a cry-baby. Can you understand him? they'd say to each other. My mother would ask why, why did I have such a difficult child. I worry myself sick over you—you'll be the death of me. Earlier it was rage, the chase with the copper stick—

I'll swing for you. Now it was all worry. So I kept the emptiness hidden, and then I'd catch my mother looking sideways at me and the helpless misery in her face, the foolish fluttering inadequacy and fear of the truth were so plain I knew she'd got it too, the emptiness. I'd passed it on. My father was immune, his schooldays had been all right, but my mother had endured the same nameless reign of terror. She could tune in to any frequency if there was suffering in it. She couldn't help herself. Behind her eyes was the secret life of real nightmares that couldn't ever be brought out into the open and acknowledged for what they were. To do that meant action, opposition, it meant fighting back. How could you fight Them? All my mother could do was endure and suffer, weep inside, bear another cross. One more. If you came near that truth behind the eyes, as I did accidentally later, she got panicky and squawked like a terrified bird, cried *Stop it!* and as a last resort turned on the tap or threw a fit of hysterics. Nobody dragged the truth out in our house after a while, it was too nerve-racking.

The sense of desolation wasn't something you could perhaps get used to, like in prison—it renewed itself with fresh force every Monday because you'd buried yourself away from it in the week-end, as a kid buries its face in its mother's apron, to shut out the truth. And the longer the escape, the more harrowing the journey back. The long summer holidays were the worst, and Christmas, when you noticed bitter reminders of happiness in people's houses, the paper chains still hung across the ceiling, the decorated Christmas trees on show in the front windows. A howling started deep inside you and you bit your lips and kept your mouth shut tight, to keep the howl soundless.

I idolised John Shelley. There was another John who was a godsend to me—John McGough—though I didn't idolise him, I pitied him. He was an object of pity. That was a blessing and a comfort, having somebody in the class you could pity. When I realised he was as immune to pity as he was to insults I started to love him. He was my anchor. At the first mental test he sank to the bottom, natural as a stone. He was bottom each term, stuck in the front row so the teacher could keep an eye on him. He was naturally dopey and naturally good-natured. He wasn't lazy, he worked and concentrated and struggled to do better. I prayed for him not to improve because if he hadn't occupied that bottom position I'd have been there. The disgrace of that bottom place was rubbed out by the mere fact of him being there in occupation. It belonged to him, you felt, in the natural order of things: that was how it was meant to be. That was because John McGough was so blissfully stupid, he had no sense of shame, he blinked round and grinned amiably when the results were read out as if to say 'That's all right then.' I liked him best of anybody in that class. He lived out on the rural fringe of the city, up a rutted earth lane, and the chaotic farmhouse interior of his home bewildered me. I liked it though. So that was it, I kept saying to myself, he was a farm boy, a country boy! His mother and his home, the whole disorderly set-up was exactly in character, vague and openmouthed and easy-going, amiably sluttish. I went home with him one night and we were supposed to do our homework together, sitting at the big scrubbed table with the oil lamp in the middle. 'I shouldn't bother any more,' his mother kept saying, slopping about in her ragged slippers, smiling indulgently at the two of us. 'I should pack up now if I were you.' Cats lay about, snoozing, and there was a dog scratching its fleas.

At the other end of the classroom, sitting in the back row in a corner against the wall, were the two stars. The teacher didn't need to keep his eye on them so they were right out of reach, a law unto themselves: they could be trusted to work swiftly and well and give no trouble. They were embryo teachers anyway. Before you could finish one set of problems these two were sitting up straight with arms folded, bland smiles on their faces as they waited for more. They were so detestable to me that I didn't even consider them as kids in the sense that John McGough was a kid. I remember particularly and vividly the buttery smiles spreading on their chops. They were adults already, pompous, assured, they were greased with cleverness, noses sharp with achievement, they couldn't get out of their childhoods fast enough. They spread their legs and leaned back in the narrow iron-framed desks, cramped by the simplicities of this world I found so hard to absorb. On the sports field it was the same story, it revolved round them, they were the stars and it was too simple for words, a game you could play with your eyes shut. They were killing time, those two. One of them, Clive Adrian, went on to play soccer for England.

Nicknames: Flash Harris, Whacker Payne, Gabby Rogers. There was something icy and ominous, crackling and electric about the teachers at that school. Then we moved from the big ugly workhouse pile at Dolphin Road to a modern, glass-and-wood low-level building at Whitelanes, near Albany Road and Stanley Avenue, not far from the iron bridge at Stanley Park and the railway junction, the goods yard, the panoramic view over the city if you jumped so that your head bobbed over the grey steel ramparts of the bridge, studded with rivets; and over there were the spires, Monkswell Green, the first world war tank, huge and stranded and prehistoric, squatting lifeless on the clipped turf in the midst of the flower beds. Whitelanes, and going home I used to push up the avenue to the top, standing on the pedals and crunching the gravel, to the posh grammar school on the corner of the main road, avenues of chestnuts, traffic flowing and the posh kids lounging on the corner, by their decorative spiked gates and warm stone and castellated ivy-covered walls.

Whitelanes. The reign of terror really began for me there, when I found myself at Whitelanes with Chirpy Birdsall. He was my new form teacher. He wasn't bald, but his hair was fair, stuck down on his large bladdery head, which gave an impression of baldness. I dreaded him so much I was afraid to hate him even, in case he sensed the hatred welling out of me. He was the kind of teacher who had antennae for picking up things like that. He exuded an atmosphere—I can't describe it in any other way. He didn't pick on me personally, he used the cane brutally and indiscriminately. He was plump and smooth and pitched his voice low, in fact it was an affectation of his, this unruffled, leisurely, cool approach. His head swayed as he walked, and even sitting at his desk marking our books, his head down, I seemed to feel the same deadly snakelike presence about to strike. He only had to come into the room and flick his grey eyes over us to terrorise me. The bond between the torturer and his victim is more intense and close than between lovers, they say. All I know is that years later, when I'd got right away from him and could have come back and spat in his eye if I'd wanted, I was buying suede shoes and a tweed sports jacket in imitation of him.

I must have been more than desperate, I must have been half out of my mind with fear and anxiety to do what I did in the end on account of that devil. Imagine it, forging the initials of a man who could make you palpitate like the sides of a mouse trapped in a bucket if he strolled up behind you and just paused a minute. My loathing was close to worship, he inspired such grovelling panic. And I did it, my ratlike, slithering, beady terror started me on a career of petty crime—I forged his initials, F.B., in red ink on the bottom of the page of homework I couldn't finish.

Mild and almost bored, he called me out. There was my crime, shaking letters, square and squat but seismographic, too thin, too dry, no oil of smoothness. The lazy inquisition :

'What's this?'

'What sir?'

'This.'

'It's . . . it's . . .'

'That's not my writing, now is it?'

'Yes, sir.'

'No seriously.'

'Yessir!'

'You honestly expect me to believe that I wrote that? Is that my F? Now I ask you.'

'Yessir!'

Murmuring and languorous : 'I must have been drunk, that's all I can say . . .' then the jaw snapping : 'You did it, didn't you?'

'No sir!'

'Sure?'

' Yessir!'

And the fantastic moment when he sighed : ' All right. Go back to your place.' How I loved him in a daze of worship and wonder, how I suffered at the deception, those barefaced lies I told him. Now I wanted to take them all back. I would have owned up if I'd known he was going to be human and let me off like that. My gratitude tormented me, and what I'm thinking now is, he may have intended exactly that. I wouldn't put anything past him, the slimy shit.

One day, as I've described elsewhere. I hung my satchel round my neck and climbed on my bike, waved good-bye to my mother and then, instead of riding off in the right direction I went round in a circle at the first turning, heading nowhere, belonging nowhere. I was playing truant, another crime, and again a seizure of acute anxiety had caused it, the unfinished homework in my satchel had forced great daring on me. The bike took me in the opposite direction from Whitelanes, into the country void beyond Sutton Common, around Alvington, the golf links, aerodrome, abbey. Now my abandonment and loneliness were absolute—this latest suicide act put a seal of secrecy on my movements. There was nobody I could tell. Riding, wandering, sitting, stationary with one foot on a grass bank to prop me up, so I could stay hunched lifeless on the saddle and wait, wait for the time to pass, I'd dream of the places that were like impossible idylls now, saturated with welcome and love and cheerfulness, places of early childhood I'd taken for granted at the time : Ashmoor, Carroll Green, Belle Vue Gardens. Flowery, summery, heart-breaking names. Ashmoor and the Alpine—only five miles out but thrilling, foreign land, past the pit and its mining village, a few ugly rows of terraces in the middle of nowhere, the bleak waste of the kids' playground, gaunt bones of swings sticking up, chains rattling, the iron wheel of the roundabout and its stump rooted in the concrete. Out into no-man's land and a looming mountainous slag-heap, colliery wheels, then the country. Scrub land, miniature precipices, the lane in shadow, overhung by big, perched rocks, the biggest I'd seen, slabs of sandstone covered with bushes and saplings, with goat paths worn by the feet of hundreds of kids who came out to scramble all over its lumps and crevices. The cleft of the lane between banks of clay; sudden panorama at the top by the church and the wooden post office. Foreign land—different altogether from the direction I knew, the rolling watermeadows and flat fields and leafy parkland of Orford, Charlcott, Wellsbourne, Stratford, and on to Evesham and its orchards, fruit stalls along the grass verges, Pershore and the soft slow river ambling under the feathery willows, striped fish in the muddy waters . . .

Ashmoor was different. I stayed with Uncle Mike and Aunt Olive, they had a bungalow—nothing on one side, on the other a space, then a lonely-looking semi-detached and its twin, like town houses that had lost their street, then another vacant strip next to a wooden bungalow, and at the bottom of the slope another towny house that was the Stores. The bell tinkled, the floor was bare planks, all the stuff was fly-blown, nobody came to serve for a long time and a baby cried in the back. There was no proper village; a garage, a blacksmith. The Rising Sun. Uncle Mike's bungalow had nothing at the back except the raw heath, his own big lawn ending at a trellis, behind that some vegetables and then a field of rough grass, his, where he had pigs, and in the middle of it, among the pits of earth where the pigs had rooted, stood a full-size dirty bell tent. Inside were more holes dug by the pigs, rotten cabbages, torn newspaper, candle-ends. And at the front of the bungalow was a flower bed and a patch of lawn and a stone fence, somehow forlorn and pointless, and beyond it just the empty lane and a thorn hedge and then nothing; the scrub land of the heath, only a few acres but it was wild and seemed huge, with no hedges, owned by nobody, going up and down under the clouds and kestrels, a dour solitude. We called it the Moor.

Carroll Green was forlorn like Ashmoor, yet it was barely over the boundary, on the fringes; in fact the double-decker buses ran out to there and turned round. It was stagnant, emptied, neither town nor country. I went with my brother sometimes in the long summer holidays for a fortnight, staying with another uncle and aunt. They lived in a brick house like a council house, and it was creepy in a nice sort of way, grassy verges instead of pavements, hardly any traffic, and like Ashmoor there would be special nights when you heard a funny hooting sound or a hand bell ringing; the fish-and-chip van on Fridays, the hardware, Wednesday morning, and the grocery came on Monday afternoon and often it was late. Dennis and Caroline were young, not long married, with no children then. Dennis would come in after work at night, softly enter the room, smile at us, murmur something friendly and go and say soft caressing things to his moody young wife, who welcomed him sentimentally, slushily, as if he was coming home from a long campaign abroad. It was good when he came in, the morbid atmosphere from Caroline ebbed away. If it was chilly he fetched sticks and stooped down at the grate and soon kindled a fire. He was a maintenance man at the pit; small, lean, fine-boned, with a gaunt handsome face—I loved the pallor, the fine stubble on his cheeks —and hair brushed straight back, springy, going bald at the bony white temples. He was gifted musically, played the piano in a dance band. In the evenings he used to sit humming softly to himself and tapping his foot. Even for work his shoes were as pointed and dandyish as his patent leather dancing shoes. He was a gentle, vacillating character, his voice low and subtly modulated. He fascinated me. He had a presence, there was an actor in him somewhere. Because he'd been ill he used his own towel. Now and then he coughed a short dry cough, and he covered his mouth with his hand discreetly.

One thing happened at their place which tainted for ever that aura of innocence. I was in the long grass in the field at the back with my brother, we had our flies open and were satisfying our curiosity, examining each other. Caroline came up suddenly and surprised us. Without a word she turned away and went back in. There was never any reference to the incident. It was just unmentionable as far as she was concerned—like the time I was staying at the caravan with Pearl, running up the steps and barging in as she was standing there stark naked, about to pull on her bathing costume. I couldn't take it in, it was unearthly, like something off another planet. Afterwards I found it impossible to remember any details of that awful revelation, only a blur of flashing whiteness and hair where it shouldn't have been. Hair somewhere. Ginger. Auntie Pearl wasn't ginger. I thought I'd dreamt it, it happened so quick.

Now at the factory the thing had a name, a woman had a hairy twat or a quim or a fanny between her legs, and it was referred to with violence and harsh contempt by the lads of my own age, as if it had a life of its own, and though they made a pretence of lusting after this impersonal twat it seemed to me they really feared and hated it. The malevolence would be transferred to the person, whoever she was. 'Look at her, the bitch—her quim's been reamed so often you wouldn't even touch the sides.'

And the jokes were the same, a mixture, often brutal, of disgust and fear and desire—like the one about the woman who baulked at the sight of her lover's erection, which was like a stallion's. So she told him to tie a handkerchief half-way up before he started, she'd take half and no more, understand? When he was on the job the handkerchief fell off and he sank his great cock in up to the hilt. 'That's fine,' she said. 'Now you can give me the other half.'

This wasn't a joke of the apprentices—none of them were—but they picked on ones that appealed to them as expressions of their uneasiness. In their mouths, in the telling, it acquired the qualities they needed to pass on, for the horse laugh of reassurance. After all, they hadn't set eyes on a fanny, most of them, any more than I had. In our imaginations it got bigger and bigger until it threatened to suck us in, boots and all, like Jonah lost in the whale.

If a man was randy, on heat, courting—this wasn't our expression either—they said he had two cocks, one in each pocket. But the last word in factory abuse, man or boy, would be literally that word cunt. 'Silly twat!' they'd hurl at you. 'Useless cunt!' Or, cold and flat, the insult to end insults, delivered full in the face: 'You cunt.'

And this disembodied, useless, evil, stupid, winking hole,

112

hung up in public and derided, spat at, it could jump into you like a bug and spread and fester and erupt. It was cancerous, it was cataclysmic. You were whole, then the next minute the fabric split from top to bottom, the dream of bread and circuses was over, the vicious war was on, peace shattered and stinking. A greasy gravy of sex dripped on the sheets. The clear cuntless eyes of childhood grew a trembling glaucoma, the innocent light dimmed and got membranous, a sort of murky twilight that thickened all day and turned into a hairy darkness at night, choking out the sun. In dirty photos it was unspeakable, a filthy brown sink-hole, stained and wrinkled, ugly as hell. Unthinkable that your mother, your sister had one. It was an untouchable, unmentionable wound opening in your mind. It sank into you, burned deep into your thoughts and took root there, scabby, inflamed, festering. No peace now—the sauce bottle shot its load, the bread was flesh-white and clinging.

The bread. I'm thinking now of that fabulous childhood bread, lily-white in our grubby fingers. ' Eric's got a piece —please Mum can I have a piece?' Eric Gaskell from next door, only the other side of the entry, but their garden fence was high-boarded, trellis on top of that and rambler roses woven in and out, impregnable as a fort. He let me go in and play on their oblong of lawn, which was perfect like a tablecloth. Very conscious of the compliment, I'd go in almost on tiptoe, on my best behaviour. We'd squat there intent, grave as old men, manoeuvring a red-painted toy crane, winding the hook up and down. The handle had a cog and ratchet and the clicking sound it made excited us. Once when everybody was out he took me indoors, and I can see him now in the pantry at the back of the kitchen— and see myself goggling at him in amazement, he was such a clean, superior, subdued boy—drinking milk straight out of the milk jug.

Either him, or somebody you really loved, say Ronnie Hooper—waiting at the end of the entry, a piece stuck in his hand. I'd get mine too and go bolting out with it joyfully, bouncing on up the road to the park or lolling at the next corner against the wall, munching those thick delectable slices of bread and jam, bread and dripping, bread and marg. Delicious, blissful, melting in the mouth because you were eating it with your best-loved friend in freedom, away from the table, in the open air with nobody watching, and you could smear the jam over your clock and wipe your mouth on your sleeve and let crumbs drop and that was part of the feast, the special flavour came from that fact of not being under anyone's eagle eye. No adults. Sauntering on up towards the park, rolling the tongue around for stray fragments, smacking your lips exaggeratedly, still enjoying the taste in retrospect long after the last crumb had gone.

Ronnie Hooper's toast, or rather the toast made at his house, that was even more ambrosial. He was my best friend when we were six or seven years old. I don't remember his homely mother, she's shadowy and so is her living-room, but I can still see and taste the toast she made. If we ever had toast at our house it was done in a rush; either burnt, wedge-shaped, unevenly cooked or falling to bits. Something was usually wrong with it. Ronnie Hooper's mother toasted the square even slices with a kind of ritualistic slowness, taking down the fancy brass fork from its nail by the chimney breast, and she'd spear the bread on the prongs almost lovingly. She'd draw up a stool like a milkmaid and squat in front of the black-leaded range, the fire bright red behind the little vertical grille, just right. The half-softened butter was on a saucer in the grate, ready, and it went on generously, fat solid nobs on the sizzling gold. I was given a full piece, so was Ronnie, we'd smile at each other before tucking in, meek angels out of Dickens as we crouched on either side of the hearth.

16

STAFF of life. The parks—we lived in the parks, and at the top of Far Whatford Street, on the road out to Compton and Worsley Pit, we had a choice of three. Or we dirt-tracked around in the back entry, oblivious to the stink of sour milk and rotten meat, never looking once at the towering black bulk of the Humber building. I wonder now if I was imitating the speedway out at Compton when I went skidding round corners, digging in my heel to make the ashes fly, making the back wheel slide and slither—my father was a speedway fan, he took me out to the track one Saturday afternoon and I sat on his shoulders in the crush, getting the fierce tang of burnt petrol in my nose, terrified by the ear-splitting racket. Later, when scooters got too babyish and a soap-box trolley was the rage I nagged at somebody to make me one. Then it was a matter of finding the right spot, a quiet hill, a strip of deserted pavement and some means of slowing down at the bottom. This was the car world now, it was a car town where even the workers had cars of their own, so naturally we needed soap-box cars for playing in. You sat there in state on the plank and pram wheels, the axle swivelled under the feet by two cords which you held in your hands and tugged as if you held horse reins. On waste ground where the grass had been worn off it was a free, hectic, bumping ride, and on a gentle slope of pavement it was slow and oiled, majestic. Certain streets had special atmospheres. Hampton Street, for instance—long, quiet and gradual, ideal for a trolley, right near home, so you could nip out before tea was ready, straight after school, gliding down slowly, gathering speed, hearing the regular bump-bump as the cast iron covers of the pavement gutters ran under the wheels—at the bottom grabbing the reins and charging up again to the the top for just one more ride. And all the time you were conscious that it was a false, special, mysterious quietness, Hampton Street, with the rush-hour traffic increasing on either side in those parallel streams of Hyson Road and Whatford Street. It gave the street an atmosphere that was curious and enjoyable. To intensify the pleasure, the good fortune, the sheer luck of being there at all it was only necessary to sit still a second and listen to the faint rumble of traffic, steady as a battle.

I'm a street kid, now always and for ever, I live in the streets and back entries and waste bits, lurk in ambush at night, heart thumping, I listen with my whole body like an animal, the switched-off torch in my hand held like a gun.

I run with the pack, scream out when they do, utter blood-curdling yells to demoralise the enemy, race gasping for cover like a fugitive. Already I'm a little criminal, treacherous, audacious—the gang spirit rules me. When the light nights come, that puts an end to the mock battles and heroics, the violent hurtling chases; the gangs break up and we drift away on our own into the parks. These are waste bits to us, the grass foreign and interesting, funny stuff, we pluck at it as we sprawl around, taste it and chew on it like a food. Fields and even the common are places you go for treats and holidays, they don't count as real like the streets. The streets are our fields, our element—where the drama is. Things happen, even in Ernaldlhay Street. I'm running somewhere and a motorbike's handlebar catches me on the side of the head and knocks me out. They carry me into my own house, lay me on the settee in the front room where we only go at Christmas and this is summer, I wake up and find strange people staring down at me. Laughs of relief, 'He's alright, look, just grazed him, he's lucky you know—don't worry, Mrs.' They fetch a doctor and I have to lie down again, on the living-room table this time, while he prods and pushes and squeezes me like my mother making pastry. Not long before this I'd had my tonsils out on this very table, creeping downstairs in my pyjamas, and if I put my eye to the boards where there was a crack I could see the whole scene below me; the table spread with a rubber sheet, the bolster for my head, covered with the best towel, the doctor and his assistant and the mysterious equipment for giving me the gas, rubber mask and pipe, all ready and waiting, our living-room invaded. No escape.

The streets meant escape; nobody could grab you for anything. On Sundays if we were going on a visit to our grandparents, the route march began in the familiar home ground streets and was soon in the avenues, Terry Avenue, Humber Avenue, the long hill alongside the railway bank and the buttercup field up in the direction of the fever hospital. The houses drew back mockingly as we marched through, our parents guarding the rear. The exercise brought out my father's army training, never failed, he scowled and shouted at us to pick up our feet, warned us to pack up this or that, let out an irate bellow or two, and got choked off by our mother: 'John, you're shouting again.' This made his temper a little uglier, and by the time we reached our destination he was on the point of lashing out at us. It was too late, he couldn't touch us then. 'Wait till we get home,' he muttered, impotent, and we didn't feel threatened. Home was a long way off. At Belle Vue Gardens it was lovely, rural, we were spoiled and indulged and everything was in league with us; the bungalow made by the sons after the first war, with no building experience—a big raised veranda like something in America; the cess-pit, the bucket lavatory, the frogs, even the currant bushes. In the front was a billiard table and a tall cabinet of yellow wood stuffed with musty picture books and sheet music, chaotic; when the doors were opened, stuff on the top started sliding out as if it was alive. Through the small windows you could see raspberry bushes and fruit trees, the boughs nearly scraping the glass. The time blossomed, the green was heraldic and yet homely.

Belle Vue was a huddle of shacks in a hollow, dirt roads between, which were no more than wide bumpy tracks full of pot-holes; a slum community of factory workers, railway workers like my grandfather, working men with enterprise and no money who'd managed to buy a parcel of ground and build a bungalow. Some were no more than sheds, hovels—Geoff always cracked the joke about the woman in one of them who'd empty her pisspot out of the window with a grand gesture. He did it with actions, his arm shot out and his clenched fist twisted, tipping the invisible piss into the garden. You could almost see it fall in a curtain. His mother's bungalow was substantial, half brick and half asbestos, slates on the roof like a street house. Belle Vue lived in the shadow of factories, Austin and Humber, and in the heavier shadow of the city itself—and it was inside the boundary yet with its own trickle of traffic, its own pulse and circulation of news and doings, like a village.

On the machine grinders too it had the same feeling of being a family, a village, scruffy and shitty and overlooked by a miracle, caught in the steel guts of a whale that spouted youths and men; you travelled in and out on its breath, too insignificant to matter. We were a gang of five or six, with a chargehand who was supposed to keep an eye on us and iron out our problems, and as well as this he had his own quota of work to produce. From morning to night he went like the clappers, ever on the trot, sweating; that was his character. If Bert Ferguson walked up behind him and asked him if he could spare a minute, he'd keep jerking away frantically at the handles of his machine, his head screwed round to talk, stuttering apologetically that he'd be right there, yes, along in half a sec. ' If I can just finish this Bert—okay?' If he wasn't in a tearing hurry it was most peculiar, he didn't look natural at all. Paddy *scuttled*. His first name, Julian, had such dignity that you wanted to burst out laughing, it was so inappropriate. Everybody called him Pad, even the foreman Mr Gutteridge. He was obsequious, ludicrous, he scuttled backwards, forwards and sideways like a crab—but much faster, like an earwig in a fit. He was in a permanent sweat of panic and embarrassment, and seemed to have been born that way. He had the best and worst qualities of the Irish, eloquence and hypocrisy. The most contemptible and shameful thing about him from our point of view was that he was so obviously shitting himself. Nobody hated cowards—who isn't one himself?—but he made it so obvious to everybody, that was the disgusting thing. Because of this craven streak he scuttled harder and harder, trying to be nice and accommodating. He crept up your arsehole and laid eggs of goodwill in your bloodstream. He had sad, pale, saucer eyes and a blob of nose, like Dylan Thomas, only he was taller, a bone of a man, there was no fat on him and no sloth, he was all speed and anxiety. There was no arguing about his skill either, and he'd done it without the advantage of an apprenticeship, getting a foothold first as a semi-skilled millwright, accepting a lower rate than the others, then watching people and picking up tips, waiting to jump in as soon as there was a vacancy, licking arses too, of course, as hard as he could go. It was wonderful though, he'd do anything for you, anything to keep the work flowing smoothly, tearing up and down with his black hair falling into his eyes.

Mr Gutteridge was very pleased with him. If you were in trouble you yelled ' Pad!' and he'd come racing up, servile as a flunkey, spilling out his lovely vowels, putting everything right and shipshape in a flash with his quick clever fingers, his agile brain.

The machines we worked were in line astern, facing the same direction, Pad leading, with his back to us. Behind me was Bert Ferguson, behind him a youngster barely out of his time, George Holloway, and at the back of him another apprentice, Ginge Radcliffe. Ginge, or Wank— he'd collected this nickname from somewhere and it seemed to fit; I mean he looked as if he was the wanking type— had nothing to say to any of us. A tall, freckled streak, long camel neck and prominent Adam's apple, he was morose, broody, encased in silence. If he was asked something point blank and forced to answer, he stared full at you, deadpan, with a venomous expression in his dark-ringed eyes that seemed calculated to curl you up. Occasionally I heard him blow up at the back of me, he'd made a mistake or the job on his magnet chuck had slewed round all of a sudden, or it was Monday and he was feeling more than usually savage. ' Bollocks, bollocks!' he'd howl, a favourite expression. He was gifted with a natural foul mouth, he swore coldly, with an icy vigour which made me flinch. Without the word fuck in his sentences he'd have been speechless. ' Got the fucking spanner?' he'd say, his arms dangling dangerously. Standing beside Bert Ferguson, a middle-aged, genial man, he'd ask him: ' Got the time you old fucker?'

George Holloway was the comic, he was corny, cheerful, laughed at his own jokes. His favourite stance at the machine was with one leg cocked like a dog taking a piss on the second shelf of his tin workstand. He'd twirl the chuck under his carborundum wheel and watch the showers of sparks, taking care and worrying but making it look very casual. He had a Lancashire comedian's accent but he wasn't funny, only by accident. I laughed in the right places, just to humour him. Ginge never bothered to hide his boredom. ' Got the tool?' he'd say, meaning the spanner for tightening the wheel nut.

'Yeah I got a smasher I 'ave, wanna see it?' George croaked, for the hundredth time.

'Stop bollockin' about, for fuck's sake,' Ginge gabbled, finding his voice for once. It was a half-choked boy's voice. Once I saw one of his rare smiles, his thick lips twisting up one side of his face before he could stop it. It was an exposure of that convulsive shyness he kept well buried. I looked the other way.

One day he disappeared, transferred to another section, and for a week or two his machine was vacant. Finally a skilled man, Freddy, turned up to replace him. What a contrast. He was voluble all right, and a performer so that he could be. He sang hymns, nothing but hymns, holding forth like a gospel soloist. Nobody knew why, as he was anything but religious. He gave a daily concert at the machine, warbling expertly and putting all the power of his lungs into the top notes, to everybody's embarrassment. We got used to it in the end and took no notice; there he was flinging his head back and airing his tonsils, and he wasn't even registering with us. Not a flicker. He could have been whistling, or his machine extra noisy—nobody turned their heads to look. That didn't exactly suit Freddy, who was very vain, but he had no option. Anyhow, far from putting him off, he belted it out louder and holier than ever. Obviously it made him feel good, hearing himself. He was a bag of nerves, but vain as a film star. Having a conversation with him was difficult—he couldn't seem to force his thoughts into words: his mouth opened and shut and nothing came out. Finish the phrase for him and he was liable to fly into a temper. Yet as soon as he burst into song the words poured freely, soared and stretched, he could do as he pleased—loop the loop if he wanted. That was why his narrow eyes flashed, his broad cheeks gleamed. He was exulting, victorious. His mouth yawned open, clean as a cat's. His voice rose out of his deep chest and bull neck, clear and pure, and he made it sob and quiver like an Italian's. You could almost see him listening to himself, congratulating himself on his eloquence.

He peddled dirty pictures—whether for money or not I wouldn't like to say. He could have passed them round for the kick it gave him, the feeling of power—there were blokes like that. It was funny in a grotesque sort of way, hearing him warbling away so angelic, pure as a nightingale, the next minute sliding the little top drawer of his toolbox in and out, hissing and spluttering as he passed out those grimy buff-coloured envelopes. He had a Hitler moustache, and his greasy reddish locks were impeccably combed and parted. He was a shiny, bristling, half-frightened and half-defiant rat. He sang well, but it was like listening to a medium, not really him. When he went off the deep end, fucking and blinding and his eyes rolling back in his head as if he was having a fit, his face turned white with fury and his head shook. It was a wonder his teeth didn't rattle, the way his rage boiled up in him. Other times he'd move jerkily like a puppet or a spastic. A real bag of nerves he was, like Pad, like Ginge, all of us. Except Bert Ferguson.

Bert was slow-witted, but not a fool. He was semi-skilled, which meant he was given the straightforward jobs, large batches of say a hundred at a time. All you had to do was set up your machine, go into a trance and keep ploughing away. He was happy to do that, the monotony was something he knew how to cope with. Interrupt him and he'd look at you bemused for a minute while he swam up to the surface. You could see him doing it. What he couldn't cope with was anything intricate and abstract; it baffled him, worried the life out of him and his genial spirits flagged. He kept going and fetching Pad, who confused him still further, unknowingly, his fingers as swift and intelligent as Bert's were slow and thick.

' Okay Bert?' he'd say, darting off to the next problem before Bert's head had finished wagging. Then I'd hear the poor bugger behind me with his head well down, concentrating, really trying hard and breathing heavy. I relied on Bert to keep me buoyed up; I only had to twist round and give him a grin for him to come out with his ' 'Ow are yer?' It was a way of saying fuck 'em all and what a war, what a life, *nil desperandum illegitimo carborundum* —don't let the bastards grind you down. A password. He had no ideas, Bert—it was the mere fact of him I seized on.

121

He was rocklike, sunny, he stood for something in my eyes. Gradually, over the year or two I worked with him, I built him up, romanticised him. Nobody else saw what I did, to the others he was only a happy bloke and a good mate to play darts with, drink a pint with: a bit thick. When he was made redundant, later, I gave in my notice as a protest and left as well. He got a job in mass production, on the track—over the road at Hammer Lane. I met him in a pub and he told me. I sat and supped the same draught beer he was drinking, that's how involved I was. Getting the sack hadn't worked him up as it had me, naturally. Outside we said all the best and went off in different directions. I never saw him again.

Another basically happy character, though with something leery underneath that would have been lost on Bert —who was wide-open, transparent—was Morgan over on the test bench. Taff they called him. Taking batches of finished work over there I made a beeline for him because he was the friendliest, the easiest to please. He rejected stuff here and there, he had to work to the limits on the drawing like everybody else or he was in trouble himself, but he let borderline cases through where his mates wouldn't, and if he had to chuck something out he'd do it apologetically. He was pleasant to deal with, and sometimes, to vary the scenery, I'd nip across to him for a quick chat, lounging against his table with the brown cork lino on top—the kind you get for doing lino-cuts at school. He was a checker, I was glad to have him for a pal; it was almost like being in with the bosses, only honourably. Until I saw he was no different from any of us. Worse, he was unproductive, and that gave him an inferiority complex. He was apologetic because he felt inferior. He sat on his arse in a clean white coat, passing judgement, and we were the ones, the producers, we were running him. It sank in slowly that these judges were on our backs. They acted like God Almighty, some of them, bluffed and blustered and it was an act, they were covering up. Attack was the best form of defence, they found. Taff, not being the belligerent type, licked his lips and said how sorry he was but you'd have to take it back and have another go. He was wary of the foreman and of wandering bosses from further afield—no end to them—and having a yarn he kept his fingers active most of the time, shifting cards and lumps of metal about on his table as if he was playing chess, keeping his eyes skinned, talking out of the side of his mouth. That was where he differed from Bert, who wouldn't give a bugger who was watching—if he wanted to talk, he talked. It wasn't a matter of defiance. The wormy fear and shiftiness wasn't in him, that's all. I idolised him for that, and it was a quality he was utterly unaware of. He hadn't a clue how rare it was. He thought everybody was the same as him. I had to be proud and tingling for him, on his behalf. I was a fraud, devoid of his unthinking fearlessness, it couldn't have been further from how I was then. This was another fascination and a bond. I set him up as a symbol, his rocklike quality, I charged him with meaning and gave him consciousness in my imagination. That was my role.

Taff was a dead loss in this sense of being material I could weave into a vision I was secretly working on, yet like Bert I'm sure he thought everybody was like him. In his case it meant being crafty, one jump ahead, and if you wanted a bit of life in the firm's time you had it on the sly. If Bert was guileless and clear, Taff was so naturally full of guile it was a kind of innocence. He was a trumpet player, a fan of Glenn Miller and Harry James. Our talks were mainly about music and instruments—I remember a conversation with him about the tone of the French horn—and I was beginning to hang my nose over trombones and trumpets in the record shops, seduced by Armstrong and Ory. If you have a valve instrument you need flexible joints to your fingers, he told me, and flexed his fingers to show me. He ran them up and down on the lino as if they had a life of their own. Another hobby of his was knitting, he said, and now he was watching me closely, allowing a little pause for me to laugh. 'Go on,' I said. Week-ends he'd knit pullovers and socks and God knows what, for enjoyment. He was small and rosy, married, with this sly side to him. The knitting was good finger exercise, too, he explained, and he gave me a nudge. 'Know any others?' he said.

His eyes slithered around while he chatted, for ever on the watch. This used to unnerve me. I didn't realise he had stuff from Freddy until one morning he slipped a buff envelope across the table. 'Have a look at these,' he mumbled, barely moving his lips. He touched his dago moustache with his fingertips and gave me a shiny grin and I knew then. I went speeding off to the shithouse with them : not the nearest, I had to have one with doors.

I felt I was heading for an interview with a prostitute, for the punishment cells, for a dose of self-inflicted, joyless pleasure. The envelope was in my back pocket—I could feel it crinkling as I walked—buttoned down tight for safety, and its power was flowing all over my body, stripping me before everybody. I got into an empty shithouse and perched on the seat without taking my pants down. Because the doors had no locks I sat with my right leg out stiff, using my toe as a wedge. The pictures waited, every second more urgent, they were ready to leap out on fire of their own accord. I fumbled and dragged them out, these greasy bits of card no bigger than playing cards, that could make you grovel. Black and white, pitiless, the players bollock-naked and nasty, their bodies lurid and starved of daylight. I bored into them, ravenous, shameful, I wanted to groan out loud. A woman sat on a chair, her legs apart and a man nuzzling at her, sucking her off. She'd got hold of another man's cock, he was squeezing one of her tits and her head was thrown back, her eyes closed and a drugged expression on her face, almost a look of pain. Hospitals, I thought of—an operation; it had that kind of surgical nakedness. One picture showed a cock in close-up, with this same woman guzzling thirstily at it, drooling, opening her mouth and lapping at the huge anonymous prickhead for all she was worth with her tongue. Others were orgies and the camera lens was defeated by arms like thighs, bellies and arses and black burrowing heads all entangled in a heap. My own cock was twitching about and I unbuttoned my flies and let it free and squeezed it, as the man was squeezing the woman's tit. That woman's drugged, suffering face tormented me for days, weeks after. I put the photos away and dropped them on Taff's table on the way

124

back to the machine. He looked mean and shifty now, more than I'd noticed before. Everything looked meaner, the blokes bent and greyish, the old ones, and even the youngsters were sickly pale. More than anything else those pictures ripped me away from childhood, killed the magic and mystery. Now I had dead eyes, I was without hope, a man. I dropped the envelope on his table, he used the edge of his hand like a rake and scooped it straight into a drawer, out of sight.

'Any good?'

He flicked me a glance, idle, not concerned.

'Bloody hell,' I said, trying to sound merely impressed. He raised his head mildly, in hopes of a chat. I kept going. I could have killed him, innocuous as he was, for sitting there so immune after unleashing that lot. The same went for the source, Freddy. I was trapped once more, a year or two later, going by Freddy's machine, and he was flicking through a whole pack of cards for Ginge's benefit, who stood sniggering his appreciation. What he'd got hold of was a series of drawings based on the strip characters Dagwood and Blondie. There was Dagwood, his startled look, hair parted in the middle as if by a bullet, a couple of hairs poking straight up on the top of his head, and Blondie had her famous gormless expression. The difference was in their antics. There they were in suburbia, they'd be fucking away in various positions, mostly acrobatic, and the captions underneath were supposed to be funny ha ha. Nobody read them, they were too busy soaking up the pornography. In one sketch, Dagwood was spreadeagled on the carpet of the living-room, looking absolutely helpless and astounded, as if transfixed by the sight of his own prick. Blondie, her dress yanked up, stocking tops flashing, had impaled herself on it or was easing herself down with her back to him, her hands on his knobbly knees to steady herself, head lifted up, her eyes round and doll-like, and facing her the door was opening and her mother coming through it on a surprise visit, carrying an armful of parcels. 'Oh hello Mom,' it said underneath, 'how nice of you to drop in!'

I saw one or two over Ginge's shoulder, a sickly smirk on my face in case somebody was watching my reactions.

They were the power and the truth, the dynamo, the missing element. Callous and vicious, they jolted you with electric shocks, bit into you with their cutting edges, sudden as blows. Cut through the dolour, the torpid heartbreak—you twitched in your pants, sickeningly, nauseatingly alive. It was worse then, it put the burden on you to do something, fuck off, and the other way was a kind of sleep, a torpor. Either way it was a bundle of sensations, starting in the dark and ending in the dark. You sleepwalked. Rode through the back gate showing your identity card to the copper who wasn't looking, but you never knew for sure, he may have been peering through the slits of his pill-box. Lifted your bike into the racks, took off the pump and clumped in, and it was getting light in the slush of the sky, kindling a dingy brightness. In the main shop everything congealed and lifeless, the belting hung slack, yellow lights shone on the myriad surfaces, and with eyes still gummed with sleep you noticed things, the matt dryness of the belts, the dry light on the papers, tables, the stagnant milky scum on the suds, the gloss of light on the enamelled casings of some of the machines, the oily sheen of others, the glitter of cogs, the tapering points of drills, the brittle curls and loops of lathe cuttings jamming the innards, frozen billowing heaps, the black mounds of swarf. The early birds were in already, propped upright here and there, reading the papers and waiting for the first hooter. It was bleak as a cemetery till you reached the spot where you belonged, then the familiarity stirred in your chest like a vague comforting smoke. The first hooter yelled a warning and the final one at eight sounded harsh as an order, raucous. Pad bustled in with a minute to spare, hopping down the gangway on one foot, dragging off his cycle clips. His face still bleary, fingers straightening the mess of his collar he nipped up and down the line scratching at his head, digging at his arse, delivering his morning greetings and salutations.

' Fit, George?'
' I feel champion.'
' Bert?'
' 'Ow are yer?'
' Morning, Ken.'

' What's good about it?'

This was Ginge, but Pad couldn't stop for an answer, he was trotting back to the head of the column, cranking away madly at the top handle of his machine, about to let battle commence. He was the pace setter and exemplar. If he didn't kick off on time, none of us did. So he dug immediately at the green button, his machine whirred and hummed. He made a few preliminary adjustments, waggled the dust suction pipe a little lower, stuck the diamond tool on the flat laminations of his chuck and turned on the magnet. He twirled the diamond under the rim of his wheel and trimmed it. A cloud of grey dust rose up. Then he was away, working, the sparks flew in showers, in purring flickers for the finishing cuts. In a sudden agitated burst and flurry he dives for his fags, in the bottom drawer of his toolbox. Lights up, and while he draws it down and sighs gratefully, he seizes the opportunity to glance round at the rest of us. He might be admiring the view, his gaze is so vague and drifting and unfocused. A thought hits him, he grabs a work card and darts off through a gap in the machines to see a progress chaser.

It may have been Ted Hines he was seeing, or one of his mates. Ted infatuated me—he was another one I had no contact with, nothing direct, other than watching him strut past, cheeky, brash, with his irresistible charm and zest, his wide grin, broad shoulders and narrow hips, a little hollow in his back and his chest out, breasting along. He was zippy, eager, his good looks were the craggy, low-brow kind, he was the open-air type, ready to talk football any time, bubbling over to tell somebody about the blinder so-and-so played on Saturday, and his reactions were dazzlingly quick, he was seasoned just right with a touch of cynicism so that his high spirits had force, they were infectious even at a distance. He was out of my age group altogether, in his twenties, which was ideal for me. It made familiarity impossible, I could get an eyeful of him and he wasn't even aware of my existence. He zoomed up and down : once he caught me at it, our eyes met and he gave me a broad wink. But he hadn't a clue what my game was. He was all on the surface; that's what gave him brilliance, such a turn of speed. He had a mass of short black hair, tight energetic curls, boyish, and underneath this mop his pale face was tough and firm, like an intelligent, gentle boxer's, and like a boxer's it manifested the power of his body. I was able to transfer the tweed jacket and suedes from Chirpy Birdsall to him, for he wore the same sort of rig-out; only his jacket had patch pockets and a couple of pleats in the back. He swaggered, swung his shoulders like a sailor on leave, with the natural arrogance of the lithe young hopeful who knows his popularity. His quick grin and high-pitched croaking voice got a welcome in the most unlikely places. I saw real tetchy old bastards with their faces cracking in an attempt to raise a smile for him. Nothing tarnished his innate modesty. Down in the club-room under the canteen at dinnertimes I'd sit watching him in table tennis matches—he belonged to the team—and though he didn't dominate by any means, his vigorous, crisp returns and the habit he had of letting himself be forced back and back, crouching, fighting a defensive battle, captivated me more than if he'd been winning. He was my star. I got endless pleasure from watching his stance, his movements, hearing his yells of triumph, his fresh happy laugh. If you have a hero, he can do no wrong.

Most of the kids I was growing up with had the usual heroes which they were happy to share, on the screens, on the sports field. I had screen ones, like them, and stars of the concert platform like George Weldon who conducted the Birmingham Symphony at the Town Hall, a handsome limping figure ringed around by students on the hard cheap seats behind the timpani, high up like gulls on a cliff, clutching tight and earnest at their scores, as worshipful as fans at a pop concert. And they yearned over him, his white ravaged face, the forelock he kept flinging back impatiently, his wild tormented antics at the crescendos, writhing over the strings, the woodwind, dragging poetry by the scruff out of the leader, who sat impassive sawing away, bland as a businessman at a council meeting as George fought and suffered, raising the pitch of life, plumbing the depths of feeling—and then the moment, the sign, the message, flung arms of crucifixion as it killed him, the cost was so great. We died with him in consummation and it wrung our hearts, the glory, the greatness; a triumph of death. The sedge withered but we'd come right through and out the other side, George hung his head and we stormed applause at him, threw garland after garland, he was dead on his feet, swaying, absolutely shagged. For us, for us. And more heroes had been forged, we were linked now in a wonderful immediacy to the dreams of epoch-striding giants, Beethoven, Sibelius. George limped away, Byronic, stepped down from the cross, a flicker of a smile on his face. Tall and dark, lame—and we stumbled down the back stairs in a daze, wreathed in beauty and reconciliation, out to the harsh light, New Street, walking on the eggshells of dreams, shattered by the everyday, wan and attenuated and lost as lovers. That was what we loved him for—he took us with him, breaking the barrier, he fought through to the realm of fabulous, splintering light at the centre of each of us, our body and soul. He heaped riches on us, made us seven feet tall. The same thing happened in jazz, only more humorous, human, less grandiose, and we had to do it from the record or with the aid of local groups who had no aura, who were ordinary dull fellows acting as mediums.

I had these shared heroes like everybody else, and I had the secret, special ones, like Ted Hines. They belonged to me, nobody else, they were my creation. One thing they all had in common was that they were liberators. And the villains put you in chains. I was in chains from the beginning, almost from birth, because everything menaced me. Villains such as Chirpy Birdsall, petty sadists, shits, they had me in chains and I was craven, I had a craven desire to crawl, be fawning—I was like a dog that tucks in its arse and drags across the floor to lick the boot that ill-treats it. Then one day I found myself face to face with a villain who sickened me. I was shit-scared of him but the craven feeling had left me. I wanted to kick back, and I did. Where I found the guts I can't imagine; I marvel at it even today. Before him I'd had a dose of Flanagan, the grey-coated foreman with a foul temper and a mouthful of rotten teeth like rusty nails, who was in charge of the engine fitters. I was on his section for six months, every day a misery. Coming up silently behind me he had the same paralysing effect as the teacher. He was a black Dickensian brow-beater, all black, exaggerated out of all proportion. 'You're doin' it wrong, aincha?' he'd ask with terrible soft politeness. Then the enraged bellow straight at your head, 'WRONG!' His roar carried to adjacent sections, heads of the curious lifted, eager for the spectacle of Flanagan stamping back to his bench, which had a sloping hinged lid. He stood with his belly pressed against it as if he was behind a lectern. He was famous for these raving, savage tantrums. I was craven before Flanagan, my loathing was reserved for the fatuous grins of the spectators, the prying eyes watching safely in anticipation. My despair soaked down to my feet, saturated me, when I had to approach him and ask for another job. He was never real to me, but a mythical fiend in a nightmare I'd wake up from one day. According to legend, he had his knife in one fitter to such an extent that the poor sod turned, in the midst of a bollocking, and let him have it, bash, right in the eye. It caught him off balance and Flanagan went sprawling. Of course the bloke got his cards. Next morning there was a brass plate screwed into the floor on the very spot, with the legend engraved on it, 'Fighting Flanagan fell here.' Everybody believed it, so perhaps it happened. It was the kind of fantasy which came alive in the very force and desperation of your desire.

17

I'M inching nearer to him, that jaundiced, kite-faced bastard of a works engineer who taught me self-respect. I ought to be grateful to him for that at least. I want to catch his full flavour, the noiseless contained prowl, his stiff scraggy neck, the head poised like a cobra's. The poison wasn't in his tongue, it came spitting out from his eyes. He had the bleak look of a killer, as if the heart had been cut out of him at birth. I was leaning against the bench one morning, either in a dream or having a breather, and like a fool I had my back to the main gangway. A finger jabbed into my ribs woke me up rudely. I swung round, startled, to find this blazing snake head confronting me. It was like a clout between the eyes. I couldn't think what he wanted, I still hadn't got the message—I thought he wanted to have a word with me about something, perhaps a transfer to another section.

' Get on with it,' he said, not raising his voice. ' We don't pay you for that.'

I turned away burning and picked up the file and started scraping away at the lump of cold steel in the vice. Up and down, up, down, in a turmoil, never raising my head, and all the time it sank into me with iron hooks and teeth, deeper and deeper, his message. I was selling my labour, the hours and days of my life, to this congealed bastard. So that's it, that's being a worker, that's what it means! I felt deeply, bitterly ashamed. I stored it up, hid it away like everything else shameful and went on outwardly the same. I looked dead, I *was* dead near enough, but inside me now there was a white flame licking round my guts, a secret rage. I didn't come up against snake head again for another year or two—I'd catch sight of him in the distance and instinctively lower my shoulders, get on with it. Then after the war, on the machine grinders we had a rush of work and the old cry of overtime went up. In wartime they had the perfect excuse, but now it was different. I got the impression that the whole section, except Pad, was sick of long hours. I was, and it was voluntary, and I'd reached the point where my leisure was the only thing that really mattered to me. Now it was being threatened. I amazed myself; I was ready to fight. They were getting at me where it hurt, that's why. And I was single, so they couldn't twist my arm there. Pad was coming down the line, after an interview with the foreman, trying to wheedle us into saying Yes all right. Nobody wanted to work over, but for some reason nobody would say so. ' I'll work if the others work,' Bert said, and so said George, so said Freddy. It was like a refrain. When he got to me with his ' How about you?' I gave him a flat no. And a strange thing happened. A terrific feeling of pride shot through me. I was a rebel—

I'd refused. Nobody had made me do it, I wasn't bending to fit the situation. For once I was actually in charge, calling the tune, standing up for my rights. I felt intoxicated with a sense of power, and it was a revelation, it went counter to my whole idea of myself. I never dreamt it was in me, this stubborn streak. Well, I knew I was stubborn, but Christ—out in the open and fighting? It was nuts, a kind of suicide for me; I had no punch, no defence, I was a skin short. It was asking for trouble, surely. The others were looking at me a bit startled and abashed, and there was even a hint of admiration. I liked it. My scalp tingled, my hands were sweating. I was the quietest of the whole bunch, no one had expected me to turn out an agitator. Pad scratched his head and said:

' You mean you won't even if the others do?'

' It's voluntary isn't it?'

' Oh yes—voluntary.'

' Well you've asked me and I've said no. I'm not volunteering.'

' I'll have to tell Mr Gutteridge, it's not my fault, don't think I'm running . . . he'll want to know so I've got no option . . .'

' That's fair enough.'

He went scurrying off and I stood there feeling heroic, conspicuous and quaky but still in charge of the situation. I waited for the next wave. The first round was mine. Fantastic how strong it made you when you knew exactly what you wanted and had made your mind up and, best of all, had nothing to lose. It was giving me pleasure because it was so foreign to my furtive nature, and my mates were all helpless, waiting for the next move. With the new threat to my free time I had an enemy, clear and visible, and I had the urge to fight. I glanced round at them almost pityingly, my mates, waiting speechless and gutless. All of them together were weaker than me. I couldn't get over it. Standing at the machine I made the motions of working, and inside I was on my toes dancing, weaving in and out, brilliant feints, ducking and dodging and throwing lightning punches. I'd drawn blood and I was eager for more. I think if that had been the end of the affair, a bloodless victory without another shot being fired, I'd have been badly disappointed.

I was expecting the foreman. Instead, a shop steward turned up—a bloke I hadn't set eyes on before. A tall, doleful, lantern-jawed character, with bloodshot eyes and a loose mouth. He pushed up close, matey and intimidating, and to my amazement started trying to talk me out of it. He realised I wasn't in the union—apprentices weren't allowed to join—and for that reason he advised me to quietly drop the whole business. As I wasn't a member, his union had their hands tied. If the management turned nasty and gave me the sack, what could the union do about it? They'd be helpless.

'I get you,' I said. 'Thanks anyway for the advice.'

'You'll work then?'

I shook my head. 'Sorry.'

'Well, look out,' he said, and gave me a sour look. 'I know what I'm talking about, mate.'

I stood there motionless, tight as a wound spring, smiling calmly, and heard myself say these astounding words:

'They can sack me if they like. I couldn't care less.'

The shop steward shrugged, obviously disgusted. He opened his hands at the same time in the gesture which meant, That's it, then, my son, if you will persist in your folly. He moved off a couple of feet and looked at me in silence, lugubriously, with the mein of a parson. I stared back with as steady a gaze as I could manage. Then he swung back, hand on my shoulder, talking into my ear in a lowered voice:

'As a matter of fact, it was the management that sent me round to have a talk with you. Listen mate, I'll be honest, there could be a lot of people involved in this. A hell of a lot. Get me? It ain't just you being pig-headed we're worried about—I don't give a bugger about that myself. D'you follow me, brother? So think it over, that's all I'm saying. Don't do anything rash till you've had a good think about it. I'm not saying you are, but you *could* be raising a precedent. It could make things very awkward for a lot of folks. Okay? Think about it, brother, that's all I'm asking.' He patted my shoulder, placatingly.

'Okay,' I said, anything to get rid of him. He gave me a big confidential wink and pushed off. I looked round quickly, and heads ducked down hastily. I was the king-pin, I couldn't back down now. A day went by, then another. Nobody said anything, but everybody was waiting, like me, to see what happened next.

Pad came darting up, pink and flustered. 'Will you go to the foreman's office please?' It gave me such pleasure, that 'please'. My workmates were watching slyly as I marched off feeling ridiculously exalted, like Joan of Arc going to meet her judges. I was shaking and shivering, but that was nerves, excitement, anticipation, not fear. My great moment had arrived. When I got to his glass pen I saw the works engineer standing up at one end, one hand stuck in his trouser pocket. He had a habit of jingling coins when he was really savage. I knocked on the door respectfully and marched in, and that was what he was doing, old Snakehead, rattling away at coins or keys. He was glaring coldly out across the vista of machines and benches into the far distance, as if bored stiff. He didn't even acknowledge my presence. The foreman, Gutteridge, looking angry and agitated, rushed up and started on me without wasting a minute. I'd been asked to work overtime in a proper manner and I'd refused, what's more I was holding up the rest of the section, urgent work was jammed in the pipe-line, it was utterly stupid and disgusting, selfish, unco-opera-tive. He barged on, until at one point I managed to mur-mur :

'I'm sorry . . .'

He must have thought I was being funny, because he lost his temper completely and screamed : ' You're not, you're not sorry, not sorry at all! Don't tell me you're sorry!'

The works engineer decided to make a move. He strolled over, bored and contemptuous, with an off-hand attitude meant to convey that he wasn't acquainted with the facts of the case, he was only there by accident but let's see what he could do.

'Tell me this, sonny,' he drawled. I looked him full in the eye, quivering from head to foot, thinking. You shitbag,

I'll tell you all right in a minute. 'Say you were coming to work in the morning, and you saw a blind man who wanted to cross over the road. Would you rush straight past, or would you stop, thinking of someone other than yourself, and help him to cross over?'

I managed a tight little smile. He was on with the same game, smiling. It must have looked comical, us two, glimmering frostily at each other like a couple of death's heads.

'I'm afraid I don't get the connection,' I said.

'You don't? It's perfectly simple. Mr Gutteridge here is in a spot. He's asking you to help him out of his difficulty, that's all. Just that. Asking you to act unselfishly for once.'

I began to feel trapped. 'I thought it was voluntary.'

The hate came up behind his eyes then, the killer look.

'He's asking,' he said softly, 'just as that blind man on the edge of the pavement's asking.'

'That's hypothetical. I don't know any blind man, I'm sorry.'

He raised his eyebrows at the use of that big word. Abruptly he changed his tack, stopped playing about. 'You a Communist?'

'No.'

'Your father a Communist?'

I shook my head, still smiling, goading. The glory feeling had come back. The tension slackened. He was miles off now, and visibly rattled.

'Read Communist books?'

'I don't see it's anybody else's affair, what I read,' I said, and for the first time felt inflamed by a sense of real injustice. He was sneaking my glory away, giving it to the Communists. It's me, nobody else, I wanted to shout. Can't you see I'm here by myself? The pride of the artist burned up in my face. All my own work. What the hell was a Communist book anyway?

'You won't help us, then, is that it?' he was saying, and I guessed by the sneering tone it was all over, I was being dismissed.

'I'm sorry . . .' I said again, lamely, forgetting the effect this had just had on the foreman.

135

The works engineer had turned his back. He jingled his coins and played pocket billiards, staring out of the window again.

'All right,' Gutteridge said wearily. What an act. He wanted me to feel I'd stabbed him in the back. I went out politely, closing the door, fighting hard against the guilt they were wishing on me.

Still quivering from the conflict, I walked back to the square foot of factory floor where I stood all day, working and dreaming violently, the spot where I belonged, felt safe, even liked—except that now, more and more it was becoming irksome. One by one, they all asked me—Pad first, he was terribly anxious—'What happened?' He looked sick and worried as it dawned on him that nothing had really altered and the situation was unchanged. And when he came up to me next morning, first thing, wringing his hands and almost in tears, saying what a fix he'd be in at home if he couldn't work overtime any more, flat time just wasn't enough to meet his commitments, pay his hire purchase, his mortgage, shoes for the kids, he'd come to rely on his overtime and he couldn't work now if I didn't —begging me outright to say yes for his sake—I just nodded and said 'Okay then—one night a week and no more.' He was in a dreadful state, making a disgusting scene as he went to pieces in a desperate attempt to put on a convincing performance. His face lit up and he scurried off mumbling how grateful he was, and I felt stupid and flat, it was so pointless after all. Yet I'd won, hadn't I? Even that seemed in doubt. What else could I do, faced with that kind of grovelling desperation? I'd won, but this turn-about-face sucked the pride out of me, and it rankled for days, the thought that the bosses would believe they'd talked me round.

I kept thinking about the questions that shitbag had snapped out all of a sudden. Are you a Communist? Now I knew he was so sensitive on the subject, I began to look on his opponent the works convenor with real respect. They said he was a dedicated Communist, and I believed it. He was pint-sized, he worked one of the massive shuddering planers, it towered over him as he watched the huge table sliding back and forth, he'd tap the tool over another fraction of a turn and the cast iron would spray off the raw strapped-down casting in a rasping fountain of hot chips. His hands were permanently black from the iron dust and he'd be seen marching through the shop on his way to the offices like that, bow-legged and fearing nobody, a tough, charred, indomitable figure, a bit of black moustache over his lip as if the back of his hand had smudged it on.

Dinnertimes, in the summer, he'd have a group of apprentices squatting round him outside on the grass verge, his back against the railings of the Ferguson empire, giving anyone who'd listen a run-through on the history of the union movement. Derek Newey would be there with a bundle of *Workers* and a tin mug for a collection, smiling down his nose and bathing in reflected glory. I could never make out this strange allegiance, the cordial, elegant and rather wish-washy young man and Alec Jenkins, his middle-aged, furrowed face and gritty, bitten-off speech, his cold blue twinkling eyes, his bitter relish for the old class war. Derek was interested in the theatre, as distinct from bookish, which I was, and for a time I cultivated him. He dabbled and wavered, and it shook me, most pleasantly, to realise that he valued my opinions. It wasn't so flattering when I got the hang of him and understood that this cultivated young fellow with his cigarette holder and his urbane, cool manner, a man several years my senior, heard me out solemnly and seriously only because I had prejudices, likes and dislikes, when it came to books and writers. For some reason he found this remarkable. He had none of my intolerance, in fact he couldn't make up his mind about anything. He wobbled like a jelly. His Communist affiliation wasn't so incongruous either now I'd got to know him better. It was romantic flirting, with no risks attached. He sat cross-legged on the grass like a Gandhi disciple near the acrid little working-class realist and it was too daft for words, like Beauty and the Beast. It was coming up to the General Election and soon the Communist candidate arrived to deliver a roadside speech. Here was Alec Jenkins' equal, an army captain recently demobbed who'd emerged from the ranks during the war, a black-haired, hard-built young Scotsman, thick neck and craggy shoulders, roaring harsh and strong against the traffic, hammering home his points with his fists, one-two, the greatness of the Labour Movement, the exploiting bosses, the solidarity of the workers. Only a handful listened, the lorries drowned him and he fought harder, croaking like a raven, with Alec Jenkins crouching at his feet, unmoved, hard and fixed and invincible. And a fortnight later we were all out, the union had called a one-day token strike. I went down in the town and joined the mass meeting, on the platform the union leaders called for a show of hands, and a forest of arms shot up. I had no idea what the dispute was all about; it was no concern of mine. It was the show of strength and the solidarity which impressed me. A strike gave you an illusion of movement and power that was exciting; it was a flag of defiance hoisted in the very face of authority, telling you to stick together, unite. I shifted position in the crowd, working a little nearer, on my own, vaguely stirred by the restlessness and discontent, taking no notice of the speeches—which I couldn't hear properly anyway. I liked the atmosphere of it and I liked my anonymity, being merely a face in the crowd, feeling the ripples of unrest wash over me. Something was on the move, it felt good. Next day we were back at work, nothing had changed, we were all stuck, we all had our different reasons, excuses for being caught by the short hairs. We were caught, that's all I knew. My real escape routes were more and more to be found mapped out in books. Nothing could beat the excitement of finding in a book the thoughts and dreams and emotions, the frustrations, disappointments, achings that corresponded with yours, whispering and confiding and trusting you like a lover. That was what I was now, a book lover. I was beginning to live vicariously, to recognise myself as some sort of exile. At Lillington during the war I used to sit in the reference library of a Saturday afternoon, the light slowly turning purple outside the steamy high windows as I opened the big tomes, the potted biographies of modern authors. A writer was somebody else —even a modern one—and I was as curious to see their photos as I was to read their life stories. I'd stare avidly at

Joyce with his black eye patch, looking sickly and piratical. I remember the fascination of the queer word Proust, that I didn't know how to pronounce though it half rhymed with *sprouts* to look at, and took on vegetable properties because of the coincidence. I held it in my mind afterwards and juggled it, fingered and toyed with it; it was crisp, crunchy, with a touch of frost, or cooked soggy and water-logged, spiced back to life with a squirt of vinegar. A short story I read at this time, by a young American, was about a lonely Negro boy who, towards the end of the tale, sat at the kerb and cried softly, and *the tears splashed into the dust at his feet*. Softly. Reading that word, and the phrase about the tears, I was overwhelmed with longing to create feelings of desolation just as powerful for myself. It seemed terribly necessary and important. I didn't ask why, I just wanted to do it—make the world cry real heartrending tears as they read my words. The same thing happened when I read Saroyan's *Daring Young Man* story, only that took me further, I wanted the sense of desolation to sing and triumph in a crazy way. There was a broad avenue of chestnuts in Lillington, leading very firmly, with a slow dignified sweep, to the main road. Either side were select, big houses, each one trim and enclosed as a mansion in its own grounds. Weekdays I cycled between the trees in the dark if it was winter, swishing over the leaves if it was autumn, and in the summer on hot Sundays I'd walk half-way up the avenue and branch off to the left up a public path leading out to some meadowland. I read *Daring Young Man* out there, lying in a nest of long grass, feeling blue and melancholy and elongated, yet part of a gay com-position—like Chagall's poet. What a blood transfusion that story is, what doubt and confusion too, what debili-tating sadness. I gathered up the swirling dizziness, the truth, the meaning, I pitied everything and everybody, I saw what was in store for each one of us. 'Man that is born of woman has but a short time to live.' The blue sky emptied, it looked blank and threatening as it does at moments of crisis in childhood. I was seventeen. I got to my feet and stumbled off home hurriedly, and was glad to be clumping down the area steps into the basement, glad to be holed up, shut off, huddling together like any family of animals for warmth and comfort.

But I knew now. These were deep secrets, closely guarded. The whole world of books was liable to be blotted out by a word in those days, it had to be fenced round protectively against the doctrine of common-sense I lived with, the material, practical routine acknowledged as real. Derek Newey's lack of awareness irritated me no end. Surely it was plain enough, the hostility of the treadmill to anything as useless as art? No, blithe as a curate he'd wander over to my side of the factory to ask my opinion of Huxley, say, or Wells or Shaw, his butterfly mind flitting to and fro delightfully. I'd handle him very warily. I much preferred to go over to his section and talk to him, I wasn't so ashamed of him over there. It was incongruous talking to him at any time, anywhere, nutty, especially in that place of formidable industry, grinding and bashing and screwing, making, churning it out—but it was no use mentioning that to him. Anyway it was all right listening to his moonshine, it made a change. I felt safe enough where nobody knew me. That was how I met Vincent, a fitter in his thirties, fair, with a big wet mouth and dirty teeth. He'd heard us talking and one day he chipped in with—'I've done a spot of the old writing meself, you know—excuse me for butting in, I'm an ignorant bastard aren't I—go on, say yes!' It seemed he wrote stories as a hobby, and he hinted that he'd had some of them published in magazines like *Argosy*. So from then on, if I was coming away from Derek's bench this Vincent at the far end would invariably collar me. He was a Dostoevskian character, he squirmed and twisted with inner contradictions and he had to expose them, humiliate himself. He oscillated between a humble-pie, Uriah Heep manner, so obviously phoney it made you blush, and a crude natural boastfulness he tried to tone down, knowing how unpopular it made him.

'Vince the bullshitter, that's me,' he'd say, breathing his rotten breath into your face. 'Now listen, don't take any notice of me, what I say. Lies, all lies. Bullshit. Ask anybody, they'll tell you. Pay no attention to Vince, they'll say. Ask Derek . . .' This was how he rounded off his accounts, or a piece of advice he was handing out gratuitously. Then he'd laugh violently, so forced it was even more offensive, suddenly switch it off and say, sotto voice, 'No, but seriously . . .'

At the very beginning I wanted to write stories rich with comedy, and the first story I ever wrote was based on Vincent. It was supposed to be funny. The elaborate, creaking humour and bombastic vocabulary, the excessively dignified style, these were lifted straight out of *Oliver Twist*, a book that had made me laugh out loud on one page and brought me close to tears the next. My story was a pen portrait of an obstreperous character who talked rapidly like Vince, who laughed like a horse, curling his lips back and baring his long stained fangs, head rearing, letting rip a mirthless whinnying sound. Vincent the Bullshitter I should have called it, but the word wasn't in Dickens' vocabulary —and that was where I came unstuck. Vincent was Vincent. He demanded his own language if he was going to live at all, and it had to be copious, flowing, spittle forming at the corners in tiny bubbles and bursting. I used to watch the bubbles and lose track of what he was saying. He was Vincent, nobody quite like him before or since, a unique pain in the neck—not Uriah crossed with Lebedev, add a pinch of Fagin and stir slowly. It was the other way round —he was the real thing, raw material, inspiration, and characters in books the pale reflection. He was a Cockney in the Midlands, he came from the hub of the world, the Smoke, and that made him more overweening than ever in this one-eyed town, and more uneasy, and squirmy, tying himself in knots with anxiety as he tried to be ever so 'umble. His gift of the gab earned him nothing but winks and knowing glances, distrust rather than derision. He was tolerated and that's about all. Instead of drying up in the face of this silent disapproval, the gab came out slimy and unctuous. It had to have an outlet, that was his trouble. He grabbed me as a likely ear, an audience. His mouth bubbled at the corners, his eyes slid from side to side: 'They're watching me, look—they think I'm delivering another load of bullshit!'

18

IT'S amazing the mates you pick up when you're passive
and drifting, offer no resistance, smile meekly, show no pre-
ferences one way or the other. I find it terribly hard to say
no to anybody; always have done. If I'd said no, can't
stop, and kept walking, Vincent would have been left with
his mouth hanging open. With other people it's not so
simple. Tony Maggs, for instance. Tony was an apprentice
I'd hardly nodded to indoors. Then on the push homewards
at night, as the light evenings arrived, he'd ride up alongside me and we'd be shoulder to shoulder, pedalling mechanically, having one of those asinine conversations he
specialised in. His yellowish turnip mush would suddenly
slide into view, his thick lips splitting open in a grin of
complicity, as if we shared a secret joke. At first I thought
he was taking the piss, but no, it was his queer manner. He
really liked me, for some cockeyed reason of his own he
thought me funny—he actually enjoyed my company. This
was flattering, and entirely unexpected, so, of course, I saw
him in a new light and even got a kick out of him for a
while, thick as he was. He had a sense of humour, I'll say
that for him. On our first night out together—we went into
town for a game of billiards and a drink—he told me something he hadn't told anybody before. ' In confidence, mind,'
he warned me, and in fact he couldn't figure out himself
why he wanted to tell me, of all people. Funny, it was. I
was the kind of bloke who listened quietly without spoiling
the yarn, he said, and another thing, he knew I didn't blab
it around.

' Blab what?'

' What I'm going to tell you.'

' Oh.'

' Am I right or not?' he asked cagily, grinning from ear
to ear.

' Go on, for Christ's sake,' I kept saying. ' Tell me the
bloody story—stop beating about the bush.'

He chortled and nearly doubled up. In his simple-

minded way he thought he was tantalising me, a big tease.
I was bored to death already, itching for an excuse to cut
the evening short. We were chalking the cues, the top half
of the smoky upstairs room in deep shadow above the wide
lights hung low over the table, bathing the emerald green
cloth. A couple of players at another table under the big
clock were talking in subdued voices. Down in the street a
car buzzed by. I screwed down the hard lump of hollowed
chalk on the tip of the cue. The dry scraping sound went
with the stale air, the lifeless quiet, the feeling of deliber-
ated movements and suspended time. Tony's confidential
act had got the better of him now, he was up close with his
face hovering around my ear. I made a feeble crack, sick
of the whole performance. It made no difference what I
said, he'd insist on reading something comical into it. Was
I a comic and didn't know it? This thought excited me, it
was a gift worth cultivating. I was still putting on the act
of listening interestedly to Tony, a stupid grin stretched
over my clock, but my mind was wandering. Then it happened, he was really telling me, urgent, his voice changed.
The story hinged on the fact that his parents had gone out
to Australia for a couple of years apparently—his old man
was a compositor, who thought he'd go out on the ten quid
assisted passage scheme, stay there the minimum and earn
big money on the *Bulletin*, then work his way home and see
the world at the same time. Tony's mother had a sister out
there. I knew this was right anyhow because I'd noticed
Tony flashing his mail around and shouting the odds. ' I
got a letter from Alice Springs,' I heard him shout, ' I got
a postcard from Bondi Beach ' or some such place. He had
to find digs while his parents were away, that was the point.
His landlady, according to his description, was a big flabby
shag-nasty old cow, old enough to be his mother, who liked
to take in lodgers so that she could always be sure of a bit.
What was up with her husband? I wanted to know. Don't
ask me, Tony said—he was a little runt, and if he argued
the toss she'd drag him down on the carpet in front of us,
stand over him like Britannia and tell him to admit defeat
and shut his row. Charming set-up. Desperate and hopeful,
she was, a slovenly old slut wandering round half undressed

till dinnertime, piling up the dirty crocks in the sink for her husband to wash when he came in from the office at night, rattish and beaten, full of suppressed venom. A Devon woman. Now we were getting it, he was half breathing down my neck to tell me the rest of it. It seems he was on his way out one morning, going past the hallstand in the passage and out came Mrs from the middle room, slopping about in bedroom slippers and dressing-gown as usual, carrying a fresh towel. The next minute she'd blundered into him as if by accident and was pawing at him, saying he was only short but so hairy that it was plain he was a man already, and was it true what they said about short men being well endowed? In a flash she noticed the bulge in his pants. 'Oh my!' she was gasping, delirious at the very thought of it. 'Oh can I see it? Oh my, what a whopper—can I get it out?' Her loose cheeks were flopping, red with excitement, hairpins working free, she unbuttoned his flies and fished it out before he knew what had happened. 'Oh God, I wonder if I can touch it!' she moaned, frantic, throwing her towel over it, glancing round madly in guilt and panic and confusion. All Tony did was stand there pushed against the wall with his cock jabbing the air, rigid as a coat hanger. She kept whipping the towel over it, lifting the corner to have another look, to make sure it hadn't got away, gasping and spluttering in adoration, till in seconds he went off with an almighty bang. His spunk shot out with such force it splashed the front door, and the landlady was down on her knees mopping at the mess with her towel—almost with her nose in it, she was so short-sighted. It looked as if she was trying to lick it off, working away with her tongue out, and she was so delighted, grateful, apologetic, babbling away to herself. 'And then—fucking arseholes!—the doorbell rang. Christ, she nearly jumped out of her skin. "Just a minute, just a minute," she was yelling, scrambling up on her feet again, still mopping away for dear life.'

When I thought it all over afterwards, it rang true except for that last bit of crude embroidery—the doorbell. Even that was possible, I suppose, but I couldn't swallow it somehow, it was too easy to add on, and an irresistible touch for someone like Tony, who had to have it laid on with a trowel. I was living it till he got to that bit. I heard him tell the whole story again later to somebody else, and 'Fucking arseholes!' he ended, exactly the same, to convey his wonder and amazement.

I think of him, and then for pure contrast think of Peter Greenstreet. What deadened and stupefied when you were with Tony for any length of time was his lack of interest in anything that didn't have a horse laugh in it somewhere. The factory was all right, the town was all right, the flicks, life—what else was there? He was content, dead as a doornail, and that damned him for me. How could anybody be so thick, such a simpleton? And I think more than anything, the one thing that got me about Peter Greenstreet— who had a very different, very enviable contentment—was his cleanliness. It was a most repulsive cleanliness that he possessed, the next-to-Godliness kind. The kind that accuses in spite of itself. He was good and kind and considerate, he was responsive, his sincerity shone out of him, he was naked in the world—like a flatfish on a fishmonger's slab. Nobody could question his utter integrity, he was worth a dozen Tonys, yet I couldn't raise a laugh in him or him in me. All I could ever do in his company was smile a watery forgiving smile at the world. No room for hate, no outlet, no chance to smash anything. After I left school I lost touch with him, then years later I bumped into him in town on a Saturday, and he seemed unchanged. If anything he was even more understanding, admirable, self-effacing. He suggested that we got acquainted again, renewed the friendship. Once again I was trapped by my inability to refuse anybody; the word No froze on my lips. I agreed to go out to his place. Leaving him I started to seethe, to call myself names for making such an idiotic arrangement. I was twenty-one, beginning to smash out—it was either that or die. I got home and rushed upstairs to the box-room, shut myself in and wrote him a letter saying I'd given his suggestion a lot of thought but it would be useless, a waste of time—I was an atheist now. What I looked forward to was the end of organised Christianity, churches closing down for lack of congregations, the cathedrals turned into museums and art galleries. I wrote this in a cold ruthless style, explaining that this wasn't so much an opinion as a self-evident process already under way. I'd been reading Shaw's *Prefaces* and I aped his calculated impertinence—it suited me to a tee. My maudlin anarchy and inner screaming threw me into incoherence. Smash, smash, that was all I could hear. This Shavian focus held in front of me was exactly right, I was able to write a letter that sounded unanswerable to me, a superb piece of logic-chopping, a cutting, devastating, inspired diagnosis, cool as a surgeon. The bit about atheism I put in to flatten him completely—it was the first time I'd used the word—and the rest was a series of body-blows aimed at his most vital parts, just in case he got up again. I finished like a real prig, telling him how futile it would be if we became friends again, we were opposed on every fundamental issue and there seemed no point in us meeting. What it was, I was afraid of meeting him. I wanted us to be opposed, enemies. Face to face he would gently listen, gently understand, gently but firmly take me by the hand and endeavour to lead me back into the fold. ' The place for criticism is inside the church,' he always told me. ' We need people like you to change things.'

Peter Greenstreet—to recall him in detail, at his most characteristic, means going through those Sunday rituals all over again. Nip upstairs straight after dinner, after washing my neck and ears in the back kitchen, bending over the yellow glazed trough with its chipped enamel bowl—brick walls still streaming with moisture, the condensed steam of that Sunday morning roast—and smelling the cabbage water, peering over the net into the yard of blue serrated bricks laid in a herring-bone pattern, on which a soft drizzle is falling. Upstairs I go to the bow-fronted chest of drawers and fetch out a clean white shirt as ordered, clean vest and underpants, laying them carefully on the bed by the side of my charcoal grey suit and waistcoat which is there already; searching intently for collar studs, cuff links, coming down transformed, feeling the stiffness of the starched shirt across my shoulders, the heavy cloth of the jacket weighing on my arms importantly; bending my knees self-consciously as I walk, with an unpleasant awareness of the strange elegance of my wrists. Marching into the kitchen with a hollow in my back to clean my shoes.

Peter Greenstreet was Sunday afternoon incarnate. The roseate glow of his cheeks, his pink lips a little too long and thin to be cherubic, his pink tongue, the pink insides of his mouth, his pink hands and scrubbed nails, pink as washed shells, his chubby knees, round and pink like fresh apples—he was the personification of the sweet soapy Christianity we were taught in that Baptist Sunday School. He sat beside me and became my friend, we were in the same class, grouped around our teacher in a halo of quiet in the dingy bare room behind the chapel, pushing back our hard chairs gingerly to avoid rupturing the sanctity. Sitting next to me with his elbows pinched in, his lips pursed, his gleaming black shoes tucked well back, exuding a mixture of prim rosy goodness and determination—I looked on him more as an example than an equal. I wasn't on his level of excellence and never would be. Having him for a friend was belittling. We were boys of the same age, but when it came to religion he had the finesse of a professional. His teeth were fiercely clenched on the good life, as if he'd been born to it. It was partly his upbringing, I found out later. He was without any swank or side, no airs about him at all, even though his father was a teacher. It wasn't Peter's fault that he was superior—he just was. When we were told to turn to a particular passage in the Bible, he had his open at the exact place in a flash. Old or New Testament, it was all the same to him—he was at home there as he was in his own back garden. Noticing me struggling, hopelessly lost, he leaned over discreetly and whispered the page number. Then he'd cough into his hand, take a spotless white handkerchief from the top pocket of his jacket and wipe his lips. Putting the handkerchief back he rearranged it as before, folding it along the ironed creases and tucking it away so that only a triangle showed. He had his own Bible, his own hymn book, his eyeballs shone with his own special brand of beatitude. Asked to read aloud, he positively sparkled. He sat forward tense as an alarm clock about to go off, and I remember what a surprise it was the first time

I heard him, when that thin reedy voice trembled out. He was nervous, and I couldn't get over that. Not *him*.

Mention his name and it swirls back, all of it—the constriction of that best suit, a first pair of long trousers, mooning up dead and blind Whatford Street on a Sabbath, stiff and correct as if on the way to a violin lesson, peering under the arch up the cobbled lane leading to a yard where they sold ice, great salty blocks, at the rear of Pemba Street. Walking correctly and feeling like a penguin, a little before 3 p.m., up the hill through the canyon of Whatford Street overhung by the Humber cliff—raincoat folded and hung over the forearm, trouser bottoms swishing, burnishing my shoes; getting nearer, feeling a kind of stage-fright. On Easter Monday assembling in the morning at the market for the parade : each church, Sunday school, scout troop a separate contingent with its own banner— those huge flapping banners held aloft between two poles, with tasselled cords for guy ropes, and the men carrying the banners had leather holsters for the pole butts slung round their necks on broad straps : the bugles and kettle drums, parade marshals, police, first-aid, the proud banners emblazoned with the name of your chapel—and as we moved off the poles lurched dangerously and I held my breath. Coming back for the morning service after that tour through the streets was tame and yet good, I liked sitting cramped in the pews and kneeling on the worn hassock with my face still tingling from the cold wind on the hills, the corners, feeling the restlessness and excitement churned up by the parade all round me, the flushed cheeks, bright eyes. The service was always perfunctory, they gave you a bun and an orange and you went winging home, a swallow-dive of joy, downhill, heading straight for the fairground on Hyson Road.

Even as a boy I was conscious of what we were doing in those processions. We assembled beneath our own flags and then marched out under the windy, wintry sky, the high winds and flurries of rain, and the sky seemed to billow and unfurl over us like the banner of Christ. The men carrying the poles braced themselves as the banners filled like sails and tugged powerfully : it was right and proper, nature had to be fought down, the indifferent streets waited sullenly as we swung round corners, bugles blazing, penetrating one district after another, soldiers of Christ on the march, child crusaders. It was a tableau, a symbolic act, but it wasn't a game. Stirring, exciting, but you weren't supposed to be enjoying it. The sweet shops, stationery shops, junk shops, cycle shops, factories, barbers, warehouses, chemists, picture houses, baths, markets, chip shops we passed were all closed—but by dinnertime the fair would be open at the end of our street, spinning and blaring loud and strong. Walking behind the banners I'd be all warm inside imagining the fair, picturing it so vividly that instead of my feet treading on macadam and tramlines they'd be crunching over the cinders flung down between the stalls. The thrill of a fairground was in sensations like that, wild anticipations—and the real surging excitement was generated with the electricity they made themselves—if you followed the rubber leads running from stall to stall where the light bulbs dangled in glaring rows you could track down the sources of power and light; massive traction engines, wheels wedged, flywheels spinning, canopies shuddering. On the road these engines pulled loaded wagons in a close convoy like a train; now they stood half hidden at the far corners of the waste ground, stowed away behind the sideshows, harmless giants, tethered like elephants among the showmen's luxury vans. No, now I think of it, the Easter procession wouldn't have been half as enjoyable if the fair hadn't been there at the end like a glittering promise. It was the light at the end of the tunnel. Otherwise it would have been grim and drab and purposeful, grim as those marches through the November streets on Remembrance Sunday. The one procession that was wholehearted pleasure, fun and frolic from start to finish was the summer carnival. There was a touch of civic pride as the floats swung into view, the lorries and brewers' drays and magnificent carthorses decked with flowers and coloured streamers, we cheered at each new burst of glory, the trades and industries all represented, unions, ambulance, fire brigade, nurses, police, a festival staged for fun and blossoming like a garden out of all the elements of a city, kaleidoscopic, a winding medley of noise and colour. What made it so intoxicating, so infectious was the craziness, the careless rapture, the way the crowds lining the route participated, yelling encouragement, cheering and laughing at the clowns on pushbikes and stilts careering down the gutters, raking the air with their collecting boxes and tins, shaking them madly like castanets. Cheery old men with nutcracker faces were giving the thumbs-up sign from the lorries, doing crazy antics dressed in pyjamas, every kind of fancy dress, and by the time the leading lorries reached us they'd have the judges' award cards proudly displayed, 1st, 2nd, 3rd, sailing past in order of supremacy. The whole thing emptied into the vast green space of Albert Park and drained away, petering out naturally, and you followed it in and forgot it almost at once because of so much else going on : car raffles, ox-roasting, gas-filled balloons taking off mysteriously into the blue with a label attached, bearing your name and address; refreshment tents, treasure hunt, bands, a play park full of sand, a tent where lost children waited for their mothers—and you stared in at the waifs and strays behind the trestle table, at their tearstained faces, examined them curiously, big enough now not to worry, then suddenly uneasy and small in that rowdy vastness, people milling everywhere, and you went darting back to where you knew your parents were sitting placidly on spread raincoats on the grass. No rain for a month but the raincoats still had to go down, my mother pressed the flat of her hand on the turf and maintained she could feel the damp—maybe the dew had been heavy that morning, she said. We hung about, eating sandwiches and drinking pop, the adults kept unscrewing the flask of tea, and when it got dark we'd move over behind the pavilion for the grand finale, a giant fireworks display. We waited patiently for hours and it was never worth it, somehow it always disappointed, perhaps because we'd been waiting too long, expecting too much. Next year we'd wait again on the same grassy bank, a vantage point, slowly getting chilled, telling each other it won't be long now. Nobody remembered how lousy it was last time. We sat listening to the breeze rustling the grasses and leaves, watching the elms blacken as the light faded, letting the dusk sadden us inexplicably. We shivered our shoulders, felt a touch of cramp in our legs from sitting too long, and began to feel deserted, last-out, everyone drifting inwards to the snug lit homes. Everyone but us. Long before the fireworks finished, we were ready to go.

19

STAND at the bay window and peer down the road: Ray's coming. He's not in sight but he's coming. It's his night. Lift the trombone out of its coffin—tubes green with verdigris at the joints. Secondhand. Try not to think of someone else's slime and slobber. All I can play is ' I Dreamt That I Dwelt in Marble Halls '. Just to sound a full ripe note, sustain it long enough to work the slide in and out, is an achievement, a good enough satisfaction. My mother pokes her head into the room to tell me it's awful, like a dying cow. That's her joke. I keep blowing.

' No more, you'll strain something,' she says anxiously, seeing my veins stand out. I stop, lower the instrument, gulp, fill my lungs with air and blow again. No good. Dismantle it, shake out the slobber, reassemble it. Can't play it but I can dream. Kid Ory in marble halls. The garden gate clicks—I wait breathless for the knock. Nothing. Is he coming or not? In looks my mother again: ' Is he coming tonight?' He'll come, he's bound to come, this front room pulls like a magnet. Shelves in the alcove full of my books, a stack of records in the corner by the radiogram, including nearly a dozen yellow-label Deccas—Beethoven's *Missa Solemnis*. Walked in the music shop last Saturday morning, flush after pay day, and asked if it was in stock. Right, I'll have it, thanks very much—just like that. Why not? What else is money for? We played it backwards by accident the first time. Wonderful. As good that way as any other when you're in love. Instead of God, it's Beethoven. Beethoven is Love. Waiting, I am waiting. Sit at the piano as if I'm composing. I am composing. I pick out notes, sad, lonely, tender, more beautiful to me than the masters. I can't play the piano either. So what? The beauty reverberates under my fingers, a secret language. My mother's head pops in through the doorway again—'Hasn't he come yet?'

He'll come, he's got to. I'm playing his music on the piano. For him. I wait pent-up like a lover. *Black, Brown and Beige Suite* ready on the turntable—he hasn't heard it yet. When he does he loathes it, can't bear to listen and I have to switch it off. It's his mood, not Ellington. All day he's been submerged in this nameless black misery . . . but never mind. At first everything's fine. Dusk of a Saturday night in July, mild lapping breeze, so quiet and peaceful. I can't sit still. I can hear the blue grass of the carpet growing. In he comes, shining, smiling. 'How's the idiot?' he says, grinning his head off, with a touch of malicious amusement mixed into his normal humour. I'm perfectly attuned to him, so it's not lost on me, this warning tremor. 'So he feels perverse tonight!' I tell myself, and I might be thinking, What a beautiful night. Slow brown Sunday tomorrow. I am happy. The idiot bit refers to the Dostoevsky I'm wading through, not me. If I can think of a funny answer I'll give it, but anything crude or unseemly would be unthinkable. We treat each other tenderly, gently, we are attentive, endlessly sympathetic. This is the honeymoon of our friendship. The ambience is undoubtedly romantic, the emotional charge high up in the chest, spiritual. 'What was that you were playing on the piano?' he asks.

'Oh, just something I made up . . .' He nods, leans forward receptively, eager to discover riches in me, so of course I play it again; a lame, halting, meagre little tune, plaintive, and each note transforms itself in the air and becomes radiant. I fashion jewels in the air. My friend sits struggling to contain a black mood, sunk back in the armchair. Soon he'll unleash his perversity, when the record goes on, and I can't help him or help myself. His very presence enhances me, changes my flow mysteriously. I am languid, heavy-lidded. I love the world, love everybody, smiling at nothing like a maniac.

I remember how the first time I went round to his place in East Street I heard delirious music coming out of a house a few doors down from him, it was boogie-woogie piano and through the net I could dimly make out this bushy-haired figure with his back to the window cascading notes like a prodigal. 'That's Adrian Levis,' Ray told me. 'He's self-taught. You should hear him play a Beethoven sonata. I used to go around with him a lot but he's engaged now. We even wrote songs once, tried to—him the music and me the lyrics. They're a big family but nobody else is gifted like him. His old man's tone deaf and his mother can't read or write.'

Mostly it would be the two of us in Ray's front room, but once or twice I was with my brother Alan who had first met Ray and brought him round. We played records, and talked books, while Alan sat there in his amazing imprisoned silence. Was he bored? Once I found a poem he'd written in celebration of a jazz player—' Blues for a clarinetist '—nothing ever more. We sat and listened, cranked up the clockwork gramophone and ate the bread-and-butter tea his mother served up if it was a Sunday—sometimes with jelly and custard, cakes and hot sweet tea. Ray would nip out with a jug to the off-licence later to get draught beer for his father. This goes on steady as a pendulum, these visits, and then he is called up for his National Service, Alan drops away and we continue by letter almost without a break in the conversation. Nothing stops us now.

I am sending long letters to Ray at Portsmouth and shorter, parry-and-thrust affairs to a married woman in the north who owns a copy of *A Season in Hell*. She reads books, writes poetry, paints pictures—I can't get over it. My letters are deliberate and brilliant compositions, failures every one—nobody suspects. I deceive as easily as I breathe, everyone but myself. I try out different styles, act parts. I'm vigorous, healthy, life-giving in my letters to Ray, strong and steady as a rock, all my vagaries suppressed. No melancholia—the words bound off the end of the nib, caustic, buoyant, no connection with me. I inspire myself, read them through and feel genuinely uplifted. It's when the reply comes and I see how successful I've been that I'm uneasy. It becomes a source of embarrassment, after the elation dies away. In the ones to the woman I am much happier, devoid of morals—what does the truth matter? I take to it like a duck to water, the male-versus-female game. I thrash about in the most calculated and provocative attitudes, I make angry, passionate, labial noises. The limits are unmarked yet I am aware of them instinctively. Within these limits I know I can do what I like. I am out to fascinate, stimulate, attract, mystify. The letters are battles masquerading as poems. Sometimes I enclose verses—they are softeners, oblique flatterers. I cultivate a cunning innocence. At one point she even asks if I'm a Negro.

On a sudden impulse I have sent out stories to a magazine. The editor returns them one by one, rejection slips underneath the paperclip, with pithy comments scribbled on them which I cherish and soon have by heart. ' Read Thomas Wolfe and learn how to temper your bitter realism with philosophy.' I can't write anything nowadays but letters. They make contact at first blow, there's no intermediary—you work direct in human materials. I'm restless, I can't stay in at night. Rake through the local paper for likely films in any district. The night-time transforms the drab streets into a luxurious solitude which ululates and parts and whispers. I slip into it each time with a sigh. Walk down under the hideous new sodium lights, the pavement falling away softly, narcotically under my feet in the dark, cross over the deserted Birmingham Road, turn up a lane of black ashes and earth trodden hard as concrete. On one side a ragged hedge of privet, allotment railings, patched wooden gates, huge gunmetal padlocks with brass flaps covering the keyholes, on the other side the steel wire and stanchions of a factory fence, buttressed and barbed. In a warm numbness now I'm on my way to see Henry Fonda at the Carlton, round the corner from the Albion Belt Works. A tightness under my heart scares me—if I breathe deeply it stabs. Coming home in a daze through the same ghostly lane I find myself reliving the marvellous Fonda walk, his grief and helplessness, submission, dignity, all manifested step by step and not a word spoken. I get home and the house is in darkness. There is a strange atmosphere of stealth—they've gone to bed but are they lying awake up there listening? The little stabs of pain

begin again. I must live, make haste and live . . . I sit at
the kitchen table and write a letter to the woman in the
north who has everything—home, husband, children—telling her I'm in love with her. I write it powerfully, like
Fonda crossing a room. Same stance, same tone, same doglike irresistible tenderness enlivened by conscience—I can
hit it perfectly, the exact note, because it resounds in me,
shakes me like a reed. Like an actor fully into his part I
am absolutely convinced that this is the truth and I'm not
aping anybody when I write ' I'm in love with you '. I
am hopelessly in need of the attentions of this mature
woman. I have her photo, know her interests, read avidly
between the lines—a thrilled exclamation tells me I'm winning the battle of letters : strike now. Back rushes a reply—
' Don't ever write that again !' Victory is mine : we make a
date to meet.

I step off a bus outside the market, in a city I've visited
only once before, as an apprentice on holiday. There facing
me at the bottom of the sloping cobbles, plastered over a
high brick wall, are the black letters of a poster—I AM COME
THAT YE MAY HAVE LIFE, AND MAY HAVE IT MORE ABUND-
ANTLY.

I wake up from a dream so powerful it pins me to the bed,
I am overcome by its truth and simplicity. In the dream I
picked up a newspaper and saw my picture, a review of
my book and the writer's first words were all I needed to
read :
    ' He is empty.'
I lie in bed wide awake trying to burrow back into the
dream which is so terribly important to me, lying still in
the warm sack of the sheets and letting its memory linger.
It is still more powerful than my waking life. Before it
fades I do recreate enough of it to decipher the full sentence which says ' He is empty as a whore '. I am full of
gratitude to the man, whoever he is, for such understanding. I am empty as a whore who can't get stuffed. An old
bag in Market Street with broken carpet slippers and a
caved-in nose couldn't be emptier than me. I know books
are nothing. I know everybody's lying, I know it's so much

straw, stuffing, I want to smash the radio, run into the street and scream ' Liars '. Defy the desolation. Find love. I prowl up and down longing to be stuffed. I take nobody's word, I believe nobody, trust nothing. If there was a God I'd say thank God for making life so empty and wonderful. When I was twenty-one I had a shattering dream of love. A very beautiful young woman had found me, gathered me up in her arms, I wept and laughed into her long hair as if taking refuge, we were overjoyed at finding each other, we recognised each other at once, I kept laughing and crying, blissfully happy and grateful, luminous with this great happiness, and when I woke up it was like a shipwreck, heartbreaking, I'd lost her for ever. Goodbye! And could have wept bitter scalding tears, but nothing would come. The dream choked me. It was a blend of ineffable joy and terrible desolation, that dream— as if I knew that time was running out and any minute I'd wake up and lose everything. Paradise lost—the anguish of the fallen angel. Nothing was said, not a word. A silent one-reeler, poignant as Charlie biting his nails in close-up at the end of *City Lights*. The Dream. I wrote it down exactly as I remembered—the first piece of writing that deeply mattered to me. A dythyrambic ecstasy. I was naked, stripped, how could I possibly show it to anybody? It's always been that way, the longing for protective colour and the impulse to strip myself naked—*let them see me as I really am*. Two desires that go on flatly contradicting each other and conflicting—the involuntary shrinking back and the reckless demand for intimacy at any price, culminating in the worst ordeal, the final disgrace of humiliation by public exposure.

And quietly, slowly, in an entirely English, unassertive, decent sort of way I was going nuts in that place. That factory, that home, that town. I had to get out. I'd see Ray at week-ends, we'd shoot off on bikes, and two or three evenings a week we sat in the front room, ours or his, never mentioning it directly, our burning predicament, but primed with books and paintings, great men, great music, primed with the future and plotting for the new life to come like revolutionaries. We'd go on sudden unplanned holidays to Wales, the Hebrides, using the Youth Hostels, and now and then he'd appear at the factory gates at dinnertimes, waiting for me to come out blinking in the strong light, laughing delightedly at the surprise on my face. I'd go off with him, Edgell Rickword's *Rimbaud* in my raincoat pocket. After he got married and his wife was expecting a baby I'd travel out to the Birmingham suburb where they were living temporarily with his in-laws, see the paintings he'd done to combat the sickening emptiness of his navy days and nights at Portsmouth—pictures of terror and innocence, soul dances, labyrinthine germinations, shooting stars, city nomad myths, done on cartridge paper unrolled on the floor of the Salvation Army hostel where he stayed at night to keep clear of the navy barracks. I read a prose poem he'd composed and called 'The Man Who Flew With the Birds'—and went dipping and gliding in pure flight on the curve of his vision. He was another autodidact, he went at everything blind. Instead of setting to work lucidly, in a civilised manner, he used his body, all his organs, holes, juices, nerves. He vibrated, made pictures, gave signs, in a pouring, helpless, signalling dance of prodigality. He was frantic, he was desperate, generous, felt doomed, no time—the fundamentals were in disorder and he was driven to these spasms of frenzied activity. Every move he made, every jitter echoed deeply in me. His wife had a young brother, and a little sister, seven or eight, who'd stare at me intently and say 'Aren't your lips red!' I'd reply 'Yes' and that would be the signal for a barrage of questions. 'Why are they? Do you use lipstick? Where d'you live? How long are you staying?' They were all crowded in this semi-detached, driving each other politely mad, and I'd say good-bye all round and leave, go trailing back to the main road with Ray, hearing him out to the bitter end, his despair so complete he could bang his head against the wall, his ballsed-up young civvy life, baby, wife, jeopardised by a chronic lack of money and free time and living room, his tribulations at the carpet cleaning factory, which was a dairy next time I went, a filling station the time after that—and I'd leave him at the corner wild-eyed, puckering his forehead, and I was sick at heart as I thought of him bowed down with worries and responsibilities at twenty, though not alone like me. I'd have changed places with him like a shot, that was the saddest and funniest part —not now, I wouldn't, but then, oh yes. Off I strode up the main road into nowhere, up the Brummagem Road walking blind, my back to the Black Country, my mind a seethe of impressions, thoughts, past the gigantic rampant tiger snarling full tilt out of the advert on the hoarding, on and on, the airport signpost looming out of the shit and drizzle and I shook my head and woke up, staring at it blankly like a sheep. Paris, that way; Rome, that way; Vienna, that way; New York, London, Brussels . . .

A Midland Red was coming, lit up, trundling along comically, two rooms on wheels—one up, one down. It scoured through the wet murk and I heard it, turned and waved it down. Not a soul upstairs. I felt empty and trembly and sick right through. The conductor came up and I stammered out something. I sat still against the window, quiet and obliterated. Going anywhere. Home. I let the bus take me, like having an Anywhere Ticket, while I travelled inwards, backwards. It was somewhere to go, it didn't mean anything more than that. I was going home again.

And I kept travelling, seeing the married woman. *Autumn Leaves* on the coach radio—' the red and gold '. Saturday night was my night; once every two or three weeks. She opened a new door on life. Her local bus would be late and I'd arrive in good time and wait on the corner, crucified. She came in for three hours: I travelled 120 miles altogether for my three-hour ration, then often her bus was late; the boy had measles, the clock was wrong, the dog had disappeared, the dinner had gone up in smoke. Domestic complications, tragedy, disaster. Two hours fifty minutes left. She came—how could she look so happy?— and then we needed another bus for the river: what time was the next one? We stood under the tin sign, that someone had heaved a brick at and buckled, tense as magnets not quite touching. My first woman. Mine—wonder of wonders. What could she see in me? She kept smiling, knowing and mysterious, the Egyptian eyes with blue eye-shadow glowed, digging into me, swallowing me. She mastered me without effort by her attack, her boldness. Her proud haunch brushed against me as if by accident. Her head was scarved, haughty, the face masked in war paint. I let out a passionate groan: ' Come on, bus!' and I could see her exult.

' Why such a hurry?' she whispered, gleaming with triumph and pleasure. Opposite, high on a tower of scaffolding, a corner of tarpaulin had ripped free. The north wind tore into it and it exploded, sharp as a pistol shot. *Crack-crack!*

Three hours she was giving me. She had nothing to lose. She was spiced and freshened by intrigue. I would go into the formalin of a poem of hers later. I'd be entered in her secret diary as an affair. She played the captivating, dangerous part in a fantasy she was weaving even as she stood there: the process continued, under my nose or wherever she was. And I took on new qualities in my own eyes. My silences became attributes, an actor's gifts; they were inspired pauses, charged with beauty and sex and death. She adored my urgency, I sensed that. So I hissed and groaned out loud to convey my grief at time passing. Displaying the anguish I felt gave me a kind of desperate pleasure. The cruellest thing was, I knew she was superbly immune. It was up to me to grab every minute that was going. My time was running away, being breathed away, talked and laughed away. The thought of it drove me wild. I was starving, she had meals galore. She was bored to distraction because she had everything. The situation ran along her nerves and she bristled excitedly. It was like the black river flowing invisibly, where we always went, the footpaths hairy with bushes at the openings, the trees spaced dramatically. She loved anything that fed her romanticism. Behind her, through the door she opened, only a year away, was Aline, with her morbidly sensitive mouth, melancholy gaze, her soft heavy thighs, her blossomy breasts set high up and wide apart, her girdle wrapped in brown paper and carried as a parcel so that she could stride better and feel free. Swaddled in a fur coat, bleakly married, she strode vigorously, swinging her free arm like a man. Her stocking tops shush-shushed as she walked. It gave me a feeling of opulent well-being to hear that dry regular sound chafing away; it was intimate and reassuring, homely and cheerful, that steady grasshopper friction. Summery, on the grisly winter cobbles. It lulled like the sea.

Crack-crack! The woman laughed richly, down in her throat. 'Time's whipping at us,' she crooned. 'Hear it?'

I heard it with tight lips, black heart. She was smiling at the imperious, swift whirling away of my minutes; she found it piquant. I looked at her, tongue-tied, struggling not to hate. I struck at her smile in my heart, to kill it. Then a 7 swung round the corner and surged at us, bull-like. At one stroke my bones were clad in a new body, I was all radiance, pride and gravity like a young king about to be married.

I muttered roughly, from my rapturous state : 'Let's get going.'

The Bliss Body

Our voyage is entirely imaginary
Therein lies its strength
CELINE

I

I'D NEVER stopped thinking of her. Going down to Devon to live with Ray was drastic enough, you'd think—yet I wasn't trying to put an end to it. No, that wasn't the idea. Or I didn't look at it like that at the time. I suppose I didn't know, when I moved all the way down there, how badly I was bitten. And instead of the distance putting the lid on it, the thing got worse. I might have got over it—might—if the letters hadn't kept coming. Those letters, in that purple ink, those exclamation marks, it was the same old game but now she could really hot it up—she had something on me. How she must have loved fashioning those letters, those ground-lines she threw out at night, baited with hints and promises for me at the other end to gobble down greedily, tugging and thrashing.

But I mustn't pile it on, mustn't blacken, I want to paint her as she was: the truth and that's all. Let the facts speak for themselves, if there *are* any solid facts to go on. I'll have to see. But no judgements: I'm not fit to judge. Nobody is.

There are things like her idea of herself—she fancied herself as a sort of artist's moll, at times even toying with the fantasy that she looked like a pro—and there was my whacky idealization of her, smashed and remade again and again in the distorting mirror of myself, meeting after meeting, her experience all docile as I cuddled it in innocence like a baby who doesn't know where his mother's been or anything about her, only that she's milky. Not that Leila was milky. She had two kids, but I don't think there could have been much breast nourishment. Powdered milk and orange juice on the National Health for them—it was just after the war. For breasts she had a couple of hard lumps the size of lemons, not much more, and

163

she couldn't have been very proud of them because she didn't let you see them. No, I can't ever remember seeing. Come to think of it, she didn't like to be touched round there at all. Couldn't bear it. She was some sort of artist herself. When you get that in a woman you're really in deep. Before I met her I was going round in a great blank nothing, my life leaking away greyly without risk, point or struggle. Leila was a road. She heaved me down it with a few naughty wriggles and I was out at the other end going somewhere. Moving. The war and peace of the road. Now and then I thought the heartache would kill me, and to make matters worse she kept smiling, the pain didn't touch her—that was because hers had happened before. And maybe it was still happening, at home. I didn't know what went on there: I only got garbled versions, embellishments, exaggerations. But it was my pain alone while we were to-gether, mine and mine only. My drama. She was audience, actress—she might even have been directing too. I wouldn't put anything past her. She let me write my little drama as we went along, and I bet she must have wet her knickers laughing about it more than once, as she put the kids to bed, warmed up her husband's dinner, let him have his rights every so often and thought over her problems, how she would tackle the next painting, the next poem, how she could do all these things and somehow find time to see me again for an hour or so, just to keep the pot boiling. The bitch. But unwittingly she was weaning me, the road unwinding, on and on, further and deeper in, after that marvellous secret entrance, hairy with lilacs and old man's beard, where she took me by the hand and I believed I was in love.

I was sick with love. It was like an ague of the guts; it shook me inside like a fever that kept raging, that nobody else sus-pected. Leila called it my fire—she loved my fire, she said. What she didn't know, couldn't, was that I was a heart in flames before I even met her or knew of her existence, hurrying

164

and stooping with my thin anxious body and this Great Fire to deliver. It was as if she was waiting, sixty miles away, for me to come out of cover. As soon as I got on the bus that Saturday and started hunching towards her, bitten into myself like the traffic, lingering, tentative, she shot into the air and waited. Hovered. Waited for me to arrive, for the bus to unload at the bus station against the market, for me to step down shakily on the cobbles near the corner stall hung with newspapers, spicy stories, crime—sick with anticipation, feeling doomed and about to die, feeling marked, wanting it to happen, the stab of love, anything but this grey death of days, this howl of emptiness. I was too early, so into the greasy café and wait, stir some muck they call coffee and watch the indifferent faces, the ugly, the sinister, the night faces, lost eyes, observe the bowed head of lust, hear the evil shuffle of a born killer—who suddenly throws back his head and laughs, a normal human reassuring fat laugh, which transforms him instantly into a comfortable family man. I laugh with him, laugh at my own fears and they scatter, hide in the shadows. Listen to conversations: the family man digs into his jowl, talks about the match that afternoon, goes into details, elaborates stupidly to the girl behind the snack bar with expressionless eyes and blank lassitude, who shows boredom in every wipe of her dishcloth on the counter. Can't he see? He keeps talking, another man shoulders in; the accents are blunt, pompous with coal and cash, the voices loud as the town. What city is this? Nottingham. I sit in a shiver of strangeness, at a glassy table in the corner which gives me a full view of the clock. Even the clock has a loud outspoken look, a Joe Blunt of a clockface that could have hung in a coalmerchant's office.

2

At the stroke of seven I make for the door. I know the meeting place, Slab Square, is only minutes away, I've found out—been down there to make sure, but I still take the wrong turn, suddenly all the streets are empty so that I can't ask, I pass shops I've never seen before and end up running. Burst into the square, the open, dazed and clumsy and brown like a partridge. In a flash she swoops, mouth glistening, eyes in a barbaric blaze, to pick me off. I am glad to die.

I must have said something facetious in a letter about mutual recognition—I'll be walking with a stutter, trousers back to front ready for a quick getaway—something happy and daft, because she pounced and greeted me like this, curving out of nowhere, sun behind her:

'I'd recognize that stutter anywhere!'

'Hello,' I said, bewildered, everything turning over.

She was a gay hawk that first night. She sprang, then drew back, laughing.

'Where did you come from?'

'The sky,' she laughed. 'Out of the sun.'

'Oh good,' I said, my words falling out helplessly but so glad, so delighted with myself because I was doing it, not on paper but face to face, actually conversing, exchanging laughs, grinning. Face to face. How easy it was, what a common joy and how I'd dreaded it, this moment. I thought up some more small talk, anything to keep the lovely circuit alive.

'Where to now,' I mumbled.

'Anywhere you like.'

'You say. You're the boss.'

'Oh no!' She was very amused, lifting her shoulders, cheek-bones twinkling. 'Do I look like a boss?'

'You know the way, that makes you boss.'

'Hah,' she said darkly, enjoying herself.

I kept glancing into the white blaze of her face and away again, anywhere. It was Saturday night, the square quiet except for the buses and their queues. The dying sunlight bled on us, warm and cidery on the back of my neck. Suddenly I was unbelievably happy, overwhelmed with what I'd accomplished. Here was this woman standing in front of me, who seemed to like me. I glanced in again, bolder.

'Where's the Castle, which way is that?'

'Over there—not far at all really. It's not much of a castle but the grounds are nice.'

'Are they,' I said, not asking.

'Very.'

'All right then.'

'To the Castle,' she said. 'Come on, I'll show you, if I'm the boss.' Laughing, glowing with her joke.

'Lead on, boss,' I murmured, wonderfully bold and transformed, thinking I must be unrecognizable—nobody would ever know me now. Every time I was amazed at myself.

We didn't touch, didn't even brush against each other. I followed her like a dancer, my whole body alert. Down short runs of steps shallow between low walls, out across the clear space of the square and over to the far pavement, the edge of the kerb. All the written stuff sank away, letters, the daring thrusts counted for nothing, the gains in intimacy cancelled out at one stroke by this first encounter. Start again from nothing. We danced along, vibrant with newness, not speaking, darting across the street by the traffic lights, sidestepping the hissing trolleys.

'Well, what d'you think of Nottingham?'

This was to make contact, like saying how's your mother, so I joked:

'I think I'm lost.'

'Poor boy.' And she chuckled, a sound I was to know and remember better than anything she said. She murmured:

'I'll look after you!'

'Thanks very much.'

'Up this street—the Castle's just at the top. Narrow, isn't it? I used to work in a factory up here—dispatch clerk. Awful. First job after I left school.'

'White collar.'

'A very grubby one. I was only there a month, then I went into an art school.'

'I see.'

'No, you don't. I wasn't afraid of work if that's what you think—I was *waiting* to go to art school.'

'That wasn't what I thought.'

'Oh.'

'I don't care if you work or not.'

'I work very hard when I'm in the mood. Other times I only work when I've got to.'

'Good.'

'But I was telling you about art school—it's a bit complicated—you see we lived here when I was small, then moved to Leicester——' she broke off to peer up an alley. 'No, that's not the place—nearer the top. I'll show you in a minute.'

'Your factory?'

'That's right.'

'Don't bother,' I said grimly. 'I don't want reminding of mine, thanks very much.'

'Will it remind you?' she laughed. 'You're here now, you're a long way away. You've escaped!'

'Till Monday,' I said, grating it out bitterly, grim as I could, for extra pleasure. And I was angling for sympathy. Instead

168

she treated me to a sudden gush of information about her husband, who hated his job too, even though he didn't actually work for anybody. He was in the ironmongery trade, him and a friend were partners, ran a shop and at the same time were trying to build up a business making caravans in a yard and shed at the back. But really he was a sculptor.

'The business is taking up more and more of his time, he can't seem to do anything he really wants. An exhibition's coming off soon in London, he's got one or two pieces in that, but he'd like a show of his own. It's a shame.'

It always is. Meet an artist and you can bet he loathes the job he happens to be doing to earn a living—whatever it is. Thousands of people, millions, can't bear their jobs either, but they aren't vociferous about it like artists, they aren't binding about it all the time, or giving their wives hell, they just keep it heroically to themselves and carry on doing the pools and watching films, or else quietly hang themselves in the toolshed one Sunday. Very apologetically. What else can they do? Sometimes they even end up pretending they *like* going to work every day—they even convince themselves. What would they do at home? They know from weekends, holidays, days off, that it's like a machine shop there at times, vacuums and washers going full blast. It's hell a lot of the time. So they make a niche for themselves at work, they learn to like it, they grow unaccountably content. The artist is incapable of this deception. He has a gift for misery. He couldn't be happy anywhere, he wants work to mean something. He's always worse off than the others, and better off, too, because he can imagine. He can escape that way. Often it's worse when he gets there, but he can't help himself. He can't bear things as they are.

I couldn't have expressed it like that if I'd wanted to—I'd never even met an artist. At the mention of a real one I used to prick up my ears: they were an unknown species I longed to know more about. My friend Ray's wife did good paintings, but if I'd called her an artist she'd have blushed bright red and told me to shut up. And the same with me, my poems and whatnot—if somebody had referred to me as a poet I'd have felt like giving them a kick in the stomach. All the same, I admitted to myself now that it might be for me, this artistic element. I might even learn to swim in it. But the gulf was there, the difference, the separation from ordinary life: I had violent reactions. It looked such a piddling little world, it had no links with the normal, I couldn't see where it joined on with the ordinary and everyday—and if it was going to put the leper stigma on me they could stuff it: I'd resign, abdicate, I didn't want to go any further. Wash my hands. Give me something tangible, for Christ's sake. I swung to and fro, curious and sniffing and disgusted when I wasn't excited, and it's amazing how long you can go on doing this before you wake up and realize that you had no choice anyway. Never. The leper taint was on you at birth.

3

AT MY side, the strange new woman was silent, loping. She didn't mince like other women. A figure flitted by in the dusk on the other side of the street, coming the other way.

'See her?' Leila cried. 'That woman?'

'I wasn't looking, not properly.'

'Didn't you get a good look at her?'

'No.'

When she didn't say any more I said, 'Why?'

She said with relish, laughing softly: 'If she isn't a pro I'll eat my hat.'

The back-street, sleazy atmosphere seemed to excite her, especially in the twilight or at night. I often noticed. Later on, in the country, in a wood, she would lose her intensity. The way she had of talking with bated breath, and her favourite mask, which was ravaged like the face of a sorrowing ballet dancer, had no power in the open. She needed streets. Night was her time. She was coming into her own as we walked, with the day cast down in the gutters. She had a gliding, hunting movement.

I was very pure and new. The woman slipping through the dusk beside me was struck dumb by my shyness. What sort of creature had she hooked out of the streets? What was he suffering from—aphasia? Wraith-like, I was delicately aware of myself and her as utterly strange, the strangeness buoying us up, floating us along on crumbling columns that would dissolve at a word, a breath. I refused to speak. We came out at the top of the sloping cobbles by a wall and the turnstile gate in front of the castle with its fat swell of green turf, gravel paths, flower beds, rustic poles woven in lattices, rambling roses. I gaped through the stone keyhole of the entrance at this other world flowing up from our feet.

I was pure. The woman was baffled, intrigued: she was trying to decide how to approach, what she could do with me. All the years at the factory, the slush and slag, shithouse legends, wartime and night shifts and the Saturday daylight at noon blinding the red bus—and the excursions—being picked up by the prostitute in London, the dirty pictures—I had come through unscathed. I was brittle with purity, I needed knowledge, weight, some dross. I looked what I was in fact, a feathered, skinny angel who would blow away if it wasn't for the lead in his boots. Helpless and shining, I looked at her. She was smiling, brilliant. The stinging gleam of her eyes held me. Deep, sharp, she sank in the barbs of her looks. I smarted with pleasure.

'What?' I said, floundering.

'Let's go in!' she said, exultant, as if there was something really wicked in there and I was a fit companion. Me! She was a marvellous flatterer, like all women. Did she think, like my mother, that all men were little boys, milksops, foolish petulant children who had to be kept out of mischief, humoured, who needed flattery even more than beef and carrots, who were liable to cry and go flat as burst tyres if their self-esteem got a hole in it? If she did, she'd never have blabbed it out like my mother: she knew better than to give away her magician's secrets. Face her with a thing like that and her eyes opened wide, astonished, innocent as periwinkles. Then you saw how the conformation of her eye gave this perpetual twinkling astonishment, that smiled and wondered while it subdued, devoured, gobbled you up where you stood. Yet she could be honest when it suited her, and she was never to my knowledge mealy-mouthed, never nice and genteel or falling silent at tactful moments. The City Snack Bar where we met once or twice later she called the 'shitty snack bar'. It's

172

true that she used to breathe out huskily 'Can I touch you?' when she meant 'Can I make you come in my handkerchief?' but romantic women can't bear to put those things baldly, even women with kids and husband, who know all the facts, straight and crooked, all kinds of queer goings-on. They'll be marvellously practical and think of everything, but there's a taboo on the words, for them. Leila had come from a working-class home, father a Leicester machine-hand in a shoe factory, her nose had been rubbed in reality from an early age, but the curious thing was that instead of blotting out romance this intensified it, blew it up, made it extreme, gave it a fierce pride and defiance. It wasn't ridiculous, like a shop girl drooling over fluffy kittens and eating platefuls of slaughtered animal, it was baptized every day in the sink of daily existence. It had to be tough, God knows, to survive facts like nappies oozing with yellow baby shit and a husband who probably farted complacently beside her in the double bed, his socks stinking like Gorgonzola in the dirty linen basket under the stairs. 'Can I touch you?' she whispered, feeling for my cock and holding it and hanging on tightly to it because it was a superbly romantic one. That was the great attraction. I strained towards her with such ardour, such ecstatic fearful life: that was how she knew. When I realized, I gave her full value for money, put more agony into it, even more than I had. Though as a rule I didn't have to fake. As the time came for her to be snatched away and the brevity of joy, that terrible fact, bit into me, I'd be sucked nearly under at the thought of losing this first morsel of woman's tenderness. I would hug her until she gasped, choking with heartache and fear and a kind of rage at being outside again, homeless. She was all right. She had her home, her husband's warm farts, the shitty affectionate kids. Bleached with self-pity, I clung to her, giving her ferocious kisses like floods of tears. She called it my fire.

She must have thought I was dramatizing, and she loved

173

drama. Her make-up inclined to the lurid: white face, plenty of eye shadow and mascara—the more theatre there was in it, the better. She was a devotee of Jean-Louis Barrault, Yma Sumac, Cocteau's *Orpheus*, painters like Dali, Max Ernst, Chagall, writers like Eluard, Dylan Thomas, Apollinaire, little magazines—above all, Garbo. She preferred Gauguin to Van Gogh—his design was better, she said, but I guessed it was more than that. She couldn't resist any exoticism. In her poems she used exotic birds for symbols all the time.

'Let's go in!'

We dared the paths and flowerbeds and rolling hill of turf together, climbed up and alongside and round the back of this scabby old blockhouse called a castle, graffiti carved in the soot, to where there was a paved space and a parapet, with vistas over the city and beyond, so ugly, so depressing they drew us irresistibly. Looked out stonily, down at the hollow pit, out over the great smoking plain, like shocked gods turned to stone as we surveyed that battlefield of industry: railway tracks, sidings, gun factory, a power station, gasworks, Boots at Beeston, university with its campus and cars like another factory, satanic mills and chimney pots as far as the eye could see. Vapours hung low over the acres of rotting terraces; it was nearly dark, and the dirty gloom in the sky seemed to be rising out of the streets, as if they had stored it up all day and were breathing and coughing it out, up the chimneys, out of the windows. It lifted off the slates like clouds of coaldust and sagged over the brown train worming in from Derby as we watched.

4

A HANDBELL was shaking itself, getting louder, and then there he was coming round the corner with it: the keeper, with his lugubrious black cap and swollen boots. Just like being back at school, or like playing in the park, hearing the bell in the distance and hanging on for the last lingering minute, stretching out the freedom. The funeral bell, another massive day buried with the sun. I looked once more down into the pit, at the sliding car life in the boulevard at the bottom, before we moved away.

'That means us,' she said. 'I think we're the only ones left.'

'Are we?'

'Looks like it.'

'Good.'

'Turned out,' she mourned, with mock sorrow. 'Nowhere to go.'

'No time,' I added.

And there we had it, our two motifs stated in almost the same romantic breath, at the very beginning, as if we had it rehearsed and ready. It was uncanny. I think I even felt a pang, a kind of foreboding brushing me, a foretaste of what was in store for me.

'Colin, where are you going to sleep tonight?' she asked, using my name for the first time as we tripped lightly down the paths, kids again being chucked out of the park.

'I don't know yet.'

'You don't?'

'Not yet.'

'But you must!'

'I'll find a place, don't worry.'

'What about the Y.M.C.A.?'

'Yes, that'll do—I don't mind where.'

'Let's call there now, shall we—get you fixed up.'

'There's no need for you to come—I can do that later, if you tell me where. Shall we have a cup of coffee?'

'Yes, but let's go to the Y.M. first. Come on, it's not far—round by the library, Sherwood Street. Or they might be full up.'

'They might.'

'I'm the boss, remember.'

'All right,' I laughed, touched by her concern. It was lovely being worried over, except when it was your mother. Grand from a stranger. She was a few years older than me, and suddenly doing this fussing and mothering she seemed a whole lot older, and I liked that. Not a girl, a woman of the world. There was the ring on her finger. Dramatic, bated, made-up, the musk she gave off, with her poems and her hard experience, hard skin on her fingers and palms from the washing-up water, from scrubbing the collars and socks—fingers I hadn't touched yet. Or her name. It was all flattering, exciting, a mature thing that I'd attracted and could hold if I wanted. Better than tremulous, unnerving girls, sulky and virginal and difficult, who made you aware of your deficiences with their gormless blunders, saying things like 'Are you self-conscious?' Leila was subtle, she could flatter, but apart from anything she said or did I knew I'd won a woman with a husband standing behind, won for two hours, and now I had the sure knowledge of the power of my youth. That was what she'd given me, a knowledge of power. I could work wonders with it, I had something to offer. The feeling welled up in me like arrogance, like dignity, fresh as a fountain.

It was full at the Y.M., but they gave me an overspill address, some digs round the corner: turn right at the Registrar's Office.

'You see!' Leila said. Without looking I'd been aware of her standing close. Now I looked.

'Well, shall we have a coffee?'

'Let's go to this place first—make sure. What did I tell you?'

'You're the boss.'

'That's it!'

Pleased, I let her take me round, look after me. I don't know who was enjoying it most, her or me. Banged on the door of this shabby sagging house which would fall down, drop to bits if it wasn't in a terrace, and there's a gas lamp bubbling out sickly greenish light to make it worse, and a factory tick-tocking away behind a blank wall at the end of the cul-de-sac. We look grimly at each other and wait, hearing shuffling slippers, a throat clearing like a rusty bolt, then the bolts themselves, the lock. I stare at the dirty cobwebs of net at the window. There's a smell of chemicals from the factory.

'Now then,' says the pot-bellied old man standing in the door. I go to open my mouth but he stoops down grunting to show me his bald head, freckled and stained like a map, and grope for the evening paper.

Then his wife paddles to the door, a little chirruping woman in a flowery pinafore, saying Dad is deaf and what was it we wanted. Yes, you can stay, yes, bed and breakfast, a good breakfast, more than you can eat, ten and six—when you come back you must sign the book, that's important, the police insist and sometimes they ask to see it. 'Wouldn't believe that would you?'

'No, I wouldn't.'

'There. You see.'

Then she drives the big-bellied old man with his Haig moustache down the passage, or tries. 'Go on, Dad, tek your paper you bin on about, you got it now, tek it and sit down— go on.'

'Shurrup,' he says harsh, going. The door crashes shut again.

We look at each other. In the Robin Hood we sit and stir our coffees and look at each other. Now we have an experience in common, not a bond but anyway a talking point. How it relaxes us, eases the tension.

'Wouldn't believe that would you?' I mimic.

'What?'

'That's what the old lady said, remember?'

'Oh yes,' and she laughs at first, then grows thoughtful. 'Looks a bit of an awful place,' she says, eyes wide, smiling, but still a bit concerned.

'It'll do for one night.'

'I suppose so.'

Then she is looking very hard, though surreptitiously, at the swing doors, a group of men jostling in, all close, as if tied invisibly together. I feel suddenly chilled, hardened. Leila leans towards me, charged with her street tension. She glistens.

'See those men? They're in a group, a company of female impersonators—at the Empire across the road. They're there all next week.'

'How d'you know?'

'Last time they came here I went to see them.' She looks straight at me, does her chuckle, really sparkles.

'Were they good?'

'No, they were naughty. Very naughty.'

'You enjoyed the show then?'

'Gorgeous!'

And she tells me why she finds them gorgeous, brimming with pleasure and defiance in this dull ordinary café where nothing exciting ever happens, nobody is ever different—using the corners of her eyes to convey wickedness, daring. I can't share the pleasure, it's all new and too civilized for me, but because she's with me now it enhances me, her difference, I feel rich and augmented, proud. I tingle with the glory of that, sitting there alerted. It's for me. For the moment I am pure response to everything she does, everything she says. I want to prove my own power, match her subtleties, point by point, give her back strangeness for strangeness. I always knew I could do it. Being ignorant is no hindrance, it helps to preserve my sense of wonder. I take the challenge, accept it and that's enough.

Before I know what's happening almost the evening is over, I accompany her to the Bulwell bus stop in the Square. She could go there blindfold by herself in perfect safety and it's only 9.30, but I'm taking her, the escort. A game she is pleased to let me play. Off she goes, promising so much with her smile through the shiver of glass that I go away dizzy with thoughts of the future, on my own in this strange town. Where am I going? I walk anywhere, mingle with the pavement traffic, so elated, intoxicated with what has happened that all I want to do is keep walking and thinking about it, juggling it around, fondling it, the amazing mystery of human communion. It's customary and yet very new, blackish green and silvery in my mind like the country before dark. I crow to myself that I am now entering the secret world of woman, no trouble. An intimate, straight in. I go shuffling around like this, gaping vaguely at the Saturday night show without seeing things, yet being with them, people coming and going, couples hugging each other's arms, wrapped round each other's necks, holding hands, some lascivious and some like children, babes in the wood: I gawp at them all fondly and feel safe and comforted and included, one of the family. I never dream that these partings at the bus stop, exactly like tonight, are going to crucify me, make me scream out with the worst loneliness I've ever tasted. Blissful, I wade about in the autumn night until my legs ache, and then make for those digs.

5

IT SEEMS worse than when I left it a few hours ago. I expected it to be bad but this is terrible. The whole street is. Perhaps what it is, I'm noticing more things. But I don't care that much, I still feel in such a good mood, ridiculously excited and buoyant, I nearly spring up the patch of sooty garden, the path laid with house bricks over the ashy ground with its grimy dry plants and sour tufts of grass. As I clench my fist and bang the door I think I see the window's dirty bandage move slightly at one corner. I could be mistaken—and this time it's the old lady opening the door, struggling and pushing, muttering angrily and getting agitated because something's jammed and it won't open properly.

'Come on in, luv, that's right, don't stand out there. It's the damp that's done it, I keep telling Mister but he does nothing.'

I follow her down the passage that's bare and damp like a tunnel; everything looks mildewed in the poor light, and we go into the back like a procession where Mister is sitting in his armchair against the back window, the paper still stuck in his fists. I call good evening to him in a normal voice, forgetting he's deaf, and he sits motionless, up straight with his heavy legs and knees wide apart, nursing the big football of his belly that's burst open the two bottom buttons of his navy waistcoat. There he sits all formal, watch-chain and fob, as if ready to have his photo taken: only his collar and tie is missing, just the neckband and stud over the stripey cloth.

'Ah,' he says.

'The gentleman's saying good evening to you, Dad, good evening!' his wife says, prodding him. She seems to shrink, and standing against him like that I realize he's a big man.

180

'I know it is,' he says.

'The gentleman's saying it to you,' she shrieks.

'I know, I heard. Shut up, you silly old woman—shut your rattle a minute, so I can talk to him.'

And while she scuttles off to fetch the book for me to sign he tells me in his flat, ponderous Derbyshire that he's a pensioner and that's why they take in lodgers, and about Nottingham and the old days, the trams, the first electric light, the stocking machines he used to work as a lad, when a working day started at six in the morning and he walked in from Colwick, walked—and the foreman wore a top hat.

'That so?'

'It is. An' I'll tell you another thing. He was there at six himself, spot on, with his watch in his hand—like this,' demonstrating. 'And woe betide you mister if you was a minute late. How about that?'

I shake my head very solemn because his fierce eye is on me, his watch still on his palm. I feel nervous as a late apprentice under the eye of a foreman, black hat like a cloud.

'What you telling him all that rubbish for?' his wife fretted, cackling and irritated, with a touch of venom because she'd heard it so often.

'It's interesting,' I said, loyal to my own sex.

Nobody heard. She was clearing a space on the dusty sideboard for me to sign the book, gabbling about the police, while the old man sat like a statue with his big hands spread on his knees. He was wetting his lips, eyes glazed with memories, in full spate of remembrance now he had a listener. Or would have been. I said I was tired out and went up to bed while I had the chance.

The old woman came groping up the stairs behind me to show me the way, still rattling and busy like a kettle on the boil; all I had to do was say yes and no and that's right. She left me on the dim landing, pointed at the door and then remembered to add, as if the thought had suddenly struck her, that I'd be sharing the room with another gentleman, not a bed-and-breakfast one-nighter like me: no, a proper boarder.

'Here for the week he is, Mister. Very nice young man.'

'Is he?'

'Well, if he wasn't I wouldn't think of putting you in his room, would I, but he is very nice, a real gentleman, you'll be quite all right in there with him, Mister.'

'He'll be in later, will he?'

'Who, him? The other gentleman?'

'Yes.'

'He's in there now.' She was scurrying off and muttering to herself, making hard work of the stairs because of her arthritis, grunting with pain, hanging on to the rail. 'Go on in,' she screeched, 'he won't hurt you. You'll be all right with that gentleman.'

In the mean light on the far side of the room a figure stooping over a bed straightened up quickly and turned to the door.

'Evening,' he said, bright and nervous.

'Hello,' I said, making for him because at that distance, in the murky light I couldn't see his features, he was in shadow, and I was confused by the bigness of the room and all the beds. Four beds, there were.

The boy—he was in his teens—stuck out his hand and said, as if welcoming me to a party:

'Pleased to meet you. I'm Chris Hampton.'

'How d'you do.'

I hadn't meant to respond in the same formal way, like Livingstone in Africa. Ridiculous, but it was done now. The boy was staring-eyed and there was a desperate look to him, close up, either the forlorn eyes or the long trembly mouth, or both. I couldn't decide. He was nervy, there was something about him that knocked you off balance. For all that he was bright when he spoke, and cultured: no trace of an accent. He dragged a rucksack off his bed.

'What's your name?' he said, soothing and plummy. I liked to hear it, and it was so incongruous in this bleak impoverished hole, in this bare room with its cold coating of lino, beds stationed at the corners like a ward.

'Colin Patten,' I told him.

He seemed to be aware that he'd made me jumpy and now he was soothing, reassuring. I liked that, liked his vigilance and the quickness of his reactions. But he had a funny, chilly, public way of speaking, as if he was making announcements.

'Please don't think I'm being bloody nosey or anything, but it makes things a bit more friendly, don't you think? Personal, I mean.'

'I suppose so.'

'You don't mind?'

'No,' I laughed. 'It needs something up here, that's certain.'

'Yes, exactly.'

He wanted to go on talking, I could see. It was the contact: perhaps he felt uneasy, or lost. Well, I didn't mind. I didn't mind anything. It was a muddy counterpoint, what he was saying, swirling through me and bound to be pleasant because I was tuned in to the music of Leila, to her voice, intimate for me, the way she prowled along, her black hair drawn back from the bony forehead and the livid look of her skin in the dark: the velvet hair band or whatever it was. The smile and quick wave through the glass as the bus slid away.

'I'm at the University,' he was saying. 'My wife's joining me next week—she's Welsh. She's got a job in the Children's Department, on the Corporation. Soon as we've properly moved in to the flat she'll be starting work.'

He was full of his news, bubbling to tell someone. When he said wife I looked harder at him. He could have been older, say twenty-one. He had bubbly dark brown curls all over his head, thick on his neck, cut short on top. He kept his rather fine, desperate brown eyes fixed on my face. They seemed to me to contradict the hopeful things he was saying. I had the feeling he was asking me as much as he dared to be nice to him, to let him talk on because he was lonely, missing his new wife, nervous in another city.

'You've got a flat then?'

'Yes, we have, and we're very lucky. There are flats and flats.'

'Yes. I'm wondering where I ought to be, which bed,' I said. 'Anybody else in here, d'you know?'

'No,' he said. 'Doubt it. I've been on my own here all the week as a matter of fact. Shan't be sorry when I shift out on Monday—or I may go tomorrow. I could kind of camp out at the flat until my wife arrives. God, it's depressing up here on your own.'

'I bet it is.'

'How d'you get on with the old folks?'

'Okay,' I said. 'You?'

'Oh yes, fine. She's a funny old bag, the old lady, but she's been very good to me. Couldn't do enough, really. Running for salt, pepper, mustard—never sits still for a minute. Trouble is, it gets on your nerves after a day or two. And you can't read a book down there or anything.'

'No.'

He went on for nearly an hour in the same strain: even when we were in bed he kept it up, like a tap dripping in the corner. He came from Kingston-on-Thames, his father some sort of businessman in the City. When I started to get undressed he fished vigorously in his clean rucksack for a writing pad and said he'd give me his new address, the flat on Mansfield Road, it was the ground floor—if I came again I'd be welcome, I could meet his wife and have coffee and so on. Obviously it gave him pleasure to dwell on these details: even to write the address down must have comforted him, brought the reality that much nearer. He plunged his arm in again to the elbow, jerked it like a lever and came out with a biro. Then he wrote the address in a fine calligraphic script like an art student: tore off the sheet and gave it me.

'Thanks very much.'

'Don't forget!' he said, and his lips twitched off his teeth, smiling. 'Just ring the bell. Hampton.'

'Right.'

I stuck the paper in the top pocket of my jacket and forgot all about it.

'Cigarette?' He had a packet of Player's in his hand.

'No, I don't smoke, thanks.'

'Mind if I do?'

I shook my head. Such politeness, and the doggy way he kept his wide-open intense eyes on me, I'd found it startling at first, pleasant, but now it was getting on my nerves. I got into bed and lay aching pleasurably and after a while made out I was asleep. The only trouble was, a lump kept forming in my throat and I had to find a way of noiselessly gulping it down. I wanted to lie quiet, to daydream myself into the streets again, the Robin Hood, the Castle, ineffable and casual moments, tracing it right back step by step—I wanted to walk in that rhythm again, the swift kill in the Square, momentous, then that rhythm, not mine or hers but something of both of us, washing through the veins so beautiful, humble and ruthless like a tide. And the taste of those exchanges, where the pauses came, the smiles, the questions: I kept trying to will it back so that I could relive it. And lying there in the dark living twice, listening to my friend twisting and fidgeting around, my body still as a washed sky, I could hear the surging background music: a dull rumble of traffic, the factory place nearby ticking quietly like a bomb. Car door slamming. Some raucous drunks at the bottom of the street—chucking-out time in

Nottingham. I was in Nottingham. To prove it, the clock on the Council House in the Square began to clang out the hour, over those tame lions, those fat pillars. Sounded right overhead. It was a completely new sound for me: Coventry had nothing like that, no swaggering civic sounds. I counted eleven. Never been here before, not to sleep. Wait a minute, yes, I had—moored up by the steps at Trent Bridge, when I was an apprentice. As soon as I began to think of this, the ambulance ride through the streets, hanging round desolate outside the Mechanics' for the others to come back from the Palais, and then in the taxi, that girl touching my bristles, easily and naturally I linked it with Ray: taking him to Radcliffe. We'd booked a boat on the Trent for a weekend, end of season, and we'd bike it, there and back, the round trip 120 miles at least. Absolutely mad. I was the expert, that was the point. I'd been there with the lads during the war, and sailing with Uncle Geoff on the Broads before that, so how good to take Ray and give him a new experience. Sailing down the river—that was the life. Enough to make you bite your lip with wonder. Great, we said. One thing we couldn't bear in those days was to be tepid in our enthusiasms—everything had to be great, terrific.

6

WE MET at Ray's house in Greenfields, my brother Alan with
me. The night before I'd wheeled the tandem out of the shed
and given it a going-over with the oilcan and rag, spanners,
propping it very carefully against the orange brick in the
evening light and squeezing a blue blob of oil on each joint of
the chain. A sky-blue lightweight job, hand-built, a Claude
Butler. Even stuck against the wall it looked classy, sleek, and
now I owned it I was suddenly responsible and it worried me,
the way it demanded care and attention. I'd bought it nearly
new from an apprentice at work who had tended it lovingly.
Going on the back for a trial spin, feeling its long lines under
me I felt swift and birdlike and effortless. It was my first time,
but I leaned into the curves when he did—and he was forging
along fast to impress me—pushed when he did, pumping away
for dear life and clinging to those weird fixed handlebars, a
willing slave as we swooped over Hammer Lane and back
again in the direction of home. I had to have it. Not long
after this I was arriving outside Ray's house at four in the
morning, with Alan on the back: a flawed bluebird now, because Alan wasn't exactly a willing slave, certainly he wasn't
enraptured, glumly stuck there behind my back, and he found
it hard to abandon the habit of steering after his own bike.
We'd be pedalling calmly and well, with considerable dignity,
then a glide straight into the gutter and desperate wobbling,
until I remembered we had brakes. We had hysterics more
than once on that tandem.

It was before dawn, a chilly morning in late September. I
propped the machine against the kerb, shivery, a bit nauseated,
and Ray must have been watching out for us the way he

immediately appeared, wheeling his bottle-green flyer down the entry with curious stealth, almost on tiptoe because it was such a forbidding hour and his parents slept over the archway. The bike ticked under his hand, oiled and beady, drop handle-bars gleaming. Off we went into the dark unknown, up the empty echoing tunnels of streets in the uncanny silence, as if the whole town had died in the night. I pedalled away in a queer hypnotic blind state, fascinated by our own gliding flight as we slipped over the boundary, dynamos whirring us along. Ray knew the way—he always did. Always had the maps, worked out routes. Maps held a fascination for him, I felt. If he could have papered his front room with them I think he would have done. I'm sure he felt that if he could find a big enough map, the right one, the key, he could chart a way out to a new life entirely. The first night I met him I was aware I think of this search he was on, and the desperate eagerness for a pattern, the need for a point of departure, that became more and more intense, as if his very life depended on it. My heart pounded suddenly, it was so different from my aimlessness, my morbid drifting, and nothing like the kids I knew who thought that life was a race and you had to get on, beat the others, move in a straight line and collect your prize.

He was after a grail, I felt, something you followed, that led you out of the swamp. It worked me up to see him, all wild with looking, wild-eyed, bashing about inside himself, nearly frantic because he was sure there had to be a clue, had to, jumping up clear as a signal, and once you caught a glimpse of that you were all right—everything fell into place. Now I think of it it's almost funny, him looking, looking outside him-self, and me locked up tight, blazing, suffocating, gnawing at my own guts and waiting hopelessly to be let out. We made a good pair. So different, and the funny thing was, we thought we were soul-mates, Siamese twins.

It was still dark and we swished between hedges and seemed

188

to be really travelling: no idea of distance at all. Ray had his head down, his whole machine pointed at the place on his map he hadn't even set eyes on yet—Radcliffe. It possessed him, for the moment he'd made it his grail. He was like that with anywhere unknown. We passed through nameless skin-disease places, a spread of red-brick for no reason on either side of the artery, endless repetitions reaching blindly for the towns. Then we were bowling along in a faint reddish light, the night sky seamed and veined, slowly cracking to let this creepy twilight come oozing out. I was half-drugged with sleep, I couldn't understand what was happening. Suddenly on the outskirts of Leicester, running into the streets which were like visions of death, rigid and blank, laid out, the amorphous mass of the town more a mood than a place, like a new ruin—I lifted my head and saw the great bars of blood, jerked a look at Ray and he was bathed horribly in blood: we all were. All of us. Bikes, arms, necks, it washed over us. It was the dawn—first time I'd ever seen one. I felt shrunk to nothing, riding along a vast papery shell under that breaking, bleeding sky, I was frightened to death by the huge weeping woe of life. What a relief when it ebbed, when the terror ran out of it, drained away and left us untouched, three kids biking down an ordinary grey road in dull morning light. It was a source of pride then, thinking on it, now I knew I was safe.

I suppose it could have been an omen, because I can't remember ever spending a more nightmare weekend in my life. And it all happened as though we'd rehearsed it, knew our parts and exactly what we had to do to bring the curtain down. When we reached Radcliffe—five hours of hard pushing, nonstop—we were done in. Stratford was as far as we'd gone before in one go. We rolled into the Yachting Station at nine, just as they were due to open, and nearly fell off our bikes with exhaustion. It was late September, the Trent was in flood, a bulging muddy swirl running high up the banks. Anybody could see it had an ugly, ominous look to it, but that didn't mean a thing to us, nor the fact that the place was deserted, with an air of desolation. Nobody else was insane enough to take a boat out, and they should have warned us but they didn't say a word: gloomily took our money and okay, there's your boat, I suppose you know what to do. I've been on here before, I said. The man nodded and stared at the ground, then went slinking off and disappeared among some outbuildings by a little orchard. No movement, not a sign of life anywhere, just the brown river in silent flood. The sky thunderous, scowling.

Once aboard and we'd cast off it looked simple, no problem, we went floating off downstream with a spectral ease, powered by the fast current and a following wind. We had the sail up, I was at the tiller like the real captain I was supposed to be and the others, my crew, sat around in the well taking a breather and smiling encouragement at me, expectant. This was the life, Christ yes, this was better than pedalling. I was too lulled by fatigue to be alarmed, only vaguely uneasy at the speed we were going. I didn't fancy being responsible either. I hadn't imagined it like this at all. Then I saw a notice on the bank: DANGER, and in smaller red lettering underneath, Weir Ahead. I didn't say anything to the others, I was struck dumb with fear. Yet I still thought I had a choice, I could do something. Ray was smiling jokily at me, Alan looked drowsy and relaxed, enjoying his trip. Sweating in my hell, I put the tiller round hard, so as to start tacking back upstream. That was the proper way and it worked, I'd done it before. This time it didn't—nothing worked. We carried on in a sickening slide downstream, sideways on, like slithering down a chute. I shouted to get the quant out, a long pole you carried for emergencies. Ray could see by my face, hear from my voice that it was terribly important. We couldn't even touch bottom with the pole, and now we had swung in close to the bank with the sign, the river was rushing us past a high stone wall and at the end of this wall I could see how the water divided, one branch into a lock and the other gurgling over a low weir. Fear can give you amazing strength, make you do fantastic things. I found myself taking a leap from the cabin of the boat to the top of the wall. I don't remember my fingers grabbing, or heaving myself up. Next thing I was on the wall and yelling madly for a rope, hanging on to it while the boat tried to drag me along, and then Ray was up with me, tugging. We made a few attempts together to haul the boat back along the bank the way we'd come, away from that fiendish chuckling weir. We were like starved coolies on the Yangtse—no strength. The marathon bike ride had emptied us. All we could do was find a tree trunk and moor up to that for the day. We stayed there all day, and at night couldn't sleep because the rope kept creaking and we imagined it breaking, strand by strand. It was so funny afterwards, we told it to each other over and over, just to remind ourselves of the craziest bits. The next morning saw the humiliation of our return, being towed in by a motor cruiser from the Station: we had to walk the length of a great field and bawl for three-quarters of an hour before anybody heard on the other side of the river, and it was no comment, nothing, just an extra charge for the towing. And after all that, with no sleep, the return ride half killed us. We parted in Coventry and the bone-tiredness was so awful we hardly spoke or looked at each other. All I could think of was crawling into bed to die. Threading the last half mile through the dead rind of houses, pubs, buses, jolting over the tramlines with the joke gone black and ghastly inside I was as full of disgust as the last rags of my strength could manage. My brother left me and went into the house, silent as ever, I fumbled at the loathsome bike with its insane gears and frame like a torture rack, taking care of it still from force of habit, my wrists quivering with weakness. I felt stamped out flat, a dead bit of metal, a cipher, I didn't want touching or looking at. My movements were grinding, ashy. In the kitchen my mother only had to glance once at my stiff face as I went past towards the stairs.

'What's happened?' she said.

7

I HEARD the clock clang in the Square, twelve times. My new pal on the other side of the room was breathing hard, asleep. I felt wide awake. I couldn't stop impressions linking with memories, I pedalled them round in my head. I must have been doing it when I slid into sleep.

In the morning I woke up to hear my room-mate getting dressed. I peered at him through my eyelashes, watched him dragging on his trousers, heard him grunt like an old man as he bent over to fasten his shoelaces, sitting on his bed in the grey bleary light. The factory was tick-tocking outside; never stopped. The student lifted his head and looked at me and I lay there like a corpse, holding my breath. I wasn't in the mood for talking, or any of that cockeyed politeness. He went out and I kept lying there, hoping he'd have had his breakfast and gone by the time I got down. I didn't have a watch but I could hear a clock working somewhere. Getting up I padded across the room, looking: it was buried in the rucksack. Nearly nine. Going downstairs I passed my friend on his way up to the bedroom again.

'Oh, hello,' he said. 'Sleep well?' He looked fresh as a daisy.

'Not too bad, thanks. You?' We were off again. I kept moving down the stairs.

'Like a log.'

'That's the idea.'

'I think your breakfast's ready down there. I think so.'

'Right.'

'See you anon.'

'Yes.'

The old man was in the back, sat up in his chair in exactly the same position, as if he'd been there all night. Except that his bluish knuckly hands were on the chair arms now instead of his knees. The deal table in front of the window had a stained white cloth over it, with knife and fork, sauce, salt, and I could smell bacon frying in the kitchen, hear the cheerful sizzle and the old woman shuffling about on the bricks in her carpet slippers.

'Morning,' I said to this baleful bald head regarding me in dead silence, the watery eyes unblinking.

'Morning, sir, morning, young man!' came from the kitchen. 'Nice breakfast I got for you, sit down and I'll bring it in. Nice breakfast, you see.'

'Think I'll have a wash first if you don't mind.'

'Yes, you come in here then, make yourself at home—here's the tap and the bowl, hot water in this kettle, you don't need me to tell you. Come on in here, sir, you won't hurt.'

I started to move, then the old man spoke, oracular, grating it out:

'Now what d'yer know?'

'Beg your pardon?'

He glared at me, deadpan. 'Yer didn't know owt much last night. Now what d'yer know?'

'Tek no notice, sir, he's daft, that old man,' screeched his wife. 'Here's your water and towel, all ready.'

I'd got the hang of him, his humour. 'Not much,' I grinned.

'Go on then,' he said, and flapped his hand at me. 'Git washed, like she says.'

When I was sitting down the old girl scurried in with a steaming plate, a mound of hot food, eggs, bacon, beans, sausages, fried bread, and the old man pointed without warning at the trailing vine of honeysuckle outside the window.

'See that bugger?' he said. 'Honeysuckle.'

'Yes.'

'Oh, yer know?'

'We've got some at home,' I told him.

'Ay.'

I waited for him to go on but he sat hulked and silent, look-ing out of the window. I picked up the knife and fork and started eating, and it seemed a signal for the old man to come to life.

'Ay. Well, last year and the year before he's not bin too bright. Last year it never 'ad a flower. Ask the Missus, she knows. Niver 'ad a flower, did it, Missus? She knowed it wor a bad job. So this year I gev it some stick. Didn't I, Missus? Chopped it right back.'

'I hope you're goin' to eat that,' his wife said. 'Nice, is it? Eat it up then, sir.'

'He could do with summat by the sight on him.'

'You shut your old mouth!' she squawked, and rushed up and poked him in the belly for good measure. 'Let the young man eat!'

He sat like a rock, expressionless. 'I can hear you, Missus,' he said, not even bothering to look at her. He was a man. Lord of the earth. His smouldering Victorian derision for women was as obsolete as the tramlines, but not here, not in this house. They weren't equal here. He put it in his voice, the contempt, looked at me instead of her and I was supposed to get this impression. But it was no more than habit, I could see that. Anybody could see who was running things now.

Then I was on my way, out in the air and walking like a dream through the vacant Sunday streets, swept clean and empty as if somebody had got hold of a giant broom. The coach filled up slowly as I sat there, drugged with thoughts of yesterday; we swung out slow and creaking and portentous, past the market, the trolleybus depot, over a canal, and the radio blarting out all loud before the driver muted it, playing 'Autumn Leaves'. We rolled across the bridge at West

Bridgeford and through the fields, and looking out over the flat autumn land, misty and rich and sorrowful, I felt weak as a kitten with sentiment, choking with a kind of grief for no reason, going away. I was afflicted with a new weakness—what was it? I couldn't understand what was happening. The sentimental song melted my bones and my grim pride, I sank back in the deep upholstery and it was a sweet sorrow. I had taken the first step and that was what it was: I belonged there, it was being left behind, the most tender morsel of myself. With every mile the rift widened, my sight fogging and turning inwards. So that was what it was.

8

I BEGAN to live for these weekends, these Saturday nights—the old couple came to expect me once every two or three weeks. Coventry was a shell, empty, a place where I worked and waited. Ray was out at Birmingham, married, with a baby; I lived with my family but I was like a lodger. I trudged the streets most nights, went to the pictures, mooned around, called in at the library and stood there vaguely, overwhelmed by the futility of books and knowledge, words on paper. I wanted deeds. Flesh I could touch. I had her photo though, a picture tucked in my wallet, and it was a token of something real, a proof that I wasn't dreaming—wouldn't wake up one day and find myself sleepwalking. I'd grab for the photo in moments of panic or disbelief. The proof. I took it out and bored holes in it, until the reality was in shreds and I couldn't believe in that either. The eyes were everything—I stared it in the eyes, in the library, the street, on the top deck of a bus. People gave me curious glances—this fellow rooted with a photo in his hand, staring. A picture on a bit of card, black and white and some shadow, but it looked on the point of speaking. A fascinating, cruel deception. The skin was matt under the powder, but I knew that close up it was thick and pocky. I wanted the photo to show that. If she'd had sores, I'd have wanted them represented too. It was an image of a face, a dream-object, the blemishes like landmarks helping me to find my way, remember, go back over the ground of those lost seconds and minutes. And I loved everything about those paths, every twist, I dreamed about them with such intensity, they were precious, I wanted nothing changed. Is that what people mean when they say love is blind?

'My chin's too big, too heavy,' she said once.

'Is it?'

'Don't look at my nose either. It's like a button—a lump of putty.'

'All right.'

'It's a joke, my nose.'

'Is that so?'

'I don't like my looks at all. I loathe being photographed. Hate mirrors. I'd rather not know. I've got an entirely different idea of myself, d'you know that?'

'Different?'

'Absolutely.'

'Oh.'

'Don't you care what I look like?'

I stammered something, not used to this directness. 'I like you as you are.'

'Why? My face is a mess.' She sounded indignant, exasperated, but a vein of shrewd realism saved her from bitterness. And I was there, wasn't I? She'd caught me.

I muttered something into the windy dark—we may have been under the arch of a bridge, in the dirty fog of a November night.

'I can't see you,' I said softly. I meant I saw everything, I saw something else, not what her mirror saw, or the street. But she took me literally, as we were standing in the dark.

'Lucky you,' she chuckled.

'Why?'

'I'm not nice.'

'Oh.'

'I mean my character.'

'D'you want a reference?'

'No, I'm serious. I'm rotten, you know.'

'I didn't know.'

'You don't believe me, do you? Listen, I could tell you a few things, and then you might not like me at all.'

'I'll risk it.'

She told me a little—not much. Bit by bit she was giving me her past, baiting me with it, and at the same time I was getting a confused blurry picture of her daytime and night-time life away from me, I felt the shut-off, solid community of it, her real life, where my existence counted for nothing—a place closed and hostile like a village: complete. From being only slightly interested and curious—I told myself it was the present that mattered, nothing else—I was drawn into this world she brought with her, that was her as much as the way she walked and laughed and made her mess of a face dramatic. Little by little the bloody cobweb hung itself on me, caught round my ankles and I remember thinking how nice, dipping in and out of the intrigue and rows like a bird, not staying, not weighed down by any of it. Later, I hated all the details but had to have them, obsessed, I dug them out if they weren't forthcoming, nagged them bitterly into the light. I needed every detail she fed me. I had so little, so I starved for the full picture, greedy now for her whole life. But this was later, when I was enslaved and messianic, ripe for crucifixion.

At the beginning and for a long time afterwards I never stopped to ask myself the simplest questions, such as what she needed a lover for: where I fitted in, what was wrong with her husband. It was enough that she was there, and willing to come again. She may have envied me and then felt a pang of resentment at my free flitting to and fro. She needn't have done: I wasn't free, I was lost in my singleness. The clinking of her domestic chains warmed the cockles of my heart. No, it wasn't that, she wasn't an envious nature. It was high drama to her, these white lies, deceptions, letters c/o a friend, and it excited her, so naturally she had to share it. I was the natural recipient. The inside story—first of all it was a game, then a

199

shared thing, and a bond. Later, when I got snared, it was a cobweb. Later still, later, I'd feel the knives and think what a hellish vengeful world I'd fallen into.

It hadn't started yet. The first time we talked art, or she did, and I listened and said something; it was a language I could use and understand, anyway. As soon as I realized it was vital to her I became a budding artist, poet, any damn thing she fancied. She'd have been most thrilled if I could have been a ballet dancer, or an actor. As it was I was dancing, making music, acting even in my tongue-tied state. It was Garden of Eden, the wild park—I was too intoxicated with my triumph to touch her the first or second time: then the third, crossing over the pavement on the bridge she grabbed my hand and we ran down the tarmac slope like that, lovers out of the ballet, into the black park alongside the river. The fog was turning to rain. On the bench, one arm audaciously round her, I could see the gleam of eyes, teeth, the river gleaming and moving. When I turned my head she had her eyes closed, waiting, a faint smile on her mouth. I kissed her on the mouth and it broke open juicily, soft and willing. My hand went up her skirt and it was the same there, lips opening like a fruit, running with juice, blood-warm and eager like a mouth being kissed. 'I'm being raped!' she gasped, gurgling delightfully, and this was her touch of inspiration to help me over my fumbling inexperience. She wanted me to think she was menaced and fearful. 'Can I touch you?' she whispered humbly, already unbuttoning me and slipping in her hand. Somebody was coming, so stiff with cold we got to our feet, she straightened her clothes and I limped along the path hanging on to her, back to the bridge, wounded and happy with this iron cock half buttoned down under my raincoat. That was how we found the draughty arch of the bridge. It was one of our spots after that, below the road and traffic and against the lapping black water. We made it ours.

'You're eating me alive,' she'd say hoarsely, after a bout of intense kissing and fingering, and give a little gasp for breath. It was her way of complimenting me and at the same time giving herself extra pleasure.

'That's because I'm hungry.'

'Oh, is that it!'

'Hungry, hungry.'

'You're shivering.'

'Am I?'

'Are you very cold?'

'Yes,' I lied.

'D'you want to go?'

'No.'

'You're shaking all over!'

'I can't help it.'

Then she shook with laughter, silently.

'What's funny?'

'Darling, you're like our dog—he shivers all over like you, I've just remembered. Sometimes when I give him food.'

'I'm a dog.'

'You know what I am?'

'No.'

'I'm a sensuous pussy.'

'That so?'

'Stroke me and see.'

Her skirt must have been up round her hips because I had my hands on her taut little bum, one on each cheek, and she squirmed it for me in the slippery panties, teasing.

'See what I mean?' She giggled like a schoolgirl.

I sank my mouth on her, eating again, chewing and sucking. She moaned faintly and let her head go back, just like the film lovers she adored.

Sometimes she sighed drowsily like an animal, almost as if she were bored.

201

'What's the matter,' I'd say.

'Why?'

'Getting fed up with me?' I'd reached that stage, wanting to hurt her slightly, provoke some passion equal to mine.

'Don't be a silly boy.'

'Tired?'

'I'm drugged, that's what. You keep drugging me with kisses.'

'Shall I stop?'

'No.'

Sometimes at the end of an evening, taking her to the bus stop, maybe sidestepping a raving ogre aglow with booze who lurched at us over the wet cobbles, skirting the shuttered market and crossing the railway on the slatted walk between iron walls studded with fat rivet heads like cysts—the glint of tracks visible through the planks—I'd be so deep in abjection it became strength: a force powerful enough to wreak changes in my very character. The shy poetic wraith hovering tenderly beside her would commit rash acts—drag her into the nearest black doorway of a lock-up shop and maul her, hands of violence dragging like claws, legs and chest and belly crushing her, covering her, blotting her out in the shallow recess.

'Are you trying to rip my clothes off?'

'Anything . . .'

'You're all sex tonight aren't you?'

'I don't know . . . I can't—I don't know what I am.'

'You are. I'm drowning in it.'

'What?'

'The sex. It's coming off you in waves.'

But it was tragic sex, salvation sex—to prevent my destruction, to hold back the night gone rancid, the leprous night faces round the corner, the deadly sick nauseating error of the streets. It was rash, raw sex, panic sex—somebody had got to witness the utter beauty of my tenderness. Toe to toe, lip to lip

I moulded it against her through our clothes, a candid vision expressed in flesh and blood. Did the glamour reach her, did the burden of sorrow? I was daring her to shun it, forcing her to acknowledge it. I'm not frivolous, not joking: let her hear the tragic shriek, take it home for supper, take it away with her. Let her be stuck with it, for remembrance. I was abject and grovelling, but deeper still I had a pride that wanted to leave some mark—not let her get off scot free. Up and down I travelled on this sickening seesaw, wanting to pour out adoration, erect beauty, up and up, before the plunge down and the urge to inflict a wound, leave a mark, a keepsake.

9

THEN one night the time was up, she was opening her bag and rummaging for stuff to repair the damage—powder, lipstick, comb, and I groaned out between my teeth:

'Oh, Christ!'

'What's the matter, darling?' she asked, startled, but not stopping the repair work. She was always a little on edge at this time of night, afraid of missing her bus.

'This is awful,' I muttered, on the verge of grief and rage.

'What is?' She was daubing her mouth and then rolling her lips together in a sort of ugly satisfaction to spread the grease, holding up a bit of mirror with one hand and staring into it with that jaundiced, disenchanted look women use on each other. The tone of her voice now made me wince: she was her hardened everyday self. Which was real? I stood there watching her, tormented by a loss of innocence.

'What is?'

'Nothing.'

'Don't look, it's too sordid,' she said flatly, slapping on powder. 'Bloody hell, I look like a pro.' Then she glanced at me, and something about my expression must have made her uneasy.

'What's wrong, Colin?' she said almost sharply. 'I told you not to look.'

'It's not that!' I croaked with my whole inside, staring at her like a maniac.

She snapped the catch of her handbag, it gave a sharp, deadly little click, like a reply. She was finished, ready to go. And watching me quizzically as if deciding what to do. She stepped up and kissed me lightly, taking pity on my martyred look but careful not to smudge her freshly painted mask. 'What is it, then?' she said tenderly, honied as an actress.

'I wish we'd got somewhere to go, that's all,' I muttered.

'So do I,' she said feelingly, a shade too brisk. 'Well, my lad,' and she threw off all pretence, 'I know where I've got to go.'

I couldn't resist it. 'Home sweet home.'

'What time is it, d'you think?'

'And always at my back I hear Time's winged chariot changing gear.'

'Very funny.'

I was jealous of whatever it was that made her sprightly, tough, indifferent, something she got out of her black patent-leather handbag with its gnashing, cold clasps. The pain of being abandoned was heightened by the sudden sight of this other side of her. There was that and the tremendous sadness of the city night, welling up in me and choking my throat. From pride I turned it into acid, a poisonous, perverse fluid I had to spit out at her. For the second time I couldn't accept and be thankful, I wanted to trap her in a shop doorway, confront her with an awareness of me as a problem, a wandering and yearning and howling soul in the emptiness. A contender. If I couldn't plant my cock in her and make it grow kids and flowers and contentment, let her have me on her conscience, a worm in her bloody apple. I felt it surge and squirt vilely in my guts, she looked straight at me, strangely, and I blurted out:

'I feel—nowhere.'

She didn't flinch, she didn't anything. I'm sure she got the message; my eyes were black with it, swimming with poison.

'I really must go,' she said.

What kind of woman is it that reduces a man to a zombie, all his days concentrated on one desire, everything emptied out

205

of him but one need, to see her again? The whole meaning of life in one hunger—what kind of need is that? Whose creation? Separated from her in Devon I couldn't stop thinking of one thing, over and over—how to get back to her again. Just to set eyes on her, just to look, that was all I asked. I was starving for a look. I didn't want to touch, to kiss—none of that. It was pure spirit, ravenous and pining, deep as the longing of a dog for its master. Even if I couldn't speak to her, or be seen, I felt it wouldn't matter as long as she was there before me, in view. No act was too reckless, no barrier could have stopped me; nothing. When the letters ceased, too risky, they were being intercepted she was sure—I got on a train with all sorts of crazy ideas in my head, ways and means of seeing her again. I'd go and stand outside the house till she came out—she'd have to emerge sooner or later. No—I became cunning like the insane—she had a boy, Jeremy, five or six years old—didn't she tell me once that because of the main road traffic she went and fetched him from school every day? Worksop, where she was living now, it couldn't be a big place, surely—and though I'd never been there I'd soon find the primary school, and then easy to stand outside in the street and take root until she came into view. Into view! Sitting on the train I shivered in my chest and closed my eyes—the train was murderously slow, it crawled over the landscape, indifferent, stretching out my pain. This wasn't love I was suffering from, it was toothache of the heart. I was rushing, I was frantic, imploring to be put out of my misery. Give us a look!

It's never as simple as you imagine. The school was on a crossroads, in a frightening cobweb of sidestreets, the houses prim and veiled, suspiciously lifeless, the whole district hostile to strangers. Which direction should I face, which arm of the cross would she come down? She might not even come as far as the school, might wait further back nearer the main road— and I'd never seen her boy, wouldn't recognize him if he walked right past me. I sweated up and down, heard the kids still imprisoned behind the dirty brick, the green-painted windows—they were chanting out arithmetic tables just as I used to do. Then the dead silence falling inside the walls, then the trickle of life, two girls darting out, a boy dawdling, kicking along a matchbox, dabbling his shoe in a puddle; then more, and the floodgates opened, I was drowned, defeated. I stood stock still and began to petrify, nerves rasped by the shrieks and laughs and the knife-like glances certain kids gave me. At each direct look I sweated and opened my mouth, thinking a miracle had happened, it was him, her boy and he was recognizing me in some impossible way. 'Excuse me . . .' I stuttered, to a little knot of girls. They kept walking, faster, casting fearful glances backwards. Then, miracle of miracles, here she comes, Leila, on the other side of the street and she hasn't even seen me, wheeling a pushchair with her other boy Simon in it, bending over him and pausing, adjusting the safety strap, coolly taking it in another notch and rebuckling it—and the sight is enough, her figure in the mulberry coat; the very look of her hands, so tender, passes into my blood, rises into my smile, fills my eyes with tears. I go across and stand in her path.

'I'm going mad!' she says, staring at the apparition.

'Sorry—is it a shock?'

'What d'you think, good God! Hullo, here's Jeremy, better be careful what we say, he's a bright boy.'

I walk along holding the iron frame of the pushchair, otherwise I'll float away. Now it's over I have to learn how to live quietly and cope normally all over again. Tomorrow I'll start that. Jeremy, a pale nervy boy, dives into a sweetshop and Leila has time to say, 'What are you going to do now?'

'Go back to Nottingham.'

'I mean, how will you live?'

'I'll get a job somewhere.' A sudden pang of fear—how

much of this situation is my own creation, my own need?
'Aren't you pleased to see me?'

'Pleased?' She makes her eyes wide and desperate. 'I'm scared stiff! No wonder my nerves are in tatters.' She adds quickly, 'Give me time to get used to it, will you? I'm still reeling.'

'I'm sorry.'

'I'm not, I'm flabbergasted. Here's Jeremy coming.' Her hand covers mine for a second. 'I'll be able to see more of you, won't I?'

'That's why I've come,' I say, murmuring like a dove.

'You're mad.' And I smile, hang my head: it's the madness that titillates, that she loves.

10

GO BACK and unravel, shake the skein—find the tangle and the mess of knots, the point where everything started happening at once: all change. Ray came out of the Navy, his demob day had dawned at last, his national service dead and done for. Out he burst, casting shuddering glances over his shoulder and scattering mad benedictions out of the Brum windows of his mother-in-law's semi-detached: he couldn't believe he was free, outside, that they weren't after him in hot pursuit. He was twenty and married, baby on the way. His letters whirled in and landed on our doormat, leaves from the storm: desperado yells for more life, in a frantic scrawl that made them look like screams for help. He'd done his two years, an innocent lad wrongly convicted, they'd put him away for nothing and now he was out, a freebooter, ready for anything. His letters boiled with dreams and nightmares, shook with haste, with the effort he was making to transform himself so as to escape from the new prison he'd landed in. War was black on his horizon, on the placards, bloated storm-clouds whichever way you looked. The turmoil he created came ramming into my quivery sails and I began to imagine qualities of daring and force in myself, to respond. My feet stayed on the ground, cautious as ever, but I felt I was flying. Ray was bursting with schemes to break loose and achieve independence, yet every move he made seemed to chain him down. He clung to an idea of my strength he'd invented, that I struggled to live up to. In Portsmouth, still in the uniform he detested, he'd got married, and, not knowing anybody in Pompey, before they could go into the registrar's office he had to find a couple of labourers in the park to act as witnesses.

Then my mother and father shocked me by doing something they'd schemed and dreamed about for years, unknown to me: they sold the house and went off to live in the country in Dorset. It was a shock, I'd never connected them with anything but a town, or anywhere but the Midlands. What was my father with his Brummy accent doing down there? What did it mean? It meant that the scrat and save had brought them to the climax of their lives, this was it, they had to plunge, it was now or never. I was too absorbed in my own affairs to have an inkling of the drama, what it must have cost them, what dreadful doubts, agonies of decision. And it happened very fast. Before I knew what had hit me I was in digs in my home town with friends of the family. My father was a storekeeper in one of the big shadow factories: he chucked that up and bought an insurance book where they were going, and this meant he had to have a two-stroke motorbike to go with it, to collect the instalments from all the outlying farms and villages, cottages buried in woods at the ends of rough tracks, some of them twenty miles from home—it was such a wide-flung area. Would it work? I wasn't asked, and no wonder—they'd reared a pasty-faced monster of tight-lipped arrogance and fanaticism. This fling of theirs into the rural unknown set the seal on my rootlessness. I'd never really felt at home anywhere, not for years, not since a small boy when a place was alive and fascinating and lovely if your mother was there, and got frightening very quickly if she was missing—like losing her in Woolworth's that day. Suddenly her hand was gone and from being a strange excitement the store was like death, it was full of animals pressing round with great holes in their noses and eyes glaring.

I hadn't felt at home for years. Now I could be what I really was, a displaced person, born to it. Homeless. It was only right and proper.

The digs were all right, a London couple with two kids, one

a boy with protruding teeth and ginger hair who seemed to have no eyelashes, who was at the grammar school and had a shed down the garden rigged out as a workshop and could assemble radios even then. They were very proud of our Rex. And they had a daughter who'd just started work as a typist. They seemed a bit frightened of her. She was a superior little bitch but she was hardly ever in. Neither was I. I flitted in and out like a ghost, and my mother told me to parcel up the dirty washing I had and send it down to her, rather than let this lady do it. The Leila letters kept coming and I got them handed to me when I came in at night for my evening meal. I'd stick the envelope in my pocket unopened and say thank you, offering no information whatsoever. Then it was a matter of suffering Joy's icy little aura or making yourself scarce for half an hour, till the husband came in. The meal couldn't start without him. He was a foreman electrician, a thin black-haired flapping man, a kind of squawkless crow. He had nothing to say, ever. Joy had inherited his little rat-trap of a mouth. I sat meek as an orphan while Mrs Schofield urged me to help myself to this and that: plump, jittery, dark marks under her eyes, a demoralized woman who'd been jolly once.

'Pass Colin the butter, dear,' she'd tell her daughter.

'Why, is he paralysed?'

'Joy!' her mother squawked feebly, as if surprised. 'Is that a proper way to speak to a guest?'

'What guest? He's a lodger, I thought.'

'That's enough,' her father spluttered, his mouth clogged with food and frustration.

About once a week we had a repeat of this performance, Joy putting her spoke in and her parents half-heartedly choking her off. Her father did show signs of genuine embarrassment, I'll say that. Not the mother. Between her and Joy I could see there was a war raging, now the daughter was old enough

211

to be another woman, a rival. The mother was losing, she was tired, the mirror told her it was hopeless. But she had to fight or be walked on. I was a mere side-issue, I'd have to fight for myself. I showed no reaction, sat there unruffled and let them talk about me in the third person. It was the only defence I had. I envied Rex, wolfing his dinner and asking what was next, harum-scarum, with nothing but wires and screwdrivers in his head.

I was living with them, part of their family whether they liked it or not, bowing my head and doing my best to look grateful for the sausage and mash we were about to receive, yet there must have been something maddeningly remote about me. It must have got under Joy's skin, the faraway look in my eye as I reached for the salt. Hope so. Hope it got under her skirt, inside her drawers, clung to her short hairs and bit like the crabs. Once I heard her in a right old tantrum in the kitchen when she thought I was upstairs, and it was all her, her voice raised up in protest, her going at her mother, who gave the odd mumble and bleat in reply as if they were playing a concerto. I'm pretty sure the subject was me. I caught phrases like 'snob—who does he think he is' and 'bone-idle' and 'lazy pig'. Even then I couldn't work up any real hatred for her, I was sunk right away, lost in the greeny deep, I could see her mouthing venomously but there was glass in between and nothing was getting through. If she'd stuck her tongue out at me I wouldn't have done any more than blink and look the other way.

I'd left the factory earlier in the year and gone to London with twenty pounds of savings, and when I came back three weeks later, slinking in with my tail between my legs, too proud to admit that the loneliness had driven me home, I still had ten quid left. That was a month before my parents tore up their roots for good and all. London was a huge map of misery soaking in September sun, like a mockery of paradise.

212

I sat on a bench and let the gongs of Big Ben crash to the ground, watched a blind man tapping through the labyrinth of the flower beds, stood against the wall at Millbank next to a blue-black negro, our backs to the offices I'd seen fill up with ants, and saw barges like links of shit float by on the oily scum. I jumped up in a kind of horror one day: London was a huge open sewer I was slowly, dully drifting down. To give myself the illusion of a routine, a purpose, I devised a deliberate constitutional: went first to the public baths at Westminster every morning for a swim—each time strange as a dream the same bald, elderly man ploughing methodically up and down, the water laving his yellow head—and from there I made straight for Hyde Park. Decided I'd stop at an Irish-sounding pub in Oxford Street each morning and drink a pint of stout, gradually build myself up. I got morbidly obsessed with cleanliness and health. Lying in the sun in the middle of Hyde Park, spreadeagled, all at once I felt I was moving, on a great hairy raft; I gazed up at the puffs of cotton wool on the spotless blue and my body rose and fell softly, drifting. I scrambled up, dizzy, moved on. Sat on a bench watching the incredible Park Lane women exercising their immaculate tailored haunches, parading themselves regally in the company of their sleek escorts, who were no more than appendages. Or taking their poddles for a walk. Or alone, sailing past in a stink of wealth, superb specimens, reeking of good taste and cocktails, chitchat, art galleries, inhumanity. I could have watched them forever, hardly breathing, so close, feeling the great privilege, as if I was brushed by royalty. These were the rulers of London Town, I felt, and the sly, fawning appendages, the men, guiding in the loot—they were nothing. Ticks in the gorgeous pelts. Bloodsuckers. The whole city, geared and churning in its oil of money provided for these queens. They took the air in Park Lane or they prowled on the deep carpets of their scented rooms, with their red shaded lamps, flower

213

arrangements, soft fleshy chairs, and they were the ones. Coming now. I watched until my eyes burned, until my knees ached: I flexed my legs and fancied I could hear the dry crackle of crystals. Day after day the same nagging ache came into my knees, always in the afternoon. In a reading room an advert told me to watch out or I'd be crippled for life, aching knee joints was a sure sigh of rheumatism, arthritis—a course of wonder-working pills would work wonders. Twelve shillings, enough for six months, the full treatment. I found the place, up some back stairs in Buckingham Palace Road, a poky office jammed with half-opened parcels, towers of card-board boxes and a typist working by the window, who handed me one of the smallest boxes and rummaged about in a tin tray for change and clattered madly at the machine again without speaking a word.

Leila sent a parcel to the doss house where I was staying in Victoria, and the sight of her writing nearly broke my heart. I shook the cylinder-shaped package and it rattled. It was a dried-milk tin with three bruised pears in it. That was before I'd even met her.

Two days after I was at Euston, meeting Ray and his wife Connie, down from Brum on a cheap day return. Fresh with friendship, each other, they came at me down the platform hand-in-hand, aglow with youth and problems. I saw them and it shamed me to be sunk so low. I felt I'd been crawling round on my hands and knees. It gave my spirits a great lift to set eyes on them as they came up, so generous with happiness, so eager to share it—as if it was a fresh-baked loaf, simple as that: all you needed to do was hand it over.

That was enough, I had to get back. The simple sultriness of the streets was theirs, belonged to them, the simple park stirring its leaves drowsily in front of the Shell Mex building just as if it was a meadow by the Avon. And happy, beautiful people wandering by, lovers, and even the sandwiches these two had brought to share with me. They'd brought it all. It was a charmed life I was offered, to taste and touch for a day. When they caught the evening train the quick joy went dragging out with them, back again, and the streets contracted. I put the death and disaster back, the livid tracks of misery leading out over the river, the bridges black with suicide, hospital blocks glowing dull red in the evening light, full of festering flesh, overhanging the policemen, ponces, pavement artists, pros, newspaper sellers, coffee stalls, palpitating traffic, all drowning like the sun in a slaughterhouse of purple light. I went threading my way through, biting my lips to keep back a scream, then diving into a bubble of decision, a last refuge. I kept hearing the lost talk, seeing it almost like a white froth, feeling the sunny splash of the laughs. Ray had the keys to all that, he could blow on his little bugle and the sun revolved. What a gift, and to think I let it slip away, didn't value it, sat and laughed and then actually waved it goodbye. A fleck of light came up in me: a decision. Saturday I'd go back.

11

BACK HOME I took a job at another factory: exactly the same kind of job, precision grinding. Went humping in one ashy Monday with my toolbox, herding through the gates and up a long private road flanked by sheds of all sizes, looking for my shed, my hole. Strips of green turf on either side, scarred with flower beds, manholes, bare earth where people had taken short cuts. I suppose it was pleasant enough at first glance, better than lots I'd seen, but my guts told me to get out, don't stay, even before I'd done a stroke—it was such a Godforsaken atmosphere. I couldn't put my finger on what was wrong, but I knew it was: the interview was enough. I was a fool to take it. Now, for some peculiar reason, I had to go through with the motions of trying and seeing.

'Think you can do the job?' the foreman had said, interviewing. He was gazing out of his box, surveying his slaves in the big screeching room—that was all it was, a room—and they faced him in rows, benches and machines, the lot. That was depressing, to begin with. And all the slaves had their heads down, nobody having a quick chat or even a smoke as far as I could see.

Before I could answer he said, 'We'll soon find out, any-way,' and turned to his chargehand with a little smirk as though to say, won't we? You won't need to, I said to myself. You can keep it. Stuff your little empire.

But I came and they stuck me near the back, an old machine belt-driven from an overhead shaft, against a window of frosted glass that was open a chink. Down below me I could make out a backyard, the outside lav and a woman coming out of her kitchen, followed by a meek cloud of steam. And, being

Monday, she was hanging out her washing, singing to herself. She'd sing and then hold pegs in her teeth while she arranged more washing, then up came her hand past her mouth and up to the line in one clear motion, one, two, and she'd sing again. I perked up and felt more human, but by dinnertime I was down in the mouth again, sitting on a wall by the green turf and the flowerbeds, gulping down sandwiches and giving it one day and no more. Next morning I only went in to collect the toolbox and to tell the foreman I'd been offered a better job elsewhere. It was a lie, but you couldn't just say the smell was wrong; you had to give them a reason. He shrugged and that was that. Wonderful then, that long road with its green borders embroidered with flowers, unrolling itself to the gate and the outside, the happy traffic zipping to and fro. Almost worth it for that, like being let out of the dentist's. The deliverance feeling. Shedding the horrors and stepping out into a world that's exactly as you left it only different—raining down blessings. Eyes growing all over you, popping open like buds. Why can't it always be like that, why can't it last? Same only different. Clock in, clock out.

It was near the boundary and the speed limit signs, that no-man's land between town and country, the grass uncertain whether to grow or not, roads and pavements fanging into the green, gobbling and being gobbled. I stood dithery and blissful at the weedy verge, heavy toolbox on the end of my right arm dragging at my shoulder, and if it hadn't been for that I'd have stayed there longer, dreamy in the light. Over the road and down a bit, towards the centre, was the house where I went to that writers' circle meeting a year or two ago. Pompous wrought iron gates and huge sash windows, rock gardens in trim terraces at the side, with a pool, stone urns and a stately white-painted conservatory. My mouth went sickly at the thought of it, remembering. Inside was like outside, the air starved to death, unnaturally hushed and cloistered. Big lemon-white rooms and grey doors and a glare of geraniums. Edith, the woman's name. She'd put the advert in the local rag and got a response, about ten of us, which she called at the first gathering 'a little nucleus'. Thirtyish I suppose, her hair and clothes in a fuzz as if she'd been combed the wrong way, but in good taste, no nonsense: she looked every inch a teacher. No rings on her fingers—I took the house to be her mother's place. Yes, her mother was upstairs in bed, an invalid—would we be quiet? Pouncing forward to introduce herself she flinched on your behalf as well as her own, high voice nearly cracking with nervous strain—she was the last person I wanted to meet. But I was in, picking a chair with a view out of the heavy window so I could switch to admiring the rock garden when Edith's agony got too much. They trickled in, simpering, sniggering, the others, and with each one she did her stuff: 'I'm Edith Wilkinson—so pleased—would you like to sit down, join the charmed circle?'

The chairs were drawn up in a semicircle, Edith trapped in the centre facing, glaring at us rawly, jerking her head like a snake and chewing her morbid lips. I can't remember anyone mentioning their writing or reading anything, except her. One man, the oldest among us, was in his working clothes, red-faced, with a great ugly curve of mouth smirking, a sore overhang of upper lip, and he sat venomous and simmering: somebody said he'd worked down a mine and been on hunger marches. Edith read us a story of hers, while we sat comfortable as if ready to go to bed, transfixed on the high wire of her voice. Her stiff upper lip froze in terror, all her own work and now she wished she was dead. She was swivelling her eye-balls at us in a kind of loathing. There was that, and a record of Peter Pears singing 'Foggy Foggy Dew', where we shuffled our feet and tittered, and I remember towards the end how she reached a new pitch of hysteria, announcing things like:

'Social activities!'

218

'We need a treasurer!'

Before that, while Ray was still in Coventry I'd gone with him to a gathering at the Tech, where there was a proper lecturer and a class atmosphere which he loathed, the minute we put our noses in. He wandered round rudely picking out books from the shelves and putting them back with a bang, saying loud things to me now and then and ignoring the discussion group. I was astounded because I'd never have had the guts to show my feelings like that. Nobody took the slightest notice of us, we lounged out before it was over and went home talking favourite books, reconnoitring. I hardly knew him then, what he was capable of. He made a poor impression that night, didn't interest me much more than the pleasant yobs at work, the slit eyes that weighed you up and the thick skin insulating them from everything. Suddenly in a matter of weeks he changed, blossomed, dropped the surface talk and the bored act. He said I was the one, I'd done it: we were at Brum one Sunday afternoon, in the Town Hall, worshipping at George Weldon's shrine in his dazzling white temple, you could hear the starlings adding their nimbus in the quiet passages. Sibelius it might have been, one of his genesis edifices building up, granite on granite, groan of ice, a slewing and groaning in the absolute frozen waste of the beginning, lifeless—I leaned over and quoted something, I wanted to put words to this music that was cancelling, smashing everything, clearing the whole damn earth of all the piddling man-made junk it carried, for a fresh start. Fresh as a skylark. Irresistible. And Ray's face was radiant, wide-open to me as he answered in the groundswell of that thunder:

'You're right!'

12

How can I bring him back, the Ray of those early days? He was quick, small, brown, a live wire, always splitting with laughs that were like spontaneous explosions at the cockeyed, daft things that happened to him and that he did, then remembered and they went off inside him like mirth bombs, his thickish lips split open and out it brayed, doubling him up. He weaved fantasies for people, in spite of himself, getting deeper and deeper in, ending up almost believing the stuff himself. 'I was buying a record last Saturday and the girl said, what sort of record player you got? One of those old wind-up gramophones I said, you know in a cabinet, but the arm where you put the needle's busted. How are you going to play this record then she said? Well I said, what I do I get the record spinning fast, it's got to be fast, then I hold a needle between my teeth and bend down and play it, see. It goes right through you at first, horrible, like getting your teeth drilled at the dentist—but after it's okay, when you get used to it, you can hear every note a treat. And you know what—honest, I'm not exaggerating—she believed me! Fancy she said, goggling at me like a baby. The only thing to watch is, I said, when you come to the sad bits not to cry, because it all drips down and wets the record and it skids. No good then. No, oh no, she said. No! Honest, if I'd told her I took my shoe and sock off and played it with my big toenail she'd have believed me, I know she would.'

There was that side to him, and then moods where he had a devil in his guts, black moods that made him writhe and despise himself, when he couldn't bring himself to speak hardly. Then the bland faces and impassive pillar-boxes and the England of the decent, nice and proper people creeping about taking care not to show any emotion or give the game away, playing the game and minding their own privet-hedged business, it used to goad him when he was perverse into anti-social outbursts, like bawling 'worst coffee in Coventry' as we went past a certain café doorway, or the time we were walking up a grass and gravel track on the edge of some allotments near where I lived and a big car swung up behind us, blaring us into the hedge with its horn. It careered past on the ruts and Ray lifted his arm, gave him the victory sign and yelled at the top of his voice:

'Yah, capitalist!'

Then we heard the brakes go on, gears slammed into reverse and the car came humping back, blunt and ugly like a tank, the driver twisted round and his face contorted, all florid and glittery-eyed. He bundled out and bore down on us, a huge black bull of a man. If we'd been a few years younger we'd have run for it. I stood there motionless, sickened, unable to look at Ray. We'd reached the age of pride, there was no running.

'Who shouted?' the man mouthed, blocking out the lane and standing over us. 'Was it you?'

He had his ham fist under my nose. I was struggling to speak when I heard Ray say:

'I did.'

The driver transferred his fist, he'd worked himself up and it wouldn't have taken him much to let fly. Impotent, I watched him stand over my friend, who looked as sick as I felt but stood there miraculously not flinching with a faint smile that horrified me when I saw it, a smile of doom and suicide. I waited agonizingly for it to be wiped off.

'See this?'

He swayed his fist to and fro under Ray's nose as if it was a monkey wrench he was threatening him with. 'Any more of your bloody sauce and you'll taste this—both of you. Understand?'

Ray nodded, his crazy lopsided smile crumbling. Then the man went plunging off, satisfied. I hated him so much for exposing us to each other, Ray and me, I started to spout fantasies of revenge in my head. I ought to have grabbed a brick and run up and belted his car all over, made it clang like a dustbin. In my dream the brick sank right through the body and in seconds it was perforated like a colander, I bashed and dodged round and round while the driver chased me, sobbing with rage and yelling blue murder. I was as nimble as Charlie Chaplin, the little man triumphant, I got the handbrake off and it rolled away down the slope, the driver half in and half out, screaming help and police. It was a desperate compensation to offset our new nakedness, cover us up. I was stripped now, we both were, walking on in a new and cruel shame, seeing ourselves in each other, frail and cowardly and never able to hit back. It was true. It was cruel and shameful and true. And much later it became absorbed in a much worse, much bigger inadequacy, so that to live at all and hold my head up, not harmed by these blemishes, I had to dream up a world where they had a place. More than that. Grass is frail but look how it springs up under the boot, endures. Nature wasn't enough though: the frail in my world had to triumph.

So that was it—so there was nothing select about us that some ugly bastard couldn't melt down to his measure with his fist. Now we knew, and we never wanted to feel select but in the nature of things it was slipping that way. Us versus the others. Without turning our backs on any of it, always very conscious of the side streets, the quiet dads, the working day and trips to the sea and fishing in the canal, all that, we'd begun exploring and pushing out to something great and wonderful that nobody had mentioned or bothered to tell us about. That they hardly knew existed. It was no use to them, but we found we could enter it. If it was a leisure thing, all right, we'd make leisure! We had to enter, let them try and stop us: and entering meant leaving. The departure cut us right off. Sibelius, Picasso, Giono's *Jean le Bleu*, the list grew a little every week, sometimes big jumps, adding on, and the message coming through was secret, just for us, you could no more tell parents and adults about it than you could about the dull burning of sex. Then a fist smashed it, hung over it, black as Monday, solid as a fact; it crumbled and left us less than normal. A minus quality. What we had was as frail as a smile. The more we were liberated, the more we weakened.

Going to see Ray after an absence of a month or two I was conscious of this straight off, as soon as I set eyes on him: the married man, father, coming to meet me with his hand out-stretched, too good to be true. Totally unfit for the world, all shine and trust and openness. Cover up, I'd feel like saying. Watch out—wait till we get indoors. I noticed it in particular when he bought the shell of an old bus for a home, had it towed to the Lickey Hills on the edge of Brum and fitted it with bunks, a slow combustion stove, some curtains: I went trailing out there on the tram, up and down on the straight switchback past the Austin empire and he'd meet me at the terminus.

'Dr Livingstone!'

'That's me,' he laughed.

'The end of the line.'

'End of the world, this,' he said. 'A bit further and you drop right off the edge.'

'Which is the safe direction then?'

'Follow me, young man.'

We went down a road of raw new bungalows repeating themselves endlessly, all the same meek little differences making them more bleakly alike than ever, meagre Englishmen's castles with their chestnut woven battlements and blank witless picture windows; then he veered right and I followed him up a ragged path to a gate, that opened on a scrubby, sour field, sloping up steep. It was ribbed like a washboard, stuck with thistles, potholes here and there and fresh dollops of cowshit. Soon we had a good view all round and I wished we hadn't: I'd sooner be on New Street Station living than these scabby unloved edges, where you can see the country being fed to the concrete, disappearing under the garbage, the whole process, and be smudged into a listless indifference that sucks the life out of friends and fields, even the light. Nothing mattered here, these were the dead lands.

'Great, ain't it,' Ray said grimly, and now I saw the bus we were making for, on a ridge near the crest of this forlorn lump of hill.

'You won't want to stay here too long.'

'I'd blow my brains out if I thought we'd have to.'

Connie had seen us through the windows. She came out on the step, smiling and comely, already the wife receiving visitors, enjoying it. Brown eyes wide and round, brown fringe cut straight, wide flapping skirt and flat brogues. A country girl who had somehow got born at Hay Mills, bang in the middle of Brummagem land. She looked calm and content, sylvan, and when she spoke it came out in a rush, agitated. But she was still at the centre, like the Bull Ring after Corporation Street.

'Tickets, please!' she shouted, blushing.

'I'll have a fourpenny.'

'You will if you don't shurrup,' she said and laughed. 'Don't talk too loud for God's sake, the brat's just gone to sleep.'

'How are you?' I said.

'Fine thanks.'

'Better on your own.'

'You betcha.'

'She can speak American, your wife,' I said to Ray.

'Oh, she's clever all right,' Ray said.

'Go and boil your heads,' Connie said, and disappeared.

Ray led me to the bonnet of the bus, lifted the flaps and I saw it was gutted, a gaping space where the engine should have been.

'The steering works, though,' he said. 'The tyres pump up, so we can move out of this dump—all we need's a pull.'

'When?' Connie said, popping her head out.

'Sooner the better,' Ray said. 'You know you don't like it any more than I do.'

'It's horrible,' she said bluntly.

'Well then.'

'I was thinking—oh never mind.' She dodged back inside again.

Ray sighed: 'She's thinking about her folks, how upset they'll be—I've heard of this site at Symond's Yat and they think it's too far, and they're worried about what I'll do for a job and—oh Christ, it's one big problem I tell you.'

'Don't forget to tell him about your mother,' Connie said, back on the running board. 'She'd have a fit if we moved that far.'

'True, true.' Then he was shaking his head and laughing at the stalemate, the frustration, misunderstanding, the stupid and ugly and what the hell, they were here anyway, living in the present, the milk needed fetching. It was a life, and it was a start, and it was theirs.

'Give me a gun, I'll finish it here and now,' he was laughing, holding his head, the problems spinning and exploding in it like fireworks.

13

Ray on his own was the friend I knew. Now he was married, and instead of this robbing me I felt richer, even if I didn't see him so much. It was early days, they were so alike in their desires they were like one person, moving into the grand adventure of a way of life, married and pulling together. For my part it gave a zest to the relationship I had, added another flavour, as I got to know a Ray who was thickening out, richer, more responsible, while I sat watching and warming my hands at the brave flames sizzling in their stove. It was like playing at families for me, and it was still a bit like that for them: nothing heavy and deadening, or there was no point. They were out for some fun, they had pride in what they'd done, young as they were to be starting out. It had to be fun and it had to mean something. 'Aren't you brave,' the woman said down below, where they bought the bread. What was she on about? There they were, the two of them, and their son: a brave new world that was theirs and it was the most natural thing to want to launch it, small as it was, to see if it would float.

Sitting in the bus peering out, sipping their tea, I felt privileged and excited, as if I really had a share in the venture of this brand-new family. The dusk gathered under the windows, a deep-coloured intense gloom hung down over the hill, full of dull knockings and clankings from the huge factory below—and slowly the intimacy increased as we sat on quietly with no more words we wanted to say. Connie would call Ray 'Raymondo' in a bluff voice that was perhaps meant to spare me, or it might have been to emphasize that he was her Ray. I didn't mind, any more than a brother would. I felt part of the family, sitting quietly and watching nothing from the windows, feeling momentous as if we all belonged in an old painting.

'I need some more water, Raymondo.'

So I went with him across the ridge and through a gap in the hedge to a rusty standpipe in a lake of mud where somebody had tossed slabs of stone around, to step on. While he did a balancing act and got there and the water sloshed into his enamel bucket with its rusted rim I looked back across the city. Looking that way in the dark, England was one big city, no end to it, streets stretching up as far as Liverpool. Black all the way. Then I saw what was really nasty about being perched on this hill, stuck up out of the frozen flood like Noah on top of the mountain, surveying the desolation. I didn't want to see the worst, didn't want to know what a grimy, greasy sink-hole it was. An instinct of self-preservation made me want to plunge back into it, because once you were in there were compensations and distractions, people, and this bird's-eye view hurt terribly, it was like a Dante vision.

I was going. 'When will I see you again, Colin?'

'I'll be back soon. Keep the brakes on or you'll roll right down into Austin's and get reconditioned before you know where you are.'

'Wash and brush up,' Ray said, forcing a laugh. The view had got under his skin too, he was coming with me to the terminus but his feet were dragging, he longed to be back in the warm bright halo of his home, his family. The raw night hurt him, he was only half with me. You only had to look at him, his eyes were uneasy and he looked slightly guilty. He was the mainstay and protector, the captain, and here he was deserting. I put him out of his misery:

'Don't come any further. See you later—in a week or two, okay?'

'So long then.'

It was drizzling, I dragged out a cap and jammed it on, rakish.

227

'You look like a Frenchman!' he shouted back, running. 'Suits you!'

Another time I arrived there with a rucksack of coal, it was the late forties, everything in short supply, power cuts, rations, and they were having trouble getting fuel out at that spot. I humped it from Coventry, I must have been mad. When I got to their door it was locked, nobody in. It was too daft for words: I should have told them I was coming, but I'd only thought of it that very morning. Spoke to my landlady and she said yes, all right, pick out some small lumps. Sitting there mouselike on the Midland Red with the rucksack on the floor between my feet I could smell the coal, wafting up strong. Nobody seemed to notice, so I relaxed and forgot all about it till the time came to get off in the Bull Ring and I went to pick it up. It was like lifting a bag of plumber's tools. And it was Saturday morning, that glamorous and vital weekend feeling in the air; I'd have liked to have gone mooning round a few second-hand bookshops—there was a Communist shop I'd found on my last jaunt, in a back street somewhere near Snow Hill Station, with copies of *Mother* stuck in the middle of the window next to a big photo of Gorki, seamed, grainy, nose like a sausage, moustache gushing and sorrowful, eyes eloquent and mournful and beautiful as a dog's, telling the whole terrible story. But with that load on my back I made straight for the tram, and didn't even climb on the top deck to see things—I thought if I did I might come tipping down headfirst when it was time to get off, in a shower of coal and confusion. We went grinding away, giving squeals of torment, blundering as if drunk on the corners, gathering speed down the hills and rocking like a ship, everything groaning and creaking, drowning the sharp hiss of the wire over the roof. Past the University, then up and down and straight on in the direction of Bromsgrove, Redditch.

I thought about leaving a note but didn't even have a pencil:

228

nothing. So all I did was put the rucksack down on the top step and go back down the hill again, back into Brum. Wrapped carefully in a sheet of newspaper on top of the coal was a book called *Lust for Life* that Leila had lent me. I'd brought it to let Ray see the Van Gogh reproductions scattered through it—and one in particular I was dying to show him, an orchard. Connie would be interested too, she did paintings herself, good ones. I remember Ray telling me once when they were courting, before I'd even met her, that she wanted contributions from people for her birthday, some money, so that she could buy some oils. And the first thing that entered my head was oilskins, and it baffled me, why a girl should want oilskins for her birthday.

I hoped the book wouldn't get pinched, it looked expensive. When they made a film of this book I saw it, years and years later. Those scenes in the Borinage made me think suddenly of the rucksack of coal, stinking like a miner, and the book lying on top of the jagged heap. Van Gogh might have appreciated that. I kept seeing Kirk Douglas instead of Vincent, he looked a wild man all right, his crew-cut all ragged, his eyes sore and his skin livid, scrubbed like a doorstep with suffering, but it was no good, he kept getting in the way, he was just too bloody familiar. Then one morning, early, first day in Provence, he pushed open his casement windows and looked out of his yellow house—nearly fell out with astonishment. The revelation poured in through his eyes, that orchard, what a feast of blossom; it turned his brain and he overflowed with it in ecstacy as the whole screen literally filled up with blossom and shivered like a basket of creamy bubbles. The blobs of fluff were caught in the twigs and branches but they were moving, stirring, a vapour of beauty on the edge of his nightmare. He only had to reach out. This was Vincent now, the mad beauty of the blossom, and it was what Ray and his

Connie were aiming their ravenous innocence at, pointing their engineless bus at it, aching to start.

It was an ache I shared, and in Ray's company, strangely enough, it wasn't doubled, it was spread out, a vision, and it led to art. It came and went, English weather fashion, like a blue sky. We got vivid flashes, then nothing there but empty space mocking, a vacuum—the only thing to do was go home in gnashing frustration, baffled by what couldn't be expressed. Many a time I'd done that, stalking back home defeated and remorseful with another chance missed, and I'd clench my fist and hammer the walls as I passed in the dark. But it got steadily better, a brilliance of flashing blue beckoning us on, and when we came to making art ourselves it fed into us like Van Gogh's blossom. Even now we were putting words to it and the words made twigs radiating out, structuring it, giving it a clear shape, and though the nearness of the state we kept trying to describe nearly drove us batty it was also soothing, pleasurable, in a way better than the real thing. We sounded our horn and it rotated, serene as Mozart, ripe and spanking and heartful as Louis Armstrong on the turntable. My ache for Leila was submerged in the boundless sky of this aching blue world growing in our chests.

It was fine to be with them, even though Ray's obsession for this other reality worried me a bit, now they were married. Because he was in a trap, he needed money, he couldn't walk in and out of jobs like I could, without setting up reverberations. Connie was his kind of girl, she blazed up in the fire of his dream, kindled to it, that was obvious. For her it was a source of pride, definitely part of his attractiveness, and it set him apart as a man, made him truly unique and hers. A man who wanted something different, who stood out, couldn't help himself even. I was happy to see her proud like that. But I saw her more realistic turn of mind beginning to hedge and baulk at the chronic lack of details, as any woman would. Better

230

than anyone, better than him anyway she knew what they were up against, what the odds were, how the world was made. She was with him all the way, whatever he decided, there was no question of that—he could call the innocence out of her, spontaneous bursts of love in spite of herself. She wanted details, that's all, while he kept talking this wild abstract talk. She started to oppose him, to try and force him back down to the ground.

'We're going to Symond's Yat,' he said. 'I can't help what your dad says, we're going.'

'Or your mother.'

'No.'

'Look, Ray, I'm not arguing, I want to know how, that's all. Facts.'

'Facts, facts!' Ray collapsed on the bunk in a spasm of mock anguish. He rubbed his eyes, groaned, held his head. 'I don't bloody well know, but I'll think of something.'

'You need a job, it's a country district——'

He shoots up, looking drawn, and in a mock-distraught voice, 'That's it, that's what I need, a job!'

He's gone a little too far, Connie is tired, the baby is teething and they get bad nights. A hard edge comes in her voice: 'Well, Christ——'

At once he's touchingly remorseful, making his peace. 'I'm sorry, Con, it's just that it's so bloody stupid that's all, stuck here, not being able to shift; you'd think we were trying to make for Venezuela or somewhere. Herefordshire—bloody hell!'

'Anyway, Colin hasn't come here to listen to our rows,' she says, still curt, unappeased. And the barb of this catches me, I take it for a warning, a reminder that it's an intimate husband-and-wife thing I'm witnessing, not to be interfered with. Fair enough.

'Rows—what rows?' Ray squirms, still clinging by his toes

and fingernails to the vision which floods on without us, sunk away in the depths for the moment and we're aground, all of us, surrounded by a heaving, rocking darkness. Connie's face is without expression and Ray's is hollow-eyed, tormented. He's going to keep on, persist, I can tell—a simple tiff is all this situation needs because we're floating over an abyss. He can't let it go, it torments him, if it ends in ruins round his feet he's still got to say his piece.

'Ah, let's shurrup yapping,' Connie snaps, in a strange cold rage, and is angrily clearing away teacups, plates, sugar bowl. We sit in the bus, a Saturday dusk settling, merging the sky into the land, the atmosphere of the discord invading and corroding us slowly, inch by inch, insidious as the night, and we might be down there in the rows of kennels, the seethe of back-to-backs, the tenements, barrack-like council flats, no difference. I know this is what is sending Ray mad, what he won't acknowledge. We've brought it with us up here even, the wife, the trouble and strife. No, he's not having that.

'I know I've got to have a job, I know that,' he says to Connie's blind back in a queer strangled voice that is half aggressive and half pleading. He turns to me, his mouth twisting; tells me about the jobs he's already applied for, Monmouth, Cinderford, that area; farm labourer, factory hand, garage hand, and nothing doing.

'I'm half a mind to just go and plonk down there, anyway. What the hell,' he says wearily, staring out of the window as if he can see the very spot: wooded, remote, burgeoning.

'There's the brat to think of—not just us,' says his wife, flat, over her shoulder.

'I'd go on the dole.'

'What about the six weeks' waiting time or whatever it is you were on about——'

'That's if you leave, not get the sack.'

He's working at the moment nine hours a day in a dairy in

town, a racketty stinking hole. He grins across at me, con-spiratorial—and it's a game again, the abyss is no more. All clear.

'No,' he says gently, to placate Connie and restore a measure of stability, 'all it means is I've got to save enough to cover us for those six weeks. It's as simple as that. Eh, Connie?'

'You know best,' she says quietly, not complaining and not giving in either. She's made her point. I begin to breathe again, push my head up. Connie comes from a household of nagging anxiety, a family of chronic worriers, and Ray's home is seething with recriminations because he's married so young, in such a horribly unorthodox way. He wonders if he'll ever be able to go home again, properly. They have plenty on their plate. In sympathy I lose myself in their problems: it's strangely comforting, lulling. Connie I can see is basically as steady as a rock. Infatuated by Ray's spurting life, she's now having to contain him, give him a firm anchorage. I tell my-self they make a good couple, knowing nothing about it—an absolute ignoramus in such matters. But it's funny how people often find intuitively the partner they need for the qualities they badly lack in themselves.

Before marriage and the child had fused them, while they were still Ray Madge and Connie Thompson, I drifted round with them during Ray's leaves, his long weekends. We'd perhaps meet at his mother's, and this Connie would be there sitting quite motionless in a dusky corner, with her radiant smile in lieu of conversation whenever I looked at her, and her convent quiet. She had nothing to say, no small talk, but Ray would come slipping in from the back with a book, or some tea, step into the glassy silence and act daft, or pull one of his faces. Connie laughed, a wonderful fruity sound, a surprise, her shoulders and head shook with it and she opened her mouth wide. It was better than any words. The first time I heard it I stared openly in admiration, as if someone had lit a fire in the corner. Another big surprise was when she dug down clumsily in the pocket of her dark skirt and came out with a cigarette holder, an amber one. Fixing it up, she said to Ray in an extra posh voice, being funny:

'Would you mind terribly?'

He took down the box of matches on the mantelpiece, that his mother left for lighting the gas fire.

'Would I mind what?' he said, winking at me. He struck a match, she leaned forward confidently, full of trust and pride, to reach the spurt of flame, and it was a proud little perform-ance, adult, intimate, which needed the funny setting because I was there watching closely and they hadn't had time to absorb me yet, into this new adult creation.

As well as me there unabsorbed, Connie herself was in process of being accepted by the Madges as Ray's first permanent girl, and she was fitting herself too into the work-ing-class terrace world, in an old ugly district of doors flush with the street and shared back yards, mere cobbled runs with drains in, where the dustbins and cats lived, the lavs in blocks of four, and washhouses, line props. A district that used to belong to watchmakers and their families in the last century—they had workshops in all the attics. Connie came from something a bit different, though not too remote for anything here to be at all fantastic. Her world was semi-detached, gravelled, chestnut-fenced, just as intense in its way as this, just as much a grid, but with important little driveways and a need for garage space, flowering shrubs, an illusion of privacy among those packed streets. But she was finding out that nothing was more private than a working-class family that kept to itself, minded its own business.

14

RAY'S mother, like a lot of mothers, lived in the back. As soon as you penetrated her territory you knew it was hers. She'd be watching the fire, the cooker, the weather if her clothes were out and flapping, catching the smuts. She was short, her broad plump shoulders beginning to hunch under the work, the marriage burden—the whole meaning and purpose of life was in the work. Kids were different—she had three boys. She gave herself no time to wonder about the child or even the young girl she'd once been; no dreaming time. Her puffy, pale face was selfless, her arms energetic, fleshed with family love. She lived in her apron, sleeves often rolled up. Beauty was for girls, another planet of existence—everything spinning in its own sky, no overlap. She made you welcome, nearly shouting with energy, anxiety. For tea it was tinned fruit, pineapple salad, bread and butter eaten with it. Always bread and butter; marg if they were short. Bread and butter with everything, the filler, staple diet. Or it was jelly and a big bowl of runny pale custard, or a jug of custard, and more jelly—'have some bread with it, look, she hasn't got any—Ray, what you thinking of—pass Connie some of that bread and butter.'

'She doesn't like it, Mum—I've told you.'

'She don't? How's that?'

'Leave her alone, she's all right.'

'Don't talk so daft, lad—leave her alone—I ain't going to clout you, am I, love?'

'This is fine, really, Mrs Madge. This is plenty.'

'Are you sure, my duck?'

'Yes, fine.'

'And look at Colin there. Have some cake, Colin. More jelly?'

Jelly anointed with custard or with tinned milk, slices of bread and butter to help it down, doorsteps. Strong tea and plenty of sugar to help that down. And for a special treat, salmon, on a flowered plate in the middle of the table, a thick section still moulded by the tin, that you stared hard at and couldn't connect with a fish once swimming in a river.

'Ever had fresh salmon?'

'No, never, Mrs Madge.'

'I did once. You, Colin? Ever had fresh salmon?'

I shifted a wad of bread in my mouth and said no, I couldn't remember ever having any.

'Well, I did, an' I never liked it. What you make of that?' Mrs Madge wasn't defiant, not really asking, but making a flat statement. 'It wa'nt half as nice as this either. That's funny, isn't it?'

Ray's dad cleared his throat: 'When you ever have any fresh?' A small, weathered, intensely still man who said little, and when he did speak it was quiet and flat: even so nobody expected it, and it sounded almost brutal, an accusation.

Mrs Madge stopped her hand in mid-air to answer, in the act of reaching for the teapot. 'Not me—what you thinking of. Where would I be on me own, eating fresh salmon? Not me, both of us did. That time in Skeg, remember, that outing?'

'No. Blowed if I can.' He was being polite on account of the company. Soon the company would cease to exist, the exchanges would toss to and fro, they'd be drawn into a fierce argument which was pure married battle, assault and counter-attack from prepared positions on habits and prejudices that never budged. They'd be oblivious of us. I'd seen it happen before. Then something would switch it off, it drifted away like a puff of smoke and you thought you'd dreamt it.

'You're crackers. You mean to say you can't remember that outing to Skeggy?'

236

'I didn't say that. Did I say that? You want to listen.

'What did you say then?'

'Salmon—you were on about fresh salmon, is that right?'

'Oh my Gawd, get on with it!'

'What I'm sayin' is, wherever you reckon you et it, it wasn't with me, 'cause I've never had any.'

I heard the front door burst open, then the middle door was snatched back and Ray's brothers tumbled in, grinning, two schoolboys hot from running or some game, pink-cheeked, eyes sharp as frost. They pulled up quick when they saw us sitting round all prim, a tea party.

'Where have you two ripstitches bin?' shouted their mother. 'You know very well when teatime is.'

'We forgot,' gasped the youngest, Michael, a lad of eight, still with his astonished baby face. Peter, eleven, to improve on this answer, said: 'We didn't know what time it was.'

'Ask then—what's your tongue for.'

'Lickin' ice-cream,' Peter said, showing off, and because he was safe.

'Go an' wash your hands,' said his father softly, speaking for the first time, turning his head. His tone was enough, off they went, no arguments, but so high-spirited and in such a stampede in the cramped living-room that Mrs Madge shouted, 'Walk!'

With all of us jammed in there, window shut because of the draught down Mrs Madge's neck, a coal fire—part of the welcome—half-way up the chimney, incandescent slabs packed round with slack, I knew Ray would be itching to escape into the street. Not exactly a din, but the restriction turned it into a bedlam that some families liked and seemed to thrive on. It was life. Not for Ray. The signs of strain showed on his face, he flinched as his brothers ripped out laughter close to his head, and when we finally let ourselves out, Connie and Ray and me, waved goodbye to his mother who stood on the doorstep until we were round the corner, he drags down a deep, melodramatic breath, filling his lungs gratefully:

'Real air!'

It's a prison to him now, that house, the suffocating little room like a stokehold, kitchen an engine for driving the family forward as a unit, his mother treating him exactly as she treats her other two sons, his father stubbornly abstracted and neutral. He was such a good boy at home, his mother has told me, dropping ominously into the past tense: when she was ill once and had to go into hospital he did everything, cooked the dinner, looked after his brothers, ran errands, and he was always bright and clever—won a scholarship to the grammar school. Didn't I think it was too young for him to think of getting married, before he'd had time to save up or look around or anything? This was when he was still in the Navy: I'd dropped round to find out if he was coming home on leave that weekend. She kept asking, asking: he's too young, isn't he? She seized on me as the older friend, steady and single, the stay-at-home with more sense, good to my mother, who could make him see reason, talk him out of it. When in fact I admired him, envied him like hell, and was at a loss to understand his mother's obsession. I liked her very much, that was the trouble, or it would have gone in one ear and out of the other. She'd do anything for you, or anybody who came. That's how she was. She wasn't asking for an opinion, she was desperate for confirmation. Agreement was all she was interested in. So I nodded dumbly and looked a picture of sympathy while she searched my face, raked it desperately for some clue to her own son, and kept asking why, why, why does he? He was the bright one, moving out, he read books, he would do things—hadn't he been given the chances his parents had never had? The first child, he'd passed brilliantly for the grammar, one of only six in the whole city, then he went into the Rates Department, a plum job. Local Government Officer. All you had to do was say 'My son's in the Treasury': it was the best there was. Now he didn't even want to go back there. Why? Didn't even want to come back to Coventry, his home town. Why, why? The hopes and dreams pinned on him—all smashed. Door to the future, that was opening like a dream, slammed shut. It was unbelievable, she couldn't grasp it, her head was in a whirl with thinking, thinking, trying to work out what had come over her son. What's happened to him? she demanded, a kind of blank stare on her face as if she was stunned. If somebody would only tell her. She spoke as if there was some conspiracy against her. Her mind spinning, she kept pouring out recriminations, fears, recollections, picking over the situation again and again for something overlooked, something vital she'd missed. Her husband was no help, he wouldn't say anything: just sat there, non-committal. Thought she was making too much fuss, a mountain out of a molehill— but how could you worry too much over your son if you were a good mother? She was a model mother, no doubt about that. The way she was going frantic though at the thought of Ray's marriage started me off wondering if her own married life had been a disappointment. But what did I know about those things? That's all he can think of, all he wants to do, get married, she kept saying. Married! As if it was a dirty word. She loaded the idea with such bitterness you'd have thought marriage was the absolute dead end. Failure and mockery, she made it sound like. And of course a rejection of the opportunities she'd fought grimly and fanatically to provide.

15

OUT we went into the street, and I was so conscious of Ray sloughing off this lot with a great heave of relief, I felt almost as relieved myself.

'Where we going?' I said.

'To the moon—it looks quieter up there!'

'It's made of cheese,' Connie murmured. 'We could nibble bits.'

'Not more food,' I said.

'It's mouldy, didn't you know?' Ray said. 'Some nights it looks real green.'

'Where's that ice-cream place,' I said, remembering something from years ago.

Ray ducked into Connie's line of vision. 'Ice-cream?'

'I don't mind,' she smiled, blithe, swinging along between us.

'She doesn't mind,' Ray said. 'What does that mean, d'you think?'

'It means yes in female,' I said, quick-witted for once in company. Ray was the one for repartee; he had a fanciful mind, and a real talent for acting the fool. I could only do it if I was with people who didn't mean very much to me. Even then I suffered from a fatal lack of confidence. With friends I was usually too eager to intensify the relationship, especially at the beginning. I was afraid to spoil it, betray its spirit, I treated it nervously, worshipfully even, as if I was handling a virgin.

'Del-Rivo's, shall we go?'

Connie was baffled: 'Speak English, man!'

Del-Rivo's was an Italian ice-cream parlour in Moorfield

Road, not far from Ray's place: little cosy booths inside and tables, cool tiled floors, and the swarthy, broad-hipped girls with loud hard voices coming for your order, bringing tin bowls full of great dollops of their speciality, an ice-cream that folks said was made from potatoes. Their secret. A funny colour, creamy brown, with a unique flavour that I wasn't sure about, whether I liked it or not, but it took hold of you and you went on gobbling, sucking it down and wanting more. I think it was the sweetness that got you—the sweetest ice-cream I'd tasted.

So we sat there or in a coffee-place, or the pictures, with a deep shyness between us that we were all adding to, unable to help ourselves. Connie's shyness with me resurrected the one between Ray and me, that we'd long ago overcome in each other's presence, and I daresay with me there Connie and Ray were acting unnaturally towards each other. I could sense a sort of stiffness. That's how it was, and it was the essence of how we were at that time, of the stage we'd reached. I got so miserable in the end that I tried to think of some excuse for pushing off and leaving them to it. Nothing would come, because in spite of everything I still wanted to be there, to hang around. And Ray wouldn't make any attempt to get rid of me. He'd say, 'We're going to see this film *The Long Night* on Sunday—feel like coming?' I went. I couldn't decide whether Connie minded or not, and meeting them at her mother's place she gave me one of her quick, eager smiles, so spontaneous and happy, my spirits shot right up and I didn't give it another thought.

In her house there was an atmosphere of upheaval, chaos, that seemed to be the norm, even when hardly anybody was in. I hadn't experienced anything like it in a household before. It was exciting, sort of free, I thought. At Ray's it was very different—there might be a din going on, or you felt smothered, but you felt things were under control, screwed down: teatime was teatime, and so on. It was a regime, warm and close, intimate, but with rigid rules of behaviour. And it was against this, partly, that Ray was kicking, that he couldn't bear any more. My mother's was more or less the same, so much so that before long my mother was treating Ray almost as one of the family. He was her kind, and though he was always laughing at her questions, even that showed an interest, a concern for her. She liked that very much. And he was very courteous to her, very gentle always. She took to Ray at first sight. Like Ray's mother with me, she soon tried to worm out of Ray what was wrong with me, what I was kicking at, what was making me so miserable and solitary and unapproachable. Something was ailing me—what was it? Only I wasn't thinking of getting married, there was no crisis, nothing in the open; so she put it in general terms, trying to ferret out what was generally biting us, Alan and Ray and me, as a group. It was because Ray seemed to be happy, always laughing and she could talk to him that I think she regarded him with more pleasure than she did her own sons; and how ironic that was. Ray's mother was looking on me the same way, as a good influence.

'Why don't you talk sense?' my mother would ask him, laughing but serious, really wanting to know.

'Sense?'

'Yes, sense.'

'What's that?'

'The opposite of nonsense!' she shouted.

He'd frown and consider, pretend to be stumped. 'Anything like incense?' he'd ask.

'You balmpot!'

'I beg your pardon, Mrs Patten?'

'You heard.'

'Balmpot? No, honest, I've never heard that word before.' He looked at her straight-faced, solemn as an owl.

'Well, you've heard it now!' she said, shut the door and left

242

us to get on with our record playing, our plotting, whatever we got up to. She'd open the door again, just sufficient to poke her head through:

'Haven't you?'

Ray says, 'Thank you very much,' and bursts out laughing.

Another thing about Connie's household that was quite new to me was the fact that she had sisters: two. And a brother. Also, on the wall in the dining-room, opposite the French windows and strip of lawn outside leading down to the fence, the line of poplars, was a picture, a big one in a gilt frame. Some shaggy Highland cattle and a sunset, all meticulous. Nevertheless, a picture. The only pictures I ever saw in our house were calendars in the kitchen, stuck up with a drawing-pin.

Connie's mother would look at me a little strangely, a bit vague and distraught, and she had a sharp tongue that sounded worse than it was. Obviously the children weren't afraid of her. 'How are you?' she'd say, and to begin with it unnerved me. Then I saw that she spoke to her own children like that, and to her husband, who was an excitable, timid man, long and thin, and couldn't be nicer. He almost dissolved with kindness, it seemed to disembody him. A saintly man. The mealtimes were fantastic, we all sat down, all talking, the kids equal with the adults, helping themselves, and I got the impression that the father was much too nice to give an order and the mother had long ago given up out of sheer fatigue. So we had absolute freedom, compared to the sitting up straight with both hands on the table palaver that I'd been brought up to think was normal. You could be finished, plate clean as a whistle, drinking a cup of tea, but if one hand was out of sight or, worse still, had slid into your trouser pocket, out lashed my father with his foot under the table. His jaw clenched, eyes glaring murder. And before you could leave the table you had to ask.

243

'Why have you come here?' Connie's sister would say, the youngest, a girl of six or seven, spreading jam and watching me intently.

'To see Ray.'

'Not my sister?'

I laughed. She was trying out the power of her directness on me, this kid, edging me into a corner.

'Her as well.'

'Both?'

'That's right.'

'When are you leaving?'

'Oh, I'm not sure.'

'Tomorrow?'

'Oh no, today.'

'Soon?'

'Yes, soon.'

'Why are your lips red?'

In a burst of boldness: 'I've been drinking blood.' And went red to match my mouth as both Connie and her mother lifted their heads, startled, Connie to give me a wide grin and a delighted look and her mother an astounded stare.

'You haven't!' the girl next to me said, screwed right round now in her chair, putting the limelight on me good and proper.

'Been eating jam,' I said, to shut her up.

'You haven't!'

'What then?'

'You've been using lipstick!'

Hoots of laughter from Connie while I brazened it out, not knowing where to look.

'Now you be quiet, young lady,' came from the mother wearily, and she did look really dragged out. She worked full-time in a welfare job, visiting sick and old people, fixing up home-helps for them and so on.

'No.'

244

'Now, Julie,' murmured the father, so gently that it was wafted over the tablecloth and out of the window and nobody noticed.

'Shut it!' barked her brother, Howard, in a tough voice that had the cutting edge of his mother's tongue—and probably the phrase was hers too.

'No,' Julie said, whining a little for her father's benefit. She was his favourite.

Ray changed in company, but not much, not half as much as some people, who seem to take on a new being with each fresh influence. When it's so drastic, it makes you uneasy and you begin to wonder which is the true self, if there is one, or just something fluid in a person that changes to suit whoever they happen to be with. I'm two-faced myself: I do it out of cowardice, to fit in, and from a ridiculous sort of consideration. Being like the others, adapting yourself completely, is like paying them a compliment. I accept you, I don't stand apart, nothing about me is critical, I am one of you: that's what my two-facedness is supposed to mean. There's the cowardice of unsure people who sway to and fro in a flux under every new influence because they're afraid to be left out in the cold, in isolation, and there's my kind of cowardice: on my own and no mistake, but covering up for all I'm worth.

In company Ray would change just sufficiently for me to enjoy a little detachment, so that I could stand back and ask myself what I liked about him. What I loved in Ray above all was his gift of recognition. He was able to see right into me, to what I was, and want me as a friend for that, as a result of that pure swoop: not for what I could do. As a kid at school I used to detest and fear games, sports day, anything that involved picking teams or sides. We'd line up in front of the two captains like slaves at a market auction and they'd choose, first one and then the other:

'Jackerell.'

'Harvey.'

'Roche.'

'I'll have Happy Harris.'

'Dobson.'

Always two of us would be left, me and a lad they called Fatso: the useless and unwanted. Quickly the others were picked off around us, till we stood naked and branded. Crucified by this indifference, I used to search for signs of suffering on Fatso's face, anything that would bind him to me against the others, establish a kinship. All I ever saw was boredom. Finally we'd be assigned to teams, and the shrug of disgust and the thumb hooking us to one slavetrader or another set the seal on our disgrace. Fatso waddled over unmarked, I burned from head to foot.

When the recognition leapt into me, it blotted out the memory of all that. Often a man goes through life without ever being lucky enough to get this from another man. It's the gift that comes with sex, that a woman has. With her intuition she senses what a man is, his essence, the love of her eyes sees it, and then the man can't help loving her for such recognition. Probably it's never put into words, the gratitude, the tenderness, it's a tactile thing: eyes that brush you, a voice stroking, a hand squeezes, and the full embrace in bed isn't so much a fulfilment as a repaying, thanking, an orison of thanksgiving. Thank you, thank you, my buried life thanks you, and your cock buries its head as peacefully as a snake and the sensualist in you begins to purr, your tenderness grows velvety, the cunt puts its odour on you, the woman bites your thanks in half, bites into your lip and you hear a sound in your ears that freezes your blood the first time, as she snaps and writhes and rears on her tail, whinnying like a mare.

The full recognition never came from Leila: nearly but not quite. It drove me frantic, trying to prise it out of her, as if that was possible, but of course she couldn't give it because her

246

husband meant more to her than she thought: more than me, much more. So did the kids. All the same, she must have thought how lovely to be thanked, how nice, and to her it was simply a matter of 'living for the moment' as she called it, being thanked, never fully but it was something, and giving a glancing sort of recognition that was slowly driving me nuts.

That's why I was often reluctant to leave Ray and Connie, why I very often went off with a lump in my throat, because they were complete, thanking and recognizing, and it was such a relief, so peaceful sometimes just standing with them. I drew near to the hearth of their charmed life. Their battles were all to come, fierce marital woundings, when they'd lived together long enough to know weaknesses and secrets, but for the moment the thing was a clear issue, their tiny world of love versus the great insanity, how to survive and come through untainted with the marvellous gifts each had given the other.

16

WE CAUGHT a bus out to a new suburb of Birmingham one Sunday evening and saw *The Long Night*, a film that seemed a confirmation of how it was for them, for me, everybody. Vincent Price the glamorous magician from the other-world, visiting the desolate industrial town, putting dark spells on Barbara Bel Geddes with his soft, sheathed hands—and naturally Henry Fonda was the tragic hero, his lost innocence trapped in a room, loud-hailers and sirens and cops milling outside under the window, riot squads, yelling mobs, then the tear gas bombs came lobbing in, one terrible error after another: all wrong, all wrong. The background music labouring, underlining, filched from Beethoven's Great Monotony. The end. Shuffling out, full right up to the throat with sorrow, a gutful of sorrow, and it hung over the seats like tobacco smoke. I pitied the weak, the sick, and could hardly walk out into the street, where the endless mistakes were joined together in houses, lives, families, births, and led us on mentally from one predicament to another. Then Connie gave a joyful little shout just like a kid, pointing up at the sky. It was sown with stars and flowering like a field of daisies, a miracle of floweriness. Connie knew a bit about constellations, she told us which was Orion. There we stood on the greasy pavement craning our necks, getting curious glances as we let it loiter down and almost listened to it like angelic melody. I suppose we let it seep down into us and feed us, until we each had a bit of interior sky lodged in us like an antidote. It was sheer instinct, a stroke of luck. We ought to have held hands standing there, like the Blessed entering Paradise. Off we went without dragging our feet. Those sort of things were always happening when I was with them—I'd never have managed it on my own.

On my own, the thing that used to pulverize me with dread was the thought of dying before I'd even lived. I don't mean dying young—though that was another fear at one stage—but actually going through the whole of your span without fully living. It was a disgusting and well-known horror for me, this idea of being finished before you'd even started. It terrified me so much I got strength from it, like someone does who goes temporarily mad and thinks there's a conspiracy to kill him off. It forced me to overcome my neurotic fear of people and made me break out, move. Forced me out of the factory, forced me to confront a girl, forced me to put the advert in the art magazine and so meet Leila. Breaking out. I probably came out of the womb like that, in a muck sweat of fear and desperation.

My mother would send me on an errand, say to take some cabbages to a certain address. I'd squirm with real pain, sweat, begin moaning for mercy inside:

'Have I got to go?'

'Now what's the matter? Go on, don't be so daft.'

'What shall I say?'

'I've told you already, you don't have to say anything—Mrs Fay knows all about it, I was talking to her this morning. There's nothing to be ashamed of, is there? We're *giving* her the blasted things, your dad's got them left over from his allotment, he grew too many.'

'Cabbages?'

'Yes, cabbages. He grew too many.'

'I can't say that.'

'You don't have to explain anything—I've told you that.'

'Perhaps they won't want them?'

'Oh go on, before I lose my temper!'

'Can't Alan go?'

249

'No!'

Once out, one thing led to another. You found the street, the house, lifted the knocker and let it fall, the dry bang echoing behind the door, then waited helplessly in torment for things to take their course. I left the factory, wrenched myself out because it had grown safe and warm and cosy as a womb, went into the Labour Exchange and there in a fly-blown display case were the jobs vacant, typed on cards and pinned up: some so ancient that the cards were yellow, the pins rusty. One asked for trainee night telephonists and it sounded all right I thought, smashing: when you were trained you did three evenings, six to eleven, and two nights right through till eight the next morning. More if you wanted. I thought that when I was used to it I'd have all the daylight hours to myself, free. At the interview they tested my hearing, made me put on a headset and take down a few simple messages, and that was it: when can you start? Three months training with pay at their special school. A session was beginning in a fortnight's time, so I settled for that.

The course was simple, just play to begin with: the London exchanges, the codes, manual and automatic boards, trunk and local and continental calls, the charges, funny incidents the instructor remembered and told us about, to keep us interested. It was like being back at school again but without any of the anxiety. Free and easy, cushy—like playing at school. Only half a dozen of us in the class, one quite elderly, one as soft as grease, happy and thick. I was the youngest. We sat in a room next to the temporary public library, a collection of rooms in a building known as the Corn Exchange. The library I'd known before the war was in a huge churchy place near the cathedral, it had stained glass windows and a ceiling so high you didn't remember seeing one, great oak shelves so high you needed ladders, back-to-back on the brown lino, long silent avenues with gaps and junctions—it was like a model city in there. And quiet as the doctor's surgery. I loved to go with Alan and my grandfather, and while he searched for his Edgar Wallaces we'd play tag and hide-and-seek in the maze of shelves and rooms. Sometimes I'd lose my brother completely, hear him creeping round in the distance, right off the track. I'd stand like a statue and smell the books. I liked the dusty smell, I liked finding my grandfather again, and seeing if he was ready, and going out with him through the panelled gates past the high counter, hearing his boots squeak. We'd be on our way to Woolworth's, for ice-cream.

They bombed the library, gutted it, together with the shops and houses, the centre, and now all the town had was a collection of donated books mostly, all kinds of scrapings and offerings, shrunk so small it fitted into this room in the Corn Exchange. The Reading Room and Reference was a mere space partitioned off. I used to dodge in there now and then during the afternoon breaks, while the instructor disappeared for a smoke or a cup of tea. I'd look at stuff like *Horizon* and *Harper*'s and *Life and Letters* and *Blackwood's Magazine*. Dylan Thomas was in his heyday—I kept coming on his poems, big new ones, his lyricism that ripened the apples and made them sound heroic. I'd taste a line here and there and then nip back and sit at my table facing the front as if nothing had happened: innocent as a strawberry glazed in Dylan syrup.

To hear it straight from the horse's mouth, Dylan's regal boom, his elegiac, Eisteddfod-for-the-masses sound, you clicked the knob of the wireless and out it rolled, readings from *Autobiography of a Super-Tramp*, from *Paradise Lost*, Blake and Clare and the *Hound of Heaven*. Such eloquence, flow, the opposite of all I was and the revelation of what I craved, the sorcerer's touch. It reverberated in the heart of my workaday world, gushed into my living-room. I used to watch my parents to see if it was having any visible effect, this extra-ordinary pomp of the soul exhibited for them in private, delivered in person, right on their kitchen table. Would it embarrass them, would it triumph? I heard the ham, the actor's organ-stops being pulled out, but behind the booming high-priest surf was an Old Testament power and glory of the prophet speaking to the earth, a thrilling bardic quaver of naked emotion. How could it fail to fall on stony ground? It was unheard-of, indecent almost, eddying round the chair legs, the toasting fork, brass fender, the ginger cat nuzzling for fleas, flowing into the incongruous vessel of our scruffy interior. 'I like his voice,' said my mother once, startling me, and that was the one and only reaction. Nobody could speak. In the Kardomah off New Street in Brum with Ray and Connie or queuing up with them in the twilight zone, West Bromwich way, to see the *Jolson Story* for the second time, I'd be bursting to really speak but silent, speechless, a foreigner with no language yet, friends who tolerated me because I smiled a lot, they allowed me to stand with them, I was no trouble, they hardly knew I was there—and back home seething with frustration I clicked the knob and began to live vicariously, compensated in a flash, quivering at the sound of my own interior drama being transmitted over the air. Or I conducted a symphony concert if I was left by myself in the house, and later, in another house, in the front room I'd more or less taken over, putting on key records and conducting, nearly dancing with my arms—it was a kind of language I was learning to speak. Whistling my teeth out, writhing and posturing, learning to sing without words, weaving spells like a sorcerer with the tips of my fingers.

The Corn Exchange was where I saw Paul Robeson in a concert one night. It was organized by the trade unions, or at least they were connected with it because a friend at the factory had tickets from his girl whose father was a shop steward. Paul Robeson sat on the platform, officials all round him, and we heard dull speeches and waited, and so did he, hunched in his chair that was too small and pinched him into a queer attitude, not at ease at all. He wore a dark suit and looked gloomy and frowning with his bowed head as if he regretted coming. When he stood up at last I had a shock. He went up and up, a huge figure, and now he was transformed, beautifully relaxed, making a crack about the newspapers 'scandalizing his name' and beaming, this was the cue for his song and he gave it, then for contrast the 'no John' ballad I had on a record. I've never been in an audience before or since that was so rapt and attentive and fraternal. We were all ages. I got as much of a thrill from the audience, the rippling excitement and burst of applause and the laughter flowing spontaneously in response to this massive human being who only had to rise to his feet and bring the house down like Samson—the songs were timed to perfection against the piano, the voice rich as an organ, bubbling up fresh, wrapping you round, teasing, but it was the feeling of intimacy in that packed hall, full of those dull ordinary people, it was the atmosphere I couldn't get over.

17

Now here I was next door, playing at schools. Those first days, while it was still new and tense and we were all eyeing each other and feeling strange I'd think of Robeson that night and his larger-than-nature body, his powerful chest, powerful voice, the whole power and ritual of his presence. And before that, standing outside the same building in the narrow street, end of the war, hearing the fantastic election results read out over the loudspeakers, the landslide that sounded as revolutionary to me as the cheering laughing audience full of fraternal love for one negro on a platform. Nothing had happened, the town hadn't fallen down, Mondays were still grim, but I was sitting here in a new set-up and that was something. I wasn't dead yet. I'd done it myself, made the thing change, shaken the pattern like a kaleidoscope, in spite of my fear of the unknown. And I remember feeling suddenly very pleased with myself, proud.

In any group like this there's nearly always one who's full of wind and piss, and one who asserts himself by sticking his feet up on the table as soon as you're left on your own. We had both these, and a dopey, good-as-gold fellow who had nothing to say but was a pleasure to sit with, very restful, his nature was so unspoiled. He was getting on for forty, used to work on construction gangs building roads and bridges until his health packed up. It was a shame to see Ted screwing up his forehead and struggling with these intricacies when you knew —and it was soon painfully obvious—that he'd never pass the test.

The man I found myself sitting beside, Spinks, was in his fifties I suppose. He was neatly dressed, shirt spotless, but a bit grey and watery around the head, and threadbare, cuffs fraying, collars wearing out, so that his genteel air always struck me as comical. All the same there was nothing pathetic about him—he was too sprightly for that. He'd been a clerk on the railways until they made him redundant; a temporary librarian before that. He had temporary written all over him. 'It's now or never, old man,' he chirruped. 'Got to raise the wind somehow. Pay the rates anyhow, this, eh what? And some cigarette money left over for the old man—with a bit of luck and a following wind. Mustn't grumble.'

'Raise the wind', 'Following wind'—these were from his little stock of catchphrases. They helped to keep out the cold, stoked up his morale. And he had his fantasies, he could confuse the ideal with the actual so easily that I often had the feeling he'd convinced himself. 'I've got a bit of property so I'm lucky,' he'd tell me. Later on, forgetting this, he'd say, 'My wife works, you see, so I'm lucky there.'

He lived at Kenilworth, five miles out, and brought a packet of sandwiches for his lunch, wrapped as carefully as his shirts were ironed and mended. One day I took him home with me and got my mother to give him a cooked meal. She liked him, he was polite, his manners were nice and he told her a little about himself. Sitting there eating and listening, I saw that he had a charm all right.

'What a nice little man,' my mother said afterwards. 'Bring him again if you like.'

But the classroom period was coming to an end and it wasn't long before we were having longer and longer spells on the boards in the Exchange, practical instruction where you had to sit at a place called a position facing the twinkling lights, stringing up cords like spaghetti and scribbling details on the charge pad for invoicing, and these practices split us all up. Instead of the group warmth and gaiety it became a series of solitary ordeals: it wasn't working out like I'd thought at all. I'd spend the whole day until six fighting down butter-flies in my stomach at the thought of all those phones waiting to burst into life and light up my board with a tangle of voices, every one a problem. When the time came to go on it was an agony like stage fright I had to overcome. It got a bit better as I became quicker, and as the clock crept round to ten and eleven and things went slack. Then out of boredom I'd plug into a courting couple here and there, hoping for some fun. Long silences there'd be, perhaps a cough or a loud breath to encourage you to hang on, and exchanges like:

'Are you there, love?'

'Yes.'

'Why don't you say something?'

And it was awful, the poor devil would be racking his brains, you could almost hear him, so you stopped eaves-dropping and slipped the switch over as noiselessly as you could and left him to it. The supervisor who strolled up and down behind your back with a handset ready to sort out tangles, he told me one night about the anonymous calls the girls had to put up with during the day, a voice out of the blue whispering in their ear 'I'd like to fuck you', or worse, and the drill was to try and keep them talking while the call was traced, so that the police could rush a car round. It sounded pretty hopeless to me. Apart from anything else, supposing they got there in time and managed to grab some-body, what did that solve? The supervisor stood over me like a detective, big shoulders, big voice, and he wasn't in any doubt at all, no problem: that type ought to be castrated. Imagine a daughter of your own picking up a call like that, he said. There was such a brisk sound to his voice, nothing emotional, that it was clear he wasn't as involved as his words implied: it was the proper stance, official line. I agreed with him that it was a nasty business and all that. My own sex was as underground and furtive as the faceless man's in the booth.

I wasn't fit to judge. If it was a problem, it was part of a much bigger problem and you wouldn't solve that with a knife, couldn't castrate it. It kept growing like a cancer.

When I think of the fairytales I used to dream up, going to and fro on my bike through the grey streets with my cock stiffening like a joystick, dream after dream and no outlet, it was a wonder I didn't burst into flame. Rain or shine, nothing could turn me off. At one time I was working on the delicate problem of how to persuade a woman to let you touch her breasts. I'd no idea they actually liked it, some of them. Marriage couldn't possibly include this, I thought. I decided that what I'd do when I was married, I'd forge a letter from the doctor—and magically the letter started to form in my head—to say that it was necessary for the husband to massage her there: that would do it. 'Dear Mrs Patten . . .' Naturally this was laughable but it enabled me to visualize the scene, make it come true, so I pedalled along steering through the dream and getting hot and stiff with an imaginary wife who was reluctant but had to obey orders, yank up her striped jersey—I saw a French magazine once in Leicester Square, a girl flat on her back with her striped sailor jersey rolled up round her neck—and show me, the husband-doctor, her milk-and-cornflour tits, each one balancing a raspberry. My tits. Owned by me. I nearly went under a lorry, it was so real. How this didn't end up in a bout of masturbating I'll never understand, but it didn't, not until I was working as a clerk and had met Leila. She started me off, and she was that way inclined herself. Always had been, apparently. So I couldn't return the compliment. When my hand went up her clothes I suppose she felt perfectly at home. Standing against a tree or pushed back against a wall she'd work away at my flies, unbuttoning, and being a romantic she kept her eyes tight shut. No need to jerk me off, it happened of its own accord; the kissing was enough. The imagination. Then back at home I'd soon be

257

wanking away for dear life. I did it everywhere, in the bath, the pictures, lavatory, and it was never any good. Always the bitter aftertaste, a mixture of guilt from the days when to masturbate made you insane and your teeth dropped out and the only thing worse was getting the pox, and guilt because it was underground sex, mind-sex, and rage and fear at the waste, your own seed slopping into the pan like piss and shit, useless as that. The feeling was rubbed in by the guilty things you had to do, making sure the slime ran down the plug-hole with the water: it was liable to get left behind, long tell-tale threads for your mother to see. I think though if I'd had to bash away at myself, that would have been the end: I did that once, jerking away like a maniac, harder and harder, till I was disgusted. It was horrible, pointless, mechanical as hell, like pumping out bilge water. In a bath was easiest with a soapy hand cupped into a socket. You lay back in the hot water and just lathered the ball—when I found that out and felt like masturbating at work or anywhere I'd lock myself in a lavatory and spit in the palm of my hand. Gob and rub.

I was amazed when Leila told me she'd done it for years in her teens: it hadn't occurred to me that girls and women went in for things like that too. No shame either with her, it was a fact and that was that. She laughed and said, 'I was always playing with my pussy in those days.' I was never sure with her, she loved to shock, it was a way of rejecting the cut-and-dried little housewife world she was compelled to live in, and as well as that I often felt she was saying things to excite me— and perhaps herself. As soon as the subject of her pussy came up, though it followed on naturally from what she was saying about girlhood and guilt, the adults who didn't want to hear about sex, who would have died of shame if they'd known of her solitary pleasures—I wondered as soon as she mentioned it if it was for a reason, if the warm sun and the proximity had made her runny. Why now? We sat on the scorched grass in the park, her back was resting against my chest as I leaned on the rough bark of the elm, a tree as wide as a wall, its giant erection keeping us both supported. There we sat innocently sunning ourselves near the public path and the Sunday morning parade wandered by, prams and mothers and boys licking knobs of ice-cream, and brawny white-shirted workers, a sauntering procession. She was wedged between my open legs, hips sunk deep in my crotch and I squeezed gently with the insides of my thighs as if embracing her fondly, in full daylight, full view, without attracting the slightest attention. She started talking about her pussy, dwelling on the subject I thought, and my fingers itched to find out if she was wet; I stirred and grew and got hard, jammed there in paradise against the small of her back. Couldn't she feel it, prodding her like a tree, roaring with spunk and blood like the sap of the tree, rooted in my groin and billowy with heat? She made an imperceptible movement of her mare's arse, a hot twitch of her tail as if a horse fly was nibbling at her lasciviously. My spunk shot out into my trousers, the hard lump at her back melted slowly, I felt bitterly ashamed for an instant and then the shame floated away tender as the leaves, soft as the breeze.

Another thing she said—another wicked and merry laugh—was that if she ever wrote a book about herself she'd have to call it *The Long Masturbation*. Which was exactly how I felt the first time I did it at work, at the Corporation job, and slunk back up the stairs and through the boss's sanctum to the room in the attics at the side of the building, wondering if it was obvious, if I looked white and shagged, black rings round my eyes. I felt that about the age I was living in, the twentieth century, machine-age civilization, these three clerks bricked up and working away like deathwatch beetles in a weird ticking activity, questioning nothing and it was full summer, the grubby windows were squares of glory—it was one big masturbation from start to finish. I was a prime example, in the right place. I loathed myself, then the place, then my workmates, then the time, the age, masturbating itself day and night week in and week out including Sundays, wanking out the roads and railways, jerking up the towns, factories, offices, crematoria, tossing off the traffics, the wars, the murders. I'd sit there feeling squalid and soiled right through like a dirty old man, unable to look anybody in the eye. But it's insane to lump everything and everybody into a principle, a symbol, and that's what I was doing: gibbering away inside myself. You can't go on living like that without point; no hope, no faith. What seems to save you when you crawl around in the dirty bilges where I was is usually a stupid remark, or a fart, anything, and you begin to focus and you see human beings again in ones and twos. Each one a world. Unfathomable. That brings you back. I used to go through the market sometimes and notice faces, shapes, colours, sounds of people, say on a Saturday morning when it was really swarming and Asiatic. Endless, staggering variety, and it either comforts you and you think how marvellous, nothing's fixed, anything can happen— anything at all—or you go half mad at the thought of all those lives, all those writhing full households, those problems, all those blind pushing snouts at the trough, all got to die, and it seems a nightmare and a gigantic screaming mistake. Running rampant, heading straight for death and nobody dares mention it or point or stop for a second to consider. Keep hating, keep eating, keep talking. Tomorrow, tomorrow, no shortage of tomorrows.

The puffy clerk behind me, Danny Spears, would hiss:
'Andy?'
'Hallo.'
'What did he say then?'
'Who?'
'Old slobberchops. Bighead. Shitface out there.'

260

'Oh him, he's on about the paysheets again. Thinks it might speed things up a bit if we did what he said.'

'Cheeky bastard! What did you say then?'

'Nothing. He knows what I think of his bloody brainwaves.'

'Cheeky sod. Let him ask me, that's all.'

'What you gonna say?'

'Say? I'll say plenty—just let him ask me!'

He'd be referring to a fellow clerk in the next office, on the same level as them but hated for his habit of suggesting improvements, sticking his nose in at every opportunity, and according to Spears it was all a means of crawling up the boss's arsehole. He'd been an airman during the war and come out a warrant officer. He sat bolt upright at his desk, sleeves rolled back and arranged in exact folds if it was summer, his pens and pencils set out in parade-ground order on either side of his snowy pad of blotting paper, like a place setting in a restaurant. I must admit I didn't care for him either, though he made a point of being smarmily pleasant to me, as he did to everybody. His name was Wilkinson—there it was in black letters in a dinky little holder, like a bank clerk's. He was an early bird, always the first one there, opening the windows, unlocking the boss's filing cabinet, having a sly look at his newspaper. Spears had to come past him to reach his den and once I saw him skipping past light as a feather while Wilkinson's back was turned, so as not to have to say good morning. The feud had been on long before I got there—perhaps for years. I liked to hear friend Spears laying down the poison in tale after tale, nearly frothing at the mouth. It livened things up for me. His pal Andy, a big slow character who smoked a pipe, was more or less an ally, but the subject didn't jerk his arms out or make him hiss like a snake. That wasn't his style. The thing was, Spears was a fanatic by nature. Get him on the subject of hanging or homosexuals and quick as a flash he'd be out of his seat and springing about in front of you, hopping up and down as if the floor was red hot, jabbing holes in the air with his podgy finger, face twisted with malice, tongue scalding and venomous. He looked and sounded absolutely cracked, spittle bubbling at the corners of his mouth—and then right on the brink he stopped, righted himself, switched over to a joke, laughing in a twitchy, feathery sort of way: it was grotesque, so rapid, and you began to wonder if you'd heard properly, if the whole outburst had been a joke of some kind. No, it wasn't. He had it in for the queers and Wilkinson to the same degree, they were the two hates of his life, it looked like. Say one little thing in favour of either and he'd be spitting and sizzling maliciously, working himself up to a war dance.

18

WE WERE in a converted warehouse, right on the pavement at the front and at the back a yard for transport, temporary sheds and rotting outhouses and Nissen huts like tunnels full of building materials, where the labourers assembled and clocked in and out. There were no cycle sheds, I had to lean my bike against a wall furthest away from the lorries, leave it there dangling a padlock and chain and bring the pump in with me. One day Wilkinson got permission from the boss to carry his new bike upstairs and park it in our room, just inside the door where there was a blank bit of brick wall distempered the usual diarrhoea colour. Danny Spears nearly threw a fit when he came in and saw it propped there, maroon and glistening, new-minted, the saddlebag still swinging ever so slightly. It had the fascination of a time-bomb: the rest of us were all primed for his reaction, Andy giving me a broad wink and then ducking his head as the door opened.

'Now—what—the——?' Spears said, very soft because the inner door was still open. He nipped over and shut it, then came back flicking pop-eyed looks at each of us in turn, as if we were having him on. His eyes were blue, with sharp points.

'It's Wilko's,' Andy said, dry as a judge.

Spears was stuttering with excitement. 'I—I know . . . I know who *owns* the bastard thing, but how the . . .'

'How the what?' drawled his pal, not batting an eyelash. He was as laconic as his friend was frantic.

'I mean, why should *we* have his fucking steed? Eh—eh? Why us? Let him clutter up his own shithouse—eh? Don't you agree? What a sauce that bastard's got, my Christ! Let him stick it in there, why not, it's like a bloody dustbin as it is. Why should he make our office into a cycle shed for Christ's sake? Isn't that bloody marvellous, it is, it's typical of that twat, I'm buggered if it isn't.' He simmered down a little, and gave the back tyre a contemptuous tap with his toe. 'Well, bugger me gently.'

'The boss said he could.'

'That twat, he'd say anything to avoid an argument.'

'You can always let the tyres down.'

Spears was at his desk behind me, I could hear him scrabbling at papers. He spluttered:

'I'll do more than that, Christ yes—I'll set fire to it! Here, who's got a razor—I'll carve a little message for him on his front tyre! Look at that lovely red paint, not a blemish, look at it. Immaculate. Who's got a sharp pin—I'll scratch Merry Christmas on his bastard crossbar.'

What a contrast to his itchy spite and menace, his seething irritation, when I took an application form down to the yard for one of the Irish labourers to fill in. Usually it was as much as they could do to write their own name, let alone remember their age or what date they were born. Most of them were old enough to be my father, yet because I appeared from 'up there' with a printed form, had a fountain pen, clean white hands and collar to match, I was treated with great respect. I was the lowest of the low, the office boy, didn't they know that? I'd be shamed by their humility and ashamed of the stupid nosey questions I had to ask. What was your last job? Why did you leave? And the job before that? What made you leave that one? Back and back, probing. I was so half-hearted about it, so apologetic, they'd stop trying to fox me sometimes and say point-blank they couldn't remember. I'd scribble notes here and there in pencil and when I went upstairs to ink the thing in I'd invent all the missing stuff, dates, reasons, even jobs. Some had been in prison for a spell but they didn't say so, naturally: it was always the merchant navy, that period.

The part that most disgusted me was their habit of calling anybody who seemed to represent authority 'sir'. It was a kind of insurance, I realized later.

'This is a lot of red tape, I know,' I'd tell them lamely. 'It's only a formality . . . I think that's everything. I'm afraid I've got to ask you to sign in two places, down here on this line and on the other side, here, if you don't mind.'

'I can't write, sir,' one elderly bloke said, and earlier, when I'd asked him his date of birth he'd said, 'I'm fifty-eight, work it out for yourself.'

If they couldn't write, I had to ask them to make their mark. They'd clutch my fountain pen in a calloused fist as if it was a cold chisel and scratch a big X: even that was painful, an effort. Just watching them struggle to drag the strange inky spike over the paper made you sweat. I used to wonder afterwards, staring at their mark, if it was better or worse being in that state of ignorant bliss. How did they manage though in this world, how did they cope with the forms, the bills, the coupons? Did they get shoved around or did it protect them, not being able to read or write? They were in another life, and the way it slowed them down, the acceptance it gave them, fascinated me whenever I brushed against it.

Cecil, the deaf old man upstairs, sitting right at the back of the office out of the way, our silent colleague, he must have been in another life too. He was stumpy, still vigorous, his skin like a lizard's, eyes rolling up into his head and he had a charlie on his back, I suppose with so much crouching over a desk. Though he hadn't been long a clerk, so I gathered: he was a cobbler by trade, and the shop where he worked had modernized, so they gave him the push: too slow. Here he had jobs where he could take his time—thumping at wage slips with a date stamp and filing pay sheets and making the tea. He was cut off from the flow of gossip and at first I assumed he was just a tetchy old bugger who didn't want to talk. Then

265

one day a typist came in and he was rattling away to her in a loud voice, like the deaf do, telling her his life story almost. 'I'm going on me holidays you see, duck, and I lost me wife last year—oh yes—so I'm on me own. I'm going down to Devon and I can't take the dog can I—well not really, land-ladies won't have dogs at no price, so me sister says she'll look after him with pleasure. Funny thing isn't it with animals, I'm very fond of it and I suppose it becomes part of the family— well they do don't they? Me sister'll look after him all right— I've got three sisters, yes. The one who's having the dog is married, she lives at West Brom. Only the other day she said why don't you come and live with us now you're on your own. It's a big thing, shifting at my age. Course there's a lot more goin' on at Birmingham, oh yes—a lot more life. Nothing much here, not for young folk that is. I'm old, I ain't bothered now. This suits me, this place. Been here all me life. Born here. So was me father. Funny, in' it?'

Another life for him. And on those summer mornings when I slipped out across the road and through the little park— supposed to be in the lavatory or seeing a labourer or posting some letters at the corner—and it was June, they'd cut the grass and there was a haymaking smell betraying you back to the idyllic camps of childhood, *that* was another life, even in the middle of town. I'd walk up Cannon Street and breathe deeply, dive into the cool shadows of a bookshop so small and carrying such a stock that you literally burrowed your way into the dusty heart of it like a maggot in a slab of cheese. I remember picking up a book of reproductions of paintings by an artist called Jack Bilbo—and I nearly started an avalanche, a couple of dozen books fell down. That put the spotlight on me and ruined the pleasure, because I never bought anything in those days, there was too much to choose from. I cleared up the mess and came back another day. The book drew me, none of it in colour either, which was crazy, but it didn't seem to matter—I read titles like 'Woman in a Yellow Hat' and the fat brushfuls of grey paint coloured themselves in my head. I was starting to paint for myself at home without any lessons, and in these reproductions it looked terribly easy and happy, carefree, the very opposite of all I'd known, all I was. It looked as if this Bilbo whoever he was—I think he lived on a boat—had got hold of a broom or a mop, stuck it in a bucket of pigment and simply swooshed it round in joyful curves and arabesques. I stared at the pictures so long I forgot the time—they liberated me like Picassos only in a more human, more accessible way. He didn't awe you, this man, there was nothing godlike about him—he probably couldn't even draw but it didn't stop him from enjoying himself, a big bearded child voyaging backwards to the beginning. Then I woke up with a jolt: wandered out casually, nice and slow and dreamy, then ran like hell downhill and across the road into work. Up the stairs two at a time, hovering on the landing while I steadied myself for a few seconds, heart pounding. Nobody said anything—old Cecil was waiting like a Buddha for the tea to mash in his big teapot with its two handles, Andy unwrapping his snack.

19

AND IT was another life at Symonds Yat, where Ray was living now. His descriptions were coming at me thick and fast, seductive reports packed with detail and yet somehow I couldn't picture it, which was queer. But the virginity of the place, that I did get, and their babe, brown as an owl, the grassy shelf they were perched on, high over a ribbon of river running white along the valley bottom, and trees, trees, tingling green in new leaf, full of thrushes and owls and squirrels, kestrels hanging over the chasm, a train like a toy chuffing out of a hole in the cliffside and threading along an invisible single track sunk deep in the bracken, going to earth again and leaving a sock of white smoke behind, lassoing the bushes with a shriek of its whistle. I could imagine it, as you'd imagine a place like Shangri La. And Ray was painting big turbulent pictures on rough hessian in the open air outside the bus, quoting Cézanne's credo to me—'I want to paint the world's virginity.' I'd sit doodling on scraps of paper when things were slack, using Andy's bald bowed head and hunched shoulders as a model, or the dirty windowframe, the tin roofs of the yard buildings, not bothering to hide these scribbles but acting as if it was my hand that was drawing, not me, wrist slack and eyes glazed in a bored expression. That way I could get quite a few drawings done unnoticed: red ink, blue biro, pencil. Not bad at all some of them turned out. Good enough to take to Shangri La and show Ray when the time was ripe. At home up in the boxroom I'd tried watercolours and oils, just stirring the paint into faces and figures like a child finding out, letting figures have no bones and squashed tomato heads if they wanted: putting the clock back. But still a bit rotten with knowledge and adulthood, seduced already by eyefuls of the masters in those glossy art books in bookshops in New Street, Birmingham: the baleful innocent Rouault, bible colours smouldering between bars of black; Vincent's scrawled signals, cries of loneliness, cries for help, his heart bare; Nolde the wild man, daubed in blood, dipping his world in the rainbow, painting eyes like eggs smashed on the pavement.

Then at last actually bold enough, cheeky enough to go into Boots and buy a stretched canvas, unsullied, carry it back wrapped in brown paper and unwrap it upstairs in secret, in the boxroom. I knew exactly what I wanted to do: paint a Cecil. Not the actual Cecil—an anonymous, international, universal Cecil. A poor man, a legendary human being sitting on a kitchen chair, telling his story without uttering a word. Resignation, defeat, bewilderment—acceptance. It was a Saturday afternoon. By Sunday he was in occupation, sitting collapsed on his chair looking stunned, wide-eyed and helpless, staring at me reproachfully as if he couldn't forgive me for bringing him to birth. I was hypnotized. To make it simpler for myself I'd arranged it so that his legs were apart and his sausage fingers splayed over his kneecaps, like an old photo I'd seen of my grandfather. He could easily have been my grandfather as a young man. My mother kept calling up the stairs that my dinner was on the table but it was no good, I was held by those gormless eyes and swollen hands, by his tragic boots planted on the bare boards, oozing weariness, hard labour.

'So that's it,' said my mother, at the door.

'I'm coming down now.'

'Who is he?' my mother said, not even looking at me.

'No idea—ask him.'

'He looks too sad to speak.'

'Think so?'

'Well, look at him!'

269

'He's struck dumb.'

'Oh is that it,' my mother said. Then she added thoughtfully, 'You know, he reminds me of somebody. Who is it?'

'I made him up.'

'Uncle Albert!'

'Who?'

'You wouldn't know him—he died before you were old enough to remember.'

'Call him that then,' I said. 'Good a name as any.'

'Albert,' my mother said, closing the door after me. 'Cheerio, Albert.'

The name stuck. It was the only painting of mine that appealed to my mother, so she was constantly referring to it. 'I like Albert,' she'd say, faced with the murky incomprehensible daubs I kept turning out. 'Why don't you paint some more like that?'

They were legion, these Alberts, the uncles and half uncles and cousins my mother would remember at odd moments— she'd cast back and retrieve them, on they'd strut, their whole dead world appearing with them, resurrected by her few words. Albert, the one I'd never set eyes on, he was loopy but harmless: he had a habit of creeping down the entry and poking his head over the gate all of a sudden, nearly giving my mother heart failure. He wouldn't come any further apparently, he was too timid. If she moved out of the kitchen, even so much as lifted the door latch, he went galloping off on his long spindly legs like a giraffe. 'Oh it was a shame,' my mother said. 'He looked so awful, such a sight, his collar all twisted and dirty, nobody looking after him. Wasn't it awful to see him, John?' I asked what had happened to him and it seems he'd gone off to London and nobody knew if he was alive or dead. There was a legend that he had a lot of money tucked away— nobody knew for sure. As well as these cracked and missing relatives it was a time when strangers came to the door in a steady stream, hardly a week without someone knocking or materializing, an apparition, a scarecrow—I'd listen as she told us and I'd remember a few myself, I was at the tail-end of it in my childhood. End of the twenties. The tramps asking for mashings, bread, holding out smoked billycans, the out-of-work navvies begging old shirts, trousers, boots, the gypsies— my mother was pitying and our house must have been marked as a soft touch: the word had gone round. I'd listen to her and think, here's a woman who's gone nowhere, done nothing, stayed timid at home by her own hearth, in the town where she was born, yet all this life flowed up to the back door, these waifs and strays, lame dogs, loopy buggers, all hitting her over the heart and getting a response.

At least two of these uncles, if that's what they were, I remembered clearly myself: Sammy Mann, very religious, and Uncle Jack, his stinking mangy old dog always behind him like a shadow. Uncle Jack was a belly and a wheeze, and of one time only—Sunday morning at eleven, trundling in, stick and dog and ten-to-two feet, on his way back from the cemetery and his wife's grave to the pub. His Sunday constitutional. Lowering himself down into the big armchair in the window, and the chair grabbed him, he was stuck. Asked if he'd like a cup of tea, he had barely enough wind to gasp, 'Yes, please, Nell.' Now and then his boots creaked. As a kid I used to marvel at his vast bulk, its dignity and authority in the navy blue serge suit, great flapping trousers, great girth: unanswerable authority, and at the same time utter helplessness. Face sweating, broad, shaggy over the eyes, tufted huge red ears, mouth reeking of tobacco. A mountain of inertia, and what a contrast to Sammy Mann, who was small and tough and stringy, a building labourer, but all spirit, almost gliding, lifting with the heavenly gas in his guts. And yet grounded forever by comical, lovable Cherry Blossom boots, huge and black and twinkling in the heavenly firelight of those Sunday

271

evenings, Sammy's time. A saintly, supremely happy man, a bachelor, untouched by his life of hardship, saved when a young man in an evangelist's tent in Bridge Street and ever since his face had shone beaming like a lighthouse. 'Here's Sammy coming!' and a groan would go up, his voice was the most monotonous droning I'd ever heard. In the end it was just too much, you were actually gritting your teeth, until he slid out his watch on to the palm of his hand and quavered joyfully, same words at exactly the same time: 'Well, folks, I'd better be making tracks!' And when next Sunday came we always knew when to expect him—on his way back from evening service.

Ray would tell me that his own childhood was almost devoid of relatives—and it struck me then that I must have been giving the wrong impression, as if mine was thick with them, milling round feverishly like characters in a Russian novel. It might have been more like that if my mother had been gregarious, but she was timid, shrinking, outraged if my father brought somebody in from the street who'd called at the door —as he was inclined to do. 'Now what did you do that for— you know I *hate* it!' she'd rage. 'Look what a mess everywhere —why don't you think?—oh you make me sick, you really do. I've told you dozens of times not to do things like that.' And he'd sigh and glare madly and be on the point of exploding, as she dug away at him. His nature was utterly different, welcoming, and so his crime was inexplicable: he couldn't grasp it, ever, what he'd done wrong. The privacy mania, keeping yourself to yourself, minding your own business, speaking when you're spoken to, it was completely alien to him, all that. He would pass the time of day with anyone, get involved in long conversations with absolute strangers, go up to anybody, a man with his head under the chassis of a car, men fishing along the canal. 'Any luck?' he'd say cheerfully to the fisherman. 'Got some ground bait down?' And doing this usually as we were on the point of leaving, packed and

272

ready, a bus to catch. My mother would be fretful yet indulgent, and I'd worry and feel ashamed—'What if they'd come here for some peace and quiet, what if they didn't want to talk?'—worrying about their privacy. Later I'd react violently in the other direction, exasperated by my mother's neurotic fear of intrusion, scurrying back into her stifling little barricaded house and shutting the door, refusing to be in contact. They had planted both these extremes in me, I veered from one to the other, compromising: shutting myself up alone in the boxroom, cosy and womb-like, or in bed in the warm byre of the sheets drawn up in the foetal position, curled round next morning with my head right out of sight, submerged—and responding to Ray, eager to match his sudden impulses, wild desires, wanting to move across the land and through towns, over England in a sweeping restless mood, to possess our heritage in one go, gulp it down and then see the bigger, outside world, break out of the island life.

20

BEFORE Ray was courting I went on a trip to North Wales
with him—he belonged to the Youth Hostels but not me, so
he borrowed a mate's membership card for me to use and we
set off, me with a steel-frame Bergen rucksack that spread the
load on my back and made me feel top-heavy and lumbering
like a grizzly. On the train it was change at Brum, change at
Ruabon, border country. Asking there about our next stop,
Llangollen, the ticket collector corrected our pronunciation—
to say Llangollen meant saying 'th' with the tongue dragged
back between the teeth in a sort of slobber. Waiting in
Ruabon for the connection, wandering past the doll-like
cottage gardens we practised aloud and got a little hysterical,
it sounded so funny. Then at Llangollen we were really in
Wales we told each other, staring intently at the hills and
valleys looking for differences from old England, tramping
over the bridge and on up the road in grand style, meeting a
postman and greeting him, saying 'afternoon' so as to hear his
accent, thrilling, the green hills and stone fences and irregular
small fields, the white torrents coming with us, new as us,
fresh as us, all the way to Corwen and our first hostel.

Inside, the warden's waiting for us at a green card table,
looking up expectantly at us approaching, as if he knew we
were coming and who we were, and Ray gives him our cards
and we pay for supper, bed and breakfast: very cheap because
it's not run for profit, an association for the young in heart of
all ages. As long as you don't roll up in a car or on a motorbike you can use the place. Dormitories for men and women,
separate, and next morning after breakfast you're expected to
lend a hand at some task for half an hour or so, say peeling

274

spuds or brushing the floor. That's fine, and hikers are trickling in, it's more or less arrival time. 'Mr Adams?' the warden says, holding out a card. I look blank, then it dawns that I'm Adams for tonight. 'Thanks—oh—thanks very much.'

On next day to Bettws-y-Coed and Capel Curig at the head of Llanberis Pass, a long trek of nearly thirty miles to cover in one day, and trudging on into the heat of noon the landscape changes steadily round us until at last we notice and gasp in appreciation and sit down at the verge to take it in properly, this amazing lugubrious world of stones, a ridge of rocks on the horizon going up and down in a jagged, desolate profile. And meeting nobody, nothing. A few sheep near the road munching at the peat. My feet have begun to blister and rub sore at the heels, I can hear a stream bubbling on the other side of the wall but I'm afraid to take off my shoes in case my feet swell up. Hobble into a chaotic little garden of a cottage that looks abandoned but there's a sign—'Tea and home-made cakes' and a dry old girl with a grey moustache and short bandy legs in twisted stockings sits us down in her tiny parlour, talking to us from her kitchen. As well as the baking odour, I can smell the damp. The cottage smells of dug-up earth, of leaf mould around tree roots in a damp wood, of wet bricks.

'Is this your first time in Wales then?'

'Yes, it is.'

'Is it really now!'

And she comes out from her kitchen-cave smiling, carrying a tray and looking us over with her small jumpy eyes. We sit feeling what we are, strangers, outlandish, too big for the furniture. I wind my legs under the chair, fill my mouth with warm floury lopsided scones. Outside on the slate path, leaving, some hens in a rotting shed move their scrawny necks and give us the same look for strangers, eyes ringed by red flesh.

On the road again, tramp, tramp, my feet giving me hell now, the barren ridge of the horizon unchanging. We watch a summer storm gather over it and rain falling, the black crust of the sky ripped open on the peaks, then clearing and bright again.

'Think you'll make it?' Ray asks, anxious.

'How far?' I say grimly, too sore to bother about sounding cheerful.

'Seven or eight miles.'

A car is buzzing up slowly behind us. Ray thumbs it hopefully and it stops. Going to Bettws-y-Coed, a middle-aged couple, Welsh. Any good? Oh very good. Sitting in the back bemused by comfort we only seem to have time to exchange greetings, express gratitude and the town slips around us, waterfalls and pretty glen on the left, leaves and lattices, shoppers, coaches, the swaying tops of bushes, foaming green trees. Out we climb, and the road takes us up in a long slow climb, three or four miles out of the town and towards the mountains, to our next hostel at the mouth of the pass. On the last mile we pass a tall thin girl in shorts, long bleached legs, with a heavy rucksack on her narrow shoulders and it's bending her forward cruelly. What we can't understand is why the young fellow tossing back his glossy black hair as he strolls beside her isn't carrying much except a knapsack—the sort of thing they had for gasmasks in the war. In the dormitory at night he says of his own accord, this dandy in his royal blue silk pyjamas with a languishing Oxford voice, that the gangling girl friend shoulders his rucksack because he has a weak heart. Now the burden's at the foot of his bed, he forages and unearths two alarm clocks, sets one half an hour later than the other and explains again, sidling the words out seductively: 'I sleep rather heavily.' Next day marching on down the pass, barren slagheaps of black mountains towering round, slate monsters reared at the whales of clouds, ripping at the sky's

276

soft underbelly—feeling like men on the moon we christen our friend of last night James Mason, he has his looks and voice approximately but it's the clubman sophistication we're thinking of, that makes us laugh. In this savage stonescape—silk pyjamas. We can't stop laughing. Until the gloom and grandeur sobers us, forces silence on us—a chilly wind springs up, ahead we can see the road vividly springing and twisting like a live thing on the strewn floor of the pass. To hear how it sounds we quote bits of Thomas Wolfe out loud: 'O lost and by the wind grieved, ghost . . .' Oh Christ my feet, I moan, so we laugh again, nervously, feeling spectral suddenly. It is wonderful though, the non-human world we are passing through. Nothing grows, hardly anything can live, only pass through and acknowledge the majesty. We are youth, chock-full of every potentiality, sad and arrogant with so much, yet nothing here and less than nothing, bundles of holes the wind whistles through. Uneasy, we step it out, feeling suddenly oppressed, all at once badly stricken, needing to see other human beings.

And on down the coast by easy stages, catching local buses, to the hostel at Harlech we've ringed round on the map. More breathtaking grandeur as we arrive, step down and take in the great sweep of the coast, the tufted dunes and white sand down below us, and a golf course down there, and rusty single tracks of the railway along the edge of the dunes, the shabby wooden halt: us perched over it, high up and birdlike, eyes drawn irresistibly by the glossy swag of sea and then aware and turning to admire the ring of mountains behind, the superb location of the castle down to the right, walls thick enough for sightseers to walk on in safety without losing their nerve—we can actually see them doing it. Our hostel is a bay-windowed suburban villa, complete with privet and an air of stuffy seclusion, as we climb up the steep twist of street and reach its vantage point, looking down on the bumpy roofs, sagging patched slates, stone cottages leaning and lurching in cold sombre alleys, snatches of Welsh seeping out of windows, under doors, the first we'd heard, and out beyond and far below, far out, the vast blue panorama of the bay and washing seas that the planted ramparts of the castle had once lorded over.

Crowing to each other, congratulating ourselves on being in this place, feeling wonderful in the last wash of sun, in we go and find the house is a bit rambling, knocked about, peeling once we're in, not forbidding as at a distance. Next day at twelve we're leaving, sitting on rough granite steps of a defunct fountain opposite the Co-op on the main road, having a snack of dates and cheese, gnawing and chewing ruminatively as the traffic whisks by, on down the coast. The night before the hostel had filled up and by the time we sat down at the trestle tables before the heaps of sausage and beans and mash there was barely room for us all there in long rows with our elbows tucked in, considerate. Everybody in good spirits, a shade too robust and healthy for me mostly, gleaming white teeth and shining eyes, almost callous with health, insolent with it like a crowd of athletes, but all friendly and swopping destinations, travel news, discoveries in a kind of jamboree atmosphere. In the dormitory the same, all one, but in the morning it seems illusory and you see them glued together in groups and pairs again, a little distant though still smiling across the gulfs, touching each other with farewell calls, good mornings, bon voyages as the communism visibly crumbles. In the street we mill at the gate and the remaining knots are cut, the morning light painlessly dissolves us. Off we go, rejoicing and single, light and airy. What a vision of physical freedom, swimming down the tilted streets in that bath of space. Natives pass us on the way up, labouring old women with shopping bags, a young mother with two children, girls, who screw their heads round and stare frankly at our loads, our foreigner-looks, and their mother tells them in a sharp voice to stop it as we swim past strong-hearted with plunging thighs and our eyes on the glassy bright sea, the terrific coast castle dreaming huge on its bluff of rock high in the yellow air, giving you a strange jolt every time you see it. A Rip van Winkle castle, fortifying the interior in its sleep.

21

IT WAS as fresh and good as that at Symonds Yat, visiting Ray for the first time, but entirely different, apart from the absence of ocean, because now Ray was a Crusoe, they were a family of Crusoes, natives themselves, and I'd roll up as a foreigner: welcome but still a visitor, passing through like a tourist, looking, not knowing the seasons like them or the changing light, the stirring life and secrecy of their hideout among the trees. Leaving them was bitter, like being turned out of paradise. It did literally seem like that, and again that was an illusion only a tripper like me could have and suffer from. They had the reality, money to find, jobs, signing on for the dole, the kid yelling for no reason, condensation from the tin roof of the bus dripping down on the beds: the virginal aspect that so overwhelmed me and was the whole of it for me, they had as a compensation. It was still marvellous, but reality was biting into it, diminishing the wonder. Because Ray couldn't find work, Connie was having to slave as a waitress in a riverside restaurant that opened up for the summer season. 'Since Tuesday she has been going out at 8.30 a.m. and coming back at 9.30 p.m., six days a week, for three quid a week. Now I know we are hard up. Across the river she is setting about fifty places for dinner while a lanky red-faced ex-army bastard manages to be the perfect uncouth manager. They say two hours off a day and two off for meals (she's not long been up and gone down again). Biggest swindle you ever saw. Just before nine at night I get Leo out of bed and in his pram and plunge through the pitch black forest halfway down that path to the station. It's like being blindfolded. The ground drops away under my feet, the pram starts pulling me over the edge.

Across the river I can see the blaze of light from the restaurant. At the point where it's impossible to go further with the pram I wait for a light to start moving down the far hillside. That'll be Con with her lamp. Then the ferry has to get her across. And at last I hear somebody coming up, a light flashing everywhere. She reaches me half dead with the climb, the darkness and the work.'

The reality of these letters, the hardship at the back of them, never sank into me, only the excitement of knowing this couple and admiration for what they were doing, their single-handed passage. What a way to live. Andy had an A.A. handbook on his desk and I leafed through the maps and then pored over the Wye Valley one as if it was an unexplored region, dark continent. Found the wriggling thread of river, and Monmouth, Ross-on-Wye, and then their place, Symonds Yat. By a town-village called Coleford, and when I booked a seat on a coach, change at Cheltenham, stretch your legs out in the snooty still streets, gaze up at the wrought-iron balconies— it was Coleford I had on my ticket as a destination. I'd turn up with a very small ridge tent in my rucksack, Ray and Connie and babe in the pushchair lined up at the bus stop waiting, full reception committee, waving when they caught sight of me at the window. Brown and laughing, unchanged, and all over again I was delighted and felt the charm of it, the luck, the fact that they were a family, a nucleus of self-sufficiency and one that held special qualities for me, and in a sense included me. I'd feel that, coming on them fresh, as if I was joining another family. A two-family man. It was rich and good, selfishly good, since I was drawing the benefits without any of the responsibilities.

The coach rolled away, I was stranded happily with them on the narrow pavement, jostled by shoppers, and Ray asked me how things were, how I felt—he knew I got sick on those big buggers.

'What was it like, galloping on that monster?'

'Lousy.' Blowing my cheeks out, relieved to be standing by scabby walls in the ringing blue day instead of lolling and sick on springs. Glancing round in wonder, lost, bits of white flying cloud overhead.

'Had enough buses for one day, I bet.' And now I was suspicious, intercepting the crafty looks they were giving each other.

'Why?'

'Because we've got to catch another one now,' Connie chortled. 'Poor old Colin, never mind.'

'Only three miles—less than that,' Ray assured me.

'That's okay, I'll be sick on the grass in front of your bus. I'll save it up.'

Now Connie was worried and frowning, just about stuttering her remorse, concern, she was so full-hearted: 'No, I'm sorry, Colin, no really—do you honestly feel sick? What? No I'm sorry, I'm a rotter, I really am . . .'

'I'm all right, Connie—good as new,' and I puffed out my cheeks in a make-believe spasm of vomiting, hanging my head over the gutter. The nausea was loosening its grip with each breath of country air.

'Are you sure though?'

'I'm fine now.'

A local bus rattled up, with a gap-toothed rustic conductress in a great full skirt plodding up the gangway to plant herself in the doorway and supervise, advancing again all fatalistic like a ploughman for the fares as we left the town and started winding round, going up in a roaring scramble of sound among steep bosky slopes of chestnuts, oaks, plantations of young firs. 'That's Pansy,' Ray said sideways out of his mouth.

'Looks it,' I laughed.

We ran out free and easy on the top of the hill, levelled off and the bus filled to the brim suddenly with yellow sunlight, so that we smiled, all the passengers turning their heads and smiling in spite of themselves, transfigured, staring down through the gaps at the heads of trees, frothing expanses of woods, as if through plane windows. Ray yelled against the engine, pointing at landmarks while Connie smiled and smiled as she watched the wonder break on my face, eyes shine, pleased and gleeful at the sight of me visibly impressed. I wouldn't have let them down anyway, I guessed how they'd waited for their first visitor to the wilds and looked forward to showing him grand sights, virgin lands almost uninhabited that they'd discovered for themselves—now here I was, very conscious of my role, hoping my face was registering it enough in spite of the mask of reticence I always hid behind—getting a kick out of their pleasure at being guides if nothing else. But it *was* very impressive, it was wild, it was scampering by too fast but I liked it, waltzing along flooded with light on the roof of the world, skimming above woods and forests, a world of trees instead of people. And what a time to be amongst it, early June, the millions of leaves crisp and green and delicious, foliage fresh as a salad that we went buzzing through wasp-like, only a dozen of us and all jabbering and jolting on the hard wood slats of the seats like pebbles in a tin can.

I wore by accident the right kind of clothes, a check lumber-jack shirt, bottle-greens and warm reds, and cotton drills, Ray wore a bright blue shirt and khaki shorts, Connie a plain white blouse and skirt of plain green, cool as a rectory lawn.

'Where's the old man of the mountains?' I bawled at the top of my voice, and Ray answered by pointing at his own chest and grinning: 'Me—last week, before I got my hair cut.'

The tin can slowed and stopped and we climbed down thankfully on the hot road in the middle of nowhere, all the rest going on down the other side to river level along the valley bottom, in the direction of Cinderford, the sign said. I'd never heard of it. I gaped round at wherever I was, wondering if it could be like this in Italy or Sardinia perhaps, and saw a wooden bungalow set well back in the hazels as if hiding, marked Post Office, and on our side of the road where the ground was dropping away to big slopes with oak trees was an expanse of short grass, fairly flat, and over to one corner at the edge of the woods a locked and shuttered wooden shack with a simple veranda, and beside it a brick wall with a green door set in it, also padlocked. No sign of human life, only birds, swooping and singing. I was puzzled because that bus of Ray's wasn't in sight either, unless he'd parked it up in the branches.

'They open that shack in August as a café,' Ray was saying. 'You wouldn't recognize this spot then, so we're told—cars parked all over this grass, coaches lined up full of trippers and the only place they can get a bite to eat round here is that café, so in they go for their cream teas and salads and ham sandwiches and pop and ice-cream.' He laughed and said to Connie, 'Sounds just like the thing we're getting away from, and she blurted out 'I bet it sounds like New Street, our kid, when they're all talking. Ye Gods!'

22

WE STOOD on the soft grass of the roadside, in the still and sunny afternoon of blue sky and birdsong and the peaceful repose that's only amazing if you've come from cities, feeling soothed by the very air, and I said, 'Well I'm damned if I can think where your bus is tucked away. Where the hell is it?'

Ray was stooped over fixing the pushchair, fastening the strap around his boy who was dozing, slumping sideways, and seeing that Connie put her finger to her lips and shushed us— you had to take your chance when you could. There was a touch of conspiracy again in the looks they were giving each other, and when Ray said quietly, 'I'll show you, Colin. Follow the path down, and turn left at the lavatory—that brick wall's a public lavatory, the bloke who owns our camping site lets me have the key—in August the Brummies will be queuing up to use that'—I saw Connie's eyes widen. It was a little joke they'd planned, I went wandering down the path as they said, Ray close behind, and in no time I found myself on the brink of a leafy cliff that plunged down four or five hundred feet to the river and distant bluish meadows. Ray put his hand on my arm, they were both laughing and he explained, 'Good job I stopped you—it's over this way, Colin, as a matter of fact, to the right, not the left.'

'You rats,' I said in pretended disgust, with Connie crying out excitedly, still unable to believe I was actually taken in and would have kept on walking if Ray hadn't stopped me on the edge—'You didn't really think it was down there did you?' It was too good to be true perhaps but it was true all right, I was a dream walking in those days, and anyway the huge drop was invisible until you were more or less on the hairy lip of it, knee deep in a miniature forest of fresh juicy bracken—fronds we'd be picking later on and stuffing in a potato sack to serve as a mattress under my sleeping bag. 'Yes I thought I caught sight of it right at the bottom there,' I told her, feeling too thick for words and at the same time glad the joke had worked, 'I was going to take a short cut and jump.' We were ridiculously, sweetly tender to one another, all of us, taking care not to wound with thoughtless actions, considerate in all kinds of ways, no doubt much more so than they were with each other and definitely more unselfish and gentle than ever I was at home in my own family. And now I can see what it was: as a threesome we were straining to an ideal, a vision we pumped life into and kept faith with as soon as we came together, that failed us the minute we separated—we couldn't seem to carry it over into our ordinary day-by-day irksome existence. It wasn't so much active love in any Christian sense, it was more a soothingness and peace and no need to say a word except breathe it in, the sky-blue life, the country rain, the ferns, trees roaring with sap, soft slatey grey mornings as still as churches. And round the corner past the brick urinal on a clearing giving way on one side to bushes and bracken and then the cliff, only less sheer, the bus nestled calmly like a natural growth, tyres squashed flat, a line for clothes strung across to the nearest tree, a basket of dry washing outside the door and a deckchair, a big rectangle of stretched hessian painted in a design bunched with life, purples and yellows exploding soft as fungi on a green ground that rippled and fluttered like feathers—this was propped against the radiator for me to notice first. And of course I did. 'God I like that, Ray—or is it Con's?'

Connie shouted, 'What? Does it look like the way I paint?'
'Well, no——'
'He hasn't seen your stuff for ages, remember,' Ray said,

and out gushed her spontaneous apologies—'No, well, I'm sorry—I forgot . . .' and sturdily, hands on her hips, suddenly blushing and in confusion—'I must put this brat in his cot while he's still asleep'—and no sooner had she said it than he stirred, snuffled, and in seconds was howling lustily, not just his mouth but all of him, all his body. 'He must have heard me, the little sod—isn't that the limit, eh?'

Later with Ray I went for a stroll, he wanted to show me things, so we scrambled and picked our way along a path around the edge of the woods, that great gambolling drop always at the side of us, drawing our eyes. It was the way the landscape opened itself right out, the slopes were space-wild and sun-drunk. At one point Ray who was leading stopped dead, whispered 'An owl, look,' and there he was perched on a fence post only a few feet away, fixed as fate. We froze and stood staring at the tawny, still shape, the ravaged saucer-eyed helmet, and I became aware of an incredible stillness my legs seemed to be sinking in. Then he decided, flew off soundlessly and one soft flap of his wings took him straight into the gloomy depths of a tree without stirring a leaf. All at once the land was savage, dark-bushed.

'How about that,' Ray murmured, as if to himself.

'Seen him before?' I said.

'No, never.'

And we seemed to melt into the trees rather than walk, following the path in a mood of almost seraphic peace, as if the owl had left a spell on us. The path took us insidiously away from the sheer cliff now, deeper into the wood, until we came at last to something man-made, a fence, on the other side a scrubby field in a queer chilly light leaning away from the sun, full of spurting rabbits.

Later still, the baby asleep, we were all outside on the grass, a cool evening breeze blowing now and again. We were throwing a ball to and fro, then it shot over the bank of nettles

and alders into a rough patch behind, a kind of dry ditch: I
scrabbled up the bank, lost my footing and balance and came
careering down backwards, arms flailing. It must have looked
funny but I was sickeningly out of control, I felt I was crashing back and back to the very edge and over. My limbs jerked
in a convulsion like a spastic's, and I heard Connie let out a
shriek of laughter and Ray was doubled up—he might have
thought I was clowning even. I sank down on one knee, gasping, took a deep breath and climbed back again stinging my
hands, I was that shaky and demoralized. Christ, I thought
savagely, a bank like this—three feet high at the most. For an
instant the whole pack of cards was in danger of collapse, the
structure lurched in the pit of my stomach, a hard ball of hate
began to congeal against them and their joint laughter. The
woods were gloomy, lonely, a long way from home: I was on
my own again. It was as precarious as that, the rapturous
silence could become emptiness, the nave of trees turn sinister,
the breeze chilly and inhospitable—then I recovered shakily
and saw how stupid I was acting. Nothing was changed. Inside the warm bus that evening watching the dusk settle there
was nothing woebegone left in me—I even recaptured a sense
of homecoming, the feeling I often had when first arriving.
We drank coffee and talked as the day died, the light failed, we
sat hushed because of the child close by in his cot but hushed
too by the momentous time of day, a white shell of moon lifting, the night itself lifting like a great bird out of the valley
and the trees. Talked our usual dreamspinning stuff, homely
and exalted, spur of the moment babblings where the deep
pauses were as important as anything spoken, thoughts steeped
in 'Story of My Heart' passions that rose up from the floorboards at this charged, emotional time and crumbled at first
light, remaking the world in the image of what we'd inhaled
outside, the sharp fragrancy of ferns, stink of dung, hoot of
owl, raising it up and up in husky fervour and majesty until

288

for Connie it was all too much, unreal, and she'd croak her protests, her desperately honest suspicions, the huddle of her shoulders eloquent with objections: 'I don't see how you can say that——' Breaking in with an abrupt flutter of her hand, dark eyes sympathetic yet persistent, asking. And Ray's flow would be halted, his loyalty tested: still longing to flow on he'd put it differently, come at it from another angle, less convincing as he got more verbose, as Connie shook her head stubbornly, hot-eyed with her inability to accept, while I relapsed into silence and waited. Maddening silences they must have been, like my brother's blank walls as he sat pig-headed refusing to say anything—but mine were more like a language. 'Strong silences' Ray called them in letters. Now and then I'd become conscious of the uselessness of words, like trying to force every music through a trumpet, crude and stupid, no subtlety. The wordless language of the whole body, not the eyes even but the presence, seemed better in certain circumstances than any words. And we none of us had much respect for thinking in a straight line, or thinking as detached activity, to and fro like tennis or any other game—the intellectual hardened against sensations, shut away from everything unthinkable. And sometimes it was just an inability to speak, like Connie's inability to agree—so that the tall, lean woman with iron-grey hair from the café at the edge of the grass in August, meeting me in the company of Ray and being introduced, told them afterwards I was 'quiet as a girl'.

There again in August I saw the transformation they'd been warned to expect: coaches with yellow-glass sunshine roofs rolling up packed, unloading and then manœuvred into some sort of order, along with cars, motor-bikes, even heavy transport. The level area of grass was now a car park, and that day I came up in hot licking sun from the station to find Ray earning a bit for himself by selling parking tickets for the owner of the land. He had a red roll of 6d tickets and a bag slung round his neck for change, and to look official. He hadn't seen me, my heart sank at the sight of his face, strained with the tension of asking, having no real defence when a lorry driver who'd backed in that minute told him 'bugger off, mate —I ain't payin' ', and Ray twisted his face aside as though struck, the yob still jeering, 'Cheeky sod, go on—hop it.' I looked at the comings and goings, people trooping up and down vacant as cows and Ray there abstract in the middle of it all. The wilds. The morning-glory world.

23

IT CAME back in September, but it had tarnished for them, the coming isolation of the winter up there made them shiver in advance, the treetops full of a rushing loneliness already, apart from the practical problems of how to survive. Already they could feel a lack of hospitality, a gloamy non-human element pushing at them to depart, at night great orange moons active and close and glaring, looming through the branches. And even simpler than that: they were missing the contact with people, human beings, creature comfort. A letter came, written on 1st October: 'If you came here now you would feel a strange place. The massive transformation is in full swing. The leaves are falling like mad. The whole landscape is changing under the eye. Each time I look out of the bus windows I see more—more colour. It's like watching a clock move. These great planes of hill-forest are riots of colour. Everything looks so solid and real, much more than in the summer. I never knew there was so much red in nature: bushes, trees, forest, on fire with a vast death. It pours with rain one day, the wind blows, the black bones start to show through. Great masses of gold. A flock of three or four hundred birds is wheeling over the face of these cliffs, round and round slow. The oilpaint is laying itself on in lumps. The contour of the earth is set vibrating in a bronzed dance. Spring we came here, the leaves were translucent: today a wind is blowing each life of a life of a leaf. And some of these leaves I know like friends. Through this window looking down the valley I have been looking at some big leaves all their life. When I think how many leaves on a tree, and how many trees—I'm dizzy!'

I'd been to see them on their planet, and Leila on hers, and they mingled and interacted in the same sky, I had them both under my skin, yet the amazing thing was they seemed to have absolutely nothing in common. It was such a Jekyll and Hyde thing that I used to wonder about myself, if I was an out-and-out liar and bag of sweet tricks when I was with Ray and only acting the responses he'd come to expect. With Leila I was in no doubt: real flesh, real despair, a cruel and urgent dialogue, clinging and tearing. There was no link that I could see, and then one day the kind of thing that only life can throw up, touching and daft—a parcel of baby clothes arrived for Connie, things that Leila's firstborn had grown out of: a gift from the other planet, the secret smiling goddess, dispenser of minutes like drops of blood. And it wasn't any good, it wasn't right at all. A joke, giving me a pang. I understood then once and for all that I'd erected a fence, I wanted these worlds kept separate. One was all blood and salt, experience, the other—nothing like that. The other didn't make me suffer and cry out, it was familiar and happy, yet so still and perfect and near that I couldn't live there. It was the marriage of these two that I was after, without knowing it, or guessing how ancient and inevitable a process it was. Or how often it looked like dirty compromise.

The excuse I made to myself for not telling them more than a fraction was that facts were no use. Facts: her real name was Vida—the Leila was one of her 'creations', or if you like the name of her *doppelganger*. She'd met her husband at Leicester, at the Art and Tech, where the exciting and truly seminal things in her life had happened, where she wore green stockings and posed nude and dished out the *Worker*, and this led her to a political-bohemian fringe and to lovers. To the middle-aged sweet-natured journalist, who was wise, introduced her to books, educated her in fact and told her of the existence of extraordinary people and things—Nye Bevan and Dylan Thomas, Dorothy Day and the *Catholic Worker*—a man who had the key to life as a whole, was intuitive, put the jigsaw together in a bouncy live way and didn't censor anything out—homos and pros and anarchists, the poor, deprived, cankers of prejudice and hate, Gandhi, surrealism. She would never forget him, she said. And the next lover—she liked parading them for me, ticking them off, these hot, close ghosts of her vibrant days—he was a pervert who ended by half frightening her to death because he wouldn't let go, was insanely jealous of her every movement, would have liked to have kept her under lock and key in a room all to himself—now she was glowing, glowing as she approached the shocking detail—and once she had to use the pot under his bed, and months later, opening his wardrobe she discovered the same pisspot with her own stinking piss still in it: he wanted to keep it forever, she said. This manic possessiveness she found terribly funny but also mad, and it frightened her so much she refused to go back to his room. He threatened suicide: she stayed away. Soon after this she was married and then the babies were coming, slips of the penis she called them—and another lover, whose friend used the adjoining bedroom in his holiday shack, only a flimsy partition between, and the friend and his mistress hurt each other for pleasure, Leila heard them letting out groans—it was like a Japanese Noh play she told me, the mockery and candour breaking through and she laughed in spite of herself. And now—what could she boast of now, to set against the kids, the shopping lists, the monotony of the dripping tap, the greasy cobbles of Worksop where she had ended up, with old-age pensioners in the park and disabled miners in the Reading Room?

She had me—I was the latest. Naturally she wouldn't have put it like that, it was insulting and patently untrue. It was fate: for all her reading, tolerance, sophistication, she was still a woman who snatched primitively at what she wanted, and there was no question in her mind of right or wrong. If she believed in anything it was a simple fatalism. The remorse and guilt she suffered later, and that too she didn't question or rebel against. Wasn't there always a price to pay? When it came to her husband a curious ethic enabled her to have lovers, even though he'd found out about the last one and been hurt dreadfully, but in future she'd got to make sure he never found out again. 'I've got to,' she said grimly. 'I can't ever risk hurting him like that again.' But no question, ever, of her turning over a new leaf: she had a flaw in her character that couldn't be mended, only accepted. 'I'm rotten,' was how she put it. She was certain it showed, and that bus drivers and butchers, men all over the place were giving her the eye because it was obvious, what she was. Pros fascinated her—I noticed that at the very beginning. She was far too selective to be one, but they were beyond the pale, the untouchables of her society: anyone with that kind of leper status had an irresistible attraction for her.

Leila wrote to tell me they were moving to 'shitty old Worksop', several miles out of the city, harder to get into the theatre, cinema, harder to meet me on Saturdays, and a few weeks later Ray had sold his bus-home to Bob Rodgers, the camping site owner, and was in Plymouth in a furnished flat. They were all there by the sea, they were swaying in luxury, it was mad, too expensive, they had ten quid left between them and destitution. Then suddenly it was out in the open, a proposal we'd toyed with and teased back and forth idly during those philosophical evenings in the gloaming, under the drenching tin roof—why don't we join forces? Now it was urgent—could I send a money order on account, if I was still keen on the idea, while they were waiting for me to chuck up my job and journey down there? This was how I liked things to happen: I needed forcing out of cover, winkling out of my shell, events taking charge, somebody else leading and me following. Off I went, following. Down to Dorset on a Royal

Blue as a first stage and staying a couple of nights with my mother and father, who had been living in a caravan outside the village while their tiny thatched cottage was renovated. They had moved in to get out of their barren field hedged with a wintry tangle of cold-glowing twigs, but things were primitive, an Elsan toilet in the earth-floored outhouse—you sat behind a portable screen and prayed for privacy. My mother poured out a story of trial and tribulation, aided by my father's Brummy accent comments, his laconic and half-admiring, half-contemptuous observations on the curious workings of the rural mind—all this in reference to the local jobbing builder, Charlie Partridge, who had been modernizing the rooms and replacing the iron range with an open brick fireplace. 'You see, I made a drawing of the fireplace we wanted, all the dimensions, design and that, oh and he'd seen the very thing for us in a house down the road, a tiled one, grey and white mottled tiles it was, lovely job—I might as well have been talking out of the back of my neck! I said, "Now look, Charlie, we're set on having a brick one. Brick. The length of that wall. Stone or brick, whichever's cheapest. We had tile where we come from, now we want something that's right for a cottage." He didn't like that, I tell you. You have to tell 'em straight, and keep on dinning it in, not once but a dozen times. You have to stand over 'em and show 'em exactly what you've got in mind—then they're okay. He's a nice bloke, mind you, Charlie, but oh dear, it's murder, getting what you want.'

I heard so much of Charlie, I started trying to picture him in the flesh. I'd got a vision of a mothy ferret of a man, then next morning I was with my father and met him in the village —fat and young, cap on the back of his curls, big yellow teeth and sly hazel eyes.

We had a drink and came back and I spent a lot of time staring out at space, standing at the front casement windows peering under thatch at a limestone wall and then the lane, then the field wall opposite and a field of pigs and far low hills spreading away beyond the main road where you saw the humped carapaces of cars glinting in the sun, moving fast. At the rear it was even more amazingly open and quiet, an earth track at the side of the cottages leading out over fields past a heap of rusting junk, a dead lorry being gutted for scrap, farm implements, a tangle of planks from some construction job at the pig farm. The track led us up to a gate which opened on a huge field, biggest I'd seen, with regiments of fruit bushes on parade, blackcurrants mostly, and beyond that lines of apple trees at attention and in the distance before a copse of firs were the low buildings of the farm itself, packing sheds and so on. It was November, smokey grey weather with stray shafts of sun glinting. Before dark my mother took me for a walk in that direction, to her favourite view, where she intended to come one day and make sketches for a watercolour if she could pluck up courage to try. 'I can't paint—I go to an art club in the village but I feel a fool, they're all better than me—but it's so beautiful where we're going that I want to try.' We were skirting a shallow gulley at the edge of pines that stood remembering hard, ready for winter. On a rough slope ridged by some old ploughing we followed the cow path with heads dipped for nettles and stones. Three heifers looked at us and started to move, wandering up curiously, and my mother picked up a dry stick and shouted in a fierce unnatural voice, shaking her cheeks: 'Gaaar!' They backed off a few feet and stood moonily considering, floating there in the softness of dusk, bronze patched with white, rubbery gleaming mouths and pear-heavy movements, still too near for my mother, who hurried me through to the spinney she had in mind. 'I think they're more frightened of us than we are of them,' she panted, clutching hard at her stick. 'Isn't this beautiful, Colin?' and I paused, we both stopped and stood hearing the stream tinkle and the peck and chip of birdsong, like reverent visitors to a church. I saw it as she did, a chocolate-box Patience Strong vision of country paths safe as streets, and no bats, and cattle keeping to the left. I was bored rather than disrespectful. Who was I to turn my nose up?

Sunday morning I set off alone for a stroll, to work up an appetite for the beef and spuds and whatnot she was already slaving over, and to see where I was exactly. On a green island in the middle of the village, outside the spongy, sagging vicarage, a shining white angel of a signpost with three arms stood up. I followed the finger that pointed down the narrowest lane into the heart of the wild, telling myself this was gentlemanly, prosperous country—a sign on a bit of white wood stuck in an open strip of flowerbed under the ivory windows of a long opulent cottage—DO NOT TOUCH THE FLOWERS. The lane twirled me deeper into the country, the village soon sank away, lost, I turned a corner by a steel gate and saw a paddock full of cows standing disconsolate and a lad speckled like eggs astride the back of one; he sprang off nimbly as he caught sight of me. He must have jumped up again as soon as I'd passed, I could hear him whooping and yelling in the rodeo game he'd imagined for himself. Soon the country changed as I trudged on, it was open now, the trees sparse, the fields rough and sombre like moorland on a small scale. I was going by a farm as it started to rain, meekly at first, so I turned round and was glad of the excuse, the gloom of the sky leaking into the dark scowling ground had begun to depress me. A labourer tramped out of a shippen as I looked, his head down, scuffling his horseshoe boots. He gargled and his mouth flabbered, then he spat on the yellow concrete. The sack over his shoulders was like a cape, almost stylish. He went back in and I saw one knee, white and fascinating, through the rent in his trousers. I marched back seeing nobody else towards the stodge and steam, the horse brasses, the brown piano with stiff keys and a sad smell, my photo on it aged seventeen, priggish with innocence, doe-eyed and Brylcreemed, neck shy over the crisp white collar, full mouth budding, brown lashes patting the mothered roundness. Wearing a suit, and—although unseen—a wristwatch with an octagonal face and chrome expanding strap, the latest. 'What a pity you had to change,' grieved my mother. 'What a difference there to that awful picture of you in the trench coat in Trafalgar Square—I cried and cried when you sent us that. Your mouth!'

24

IT'S FUNNY, the pang I felt leaving that place, when my mother took me down past the pines creaking overhead like a boat on the corner, down to the main road to pick up the Royal Blue. Monday afternoon, my father out on his rounds — it was worse than leaving home for London in the days of soundless wailing and gnashing of teeth. I felt I'd lived there all my life, yet I hadn't lived there at all, only visited. I didn't understand why I should feel so awful. And I was only going on to the coast, I'd be nearer home in Devon than I would in the Midlands. Nobody had asked me my plans or anything, those days were over; they waited for me to say, and if I kept quiet there were no questions. Sometimes I wished they'd come out and say so, voice their disapproval if that's what it was—but no, they'd decided not to say anything, and it must have been my mother to wilfully *decide* something like that, come to a decision and stick to it, for the sake of her peace of mind. What had they decided? It was my life, my own business, it was entirely up to me, what I did: my mother confided this much to me, as if to say—Make a rod for your own back. For all that it was a remarkable decision for a mother like mine to make and stick to, when her whole nature ran counter to it. Yet she was pulling, pulling as hard as ever as I looked at the pine needles scattered over the grass like fish bones, as the express coach yawned open and swallowed me, swept me away in a cloud of comfort and the passengers lowered their heads cowlike again to papers and toffees, sandwiches, thermos flasks, or went on chewing the cud and waiting to empty their bladders at the roadhouse the other side of Honiton. All I could do was sit back still as death nursing the stone of grief, shooting through the bony avenue of trees on the first ridge as oblivious and deathly as a space traveller. Nothing to be done except die the deaths and hope to rise, cling on forlornly and gaze out half blind at the hedges gone venomous, plants with saucer leaves and creepers like seaweed hanging broken in the blood of the berries, the world filled with melancholy like a stone urn, the same one that was dew-fresh and all frisky youthfulness yesterday or the day before that. The poison spraying out of my eyes, right and left. Until I lay back sick with self-disgust, drowning in mocking petty talk that seemed maliciously aimed at my ears, my head and I could have swung on them in a fury of loathing, devilish, chattering my teeth like a cat at flies crawling on the window.

Sitting there I slowly hardened into indifference and great age like a toad. And perhaps I was being warned, because I was heading for one of the worst times of my life, and through no fault of theirs the new life with Ray and Connie ended up a fiasco. Leaving Exeter on the last lap I rose wanly from the dead, and rolling through Devon into Plympton and Plymouth I was almost normal again, the coach pushing now like a bull instead of galloping and regal. I was glad to see a worried Ray whose family was mysteriously sick, Connie huddled on a deep sofa nursing the baby, both swaddled round in a plaid tasselled shawl, whey-faced and silent. The flat was sunk in the ground and spread with carpets in all directions, with fat chairs and cushions, folding screens, gas fire plopping and seething its red skin, all manner of shiny luxuries. So much thickness under your feet you felt sinful, the gas fire whispering like a serpent. Ray had a plan, he'd been busy making inquiries and answering adverts in the *Morning News*, he'd found us a cheap furnished cottage out at Newton Ferrers, and if Connie wasn't too groggy tomorrow we could leave this posh lugubrious dump that sucked away your savings at an alarming rate and move in: it was all fixed. Only three rooms and a galley-kitchen but all to ourselves and a marvellous spot, right on the water's edge, an estuary, and round the corner almost was the open sea, the Mewstone, looking across to the first headland in Cornwall and right out to France if your eyesight was good enough, or your imagination. He infected me with his enthusiasm, so much so that it seemed a crime to tarnish it with problems like jobs and money. Sitting around the fire that evening in our luxurious dugout, Connie off to bed early to try and sleep off her sickness, the subject was broached and even welcomed, it gave added pleasure to the warmth and leisure and comfort we were enjoying. Like rain on the windows when you're snug and dry.

'I'm still chasing jobs, Colin. Been after two shop assistant jobs today.'

'No good?'

'First one wasn't—no experience, no job.'

'Where was that?'

'Burton's. Second one a bit more hopeful—had a long matey chat with the manager—but I can't say I cared for his parting words much.'

'Don't come back!' I shouted and we doubled up, it was like old times, even sunk in the foundations of that haunted house, furniture breathing in the dead shadows.

'No,' Ray laughed, 'he told me to call on Wednesday again but *come in dark clothes.*'

'Oh Christ—what have you got?'

'Nothing, not a thing, not even black shoe laces. No, I've had it there all right. Con's just written after an office job—I told her if she can get ten quid a week we'll mind the fire and make up the baby——'

I had a sudden thought: 'I sent my bike down by train——'

'Yes, you wrote and said—it ought to be at the station by now. Tomorrow we'll go and have a look.'

301

'And I'd better call in at the Labour, see if they need any clerks.'

Ray stuck out his bottom lip, shook his head. 'Doubt it, but no harm in trying. What we'll do tomorrow, we'll go to the station first, then over to the Labour Exchange and back here to pick up our stuff. No point in lugging that round with us.'

'Okay.'

In a nasal, Brooklyn Kid voice: 'Check!' And he flopped out on the velvet sofa, dragged down his cheeks with the palms of his hands. 'Boy oh boy—problems, problems.'

In the scruffy, peeling Labour Exchange stranded on a corner with a strip of pavement all to itself because of the bombing, it was grisly marching in spruce and sprightly to ask the dole man for something you didn't want, but it had to be done.

'Clerical? Not a chance, old man. Call in again in a month or so, if you like.'

The voice was slow, and it sighed back with a fat sound, Devon-creamy, mouth smiling like a dead rat. In a month or so! If I liked! It was so preposterous I went out bubbling—wait till Ray hears this—instead of feeling derelict like the building and the wall outside. 'It's all right, I'm saved—call back in a month they said—think we can leave off eating that long?' And we dived down a side-street chanting a catch-phrase out of an Albert Cossery novel at each other—'A black day for us all!' But life was earnest, no laughing matter, the thought of Connie's expectant face was enough—and the rent book, the owner of Apple Tree Cottage who looked us over carefully and nodded warily, showed us the slot meter, told us how the last tenant had clogged the drains with sanitary towels and tea-leaves, then as he left us to it he lifted his clenched trilby to Connie and we saw a huge white parting running livid over his scalp between black stuck-down hair. Last of the Mohicans he was nicknamed, no hesitation.

We poked through the little rooms and in one a patched cat leapt out of sight, giving us a shock. The landlord's ghost, Ray said, but I thought of the dole man. Opened the plank door at the back and went stooping out, and there was the old apple tree in a gape of bare earth, bashed sideways by gales with its face scraping the ground. A row of kale went frilling away to a corner, pinned up with rain jewels.

25

WE HAD to find something, pay the piper somehow. Ray succeeded first, starting as a parcels clerk in a windy goods yard at Devonport, coming home with descriptions of the open-ended shed he shivered in, the cold sinking into his bones. 'I'll have to find something else before the winter really comes—wonder where they buried the last frozen clerk.' I was in a tight corner, nothing available except factory work and that was the one job I'd sworn never to do again. Back in I went saying it was temporary, a stopgap, mass production in a machine tool factory, and in a way it was new all right: they had to train me for it. Transplanted from Derby, most of the key jobs were held by northerners who were also there to train the local recruits. I heard of a vacancy in the offices and told Ray—he jumped in like a shot, just to keep warm. He'd walk into the screaming machine shop where I stuffed steel and brass rods up the arses of autos and a curtain of oil descended, drills darted in like minnows, teeth chewed, knives sank, the shiny nipples no longer than the nail on my little finger dropped in the tin trays—Ray would be there beside me and I wouldn't even know, his mouth opening and shutting, a pain between his brown eyes which were clenching against the hard high shriek. I'd have to shrug, point to my ears. I hated him to creep up on me in there. I was in hell, I'd stick it because it was temporary, but I didn't realize I was being degraded till Ray appeared and I found I didn't want to see him. Then I knew.

And it was as clear as day, every time I clocked out, bashed the buff card and dropped it in the slot against my slave number and began the long weary ride into the centre on one bus, out again on the long jolting wind up and down to the beautiful creek I was already beginning to hate: I ought to have gone in the other direction, I had made a terrible mistake. The south was beautiful, ideal, dreaming on its seacoasts, primordial, Garden of Eden mornings folded in its navel, joggling in its rolls and rills, but where was it, where was I? It was nowhere, a lichen-infested crazy cuckoo land. I was dying, moss and fungus covering my limbs: on Sunday I sat on a bench high on the timeless cliff reading one of Leila's letters and watching the herring gulls float in a perfect white dream, I sat filled with slow loathing for the slow puffs of cloud, the perfected curving coast. It was nowhere, outside the circuit of things. It stopped the clock of your blood. The north with its slimy streets that drove you out, choked you, gave you the horrors, I had to flee back to it soon—it was my own reality, it was Leila in the shitty fog tilting her chin and surveying the damage in her bit of mirror. I couldn't stay here like this, green and wooden, flapping weakly with the days in the effort to embrace the fiasco of the new life on Sundays, a grease gun aimed at my stomach, overalls stinking of machine oil in soak in the galvanized bath under the sink. And in the doll's cottage I was on their necks every night, sitting morose in the only living-room and hankering secretly to be off on the journey north, or at the deal table with Ray working at a slaughter-house-style watercolour, daubing away in friendly competition and to justify my existence. The artist life. Or writing a letter with fierce desperate strokes, a love poem, shaking the table— every week the atmosphere a little more strained, a little more uneasy, and no wonder. No good, nobody's fault, no need to say a word. Connie's eyes would be red-rimmed after a long spell upstairs, she'd pick up some sewing and bend her head so as not to be seen, and I'd go out the back to the lav, in a tiny cobbled yard under the stars weeping icy light, where you could hear the sea thumping and sucking senselessly, day and night. I could have been on the moon. Then I'd catch sight of the dole man's ghost spying on me from the vegetables with his white pin-cushion cheeks, and laugh, and fill up his ghostly saucer.

Towards the end of February Leila outlined a plot, broke into exclamation marks again and again as she put forward her most audacious proposal: she was visiting Leicester her home town the following Saturday, taking her youngest boy, Simon—just a name to me—to spend the weekend with her mother. That was the arrangement so far as anyone knew, but if I came she'd meet me at the bus station café at twelve noon, we'd have all day to ourselves and spend the night in a guest house or small hotel—nobody would suspect anything. Simple matter for her to fix it with her mother, give her some reason for not turning up. 'Come if you can—please!—but don't reply to the normal address for God's sake whatever you do—it's not safe any more. Julie who passes on your letters is my dear husband's mistress! Suspected this for a long time. Intrigue, treachery, double-cross—it's like the Borgias. I live on my nerves daily, expect the worst, I'm a wreck—you won't recognize me. Please come if you dare—and if you aren't in the café I'll know, darling.'

I shivered in my chest, alive and suffering again, and Friday went to work prepared. The day before I had to rush into town at dinnertime and buy my first packet of french letters. Tore straight into the rubber goods shop and it was empty, nobody behind the counter, and by the time the man in white coat, white hair and specs had shuffled out from his lair, his sly shoes going suck-suck on the lino, my dutch courage was in tatters.

'One packet?'

'Yes, please.'

'Lovely day for the time of year.'

'Beautiful, yes.'

306

Wrapping it up nice and cosy in *Old Moore's Almanac* and into the plain buff envelope, dab of sellotape, he looked at me over his glasses:

'You know if you have five packets it's ten bob?'

'No—no, I didn't.' Five packets, I thought to myself, what would I do with five packets?

'Worth remembering, that.'

'Yes, it is. Thanks.'

'Any jelly?'

'No, that's fine, nothing else. Cheerio.'

'Afternoon sir,' brisk and respectful, and he sponged up the money smiling, as if I'd bought a buttonhole.

In work I thought I'd better find out how to use one, so before the hooter went I slipped into the modern shithouse with my hands still clean and sat on the seat trying to get an erection. There was some doggerel on the door about the adventures of the vicar's daughter: I read that hopefully, it was about her being frightfully ignorant and sheltered, not a clue about what it was for, names or anything else. I thought it was lame and pathetic and I'd read it already. I concentrated on Leila, shut my eyes and lusted violently and at last got it hoisted, except that it was soft as a banana. Hastily I unwrapped a french letter and popped it on like a hat, rolled it down in a sudden inspiration as if rolling on a silk stocking, then peeled it off again. I could do it, easy, no bother at all. It was the one thing that had been worrying me. It was like kissing for the first time, wondering what you did with your nose. Now I was happy, laughing at myself. Amazing how difficult every damn thing was if you thought about it long enough, how easy if you stopped thinking.

I CAUGHT the night train from North Road, midnight, pulling into Birmingham on clanking chains of fate before dawn, staggering into the streets with drunken legs like a sailor ashore. Too early for the first bus, so I found a transport café open in a street not much wider than a stone passage, down from the Bull Ring and fish slabs—the room a grim greasy cave, but warm, full of iron-faced men, stringy wrung-out men, frowsty, glowering unshaven men, all implacable as the winter streets, bunched shoulder to shoulder at the square dolls' tables under clouds of rising steam, clouds of breath, swag-bellied brown clouds of tobacco smoke. Anybody who opened their mouth either belched or swore, and it was impersonal as a doctor's verdict, naive as a child looking at stars, they weren't curses aimed at anyone. It was a comment on a foul existence, a vile fate, at that time in the morning especially. Everybody swore, the verdict was unanimous. What a fucking life. I huddled frail and sickly in my grey tweed overcoat yellowing at the collar, it was belted and held me together. I sat in a corner struggling against waves of nausea from the smell of bacon frying that early, and from the train, dragging and grinding through the black arctic night, oiled and flashing, the glimpses of yellow street lamps bathing the concrete roadstrips of endless housing estates, the lit glass cages working a night shift by the side of the track, and ghost towns with viaducts and blind tatty shops and nightmarish empty streets sliding by, traffic lights winking on and off for no reason, red, orange, green, not even a dog crossing over. I sipped tea and looked blearily at the lorry drivers blundering in, bull men, weasels, the ugly mugs of the advance guard of

Saturday's market. We were all the same, in garb and servitude, bleak as a convict colony. The face opposite me had small red eyes screwed into its leather and a smile that made your scalp creep, it was all stitches and rivets.

I caught the first workmen's bus, a double-decker, it lumbered red and fat and half asleep to start with, nudged around a bit anxious with its dopey cargo as if it had a bedroom in its belly and must take care, then went blundering off over the cobbles that were slimy with frost, down the slope away from the big cindery church and blackened railings, dropping through long black alleys like coal chutes. Coventry was less than an hour's run—it was still before seven when I got there. I could have stayed on all the way to Leicester but I had time to kill: may as well get out, wander around. I found another transport caff open. A bloke squashed up against me leaned for a light.

'Sorry, don't smoke.'

No answer. Not even a grunt. He was stuck with sleep, middle-aged, his crumpled round face covered in grime. Must have come off a night shift. The place was too small for the crowd, men pushing in every other minute with pinched bleary faces, rubbing cold hands together that sounded rough as emery cloth. From the counter a little leaf of a man was making for his table with a fry-up, plate in one hand and tools in the other, taking them through the crush carefully like horns. He got there and sat down and pointed his elbows sadly, next to his mate who was stoking his pipe, fingers feeling in the dark shag. I noticed a change now, perhaps because it wasn't so early: more animation, lifting spirits, even a joke or two. The cursing went on just the same as a matter of habit, but with less clank in it.

My rendezvous was a small restaurant in a low building with a clock on the roof, tight against the bus depot. Public lavatories were in a block at the end, and a booking office.

Opposite was a car park, public baths, then a short hill of factories and warehouses, both sides. I'd been walking my legs off all morning and it was still five minutes to go. I went in and sat down at one of the paintbox tables in the yawning space at the far end and felt the old fluttery shiver in my chest again. Empty: a waitress sauntered across with her cheeky pad and pencil.

'Can I order in a few minutes—I'm waiting for somebody.'

'Suit yourself.'

She was ten minutes late, hatless, stooping over her child who was toddling, wearing baggy corduroy trousers. From this stooping position she glanced across, searching, she saw me in the far corner and smiled faintly, triumphant. As they approached, steering between the blue and white check table-cloths, the triumph and gaiety curved her mouth. I sat in full view, feeling round and obvious and foolish and yet sharp like a new penny. What a smile she had, tempered in fire and ice. Face white, eyes wide open and staring, almost cruel in their fierce expectancy. I trembled at the recognition, it was what I'd dreamed of—never hoped to have. I can make no separation between the cruelty and the love, the dream and the reality.

'You made it then,' she says, stroking with her voice. Love is power.

'I think so. Just about.'

'This is Simon. You don't know Simon, do you?'

'I don't know anybody. Hallo, Simon.'

Simon is eighteen months old. Brown liquid eyes, Blake eyes, the pure innocence that regards in silence and sees all, the whole story, reads it like a book and is struck dumb, ravelled in the knowledge and dust of centuries. And no words; never any words. The drophammers of education will soon be pounding his little skull and there still won't be words. He watches me like a thrush.

'He's not talking yet.'

310

'He knows though.'

She chuckles wickedly, flashes me a knowing look. 'My God, yes. He frightens me sometimes, the looks he gives me. Wait till I can talk, I'll spill the beans good and proper—that's the kind of look. There—that! He's going to be a devil I tell you when he gets older.'

'Then what will you do?'

She laughs again. 'Deny everything—to the bitter end!'

I order lunch and when it comes she picks at hers—she's been eating something at her mother's, she tells me. She concentrates on feeding her boy.

27

OUTSIDE, the streets are ours, the city. My heart pounds and she knows it, she has Simon by one hand and me by the other. Off we go to the guest house like that, a family, and book a room for the night. The situation really intrigues her—she can't help reminding me:

'Well, husband?'

'Yes, wife?'

'What's it like being a father? Do you feel like one?'

'No.'

'Well, you should.'

'How's a father supposed to feel?'

'Responsible.'

'What's that?'

She laughs again, delighted. 'Aren't you hopeless!'

'We'll see.'

'Oh we will, will we?'

'Yes.'

'When?'

'Tonight.'

We stop in the street and kiss surreptitiously, fugitive. Then a chill grips me and my heart goes down, I look at her and I'm terrified, agonized, time whirring out of control, flocks of minutes bursting round my head and I'm going away, it's over. I look at her, hatred in my heart.

'I'm looking forward to it,' she's whispering, then notices my face. 'What's wrong?'

'Nothing's wrong.'

We are too close, she is in my rhythm, there can't be any deception.

'Tell me, please.'

'It's just . . .' and I choke with self-pity, it's over, I climb on the train that goes south, the train slides out, I'm waving goodbye to myself. 'There's no time,' I mutter, crushing her hand with hopeless rage, till she cries out. 'I'm sorry, I'm sorry——'

'You're a funny boy,' she says quietly.

'Oh, I'm a scream.'

'We've all the night before us haven't we?'

'You make it sound real vast. All!'

Now the bitterness and the dread is showing but it doesn't make her angry, not this time. For one thing, it's too flattering. Her low voice soothes at the fear, murmurs throatily, her hand squeezes. 'Come on, silly boy—there's an art exhibition I want to have a look at. Shall we?'

'If you like.'

'Come on then. Think how lucky we are. Come on, Simon.' She kisses me lightly, she has me by the hand, I walk beside her without any fear and she swoops her face round, eyes astounded: 'Did you see that look he gave us, when I kissed you? Oh what a devil he's going to be, what a devil!'

I feel perfectly all right, we go springing along fresh and eager as honeymooners, she is telling all sorts of things obsessively, fantastic things I can't properly take in—telling me that her mother knows about us but won't say anything, the secret is safe there, no it's Julie she can't get over, Julie her best friend, finding out was like a slap in the face and now she trusts no one, will never trust a woman again, and what torments her, drives her mad, is being in the dark, not knowing how much her husband really knows and how much is bluff— When he drops a remark so close to the truth that she breaks into a sweat and closes her eyes waiting for the axe, is it accident, coincidence, sheer fluke or does he in fact know *everything*, is he having a fiendish cat-and-mouse game with her? She stops and smiles challengingly, proudly and I sense the intense satisfaction this mesh of lies and mystery and suspense is giving her. We sit back on the leather bench against the cool white walls of the small gallery, she lights a fresh cigarette and abandons her narrative to consider the paintings. And now I fall helplessly into a ridiculous state of jealousy, I hate the paintings for absorbing precious time, soaking it up like sponges that hang there malevolent, arranged weeks before for this specific purpose. They rob her attention and I can't bear it.

'Shall we go?' I say sullenly, but she rises and walks to and fro, smoking, insatiable as a child: it could be a normal outing instead of the eve of the one night, the one and only chance before time washes us away . . .

At last she's had enough, at last we are walking up the garden path to the ordinary blue front door of the guest house, a house engulfed to the eaves for me in absolute mystery, profound significance. We go in, sign the register, make bubbles of conversation with the proprietor, then his wife darts up, very small and birdlike, to prod us into the lounge with her sharp nose. She is necklaced and neat and the lounge is all brown, like her dress, which has red and blue deep in it like hen feathers. As soon as she leaves us to make tea I lean over to Leila and hiss: 'Can't we go upstairs?'

'How?' she asks, radiant and willing, touching my face with her fingers.

'We'll say we're tired—been travelling—what time is it?'

'Just gone eight.'

'Eight-thirty then, no later.'

In the room at last, facing each other, the sudden miracle of privacy makes me shake all over. I can't speak, can't move. She stands in front of me in her neat suit, utterly available and ready, pure gift, yet imperious, final as fate.

'Kiss me,' she says.

314

We put our arms around each other and it is the moment I think I have been waiting for, dreaming about all my life, and now it stabs me with its unutterable tragedy and loneliness. I hold her tighter and tighter, crushing desperately, tightening my arms and burying my face and can't escape the anguish of being separate, can't change it, we are born and we are alone and we're going to die. To her this is fire and passion, all one, we are in the bed naked and dying, ecstatic in the clean sheet smell, I make no attempt to make love, just hug and hug body to body, skin to skin, drown in the sheer sensation of nakedness and abandon, staying awake the whole night like a condemned man, afraid to lose a second. Simon is over in the corner in the cot they've provided, punctuating the delirium and grief with sudden piercing squeaks of his rubber toy. Leila is convulsed in fits of hysterical giggling, I laugh too at the squeak and her 'Oh Christ!' and now we're more human, reprieved, though I still force myself to stay awake out of fear of the dawn. Leila drowses and then another mad squeak in the woolly blackness wakes her and this time she has to stuff the sheet in her mouth, it sounds so hilarious, so incongruous, buried in a bed of hot love and romantic agony and suddenly hearing that. 'It could only happen to me,' she gurgles, clutching at my waist.

There is more agony to come. She has to start back for home that same afternoon, after we've had breakfast and wandered back into the town. As the hours dwindle I can't bring myself to leave her. I am shamelessly craven, begging for crumbs of time, extra minutes. 'Don't go yet.' It's terrible to be naked, at the end of the world watching love dwindle like a train, pierced through with sweetness and whole streets, whole cities congealed into purgatory. I don't know where to go, I can't face the thought of living anywhere away from her. 'Don't go yet.' Alarmed, she lets her bus go and climbs on mine, keeps me company on the first lap of my return journey. At Birmingham I cling on helplessly, beseeching her with my eyes like a

315

stricken dog, the bus is backing and turning, filling up, we stay on it and ride back to Coventry, then through to Leicester and it makes no difference being back again, the pain is worse now. She transfers to her coach, I kiss her and Simon, she gives my hand one final squeeze. 'Write to me,' she murmurs. 'Write, darling.'

I turn my back and face south. That's the last I see of her. The last I'll ever see, I tell myself. All over. My own bus rolls out, and the sudden stabbing horror of this calamity is too much, I begin to weep. It is some time in the evening, black as midnight outside. I turn my face to the glass and creaking woodwork of the window, the black night swallows me up as I lean sightless in the corner. The misery fills my throat and in the reflection I can see my mouth, forced open in a soundless howl. Everything is a terrible mistake, this bus, these insane passengers—where are they all going? There's no reason for them to be going anywhere or doing anything, no grain of sense in all this frantic activity. Because movement, travel, distance have inflicted these wounds I want to obliterate them forever, the mere suggestion of movement sickens me to the heart.

In Devon the following morning I can't remember how I've got there, I don't understand afterwards how I changed trains at Bristol, how I managed to crawl out of the station at North Road and find a bus to carry me to Newton Ferrers: I must have been an automaton. I had lost two nights of sleep, my legs and arms ached, so did my spine, my teeth chattered, I felt sick in every fibre of my body. I must have stood in the doorway of the cottage that Sunday morning like something hideous the tide had washed up. No questions, no need to be shamefaced, they quietly got me into bed—I had a fever and stayed there a week. And slowly, slowly, because I was too weak to do any other than lie on the beach of the nightmare and let things rot, let the hours ebb and flood, the light die and be reborn, little by little reason trickled back in. I got up all wobbly and etiolated and unshaven one afternoon and walked through a pool of watery sunlight on the floor back into life; all saved, all solved.

One day soon I'd get a ticket, one-way, for the north.

Flesh of Morning

I

WHY IT happens I don't know, but every so often I want to go swinging back, link up with childhood again. Live it again, taste it, walk in that light. Not that it was all light, Christ no—but the issues were so much clearer. It's as if there's a vital clue to the present misery I need to find, I've lost it somewhere, so I go combing through the succulent young grass, the pure snow, sifting and searching. Was misery inside or outside then? Did it come seeping out of the bricks, the ground, leaking down from the sky—or am I reversing the flow? I'm asking, is it me or them? Is the world a poisoned and tragic place now, so that the only hope or virtue is in being nimble enough to sidestep the fall-out, tucked away in some uncontaminated spot, no radios, no papers, head down and the fog billowing over? I'd be a liar though if I gave the impression that every swing back into the past was a deliberate attempt to find out how this stone wedged in my chest came to be stuck there. That's daft: life's not a bloody detective story. Going back is pure instinct with me: begin at the beginning.

That time when I was ten or eleven and I had my brother with me, we took a small ridge tent, just big enough to lie down in side by side if you kept your arms straight, and we had sandwiches and fat bottles of coloured pop, rolled groundsheet, all distributed carefully in the two haversacks slung on our backs. The instant I got mine on I felt grave, responsible, older. Off we went stoutly to catch the bus, mother waving on the doorstep. I had the most to carry, being the elder.

'Watch the traffic, Colin! Look after him!'

She waved us out of sight, dwindling pathetically, and this always undermined me at the outset, looking back as we

321

turned the corner. Goodbye! We could have been crossing continents, entering jungles, instead of tramping down to the bus station for the 28 to the boundary. It must have been my idea to go in a field not far from the aerodrome, and what made it momentous was the thought of staying the night— we'd got permission, we could if we wanted. It was August, dry, windless: the foliage had run riot and exhausted itself, huge dusty nettles in the ditches, dock leaves, the summer bolted and gone to seed. It all hung there, that was the feeling.

You got off the bus and walked for a few minutes, went over a little hump-backed bridge and there was the field to the right, where we'd been with our mother and father once on a picnic. The ground was rough, a wilderness of spiky thistles, tall thick-stemmed brutes, and so many nettle beds you had to pick your way like a goat. It was worse than I'd remembered, so bad that I began to wonder if we'd gone wrong somehow—and then I saw the dried-up stream choked with big jagged stones, the baked mud full of hoof-holes where the cows had trampled down the low bank for a watering place. This was the spot alright, only now it was changed subtly: no parents, no protection, now everything bristled, looked hostile. My brother stumbled, twisted his foot in a rut and whimpered. When I glanced at him he looked away.

The very silence frightened me, and the strange air of desertion. I hated it, the field was ugly in a malignant, menacing sort of way, I wanted to run off home. What was happening? Without speaking we unpacked the tent and started to put it up: it was so small the steel pegs were like meat skewers, you just shoved them into the ground with the heel of your hand. But it hurt, the earth was iron-hard: one after another the skewers bent. More antagonism—the field didn't want us, I felt. Biting my lip I went searching for a softer spot, the blackness congealing in me, while overhead the sky was clouding and lowering like a lid, all without a breeze, and in absolute silence.

'What's up, Alan?'

'Nothing.'

'Foot hurt?'

'Didn't hurt me foot.'

'What was it, then?'

'Ankle.'

'Alright, is it?'

'Suppose so.'

We pitched camp again, desperate now, made our hands sore getting the skewers in, spread out the groundsheet as if we were really staying, but I knew we weren't. I was the elder, I had to bluff it out. We sat nervously in the mouth of our tent, doorflaps rolled back and tied with the tapes and inside that snug, womb-like look a small tent has, the yellow filtered light on the smooth groundsheet with its rubber smell, sleeping-bag laid out—it really looked inviting. I sat there hugging my knees, munching the soggy tomato sandwiches and guzzling the fizzy strawberry pop—I couldn't wait to get away from there. The weather was my excuse; not that Alan cared. He was scared too, I could sense it, either by the silence or the field itself, the ugly look of it: or he might have caught the feeling from me. What had I caught it from? I didn't stop to ask, it was such a relief going.

In a way it was like a sudden attack of homesickness, very treacherous: like going away on a camp with the scouts for that first time. Devon, a lush creamy landscape opening and folding, all its flesh overripe, steep ferny hills, marching up the green rooted lanes sniffing waves of fragrance, and suddenly out on the crest of an amazing new world, the sky hitting you in a great stroke of surprise, the sea far below shivering like an animal—and the light. The clean sea air inside your shirt, up your legs. To be tipped off the lorry with all the tents and equipment into a world like that, lying in the dim bell tent, feet to the pole, and all you could do was ache for the dirty scabby street where your mother lived and nothing else, blind and deaf to it all, your whole being tuned to one far-off point of departure . . . And what a labour camp they made it, our beloved leaders. Up at six digging latrines, getting breakfast, running cross-country races, while the senior scouts and rovers lolled on the grass drawling out orders, sunburnt and handsome giants with their fat thighs and hairy forearms. They lorded it all the week, joking among themselves, very conscious of being an elite. And no resentment from us, not a crumb—it was the same old pattern of school and home we were used to: anyway we were too young to question anything. At night we bought chocolate and slabs of toffee from the tuck shop and lay in bed chewing till we were sick, and I never stopped longing for home, every waking second, all the fibres of my body.

2

THEY SAY, oh I didn't know you wrote things, and immediately you feel wrong, disgusted. For all kinds of reasons and nonreasons. Number one: they haven't read anything and they're not going to, even now—the important thing for them is that it's printed and you get money for it. Money spells importance. All the shit that gets printed daily, surely they can see there's no honour in the mere achievement of print. I want to tell them, you wouldn't have come up glowing to know me when the stuff I was writing wasn't being printed . . . and then I think, how stupid, they wouldn't even have known of its existence: I made sure of that. Not even my brother, my mother and father. There is the same instinct now, maybe even stronger today, to disown the art that comes out of me. Something is not quite right about it, and buried deep in a drawer it doesn't matter, but when it's out and read and the tiny accumulations of comment testify to its existence, then that's terrible. You want to howl at them to shut up because they're ignorant of the reasons, there are reasons they'll never know about. Can't they tell that?

Art needs to be handled gingerly, it isn't safe. Artists are liars. Better to be just a national insurance number. I'd rather dig holes in the road, it's more honourable. Always this finger itch to make a pattern, to order the chaos, find out why. Going up to Nottingham, no job, nowhere to live, just to be near Leila and continue the agony. Why? Because of the chaos, and the ice age we're in, swarming millions walled in, roads everywhere and no directions, and in spite of that a woman could warm you up with a flick of her eyelashes, could touch you with her voice in a way that made you tender about the clothes she wore, the rooms and gardens and streets and weather she moved through to reach you. Regal, fateful, powerfully coming. Sure as fate. I wanted more of that. I had just discovered what it meant to be intimate with a woman. Trust me to pick one who didn't belong to me, who liked me alright but only wanted me for an affair. What's an affair? Well, I'm jumping over great gobbets of misery, no end of twists and turns before I finally manage one night to box her into a corner and make her cry. How women loathe to face facts when it doesn't suit, how direct they are with them when it does. So she stopped fencing at last one night and said, calm as you like: 'I love my husband.' Or words to that effect.

'Oh good,' I said bitterly. 'Where does that leave us?'

'Colin, it doesn't make the slightest difference,' she said, smiling. I stared amazed, eyes burning back into my head. I really thought I was mad at last.

'It doesn't?'

'No, of course not.'

'Sorry, I'm lost.'

'I love you both, in different ways,' she said, perfectly serious.

'Do you really?' I could hear myself saying, eking it out. Punishment was all I could give. I got ready.

'Yes. I mean it, Colin.'

'Christ yes, I'm sure you do. How bloody convenient.'

She took it, I hunted over her face for signs of anger, hurt. Nothing. For the first time I was humiliated, but the despair kept talking.

'I'm lost,' I said.

Loving her to excess had sapped my strength. Now I was weak and dangerous. And this was the beginning of the end. But we kept on, grimly. Then the amazing thing happened, the meeting with Aline, with absolutely no effort or act of will on my part, the first time it's ever happened like this.

326

Go back a bit: that meeting is too important, crucial, I mustn't rush at it. Go back to the hallucinatory few months in the cottage in Devon with Ray and Connie, one night of delirium in Leicester and then the collapse, the fever. On with the grind again, though instead of the screaming factory I'd found a builders' merchants in the city and was a warehouse clerk. A pricing clerk, they called me. Strangest, most demoralising job I've ever had. I was there four weeks and at the end of it I still didn't know what I was supposed to do, except look busy. Why they took me on in the first place I'll never know. Nobody spoke to me by name, I went in and out of that dump like a ghost. Yet it was interesting, if you could summon up enough detachment—an Aladdin's cave on several floors, stacked to the roof with bins of nails, cleats, ragbolts, racks of S-bends, gutters, lavatory pans, and for dozens of items they seemed to have a secret language. Only I was too young for detachment. Also I was obsessed by time, and in this place it dragged terribly. If I could have wandered about exploring, peering in all the musty corners, it wouldn't have been bad, but I was supposed to be pinned at my desk fluttering papers, doing nothing and looking busy. I had a few bills in front of me, to work out the prices—eight bags at fourteen and sixpence—and there were half a dozen items on each bit of flimsy paper and the whole lot took me about twenty minutes, dragging it out. I asked for some work once, really desperate. The chief clerk looked at me as if I'd said some dirty word or left my flies open—I swore to myself I'd grow roots before I asked again.

Even in those days—especially then—it came as no surprise to me, the situation. I'd suspected for a long time that for all its apparent order and efficiency the world was definitely unhinged in some basic, never-to-be-admitted way. You had to humour the bastards, that was the game. Because they were the ones who doled out the bread and butter. So here I was stuck in this long slit of an office, windows so small and high that you couldn't have seen out even if the muck had been scraped off them, here I sat picking my nose day after day and getting paid for it and it didn't strike me as at all peculiar. Just the way of the world. It was stupid to get angry but I did sometimes, seized up with rage suddenly for no reason, which made me lurch to my feet and go slithering out to the lavatory, a prison cell down on the next floor with the usual window too high. At least it was private, with the bolt across you could just stand there like a bloody stork and go into a trance. That was a great luxury, not having to look busy. Worth a ten-bob rise, that. And by standing on the wobbly seat you could see a corner of the building opposite, another warehouse, a bit of the wavy asbestos roof, a scrap of sky. Funny how you felt the need to convince yourself that there was an outside. Amazing how attractive it looked, even the few scraps you could catch sight of—how it beckoned, seduced you: the sounds of kids playing, rag-and-bone man howling like a wolf, women's voices. They drifted up and your eardrums would snatch at them, suck them in of their own accord. You got a thrill then because the walls melted, you were out, liberated, in those few seconds as the sounds hung there in your head.

Nothing on the walls to read. I wrote letters to Leila in there, and to my mother. Ray was still with me in the cottage: nobody else to write to. The amazing simplicity of my life, so uncluttered and so pointless. That was what the seizure of rage meant—I see now. The job fitted me like a glove, it expressed me perfectly. Then it wasn't possible to do anything except react, pour out the love-letters spiced with sex and longing, topped with poetic sauce, own brand. Say good morning, evening.

3

ONE DAY the chief clerk lifted his head and I finally became aware that he was staring at me. This is it, I thought, cards. The bullet. And for some insane reason felt guilty. Still staring, horn rims glinting, greasy black hair glued flat on his skull, parted dead centre as if by a knife. A sharp, short-arsed Liverpool lad, promoted and shipped down by Head Office, so the locals hated him: the new broom, there to streamline the system and galvanise the sleepy south. Now it was my turn.

'A moment?' he was saying. To me. No, he wasn't being sarcastic, he actually meant it.

I stood there. He had a bundle of papers for me.

'We'll put you on checking,' he said, hands ferreting, eyes down. They nearly all have this insulting habit of not looking, when they get you there. 'See Jim Foster,' I heard, so I shoved off.

Jim was a fatherly Devonian, he grunted like a bear but was amiable enough, even on Mondays. He was a family man: written all over him. He plodded, conducted a choir; sometimes his left leg hurt, a legacy of the war. Then his big round body moved a bit irritably and once he swore softly, only once, being a churchman. I looked at him, interested, hopeful, but he was sunk deep in his family fat, impregnable, no winkling him out. What happened on the surface was incidental. I sat next to him every day for the last week I was there while he patiently sorted out little problems for me and I knew he was wasting his time. I wasn't staying. Any day now.

He'd been in the army, Libya, Tripoli, Tobruk, Alamein.

Got wounded and taken prisoner in '42. 'Lovely job that was. Lucky to be out of it.'

Soon he would have clocked up twelve years of service with this firm. I reckoned up. 'You came here straight from school then, did you, before the war?'

'That's it, me 'andsome.'

'Twelve years, in this one room?'

'You've got it, me lover.'

Queer that he never got curious about me, I thought, marvelling at this matter-of-factness, his warm muddy nature which oozed placidly like his body. Then once a prickle of awareness told me that he was mildly curious at last, even before he hauled up the words:

'You aren't from down here, lad.' Speculating, you could hardly call it questioning.

'No, Black Country.'

'Up the line, eh.'

'Straight up till you get to the Bull Ring,' I said and grinned, seeing the same single-line track to the north whenever they trotted out this phrase.

Things livened up momentarily when the reps breezed in on Friday mornings, the room filling up, suddenly taken over by expansive, blustery back-slappers, freebooters flaunting it in front of the desk-chained clerks, lighting up the room with jaunty talk, broad smiles. Some with beer guts, belly laughs, some thin scrannels, one dark Irishman with burning eyes, Red Indian cheekbones, but most of the eyes were shrewd and dead, shamelessly worming straight in. All the same I liked the reckless air that came wafting in at the door on Friday, heralding the weekend. I liked to hear the door bang open, no respect, with Liverpool glaring through his goggles and being ignored: they had no time for him.

'What d'ja know, Jim, old cock?' a man they called Smithy would shout—he was the loudest.

'Not much, or I wouldn't be here,' was the stock answer.

Hearing this bovine character say it made me raise my eyebrows: somehow it was too flip, too cynical, as if he was trying to imitate the tone of the reps.

They were from the outside, so it gave them a shoddy glamour. The freedom of the road came in with them, and it disturbed me for the rest of the day. I felt effervescent, I sighed like a lover, I sat there with ears flapping for news of the outer world. Listening, I was doubly sure. I was on the road out. I sat mouselike and checked and cross-checked, next to a bear who grunted and rubbed his gammy leg, who didn't know much or he wouldn't be there. Drank my tea—one sugar please.

Got to dinnertime and I'd be out, rain or shine, roaming the backstreets, aimless, stretching my legs, sucking down air and liberation, then because the freedom was sandwiched between bouts of prison it was soon a mockery and a burden, a dreary killing of time. What time is it? As a kid out walking with my brother we used to ask old men with watch-chains showing on their stomachs 'Have you got the right time please?' just for the pleasure of it, and to see who guessed the nearest. I still didn't have a watch. Had one once in my teens, when I was a bit of a fop with a flash strap of expanding chrome steel. Felt strangled: couldn't bear one on my wrist. Hated the symbolism, the insanity of minutes, seconds, life chopped up and regulated like that, tripping down the drain with a goosestep rhythm. So I was always looking for clocks on high buildings, peering into the interiors of shops and getting queer looks from shop assistants, asking passers-by.

Out at dinnertimes into a sleazy district, a clutter of backstreets, a rag-tag of roofs and chimneys, bolted on like a rusty grid to Union Street, famed for its herds of sailors of all nationalities, aiming them straight and true for the Halfpenny Bridge, the sailors' barracks, Aggie Weston's, the Salvation Army and the docks. Or the town if you were going the other road. Once famous for drunken fights, coppers prowling in pairs, now it was tame and just dirty, bashed about by the war and the stuffing littered everywhere. Gaping holes, piles of rubble, valerian sprouting from the mortar, fireplaces rusting out in mid-air. Buildings going up here and there, behind the corrugated palisades. It was winter, pinched, often raining and blowing. The windy city. I mooched about with my collar up, sometimes with a pasty stuck in my fist like one of the regulars. Out from Tavy Cottages into the Octagon, along by the gents' outfitters—short and tall, we fit them all—and the barber's, pub, tobacconist, a brewery, and cross over to look at the pulp magazines. That meat. Junk shops, taxi office with a scuffed counter and some weary-looking fireside chairs, all different: man behind the counter grinning out vacantly with every tooth in his head. A tattoo artist. Stand and gaze at the fly-blown photos, most of them known by heart. Elderly man with thin white arms embroidered thickly from wrist to armpit, a dragon billowing up from his belly-button. The skin of his body corpse-white. Women with bone-poor faces and childish eyes, smiling, naked but clothed in intricate design from head to toe. A young woman with a face case-hardened by experience like a pro, stripped to the waist and bloodless like the others, full breasts decorated in flower petals round each nipple.

Down Battery Street to Peel Street, past the chaotic little shop filled to the ceiling with bikes and lumps of machinery for the breakers, the notice still in the window with the comic spelling: 'Wanted, Washing machines, dryers, iol heaters, hand sewing machines, radios, friges, vacuams, ions. En-quireries, 37 Alma Street West.' Felt the destitution like a curse.

Find myself one day outside the big ornamental gates of the naval hospital. Bottle-green ironwork towering up, the coat of arms, anchors, tridents freshly gilded, and not far inside I can see a rack of punch cards and a clock, the commissionaire's box, the flower beds and the cushions of turf, lime trees, and planted in the middle of the grass a white-painted ship's mast with rigging, rope ladder and crow's nest, where they must run up the damn flag or whatever they do. I stared in through the railings like an urchin. Read the notice in the glass-fronted box about visiting times to all wards 'with the exception of Zymotics Ward'. Signed by the surgeon admiral. Going away, following the long stone wall back to the granite warehouse and my chair, desk, papers, I kept telling myself to remember that word 'zymotic', God knows why. The very sight of it up there on a public board struck me as fantastic, and them expecting you to know. Well, you might, if your friend or relative was one. A zymotic! More likely I wanted to remember it for Ray, to try it out on him. If the mood was right. You had to be in the mood for a word like that.

The men of no fixed abode I used to see in the streets, hanging round the steps of the church hostel in King Street, by the scaly old railway arches running with slime and dog piss: derelicts, crazy buggers, homeless old men. I used to admire them, underdogs and outcasts, they were free, they weren't in the clutches sitting stupid in a sunless room all day, they were out in the weather. Wanderers. I didn't want to see how they were chained to the gutters, noses rubbed in the stink of dustbins. Youth grabs what it needs and bounces away, marvellously elastic. Now and then I'd see a city tramp they called Claude, short, shambling, thing like a baseball cap rammed on his skull. Under the peak his charred face screwed up in a permanent ferocious squint. Shirt open to the waist, winter and summer. If he wasn't foraging in a litter bin, arm plunged in right to the armpit, he'd be swaying on the edge of the kerb spewing obscenities at the traffic. 'Fuckin' bastids, bastids!' he screamed. Never saw him without his potato sack slung over his back like an unspeakable Santa Claus. At the newsagents he read the racing results from a paper in one of the wire racks outside, lifting up the corner with one hand and aiming his squint through a magnifying glass held in the other. Once he was straightening up from a bin with a squashed tomato he'd rescued—an old lady said 'here' and held out a bun to him, as you would offer one to an elephant in the zoo: not too close because of the stink, the strangeness. He sent it flying with one swipe and swore at her.

What about the poor bastard they said was a shellshock case – twice he nearly gave me a heart attack. He had a habit of breaking into a wild gallop, leaping in the air and letting out a loud hiss between his teeth like a blown pressure valve, all at the same time. And he had one of these mad fits as he came level with me under the railway bridge, coming up from behind. My shoulders twitched up, my guts wrenched, heart gave a sickening lurch. Twice he caught me like that. Tall, gangling, a lopsided face with a coconut tuft of gingery hair, expression like a frightened schoolboy. As if terrified of himself, what he might do next. 'Isn't it dreadful,' you heard ladies murmur. 'He has a wife and family, you know, oh yes, lovely woman, she won't live with him any more. Wouldn't you think somebody could do something?'

Going past a gutted shop, only the front walls and a broken window frame left, I saw the sign on the square of red tin poking out in the street like a railway signal: Drink Vimto. Took me back in a rush to pre-war, to those summery evenings around Harbourne. I sat meekly in the back of the big Siddley my uncle drove for his firm, my aunt beside him, queening it, and in the back with me wallowing in the brown leather was my cousin Margaret. Well away in her corner, plenty of space between us—I was the poor relation. That didn't matter, I wasn't bothered: not then. It all went with the car, the sumptuous walnut dashboard, my uncle's elbow out of the offside window and the panache of his driving, strumming on his knee with his left hand. Early as that, young as I was, I knew the smell of power and money, the assurance that went with it, the swank and ignorance and fish-eyed patronage. Nobody heeded the vast pure power of the sky and the stillness that belonged to that, the day running out calmly, trickling away like the last of the tide, leaving this enormous peaceful feeling in the wash of sunlight. The land glowing beyond the hedges in flakes of gold, scorching a wood. The leaves smouldered, went out. We went wafting on rich springs through the lanes frothing to the rims with pale umbels of cowparsley, hemlock, angelica, with elders, hazels, stirring the verges and making the cows stare. Suddenly Margaret yelled out, 'Stop the car, daddy, I want a Vimto!'

Not please or can we stop. I could have seen my father stopping. We swung in at the Red Lion, pulled up with sedate majesty in a crunch of gravel and as my uncle climbed out he said over his shoulder, 'What does Colin want?' When she didn't answer he said a little peevishly, 'Margaret?'

'How should I know?' she screeched. I was used to these situations, but I still squirmed. They went with the car. My uncle was alright, I could get on with him fine when we were alone, it was the family man side I couldn't stand: the three of them together. This was the man who stuck his face in the window and said, wagging his sleek head, widening his watery eyes, 'Will my family and nephew for Christ's sake tell me what I am required to fetch from this hostelry?' Which was nothing much, but the tone was poisonous.

I'd have one of those fruit drinks, dark and sugary, the Vimto thing, sucking it up through the straw and holding down the belches. My uncle drank his beer with a big facial performance, lip-smacking noises, ahs and ums, and then he belched. 'Jack!' his wife said, from force of habit, or it might have been for my benefit. Margaret cuddled into the corner with her bottle: she was my age but she liked to act babyish. She was soft-looking, a girl. She smelled different. Strange. I wanted to poke my finger in her flesh, to feel the difference.

4

GIRLS. I went to see the girl from Leeds, the art student who was working at Butlins for the summer. She had a vacation job. Pwllheli. Looked on the map to find it, up and down the Welsh bulge—ah yes. Over twenty-one and still hadn't met a girl I could talk to, be with. Christ, you had to be desperate to go to Pwllheli, wherever it was, just to meet a girl. I was desperate in a quiet way and I had the photo to go on—dark hair, eyes, uptilted face looking a little arrogant for the camera—and the letters were friendly, though I had to admit, cool. Hell, what would I be doing all holiday anyway except mooning about the house, going for melancholy walks to the edge of the streets and across a stile into the meadows on warm evenings, taking a book, say Rimbaud —'melancholy golden wash of the setting sun'. Look on the map and find Pwllheli, trace the route. Send a note and then go before she had a chance to say no—nothing to lose. Meet her, see what happens. The will and the desperation forcing to create meetings, against the hermit instinct and the gag of shyness. The will won the first round, always, then drawing nearer the awful conflict fought itself out in my guts. White and sick and sweating, vowing never again. But I get there. The fear of failure worse than the dread of disgrace.

My mother showed remarkable restraint whenever I said I was going here or there. Strange journeys, visits, with no reasons ever offered: surely she must have been dying to know. She didn't ask. Wouldn't. I was grateful, but it was unnerving and in the end left me more guilty than a row and recriminations would have done, because this way there was no opportunity for anger. I couldn't rage righteously when they refused to pry, couldn't rebel against the stupid restrictions and narrow minds. No opposition, nothing. A clear road. Well, I knew that was a lie, but I kept quiet and just hopped it. Held my face straight and said, casual as you like:

'Going to North Wales for a few days. Wander round a bit.'

'All right. You'll need some clean underwear—when were you thinking of going?'

'Oh, Monday I think.'

As soon as she became concerned over anything, she frowned like a girl.

Afterwards I thought, the letter postmarked Pwllheli which came. She's not a fool, my mother: though I doubt if she'd ever heard of the place. It wasn't that, it was just her knack for putting two and two together.

The train journey was dreamlike, now I think of it. I went across from the Midlands, changed somewhere and was blind to everything, so preoccupied with the struggle inside. All inner attention, like a man near to being mad. The only thing I noticed was that the Pwllheli place was as far as the train went: terminus. First time I'd seen a railway track ending at a pair of buffers inside the station, except for London. It made the whole thing so ridiculously portentous, me getting off at the end of the line carrying a handful of things in a weekend bag—like a bad film. But the station almost cheered me up, light and airy and clean, small, lots of painted wood, sun shining gaily through the glass skylights, and going through the ticket barrier to a completely new town. It began to feel good to be lost.

I walked about for an hour getting the feel of the town, wondering vaguely where the sea was, not caring a damn about it, still dominated by the stifled tug-of-war in my chest, the endless warfare I kept trying to blot out by a refrain that went roughly like this: if anything happens it happens, if it doesn't it doesn't—what have I got to lose? Jesus, here I

337

was nearly falling off the end of the peninsula and they'd got a Woolworth's, a seasidy, country one, bare clattering board floor and antiquated counters. And bang opposite was the Co-op. Stone buildings, short twisty streets, nothing much to it but for the moment I couldn't sort out the pattern. Suddenly I felt drained, dragged out by the strain and strangeness. I went in like a dreamwalker through the glass front of a café and sat drinking tea, eating a piece of sawdust cake—jukebox playing 'Put another nickel in . . .' A gang of kids, youths and girls, tumbled in and started fooling about, letting out self-conscious squawks and giggles that set my teeth on edge, drawing attention to things I thought I'd accepted, the bubbly bleak music, stamped-out plastic cups and saucers, candy-floss pink walls and lollipop people. But it was the plate glass I really loathed. I sat by the glass wall and I could see out, only I wasn't out. A lie. A trick. As if it didn't matter whether you were in or out of the horrible bloody dump. Soon we won't know the difference, it'll be painless. I got up and went out, saw a sign that said 'To the seafront' and started walking that way in a trance, looking in front windows of houses for a bed and breakfast sign. Soon found a trim little terraced house and was going up the doll's house staircase inside to approve the room.

'That's very nice,' nodding.

'When would you like your breakfast?' the woman said. 'What time?'

'I don't mind.'

'Eight, is that too early for you?'

'Oh no.'

'I'll give you a call, shall I?'

In the soft fussy room I lay still, smelling camphor, staring up at the plank ceiling, the nails, the joints, telling myself that this was Wales, a morning in Wales. Nothing seemed much different: I always expect dramatic differences. The woman's singsong was hardly noticeable but she had to

338

bring hot water in a tall white jug and leave it outside the door. I heard it then, Wales.

'You'll see the washbasin,' she called. 'Young man?'

'Yes, thank you very much.'

When I opened the door for the jug I could smell the bacon, even hear the busy sizzle. I was hungry, I was here, I'd nearly done it. My spirits began to lift, the mere fact of being here rejuvenated me. Life was easy if you just let it happen. I was cocky now. I poured the hot water into the basin, touched it with my finger. Too hot. Then I spotted another, even bigger jug, a tin one, under the marble-topped washstand. Cold water. Life was simple, hot and cold, one problem at a time.

Found the post office and bought a letter card: sat on a bench, a warm sunless morning, and wrote to her. Dear Julie, I'm here, when can you meet me and where? Just say the time and the place—don't work too hard. Probably nothing like that but it was brief. I hadn't got into my stride writing letters to her from home. Had to meet her first, I kept telling myself, but something in me sank like a stone at the thought. Those replies of hers, they were so bloody dead. And ominous. What the hell, who cares about letters, I don't want a pen friend, I want a girl. Flesh and bones and blood. And so on. Inside I was far from hopeful.

That afternoon I went into a stationer's and there was a table of books for sale, remainders, paper jackets soiled. Walked out with one called 'Why Abstract' and followed the sign to the coast, meaning to sit on a bench and read my book. Went by a large guest-house on the corner, black-and-white painted windows, stranded between the sea and the town, and then there was nothing, nobody. The road curved to the right beside the sand dunes, full of purpose, then it ran on blankly. I sat on a rock and stared at the sea, watched a seagull which happened to be directly ahead, offering itself to the horizon, and for the life of me I couldn't bring myself to move my head one way or the other, it was such a desolate-looking coast, such a Godforsaken spot. Like sitting at the edge of the world. It was warm in town, but not here. The breeze had a bite in it, the whole feel of the place was abrasive, cold, inhospitable. I was beyond feeling a repulsion for it: just frozen. Got up and turned my back, walked almost eagerly towards the town, the knot of streets, shoppers and loungers, the holidaymakers gawping, scribbling their postcards, hunting down gifts. I went and sat in the snack bar again. Wales for the Welsh. Dear Julie, hurry up and I hope to Christ you've got a friendly face. Collecting my egg and chips I even smiled wanly at the girl behind the counter, one human being to another. Not a flicker. Deep freeze handmaiden.

Julie turned out to be the same, expressionless. I met her at seven, after her day at Butlins—perhaps that was the trouble. And she could have been bodiless as we went up the same blank road to that wind-scraped coast and I gazed ahead fixedly, numb with the cold, the icy aura of her, and struggled to wring out words, make contact, when the truth was I couldn't wait to get away, none of it meant a thing, we were wasting our time.

She was making me more and more insipid; I hated her for that.

'Had a hard day?'

'Oh, so-so.'

'How long will you be here?'

'Another three weeks yet.'

Halted, crossed over, walked on, burdened by defeat.

'Like it here?'

'What's that?'

'This place, do you like it?'

'Not much.'

She looked neat and unruffled in her cornflower blue, but her indifference was showing. She wasn't amused by my persistence, she wasn't anything.

'You the only student?'

'Where, at the camp?'

'The camp, yes.'

'Oh no, there are six or seven. At least. Two French boys. They're nice.'

That's how it went.

5

IT WAS more or less the same fiasco with Connie's friend Jan when she came for a holiday that time: it must have been Easter. I was in the cottage with Ray and Connie and the baby, sharing—first of all sleeping on a camp bed in the living room because there was only one bedroom, then a couple in the village let me have a bedroom for a pound a week, and that was better, we could spread out a bit. Fact was, the good life we'd embraced so innocently had begun to crumble. Our jobs had undermined it, Ray's and mine, and in the evenings I was stuck there night after night, too tired to move out, blocking their marriage with dreams of adultery. The woman up the line, beckoning, intriguing. I might even have been writing a letter to her when Connie suddenly sang out: 'Hey folks, listen to this – Jan's coming!'

Ray lifted his head, startled. 'How d'you mean? A holiday?'

'Of course,' Connie crowed, 'what did you think I meant?'

'Isn't she working then?'

Connie gave one of her big yells of laughter; she was really zooming about inside with her news. 'It's Easter next week, daftie!'

And naturally Connie was bound to feel gay: for weeks Ray and me had been going in to work together, sometimes meeting on the way home and anyway swopping talk and ideas at night, jawing on about books, writing fan letters to one or two writers and speculating endlessly on their lives, struggles, developments. Utterly dreamy, ridiculous, up-in-the-clouds thoughts, the kind of idealistic boyish un-worldly guff that women hear mostly in silence, sitting in a corner. When they get their heads together it's for something much more personal. Either that or gossip. It has to be of some concern to them, to affect them personally.

So Jan was coming. This would even things up for her. I imagine too that she thought things might end with me fixed up with a girl friend—let's say at least that the thought crossed her mind—and then I'd be off their necks for a while, thank God. Who could blame anyone for hoping? Only it wasn't to be. I hadn't met Jan, so naturally I was curious, and the night before she was due we decided to make the room festive and tack up the watercolours we'd done that winter. We had a pile of daubs between us—up they went all round the fireplace, the window, even on the door. Seeing the brave show, nipping outside to peer in at the window at night just to observe the effect, a cave of colour, a jewel box (like that flash of glory in the glimpse of Gauguin's hut at the close of *Moon and Sixpence*—or did I dream it?)—it looked so inviting, token of the good life we'd nearly talked away down the drain, that I began to wish I wasn't leaving after all. I'd more or less decided, secretly, to go straight after Easter.

When I say the same fiasco I don't mean that Jan was in the least like Julie. On the contrary, they couldn't have differed more, those two. Julie the typical self-conscious teenager, knowing, face gummed up none too artistically with make-up, and under it the frozen virgin. Sealed and waiting for the one and only, the man she would marry. He would unlock her, no one else. But Jan's effect on me was equally disastrous, simply because she was vulnerable, shrinking almost visibly from further hurt, and for me that made her virtually untouchable. I couldn't bear to be the one, her awareness filled me with anguish, I shrank back instinctively from the responsibility. Not me. Yet how tender she was with the baby, silently bending over, and sensitive in her listening to people, withdrawn and yet you felt she was registering nuances, tones, her small intense face had that kind of quick snatching intelligence. She could be a bitch too, I was sure,

343

from one or two stinging answers she gave—though as a rule she sat quiet. Cramped up in silence. You longed to say the word that would unlock her, make her life pour, and ended up horribly afflicted instead with the same disease if you had any tendencies that way yourself, as I did. She was contagious. I was afraid of her. Her silences were glutinous, they made me feel sick. She was the last thing I wanted. Tall, awkward, large-boned, a tortured Yorkshire girl. I went one night into town with her to see a film, it was *Mr Deeds*, on at the Scala, one of those enormous baroque picture palaces they used to build in the thirties, heyday of the cinema, gilt and velvet and plush everywhere, a scarlet and gold heaven to keep the workers happy in their back-to-backs, enough room in there to seat a thousand. Off we went to catch the bus and there was Connie in the hall making sheep's eyes at us, chortling over our 'date'.

'Hurry up, you'll be late,' she hooted, looking meaningfully, private-public, at Ray, who was doing his best to stay non-committal.

'I was born late,' I said.

'Keep your hair on, we're going,' Jan said, flinty-eyed. They'd worked together in the same office somewhere, once upon a time. Bits of old slang and familiarity kept popping out. They enjoyed this. They had their own relationship, connected with this, which they liked to revive and renew every so often with the old language. And their own brand of humour. This way they could assert themselves, escape from Ray and me if they wanted, thumbing their noses in the process. We couldn't follow into those thickets, or at least I couldn't, I didn't know any of the code.

The film we'd chosen to see couldn't have been a more ironic choice, for in it shyness was enshrined as a virtue, as the most paramount shining thing. All the way through it was integrity and lump in the throat and fumbling, butter-fingered innocence in the midst of corruption, a triumph of

344

the ordinary speechless man who has his values straight, who recites bits of poems on doorsteps, then falls over the dustbin in confusion, love and confusion. That sounds like sarcasm, but at the time I loved it and the Gary Cooper hero passionately, in fact for years after. Went to see every film he appeared in, though I never experienced that kind of thrill again. It was fantasy of course—shyness cripples, it never triumphs—but how it encouraged and pampered me, gave me a super-ego to live up to, made me glamorous! Until the lights came on, that is, until we shuffled out and the reality was there lined up, painted even more venomously in shit-colours for us to drag through, debilitated beyond words. Well, I speak for myself. As if to rub it in we passed a couple of morons at a street corner who kept lunging at each other and then one would let rip a rasping ugly laugh, and on our way in to the bus station a pack of kids on motorbikes came blarting up in full cry. I looked at Jan, who was plunging down the ramp on long strides, remote from me. I screwed up my face half-humorously at the din to convey comment— the skin of the world was corrupt, but that's nothing—and she just smiled faintly in a far-off, mysterious sort of fashion. Once again I was being tormented by a sense of failure, unable to make any contact or decide whose fault it was. This time at least it was obvious it wasn't just me to blame, but why couldn't I take the initiative, break through? It took passion to be heroic. I told myself glumly afterwards that I might have made the effort if she had interested me that much, which wasn't quite true as we sat side by side in the cinema, not touching, then on the bus locked in difficult, painfully stilted conversation, but by the time we'd walked through the village on stiff legs, past lighted windows, voices, a snatch of song from a radio, it was the truth. My personal universe was waiting, all I wanted was to plunge back into it.

The ache of remorse as I went to bed didn't last the night: once I'd let go of the nagging uneasy notion of us as a pair, things were much better. The whole menage seemed to relax and we either did things on our own or collectively that holiday, wandering on the rocks and pebbles of the beach looking for something special, glass, bits of driftwood, stones bored through by the sea, then on Sunday out for a jaunt to the Point—if you craned your neck you could see it from the cottage window—and we took it in turns pushing the push-chair up through the trees, the long peaceful track with its ruts and gulleys full of leaf mould, sea churning white in the steep rocky inlets below our feet. We'd get lungfuls of air and space, smell the leaf mould, Ray making mental notes to bring his saw as we sailed past thick branches lying dead and encrusted with lichen in the ferns. We went faster, tugged by that Point which always surprised us when we broke out of the trees and the gloaming on to the turf and outcrops—like being shot suddenly straight out to sea, or on the deck of a ship. Not a bay, not a cove, the open sea! Turning our backs on that and returning to the cottage, coming indoors to make a meal, involved a shrinking, it often seemed to me—we were so expanded and pleased with ourselves up there. Connie voiced it exactly, more than once, pouting and moving her limbs angrily, unbuckling the baby's strap and standing up with him seated on her forearm, bland as a Buddha.

'I don't wanna come in. Bloody cooking,' she'd say.

'Let's starve, then,' Ray said once, taking up the challenge. He was bent over folding up the pushchair flat like a sand-wich, and I remember holding my breath for a second: I was hungry.

6

I'M WELL aware now that married women were my salvation. Girls were either too pure or too cagey, or a baffling mixture of both. How could you bring yourself to touch a girl who was so unsullied, who flushed and looked down at her feet or waited quivering like a sacrifice? And worse still were the brassy ones who had it all worked out in detail in advance, there it was ringing up in their cash-register eyes, your whole damn future: bungalow, carpet slippers, the little paddock in the rear where they let you canter to and fro with the lawnmower. Women were better. Women who'd been through the mill enough to be saddened, but they weren't defeated yet, only sharpened a little and wiser a lot: these were the ones with love and madness and generosity to spare if you could only find them.

I didn't find Aline, she was sitting quietly in the back of the junk shop. The printseller, that's how he described himself, introduced us. I knew him slightly, and it seemed they were old friends.

'Come and meet Aline,' he said, eyes gleaming. He liked to provide distractions for people.

There was no blinding flash or any of that nonsense, in fact we didn't go for each other at all at first. I made no real impression, she told me later. Honesty in a woman was something I hadn't encountered before: not this frontal kind.

'I wouldn't have looked twice at you in the street, to tell you the truth.'

I laughed: I knew I was safe.

For my part, I noted a pleasant, intelligent-looking woman with big eyes looking at me very steady and direct, with no particular curiosity or interest, nothing to spark me off.

'You had that vile blue serge suit on, you looked common, you could have been anybody,' she said.

'Clothes don't matter, do they?'

'They do to me, oh yes,' she said firmly.

'Alright, I'd got my disgusting suit on.'

'Then you and Lou invited me up to your flat for tea that Saturday and you came down the stairs to let me in—you were in that dark sailor's jersey thing, your brother's. You looked . . . different. What a difference! Soon as I set eyes on you that second time I thought—aha, what's this?'

I laughed again, felt absurdly privileged. It was a gift she had.

And it was letting her in from the street that I woke up to her, the luxuriance of her throat and shoulders, which the string of pearls seemed to confirm, the vibrant eagerness that wasn't flushing but a slight bending forward of the head, very young and touching—yet at the same time she was subtle, contained, rich and sad with her store of experience, smiling. It was a dank November afternoon, drizzly, but she was hatless, giving an umbrella a quick shake as she entered the hallway and presented me like a child with something in a paper bag: something heavy.

'My contribution,' she said happily.

'What's in it?' I said, surprised.

The stairs were narrow and she hadn't set foot in the house before so I led the way, the back of my body tinglingly aware of her.

'Nothing exciting—a tin of fruit,' she laughed.

'Ah yes, for the tea-party.'

'Is that all right?'

'What's that?'

'Is it enough? It's not much . . .'

'Yes, fine. Didn't expect anything. In a minute I'll just nip across the road for a loaf and some cakes.'

Gulping it out, but I had the excuse of the stairs.

And we'd got to our landing. I was aware for the first time of how poor it looked. Turned the corner to find Lou waiting in the doorway in silence, almost a resentful expression on his face. He'd heard us coming up.

'Here she is,' I said.

'Hallo,' she said brightly, if a little guarded.

'Cheers,' he said, ducking back inside.

He was there first, installed and waiting, so that gave him the upper hand. As if sensing this, Aline pushed out a remark to placate him.

'What do you do on Saturday afternoons as a rule?' she asked.

'Me?'

'Yes.'

'Have a snooze.'

'Oh dear!' she said.

He looked at her briefly. 'Why, what's up?'

'I'm disturbing your snooze.'

He shrugged and dropped down on the sofa, bang.

'Am I?' she asked, cool, her eyes animated.

'Don't be daft,' he said.

He could be like this, withdrawn, yet you could go on being relaxed and intimate with him as long as you knew the signs and didn't come too close. I'd seen him like this many a time. The touch of resentment could have been anything, perhaps he wanted to work, or wasn't in the mood to talk. I didn't care, it was exciting to have her in the room. It wasn't a room now, it was a stage: charged, electric. We made entrances, exits.

For a fortnight we'd lived in it, Lou and me, like a couple of monks. We had two rooms looking downhill to the station with its clock tower, and farther on the Council House, the trolleys went hissing past with a sound like acid spraying, the trees outside the big black church looked delicate and mysterious in winter, twigs lit up from underneath at night by the street lamps, half lost in fog in the mornings. Across the landing was the kitchen we shared with the Hungarian and his English wife, the couple who sublet the rooms to us. Lou was lolling on the lumpy old sofa with his legs spread out and a funny bent grin on his face: something was biting him. I began introducing him to Aline properly and she said, 'We know each other, Colin.'

Two surprises—the unexpected use of my name, which gave me a shock and I came very alert to her, and to find out that they were acquainted. Why hadn't Lou mentioned it, when I told him she was coming in for tea? I looked at him with fresh interest, puzzled, and he had the local paper spread on the floor in front of him and was hanging over it, reading—he liked doing that.

'I didn't realize that, Lou,' I said.

'Only to say how d'yer do—since going in the shop, like,' he mumbled, not raising his head or bothering to put any expression in his voice. He was a hard man to stare in the eye if he was set on being evasive, and this was one of those occasions: though his manner generally was flitting and quick, a will-o-the-wisp approach to life that kept him uninvolved and free and rolling, on the move always: like the buses he sprang into. He wouldn't walk anywhere if he could help it. In Nottingham you could walk down a street with him anywhere and see him nodding or waving to somebody—he seemed to know hundreds of people. So it was no surprise, when I considered it, him knowing Aline, and not to think it worth a mention was characteristic too. This apparent gregariousness which kept him (I nearly said saved him) from real contact with anybody, was it a philosophy he was working at, forming and nurturing it within himself, or a blind fear that was driving him? It wasn't a question you could ask him direct, he'd slip away under some jokey half-answer.

'How's the bread situation?' I asked him.

'Afraid the cupboard's bare, mate,' he said, still with his

head down and not a flicker of interest in his voice. You're overdoing it, I thought. Then he sat up: 'I could do with some fags if you're going over the shop. Hang about, I've got a quid here somewhere.'

'Have some of my cigarettes. Here!' Aline said, opening her handbag, and I flinched, she was being too nice to him in the mood he was in. He sounded curdled, best to let him be.

'Tips on 'em?' he said.

'Yes—have some, will you? Please.'

'Not tips,' he said shortly. 'Like smoking nowt.'

I was in sympathy with her big-heartedness, losing patience with the mingy spirit he was indulging.

'Shan't be a minute,' I said at the door and left them together, slipped down into the street that was quieter now with dusk settling into it, people going home to tea, a lull on the pavements, and I looked up at the living-room window, still unlit. I felt strangely elated at the thought of her up there, waiting.

Back up the stairs, rapid, and Lou was still at it, reading the bloody paper, but no sign of Aline. I tossed him his packet of ten and he said, 'Ta,' and I said, 'Where is she?'

'In the kitchen or having a slash, I dunno,' he said, still doing the hard act in a half-hearted way. I gave him up and went to look for her.

She was filling up the kettle at the sink, there was her fruit salad tin lifting its lid, she'd opened that and even got out plates, cups and saucers, cutlery. Home from home.

'That was quick,' she said. 'Shall I have the bread?'

'If you like,' and it was ridiculously easy to be with her, no strain, I couldn't believe it was happening to me. I avoided looking at her, this woman who was at my disposal.

'How do you like it, thick or thin?'

'Oh, average.'

351

She worked away, smiling faintly to herself: I saw that much.

'You don't come from around here, do you?'

'No,' I said.

'D'you like it, as a town?'

'It's not bad.'

'I grew up here. I've never been anywhere else,' she said simply.

I lit the gas under the kettle while she went on with things, and some silly chat passed between us about the shop on the corner, Gault's, where I'd been, and the treacle tart they sold there.

'You want to try it sometime, it melts in your mouth,' she said.

'I've got some,' I said, and we laughed. 'You must have been concentrating on it while I was over there.'

'No,' she said quickly, 'no I wasn't thinking of that.'

Something in her voice made me look at her, her eyes shone with her secret, and a kind of challenge, a tense defiance to her face that was beautiful and bare, shining like a knife blade. I couldn't face her, the kettle was on the boil so I saw to it, while she found the tray and loaded it up with our feast.

'Quite a spread,' I said, murmuring it. Whatever we said now was intimate, a sort of touching. My voice did it of its own accord. I couldn't help myself, I moved over to her by the kitchen table and picked up the tray, bowls glowing with glazed fruit in the thick white crockery. As if helplessly she reached out and touched my cheek, watching my face. I felt my eyes dark and soft on her, I was lissom, I had power and beauty for her in that moment, it went rippling over me. I astonished myself.

7

LOU COLTMAN was an elusive lad from the very beginning; pale haunted eyes that cast an immediate spell on me,
said come on, live in a blaze of glory, it's all ours: he revelled
in the power of his youth. His gift of intimacy came natural
too, his whole face invited you, he couldn't help being personal, like the notes I had from him—then when you got
there he'd gone, slipped away from you mysteriously. He'd
always be a ghost. Small, lean, fair hair like a scrubbing brush
on his forehead and later on a fringe of beard which made him
somehow more boyish-looking than ever.

I'd been in Nottingham for months and I went one night
to the Co-op hall, desperate for company, unable to bear the
bed-sitting-room life I was leading, the creeping, creaking
noises of other tenants, chained and padlocked doors, a
woman sobbing one night, shouts, the hand-wringing despair I imagined: worst of all the four utterly blank walls of
your own room as you opened the door at night and walked
in, put down the milk bottle and it went *clonk*. The effort to
accept that room sickened me, the terrible blankness of those
walls drained the fight out of me. On the walls now were two
watercolours I'd painted in there, God knows how: one a
Pieta head, long big-nosed Mediterranean head in lime greens
and bilious yellow and brown-pink, done blurry out of
ignorance on too-wet paper and then liked for the effect.
Thought I'd stumbled on a new technique. Now they looked
dingy and in keeping with the general dirty-rags wretched-
ness of the house, unspeakably sad they looked at times like
the chest of drawers, the blankets. I stared at them—the
other was a bowl of fruit—and groaned, like a man who
realises he's caught a dread disease. Melancholia. Leila said,

Do some painting, now you've got a room of your own. Or she may have said 'work'—I'd like to see some of your work. She spoke about art like a professional, had a great respect for it, whereas it seemed grotesque and choking to think of it in any other way except as something you did on the run between cataclysms, like making love. Thief art. But it was her prodding undoubtedly, my two-hours-a-week visitor from outer space—these meagre efforts were products of the old dispensation. Aline saw art as oceanic, a lush oriental sea growing, rising like wheat on the landscape, and her own melancholy would have told her that nothing grows in a bed-sitting-room.

And it was the same with writing, the impossibility of being a Writer today, complete with study and desk and wifey: surely nothing could be more absurd. Because there were connotations that went with that tranquil picture, you had to avoid like the plague those shameful inferences of authority, of speaking as a man of substance and weight, a little place in society and a little platform to clamber on, the spokesman, the man who judges, establishes directions, morals, gets listened to, taken account of. It didn't wash any more. Apply it to yourself, even with your eyes and ears shut tight to all the chaos, and you saw at once what a load of shit it was. Any writing had to be on the sly as it were, you weren't fit to judge, nobody was: the only thing you could possibly offer were mad songs, temptations, rules of survival for yourself— if anyone else found a use for them they were welcome, but it couldn't ever be created with a public in mind. No more, no more. You walked backwards and obliterated your footprints as you went, swearing blind it wasn't you, they must be mistaken. Artist? He went that way. Not me, never. Wouldn't be seen dead with him.

That was the message I had from Lou Coltman that night at the Co-op hall, and in some strange wafting fashion it came across without him saying a word, before the play-reading even started. I got very excited just looking at him. He was like a book you put off opening. You postpone it, you know what's in store for you. Sitting on the hard ordinary chair with his copy closed and such electric intensity about him, his hands and his head, I could hardly believe it. I wouldn't have cared if he hadn't opened his mouth all night, I sat gobbling him up. He sat there, composed, the essence of restraint, then it began and he was coiled like a spring, ready for freshness, savagery, abandon. What was it I found so riveting about him—they were reading this Strindberg thing, spiky and malicious, you tensed yourself for cruelty and got pierced with tenderness—what was the galvanic quality he had surging off him, a mixture of nervy, abject panic and the most devastating contempt and rage and held-back passion? He was the producer, too: I might have guessed. About forty of us in the audience, no more, and I kept glancing to left and right through the performance but not a flicker of the electricity I was receiving seemed to register on the others. Sat there like lumps of wood, clapped dutifully at the end as if measuring it out on their palms, and I wanted to grab their collars and shake a storm of rapture out of them, I wanted to signal a message back, acknowledge that here was somebody aware of an extraordinary event.

What I actually did, I slunk out with the rest of them into the pouring rain, tramped back to my room, splashing along pavements hunched up with my raincoat collar turned up and buttoned, conjuring up in my head his appearance, movements rather than the tone of his voice, trying to fathom the nature of this amazing throw-away power of his. I ended up scribbling him a fan letter: really a letter of thanks for existing, making it happen, whatever it was—it came out pretty incoherent so I left it like that. Why not? What was there to say after all except thanks and how fantastic to stumble on an oasis in a city I'd thought was dry as a rock?

Next thing was, the pallid pop-eyed lady on the ground floor, half out of her mind with her seven kids and her husband in the navy, she was yelling up the stairs in the frantic hysterical screech she used for her family to tell me to come down, I had a visitor. Saturday afternoon; it was a wonder I was in. Thought it must be a mistake because I didn't know anybody: apart from Leila, nobody knew I was here, I might as well have been dead. I was like a ghost walking, no name, no identity, if the front door had been locked I could have floated through the walls. Who the hell could it be?

Lou Coltman stood on the pavement, hanging back, half defiant and half indifferent, or sheepish—I was never sure. Smaller, slighter than I'd remembered, slouchingly cocky about the head and shoulders, fag in his mouth.

'Got your note,' he said, and twitched slightly round the eyes: very slightly but I saw it.

'Yes—I'd forgot—can you come up?' I gabbled.

'After you, mate,' he said, coming forward. Just a touch of mockery, but no sneering. Friendly, curious, and when he moved, eager. Hair creamed and not having it, bristling up at the front, shoes sharp and scuffed, trouser ends a bit tatty-looking. Crisp white shirt and dark tie like a piece of rag, knotted anyhow.

Upstairs he seemed utterly indifferent to my ugly room. Sat on the edge of my bed, on the grey army blanket, leaned forward with his legs apart and concentrated on his cigarette: or on whatever he was thinking. Staring down at the floor. I waited, swam around in the silence, bathed in optimism, saying things to myself like this: Look who's here! Look what the wind's blown in! He was sitting and smoking. It was funny—I began to wonder what he'd come for: maybe just a sit down. But it was merely to establish contact. He did that all the time, made contact and then waited. His philosophy, if you could call it that, was summed up in one rule: Never push anything. After a while I found his waiting game un-nerving and said, 'How about a cup of tea?'

'Coffee me, if you've got some,' he said flatly.

'Yes, plenty--I'll put the kettle on then.'

'No milk,' he said.

The cooker was outside the door on the landing, a com-munal one, my Woolworth's tin kettle on the flaky iron grid, up to now my one cooking utensil. Might get a saucepan one day to boil an egg in, but I recoiled from any suggestion of permanency, anything that might look as though I were setting myself up in this house. I was finding out how super-stitious I was, afraid to tempt fate. Hop, skip and jump down to the turn in the stairs, where a yellow triangle of sink was snug in the corner, under a narrow window—that's where I had to go to fetch water. Twist the tap and it sput-tered and slushed like an old man talking through ill-fitting dentures, then it filled your kettle in a series of steady retches. Or if somebody had a tap on somewhere in the depths of the house, all you got was a faint strangling sound and you had to wait. Water this time, retch, retch, and it almost had a merry splash to it now, with a visitor waiting upstairs. My first. Life could be something, even here. I didn't need to look, I could tell by the weight when I had enough water in.

I offered him some bread and cheese, tomato, lettuce leaf, but he wasn't interested.

'This is smashing.'

Thighs parted, he sucked gingerly at the hot coffee, glanced sideways at the newspaper he'd laid out on the blanket be-side him, poking vague disinterested questions at me, long intervals in between.

'So you wrote me a note,' he said, 'just like that.'

'That's it.'

Now and again he flicked glances at me surreptitiously. Sly or shy, I couldn't decide.

'Often do things like that, do you? Straight off, I mean?'

'No, not exactly,' I laughed. 'Never done it before.'

Which made him look properly, with real interest and respect.

'Good, I like that,' he said with relish, and I sparkled, felt good, responding at once.

'You do?' came out of me, and I despised it for what it was, worldly, cagey, nothing to do with how I felt.

'Yeh, that's how I like things to happen, off the cuff like that. Random.'

'I know what you mean,' I said coolly, waiting.

He stuck his pale young face forward, pugnacious, alive to the implications of this idea, suddenly very positive and breezy, evangelistic even.

'If you'd gone away and thought about it for a week, mulled it over, considered it from every angle and *then* done something about it—supposing you had—it wouldn't have been the same at all,' he said.

I considered this speech: it was quite a mouthful for him.

'Wouldn't it?' I said (or some devil in me), merely to egg him on.

He shook his head very seriously, swelled out his bottom lip, juicy red, grotesque.

'Not the same.'

Abstracted, his eyes wandered down to his newsprint again.

To jolt him I said stubbornly, 'Not if I used exactly the same words?'

Again his head shook in the stubborn veto: 'If you get a sudden impulse and say to your girl friend, luv ya, that's not like going off for a fortnight, weighing up the pros and cons and then posting it in a bloody letter, is it?'

I grinned. 'You said a week.'

A second ago it was as if the living universe hung waiting for answers, now he slumped over on one elbow, rummaging for fags in his right-hand pocket, affecting a bored air. 'Don't let's flog it.'

'No,' I said.

I felt the lonely shiver in the chest that comes with withdrawing, with presuming too much, too soon.

'Good cuppa.'

'Fancy some more?'

'Not me. You have what you want.'

But I just waited emptily, not unhappy, while he smoked and furrowed his forehead, tussled inside himself and finally came up with—'Each day ought to be a blank sheet of paper in front of you, waiting for scribbles, nothing mapped out beforehand. That's how it ought to be.'

'It is for me, more or less.'

With a queer touch of contempt or pique, as if I'd tried to steal his thunder, he said, 'You're home and dry then, no problems.'

'Think so?'

He nodded vigorously, inhaling.

'It's the forcers every time, they're the ones who bugger things up.'

Afterwards he said restlessly, 'Coming in town?' and this again was typical. He had to have movement, people, talk: city life was a river and he was an out-and-out city man, a nomad, he liked to feel it swirling round him and be in touch, yet left free. He was sure of himself. His element was rootlessness, he was born to it. For me this was a completely new attitude, it meant that the amenities of a city were there to be used, exploited, they were on tap like the water and electricity, waiting and ready, you switched on, plunged in. Dipped in and out. Got on a bus and swirled into the centre, lying back on the side seat as Lou did now, looking as if he owned the place. The bus was his. He lolled back, impudent, a kid of twenty-odd. The interesting thing was that this attitude didn't make him international, but intensely local. A local patriot. He took a pride in the streets, pubs, buses, these things he used like an owner. In the next county they were different. He wasn't there, he was here. The environment he was using became his, made over. Not the planners, the builders, but the users created the cities. Knowing this gave him his local pride.

I'd always felt hostile or bleak or unspeakably dreary in cities: now I saw they had a certain glamour. I looked at Lou and grinned. Never push anything. He twitched his lips faintly and let his eyes rest on me for a second, then he was gazing out of the window again.

8

WE GOT off in the square and went drifting across the open space from one side to the other as if we weren't going anywhere. I kept with him, we exchanged one or two basic questions—'Been here long?'—'Where you from?'—and it turned out he'd been a student teacher in Coventry and chucked it after the first taste of teaching practice. Now it was summer, the evening had that suspended feeling warm air brings, the sky pearly-feathery and absolutely still over the Council House, but Lou hadn't seen it. He was hunched, down-looking. Nothing higher than a poster interested him: certainly not nature. For landscapes to mean anything to him they had to be man-made. I asked him why he jacked in the teaching and he shrugged, off-hand, without answering.

'The pub up here near the castle's alright. Depends which night though. What day is it?'

'Saturday, thank God.' A remark that was more habit than truth. Since coming here and living in a bedsitter I'd come to dread the yawning hole of the weekend.

'Saturday's alright as a rule.'

Then as we went mooching uphill in a queer silence he suddenly started on my question, saying as if to himself that education was a waste of time, he had a built-in resistance to it, like religion: the instant he got inside the school on his preliminary visit and saw them herding around as if it meant something deadly serious, it frightened him. He'd escaped from this world, he'd forgotten what a straitjacket it was. Without knowing why, he'd been running ever since, become a freedom addict. Seeing them in Assembly being screwed into rigid rows and hushed and then told to sing loud, sing properly or else by some thin-lipped, pasty-faced grizzled

361

fogey, it was too much, it took him back in a sickening rush to his own schooldays which he'd loathed and dreaded and then immediately forgotten.

'What did me good and proper though was the Staff Room.'

'How's that?'

'That's where you saw it was a job of work and nowt else. I mean these teachers were trapped in a situation and trying to make the best of it, to get through to pay-day, pension-day—they cuffed kids round the earhole if they were that sort, they gave 'em debates now and then if they were that sort, but you only had to see them there stirring their mugs of tea for it to hit you that they weren't no different from you or me—or the bloody kids. All the guff about marks, progress, improvement, Johnny's got it in him if we can only winkle it out, you saved that for Parents' Day and Speech Day and when you put in for your next rung up—nobody believed in it for itself. It really got me, and it was so plain, and no need for a soul to mention it. You just looked.'

We pushed into the pub, which was dingy and brown, iron stanchions at the corners of the bar, those chairs with round plywood seats and holes punched in a pattern—the kind they used to have in offices—and an old upright piano, lid down and locked, in the corner black as a coffin. There was a fire-place, grate full of ashes, an old woman sitting up close to the hearth as if she could feel the warmth of last winter's fires, sucking down a Guinness slowly and twisting the scrag of her body to look at whoever was coming in, with a kind of blind beakishness. The public bar this was and it looked deserted, just the man behind the counter wiping a glass and giving us a nod, thin and yellow like a candle with a meagre black wick of hair, shirt sleeve dragging in the wet. This was the old-fashioned brown pub, the local, it had regulars and was tucked away in a back street, in a district marked down for slum clearance in the foggy future. We went around a glazed screen and down an alley of a passage, stone-flagged, into a poky room with wood settles.

'Take a pew,' Lou muttered, moving over to a corner, 'and meet this bloke, Woody . . . I'll be back. He's a good lad, Woody.'

And I'd lost him, he went and attached himself to one group in the middle of the room, said a few words, stood listening at their elbows and merging, hanging his head, completely unassertive and colourless, then went drifting off into an elbow of the room where I couldn't watch him. Not that Woody gave me the chance: he was the buttonholing sort. I began to wonder if I'd bumped into him before, but of course I hadn't. Apparently the mere fact that we both knew Lou Coltman was enough for him. I took a dislike to him on sight, that narrow face and flushing skin over the cheekbones, china-blue eyes and a corrupt loose little baby mouth curling up at one side as he poured out talk and appreciated himself—'I tell a fucking good story, don't I, bloody amusing, don't you think I'm clever the way I em-broider it, on form tonight I am'—this was what his wide eyes with no bottoms to them seemed to be saying. I sat listening to him or pretending to, let him rattle on, searching for Lou out of the corner of one eye and trying to work out what he saw in this mate of his. Woody lowered his voice, confiding.

'If you want a woman,' he was advising me, 'I can put you on to a beauty. She might be in later: I'll introduce you if you like—but you want to watch out, there's some real old rampers come in here, really thick they are. I mean, you don't want to die of boredom getting to it do you? I know I don't. If you fancy coming to a pub called *The Odd Wheel* down Alfreton Road I'll show you a bitch in there I went with once—just for a laugh, you know? I'm a writer, did Lou tell you? I work on the *Post* but I don't mean the sort of crap I do in there for a living—I'm writing a book as a matter of fact. You'll get the impression I'm a big-headed bastard, but listen, Colin—can I call you Colin?—I only mention it because I like to observe people, if you know what I mean. Anyway there's this gin-drinking fanny at *The Odd Wheel* who always comes sidling round me, jigging her big tits in her jumper—no brassiere, you can see the nipples stuck out— rubbing her thighs up against me on the seat, you wouldn't believe it if you didn't see it for yourself. Forty if she's a day and one of those bloody stupid pony tails in an elastic band, and when she opens her gob, oh my Gawd. "Hallo, duck, interesting place this, isn't it. Haven't seen you here before"— incredible make-up, pure fantasy, and out of it comes this mashed-up accent, and I think, "Who do you think you're kidding, you're on the machines at Players you are, Clara" . . . That's her name, Clara, believe it or not. So one night I'm half sloshed—I mean you'd have to be—and we go up to her place, a flat she calls it. What a slut, you'd think there'd been a murder in there, it was pure chaos. Kids yelling in prams in one corner, plaster seagulls going up the wall, sink jammed solid with dirty crocks and in the midst of all that she disappears and comes trapesing out half stripped, nellies hanging out of some gory red lace thing—and she starts clearing the debris off the settee. I made some excuse, I just couldn't stomach it, not even pissed . . .'

'Sounds nasty,' I said, grinning him off, and for something to say: but he was eyeing a couple of girls, newcomers, working up a little spiel on them. It was going to be the same lip-licking, eye-gleaming performance, and the thought came: there's something not quite right about you. As if he hated women almost, was intent on having some sort of revenge. I spied Lou weaving through with the beers and packets of peanuts, flushed with all his encounters.

I sat on the bench as Lou came up and Woody pushed himself up closer to say, dropping his voice intimately, his eyes leery, 'Lou said you'd written him a great letter.'

I mumbled something, fobbed him off with false modesty,

364

but he humiliated me obscurely and I didn't understand why. There's something nasty about you, I thought, and left it at that. I understand better now. Without knowing a thing about me he was itching to pay me compliments, flatter me, for some weird reason of his own. Praise of any kind makes me uneasy—who can sit inside me and measure the worth of what I do or am?—and senseless praise that sucks up can take away your pride and self-respect if you aren't careful. Praise me and I duck, back away, make off for cover. To be recognised is my constant need. Praise implies blame, the same critical coin: somebody is coming up warily with a certain detachment, carrying calipers and a little book for your measurements, notes on your performance. For the future. Never for what you are. To be recognised is to be loved for what you are, for your weaknesses. Recognise me and I sparkle, begin to recover, want to excel, to expand.

'Now then,' said Lou, introducing, 'you know Woody, that's him you've been speaking to, and this is Bob, him with the big glass and nothin' in it—and next to him there looking angelic, only she ain't, is Maureen.'

'Shurrup you,' Maureen said, blonde and gormless-eyed, heavy low fringe touching her eyebrows. She had a bewildered expression. She giggled. She seemed to like Lou, but wasn't anything to do with him. She was with Bob, a big brawny fellow with a hot baked face and scrubby Van Gogh beard, in a thick green sweater and no shirt. He had his arm draped round her shoulders, they made a placid peaceful couple on that side of the table.

'Who wants a nail in 'is coffin?' Bob said genially, offering his packet of Capstans.

'Don't smoke, thanks,' I said, thinking for the first time that it would be hard not to in a gathering like this, if you intended to stay friendly. The sociability of this man came off him like a heat. I felt a pang of shame at my meanness in denying him pleasure. Cigarettes were passed out, the others lit up, and then I was aware of being fixed. It was Bob watching me with all his head like a dog, eyeballs bulged in concentration.

'Let me guess,' he said, smiled, rubbed the side of his face and it rasped.

'What's that?' I said warily, a bit foxed by the way he'd said it, importantly.

'You ent local?'

'No.'

'Brummy?'

I nodded. 'Near enough.'

'See?' He turned in triumph to the girl. 'Good, en I.'

'Tek it easy,' she said. 'Steady on, kid.' To me she said confidentially, 'Don't worry, duck, he don't mean no harm.'

'Harmless, is he?' I laughed.

'Wanna try me?' Bob said to the girl.

She blew smoke in his face. 'Hark at it,' she said.

Bob wasn't finished with me yet.

'You're an actor,' he said.

I shook my head. Maureen let out a shriek. 'Yah, clever dick!'

Bob shook his head slowly, sank back away from me, vaguely friendly but puzzled. I was glad the pressure was off.

'I could 'a swore you was an actor,' he said.

Then he lost interest in me.

'Anybody who wants to buy me a pint, don't worry about hurtin' me feelings,' he announced, cheerful and clomping. 'I'm broke I am. Broke an' happy.'

'On a Saturday?' said Lou, already on his feet and reaching for the glass.

'Had me pay packet pinched, all but a quid,' Bob said, without a flicker of complaint.

'Why didn't you say so?' Lou said, going, and when he got back he said, 'That'll teach you not to trust your fellow workers.'

The man was on building, a labourer, but apparently he'd been a skilled fitter at Raleigh's and couldn't stand the indoor life. I was sitting with eyes and ears wide open, all my senses, as you tend to do when nothing's happening, you seem to be drifting pointlessly, yet sense the possibility of creative moments. Lou was the unknown quantity, that was his fascination—he was attending and yet looking out for somebody, another person, a further ingredient. 'That'll teach you . . .' he said softly and then ducked over his pint to listen and wait, as if he'd dropped in a catalyst. I saw what he was: a ginger man.

'How d'you mean?' said Bob, genuinely shocked. 'I got some good mates on the job – one sneaky bastard don't change everything. What d'you mean, that'll teach me?'

'Well, it will, won't it,' squeaked Maureen, and I looked at her and then saw Lou with such a secret little smile at his mouth corners, his head down. He'd started something, it was fizzing. Trivial, but he had to have a stir around him. And he was passing time, expecting others.

'Teach you not to leave cash in your jacket,' put in Woody sarcastically, but he wasn't really interested.

'Agreed,' said Bob heavily. 'But that's not what Lou said.'

'I take it back,' Lou murmured, then became suddenly emphatic, intense: a startling transformation. 'Would you trust this bloke?' he asked, and gave a nod at me.

Bob put back his head and laughed. 'How the hell would I know, I never met him before!'

'I mean by looking at him,' Lou said.

I sat squirming while they all focused on me. If I hadn't been on the receiving end, if it had been someone else, it would have been comical. I might even have enjoyed it.

'Yes,' Bob said at last, 'I would, mate.'

'How's that, then?' Lou persisted.

Bob looked puzzled, he frowned like a boy.

'What makes you so sure?' Lou said.

Now it was the other's turn. The limelight scorched him. Watching this Bob and grinning at him encouragingly, I suddenly noticed his wide belt round his trousers, it was made of red webbing, a big brass buckle at the front: a fancy belt. I looked at him with fresh interest and thought, he's not just a clod, this one. He fancies himself. Somehow this new aspect of him caught me by surprise because he sat all in a heap, unshapely, no self-consciousness and no vanity. But I'm wrong, I thought.

'How?' he said, mouthing. 'It's easy. It's bleedin' obvious, I'd say.'

'Yeah, but why?' Lou urged, not asking so much as extracting, like a hypnotist with his trance victim. It was amazing how he could soothe and stroke with his voice and at the same time convey force, insistence, the pressure of his will. I kept my ears cocked, marvelling. Bob was too thick to respond, I felt: it was me, watching, I was the one who sat spellbound.

Bob itched about and worked his shoulders uneasily, he would have spat in his hands if that could have helped. He stumbled blindly into speech, saying in a harsh voice that the police only bashed you up if you were a certain type, they knew who to pick and who to leave alone, and it was the same with him, he could smell the bastards who would shop you, shit on you . . . He sat back with his glass in his fist, white curds clinging to his lips, his speech floundering. 'It's obvious, Lou, obvious,' he said, almost fuming.

Now, as Woody opened his mouth, Lou looked over his shoulder again for whoever he was expecting: maybe hoping to see somebody he could borrow from. In seconds we'd be in the middle of a hot debate on the police, whether you needed courage to be a copper, the brutality, the squalor of the profession, was it forced on them or did they lap it up, and what rights did you have, if any, when they grabbed you and you were broke and no fixed abode—what chance did you have?

I had little to contribute, apart from a bobby jumping out of a hedge when I was a kid, riding a bike down a country lane and not stopping at the halt sign. I was with a great friend, a boy several yards behind me, who had time to brake. With him as witness, my pride flamed up and I found enough courage to act stubborn when the copper tried to make me look foolish. 'Now then,' he said, planted like a tree before my front wheel, 'you could see the sign, you're not blind, so why didn't you stop?'

'I didn't see it,' I said, which was the truth.

The policeman let his gaze rest on me for a long time but I didn't wilt, not with my friend watching. 'How old are you?' he said, heavily sarcastic. I went hot in the face and said, 'I don't see what that's got to do with it,' and in a flash he dropped his baiting game, yanked out his notebook and took my name and address. My old man paid the fine. I mentioned this when Lou brought up about power and how it could corrupt. But *he* had a power, I felt it. He kept looking towards the door but his other mates didn't come. After a while he muttered something about making a phone call and disappeared. He was gone for an hour. The others thought he was round the corner in *The Iron Man*, another pub he was known in. When he came back he was edgy, strangely subdued: at closing time he was ready to shove off with hardly a word. I asked for the address where he was living.

'Hang about,' he said, ransacked his jacket, which looked slept in, and came out with a crumpled buff envelope. I gave him my pen and he scrawled on the paper, using his palm as a rest, holding the pen lightly and a long way from the tip. I wasn't surprised by this fastidiousness, nor by the nervy style of his handwriting. 'Cheers then, mate,' he said, already loping for a bus he'd spotted. The bus stop was right down the street but he made it. He didn't look back.

9

A MUCH more uncomplicated man is Davey, who comes later but can't wait . . . 'a fanatic', his girl calls him. She doesn't mean that exactly, she's referring to his mad impulses, and when I say uncomplicated, compared with Lou, I don't mean he's simple. I often wish I could have seen them together, but never did: just have to accept that they knew each other.

Like Lou, Davey has the gift of immediate intimacy, you trust him, but unlike Lou he overwhelms you with warmth, fraternity, opens up like a child, gives himself away completely. Lou's personal alright, but even when he appears to be revealing, stripping, he conceals. Every step he takes has the effect of covering up his tracks. So with Lou I'm none the wiser about him, I still don't know what makes him tick. Davey is utterly transparent, all his actions betray him: it's impossible not to know. And right from the beginning I was aware of him physically, still glowing all over with the nimbus of adolescence, though he was twenty-three or four, his voice very expressive, huskily emotional, his whole attitude to life ridiculously fragile and tender, so you caught your breath and thought, what's this: I must be dreaming. As if to counteract this—though you couldn't say he was aware of it as a grave weakness, he was one big weakness—he'd anchor himself, prevent himself from floating away in sheer joyousness, or sad smoke-rings, grievings after childhood idylls, by slinging dollops of verbal shit right and left. And by a nimble goon humour of his own, and being a clever mimic, he could mix his qualities on his tongue and achieve a union, though it sounds crazy, impossible. He was an earthy romantic, an idealist who farted, who had to keep drawing your attention to the sheer shittiness as well as the creatureliness of existence. If it hadn't been for the laugh that went with it you'd have sworn it was a kind of disgust he had for reality, a rage. His dreams flowered, the heroes of his youth were glorified in the news cuttings he showed me, then the world he saw through the window shattered it, outraged him. Except that he laughed a lot, sparkled visibly, groaned with pleasure when he was hungry and his girl Judy shoved a plate of beans and chips in front of him, some doorstop brown bread and a mug of hot tea, syrup-sweet. He'd scoop up a mouthful on his fork, load his bread, take a huge bite, groan, mumble 'Ah lovely little un' and put his arm round her waist, then curse when she sat down with a bump on his lap before he'd finished, maybe banging noses as she coiled like a cat and tried to kiss his greasy mouth. 'Not on me chops, not when I'm eatin'.' He'd jab her away brutally and say 'Gerroff, you stupid bitch, now look what you've done!'

I'd wait for the bang, knowing her temper, just sitting there as if invisible, but it was amazing, nothing happened except a slight feeling of strain in the atmosphere, and Judy would be back at the cooker or the sink and Davey would clumsily, sheepishly begin to mend the relationship. 'Sorry, little un,' he'd say, still eating, 'you know I ent got much time, I got to get back to the fuckin' grindstone—you know that, don't you, duck?' And she'd come back, coil on his lap and perch there, still as a dove, and I'd blink and grin my head off, I couldn't help it; but nobody would notice me, they'd be cooing and kissing and he'd say, 'You're so bloody clumsy that's your trouble—oh Christ me nose still hurts' and she'd croon, 'Oh Davey, I'm sorry, does it,' and soothe his hair. Then the kettle would boil over and he'd yell, 'Now look!' Suddenly he'd take care of me with a warm glance, a tender grin, a solicitous remark—'How's Colin in the corner—fancy another cup of tea, me old wack?'

Lou was elusive physically as he was in other respects. I

once saw him stripped at the sink in the kitchen of his mother's house, having a wash down, and there was nothing deep-chested or athletic about him but he was surprisingly muscular round the shoulders, and dangling from his neck he had a St Christopher on a chain. His vigour in some curious way didn't make you conscious of his body. Whereas Davey was a body in blossom, he flowered from the waist, his life branched down through his long legs to the girls he needed, they sapped him or renewed him, he was never sure whether it was death or rebirth. He thrashed his arms, held his head, complained bitterly of their possessiveness. A tender, big-hearted animal—then you noticed his hands, his fingers, delicate and shapely and narrow, feminine hands, and it was this that reminded you of his agile mind. I met him first in the summer and he wore nothing much, cotton drill pants and a sweatshirt, baseball shoes. I could smell the salt on his skin, he'd roared off to Skeggy on his motorbike. His blond hair was in spikes. 'Ain't it funny,' he said, 'they let you swim in the sea and yet that water's international. Touches all them countries. You'd think they'd want to stamp your bleedin' passport before you put your big toe in even.'

He drove a bread van round the country districts outside Derby, but he'd been a factory apprentice like me and jacked it in, then he was a signal-box boy on the railway and loved it, gazing out of the window high up on spring mornings, hearing a blackbird every evening pouring out liquid ecstasy. That was when he started his dreams, buried in that cutting, lovely, with a signalman who reminded him of his grandfather. They transferred him to another box, the man there was a mean pot-bellied bastard, too miserable to live, Davey was on early shift and kept turning up late, so misery-guts soon had his knife into him . . .

I'm missing something out that's vital, I still haven't got the picture. Those hands. The strangeness and beauty of his voice sometimes, when he was rapt, quivering to communi-

cate a memory that had grown precious, a key to his world:
yet he just missed being a street-corner yobbo. His heart
would swell and choke him just before his hips began to
swagger. He had a funny collection of pals: delinquents,
thickies, students, misfits like me—his warmth didn't dis-
criminate. Slowly it dawned on you how gregarious he was,
how you were part of the swarm, the changing pattern, and
this hurt, because you could have sworn the intimacy had
been personal, secret, just for you. That was laughable, you
saw that in the end. He made contact all over his body, all
the time, gave off a kind of helpless love: did it as easily as he
moved through the air. Before he knew what had happened
he'd be clustered with mates, stuck with them, all kinds, like
burrs on the legs of your trousers, and another side of him
would surge up in reaction—the solitary. 'All I want is to be
by myself, think my own bloody thoughts,' he'd say, confiding in me because I didn't seem a threat like the others, I
left him free. But I was the biggest threat: I loved him.

I saw him as physical all the time, his hair growing down to
his neck, his jaunty-bashful walk, shirt open and no vest, the
run of blond hair coming up from his belly-button, but never
myself bared to him physically as a homosexual does. The
girls took him naked and emptied him, he poured out his
love for them from between his legs, complete and utter, and
I was the same, my balls and cock ached after the moist
secret entrances of women. Once he said to me on a brief
camping trip, we stood shoulder to shoulder unpacking stuff
and his voice came small and colourless, his face rueful: 'Ah
Colin, there's no way to express your love for a man.' He
wanted to put his arm round me, it was spontaneous and
beautiful and I couldn't help him, I was paralysed by the
unwritten rules. Afraid too of looking a clown. It should have
been natural, it could have been. It was fraternal.

Judy was his regular, he more or less lived with her, but
girls and women fell for him all over the place and he just

responded: nothing nasty or grabbing in him, he loved their girlness, femaleness, their pliant bodies, willing natures, the sympathy that shone in their eyes, their tears, and oh their smiles, how he loved the way they smiled at him. He would have gone through the world of men cutting the same kind of swathe, I'm certain, except for the hard edge of male assertion he came up against, and of course his own male will clashing, conflicting, bringing a vindictive, bitter streak out in him that I hated to see. He approached everyone, male and female, young and old, as if there was no difference, he melted them if he could with his warmth, he went forward bare-breasted, all heart. Mere humanity in a person was enough to inspire generosity in him, and the more lavish their weak-nesses, the better he liked it. He responded to anything generous, he expanded visibly. Naturally he was bound to get in a mess and it couldn't last, the world being what it is: he spoiled rapidly as the adjustment twisted him, he fell into ugly jeering moods and you felt it was indecent to be with him, a silent witness. Then he'd recover and come bursting into a room and it was like old times, he'd be radiant, open-faced, he'd sweep you off your feet.

10

If I had to put into one word my loathing for the society I grew up in, I'd say, without hesitation: sex. To find sex torn out of context and isolated in medical books, picked over by psychologists, worst of all hung like bloody meat in shop windows, stamped for sale and paraded on the slave blocks, made over into a pornography of precision and detachment by cameras—here was the root of my hatred for adults. I saw that thrillers, gutter press, advertising, they were all at the same game of striptease, the whole masturbatory culture we have now at full blast was just getting under way. But the disembowelling was still to come. The snouts in the money-troughs hadn't yet understood that a new source of wealth could be made to flow, that all it needed for the fires to burn, for the revolution to take place, for the smelting of sex to begin, were a few hundred furnaces of sick lust roaring away up and down the land. To grow up to manhood in the midst of that burning lava is to be in hell, is crucifixion. It's the beginning of the end when sex is separate, when it carries a price tag. We're going to hell when you can pick sex up in your hand and fit a french letter on it. We're sex-mad because we think sex is detachable, like a dog running round in a frenzy trying to gobble its own tail. What we call sexy is something we can lick up off the surface of our skins with our tongues, an oily sauce which is no more than the sweat bursting from us as we run between the furnaces.

When one desire in your blood runs hot for the throbbing image of bloody meat hung on hooks in the shop window, the sex thing smelted out by the furnaces, and another desire burns for the love of a particular woman, for her voice, her tender solicitude, her proud haunchy walk, the hollow of her back, the thoughts in her head, the laughter in her throat, the spittle in her mouth, the shit in her colon, then you are torn apart in the very centre of your being, you are crucified.

I was twenty-three when I went with the prostitute. London was the right place, ripe and rotten with prostitution: everybody was at it in one way or another. You could smell the sex-and-money mixture, it had its own sound, tinkly and clanging, the stink of petrol and steel and burnt rubber in the streets went with the Cockney rat-yap on the corners, the cold shoulder in the tube stations, the boot in the alley. Everything on sale and going cheap, even death zipping in and out on wheels, blaring like a car roof in the sun.

I was in a crowded tube with a suitcase, it was the rush hour and passengers stood up like skittles all round the doors. We slid in to Earl's Court and a weasel of a man lashed out viciously with his foot at my case, snarled 'Get it out of the way' and came bundling through, using his shoulders, making for the door. I was too flabbergasted and at that time too timid to answer, I just felt sick all through my blood, wished him dead and loathed the whole carriageful of wall-eyed zombies, myself included. Then the curving posters on the tunnels with their chorus of con-messages, then the multitudes on the escalators, the maniacs who have to run, the ticket collectors who look malignant, the sophisticated, bored, languid and predatory faces, the cigar in the juicy red mouth, the glossy briefcase, the jewelled finger dripping blood, the blazing arrogance of the poor: and you get out through the nearest bolt-hole and it's no different, but at least there's the sky with its space.

For a young man longing for something wonderful to happen to him there's a terrible atmosphere inside even a feeble place like the Windmill, for instance. Coming out he feels soiled right through, tainted for ever. What's worse, the wonderful something he strains towards with his longing seems a kingdom he can't possibly enter now that his purity is lost. He's corrupt. All he's done is sat in this crappy old theatre where the nudes aren't allowed to move, and no opera glasses, no cameras, illustrated programmes are five bob at the entrance, the show's continuous (we never closed) and at every interval the old rams at the back go leaping over the seats in a mad dash for the empty front row. For the young man the show is one long humiliation. He's from the provinces, nobody knows him in here: even so he feels conspicuous. He sneaks glances to right and left. Men only, in all directions. The comedians hurl themselves on and they grimace with pain, struggle desperately, laugh bleakly at their own jokes, up against a blank wall of brutal indifference. The rows of Shylocks wait like butchers for the flesh. Their eyes sharpen. On it comes, prancing and oh so English, titties fresh from boarding school bounce gaily in the transparent blouses. You can see the cherry doing a jig, mostly civilised, one or two really loose and frantic, but even so in the best possible taste. You don't know which to concentrate on. The singing which falls out of their chops as they pant up and down in a line is excruciating, the accents so genteel that you have to make a conscious effort to ignore it: like the piano twinkling in palm court style through the set-pieces, where they have a nude standing motionless at the back being bathed in coloured light and you try to tell yourself it's a woman, she's bollock-naked and that's her belly-button but it's no good, she looks no more real and warm than a bronze lump on the Embankment.

You're only young once, they tell you, but being young can be agony. Funny as well, when you look back. A pal told me he had a girl friend in Leicester who was churchy, and when they were lying in the grass one summer she asked him, 'Do you believe in intercourse before marriage?' 'No,' he said, and he had a stalk on him halfway up to his neck. 'No, neither do I,' she said, and took him home to tea. Somehow he got his erection jammed in under his belt or somewhere, and he sat there squirming in the sitting room with her mother's beady eye fixed on the stain between his legs. 'Oh bloody hell it was funny,' he said, telling it, and I'd like to bet it wasn't.

I didn't know where the prostitutes hung out, I hadn't asked any of my mates at the factory: that would be giving the game away, and the truth was, I hadn't admitted even to myself that I was going to try and get picked up by one. Even in London all day, mooching past the galleries and book-shops, squatting on stools in the snack bars and watching through the mirrors, the swarm and blur of the crowd, I still didn't know. When it got dark I began to know. Went drifting down those side streets behind Piccadilly like one of the damned, then it drizzled and the black road between the pavements glazed and ran. I stood in a doorway watching the odd car swish through, heart thumping up violently whenever a woman went past. I was doing it, I knew now. Waiting. I wanted the vultures to swoop and pick me off, I was that tense and desperate. A car swung in to the gutter opposite and stopped, engine throbbing, a figure moved out of the doorway, the car door opened and closed, they roared away. A pick-up. So this was it, it was here, I was on the circuit. Still nothing happened. A young couple went by, lovers, coiled together and heads bare, heedless in the rain. I watched dumbly. Their innocence pierced me, the cruel simplicity of their lives, they splashed round the corner and I stared into the utter bleak emptiness of the street. In the factory an apprentice would say of his sweetheart, 'She's fabulous.' He'd have to tell you. Then he had to coarsen it, and the acrid touch, the humour and contempt. 'She's fabulous,' he'd say—'I could use her shit for toothpaste.'

When she came up I wasn't ready: I didn't see where she sprang from. There she was sauntering by, perfectly natural, saying 'Chilly, darling?' or some such stock phrase.

Holding an umbrella. She sounded foreign. I nodded, perhaps mumbled a word, and it was fateful, overwhelmingly important as I stepped towards her and she held the umbrella over me.

'What a miserable evening!' she said brightly, as we walked on side by side like husband and wife, the umbrella floating above our union, while I shivered in my chest and moved my legs in a tension. It was happening, happening. You moved your legs and it happened.

'Here we are!' she said, stopping at a green door, and from her handbag she took a key. 'That wasn't far, was it?'

Now I was her child: she was mothering me. I followed her in through the doorway obediently, she called up to the first landing in a foreign language, maybe French, and I saw as she went up the stairs that she was a woman, not a girl. I went up behind the full curve of her hips, the dark skirt. Up she went fast and confident, blatant. I was speechless with admiration.

I sat on the bed and felt nothing, no desire, only a great gasping fear because I didn't know what to do and a gulping fearful excitement at doing something so forbidden, unspeakable, unimaginable. I was with a pro, a woman whose trade was with men below the belt: no shame, and what a relief that was, a woman smiling indulgently at the cock bulging in your trousers, the terrible fact transformed, no longer ugly. She was there to be blocked, the price was fixed, no arguments. Take it or leave it. And it was alright and you were grateful, the guilt ran out of you and you sat on the bed smiling and felt no desire, in some curious way it had got left outside the door with the top half, the part above the belt. You sat numbly, without feelings, just a swirl of fears and a stirring of shame because you'd paid and the woman was there ready, she was an expert, a professional, she had her pride. What the hell was wrong with you? Why were you such an insult?

She dropped a little shower of dirty pictures on the bed and left the room. My trousers were round my ankles, I sat looking at my bare legs and they looked foolish, helpless. I was half-hard, she came and sat beside me in her slip, stockings rolled down, heavy white thighs inert. She stroked me between my legs and I lay down on the bed and nothing happened and she said, still patient. 'Don't you have a sweetheart to do this for you?' Her words stuck in me like a thorn, bitter, sharp.

It must have been how she said it, the touch of amusement and the pity, or it may have been the dread of catching the pox. I sat up and started to cry. Then she was furious: her face shrivelled with rage. She stood up, dragging on clothes furiously and shouting 'Don't do that, don't be so stupid, stop that! I can't waste any more time, I've got somebody else waiting to use this room.' She disappeared, and a maid came to show me out, very polite, like a sedate waitress in a teashop.

'Will you pull the door shut at the bottom of the stairs, sir?'

I gave her a tip.

Outside in the street I was completely lost, I felt mad and emptied and lost, I wanted to run, to yell. The rain had stopped and the sky was ragged, trailing moonlight. With my head back I looked at the sky and ran, bursting with a desire to apologise, to ask forgiveness. I turned back and ran up and down the street searching for the green door and it was no good, I couldn't find it. Nothing looked the same; the whole thing was like a dream.

I I

LONDON. Saturday in Nottingham a yawning pit to cross
over, so one weekend I catch an excursion train, flee to London. The regal arches of the station are always exciting. The
great threshold. The pomp of the capital awaits me. I leave
the station purposefully, as if I'm going somewhere. Walk
my legs off getting lost, keep going, catching the crowd fever,
the million-footed tread. The rhythm drugs me, the pleasure
of drowning in the sea of crowds, drugged by the amazing
variety of faces, the richness of unknown lives, staring into
faces, looking for God knows what. That's all I ever do in
London.

Back to the station at midnight more dead than alive to
sit exhausted among the dregs, the derelicts. Go underground
into the stale air of the white-tiled cellars for a piss and nearly
fall over a man, only young, dark round head and slender
body, stretched out asleep on newspapers on the tiled floor,
head pillowed on his arms.

No train for me until five to one. I go into the buffet and
buy coffee and cake at the wet steely counter, sit at one of the
round tables in the institution-like atmosphere that station
eating places have, the woodwork heavy and dark, oppressive, the ceiling high and grimy, weary as an old yellowing
biscuit, floor scummy and littered with the day's traffic,
sloppings, spent matches, ash, crumbs, fag ends. Two of the
tables occupied by silent engrossed couples, the rest vacant.
Then I notice the old drunk slumped over a table at the back,
he starts mumbling harmlessly to himself and I notice him.
It's like a stage set; above him there's a grill giving a view of
the pavement outside, feet and ankles going by occasionally.
A policeman stoops down, looks in—obviously he's made a

habit of peering in from up there. In a matter of seconds he's downstairs to the entrance and marching in, young, truculent bony jaw stuck out under his bucket helmet, slamming down his feet in an ominous manner as if he's leading in a regiment. He makes straight for the drunk and stands over him, bullish and planted, his face set.

'I told you before,' he says, 'and I shan't tell you again. Now get up.'

I watch over the rim of my cup, trying to imagine the crime the old man's committed. He sits mumbling to himself and whining, he hardly knows where he is. Then the Law has him by the arm, dragging him to his feet.

'Move,' the Law says loudly, even glaring angrily about to see who else he can tackle. I keep my eyes down, sickened, heart pumping black blood into all manner of crimes I'd love to commit.

'Did you hear me?' he bawls in the old man's ear. 'I don't want to see you in here again. So move!' The old man sways on his feet, hopelessly fuddled, hands pawing the air. He gets a violent shove in the small of his back to help him along, blunders forward in a rush off balance and goes down, sprawling between the tables. Infuriated, the Law bounds up and yanks him to his feet, bundles him out of the door with his jacket bunched up round his ears, shouting what he'll do to him next time. I give them time to get clear because I can't trust myself, twitching about on the chair, unable to sit there any longer. I want to rub London off the map, heave it out of my guts. The glittering vitality of its streets is a mirage. Somehow this scene has summed it all up; the gigantic proud engine of the city is full of ashes, cold ashes. It's a dustbin.

My train is still a good half hour away. I go and sit on the benches for waiting passengers under the big clock, on the platform in the open. Better than the waiting room, which is lugubrious, like a foyer to the underworld.

More slumped rejects scattered on the seats, snoozing, one

eye open for coppers. I'm glad to be sitting among them. Never more sure where I belong.

Farther along the same bench a well-dressed woman, small, middle-aged, is bent over sleeping, clutching tightly at her black shiny handbag. A kid of twenty in a pink shirt, grubby but with a fastidious air to him, comes up trailing a beefy young bloke in a dark suit who grins round at all and sundry good-naturedly.

'Christ Almighty, look at her,' nags Pinky, gazing down at the woman and tut-tutting. His pal sits down on one side of the woman and him on the other. They want to be together but there's no room, the woman's in the way. Pinky is close to me, his bleached curly hair wags censoriously over the unconscious woman.

'Isn't it disgusting?' he bleats to me, gives me a hard look. Close up he looks twitchy and drained, beaten.

'Is she drunk?'

'Yeh, oh yeh,' he says. Lighting a fag, his hand trembles. 'If it's one thing I can't bear to see it's a woman drunk in public. Bloody awful, it really is.' And he keeps wagging his head, agreeing with himself.

'You here for the night?' I ask him.

'Who, me?' he says warily, suddenly sharp. 'Oh yeh, yeh I am, that's right. Here for the night, actually. You?'

I tell him I'm waiting for the next train to Nottingham.

'Is that so? Go on. Nice place, Nottingham, oh yeh. Worked in a hotel there once, Black Boy is it? Ever heard of it?'

His eyes never still, his head twitching and wagging, and a large part of him absent when he talks, like a somnambulist. Fatigue is creeping through him but he shrugs it off, refuses to relax.

I ask him if he comes here most nights.

'Yeh, I do actually, as a matter of fact.' He puts a more pettish, acrimonious note into his voice, his eyes swivel over the platforms. 'Well it's like this, you see, I get sick and tired of paying two pounds a night at a hotel, it's such a bloody racket. Isn't it, really? I mean, you think: up at seven in the morning, swallow a cup of tea and out to work all day just to pay for your hotel, it's never worth it is it, really?'

I murmur sympathetically.

'Sick and tired of it I am, as a matter of fact.'

He sits musing, smoking, drifting off again.

'Don't blame you,' I say, thinking You're a liar, but if you want to put up a front it's all the same to me. 'I wouldn't pay those prices.'

'No, it's not the money,' he says quickly, 'it's the bloody principle of the thing. After all . . . Christ Almighty . . .'

'Yes, you're right,' I say, nodding now as regularly as him, catching the habit.

'You a Londoner?' I ask him.

'Me? No, Irish,' he says dreamily, like a man speaking of a place he can only dimly remember. 'Bray, outside Dublin...'

He reaches out and gives the sleeping woman a shake, spitefully.

'Wake up, Missus,' he says conversationally, 'the platform's going out.'

His pal laughs from the other side, watching, the woman unfolds, groans, opens her eyes painfully, croaks, 'No bleedin' peace,' and begins to sing, as she rolls to and fro and opens the clasp of her handbag, fumbles inside, fetches out a flat bottle in a crumpled paper bag and unscrews the cap.

'Oh my Christ,' mutters my friend. 'What have you got there, eh?'

And he leans his nose over, sniffs at the top of the bottle.

'I thought so,' he says, wrinkling his nose in disgust, the woman swigging away from the concealed bottle between snatches of song. 'Meths.'

He smokes and stares straight ahead, his body lifeless as a statue but his white face afflicted with nerve tremors, eyelids fluttering. He draws in his head, he's a bird of prey. His profile listens. 'Christ yes,' he says softly, as if to himself, 'and she's got another bottle of medicine in her handbag. See that? Two, she's got.'

He leans over the woman, nods with his long nose. 'I see you got another in there,' he says loudly.

She snatches her bag out of reach. '. . . . your own business . . .'

I get to my feet stiffly and go off for my train. 'So long—time I went.' Going, I wave at him.

'Is it really?' Pinky says, waking up to the fact of me now I'm going. 'Bye bye, old man,' nodding his farewell politely, watching me with mocking eyes.

12

BEFORE I met Lou and for a while afterwards I had a clerk's job out at Banstead, the huge ordnance depot on the edge of the city. I'd leave my bedsitter furtively, slip out past the closed doors like a burglar and get the bus at the bus station, feeling utterly nameless, nothing, as we went nosing out through the grimy brick channels. It was the first time I'd ever worked away from home, in a strange town. It was spring, it could have been any season.

I sit clutching my money: half-past seven or a bit later, shivering in the damp air, speechless, nothing but a busload of cargo. That *Modern Times* shot of them all funnelling into a factory in thousands, changing suddenly from people to sheep at a cattle market being herded between the steel fences—it's not like that when you're one of the herd. You sit on the bus as if alone, you nurse very carefully this gnawing emptiness as though the bottom has dropped out of life. It's you alone: the others might not exist. You shrink away from them, especially the veterans, the pipe-smokers, tough leathery grey-heads with impassive expressions who reinforce the general picture of normality—their set shoulders, the placid, regular puffs of smoke—and you want to bow your head like a man entering Dartmoor who is crushed by the sight of the walls, their thickness, worst of all their terrible permanence. The relentless forward thrust of the bus affects you: it'll never break down, never get lost. It doesn't, either. Drops you neatly outside the gates and still you have the choice. Everybody has. What carries you in on clockwork legs isn't the others, as it seems on the film, it's not the rising of the dead or the rush of the lemmings; no, everybody acts for himself. Everybody is convinced and crushed by the efficiency of the arrangements, the streets laid out symmetrically in a rigid pattern, the unhesitating bus on its cold timetable, aimed like a projectile for the gates, loaded and ready. You can't beat that: nothing is allowed to dawdle. Soon you don't even question it. Far easier not to. The system's fixed, immovable, vast, the structure you go threading through was in existence before you were born. Foundations all over the world, enormous girder-work sunk deep and set in the concrete of centuries. It'll last for ever . . . amen.

You rise with the others. Somewhere like a bomb ticking there's a woman planted: only a woman could make this lot crumble. In your dread you seize on that, weave fantasies, you rise with the dead and buried deep in you, secret, something frantic snatches at a bit of warmth and freshness. You go in.

I got to hear of the job because of the man downstairs who collected the rents and did odd jobs for the landlord, slopped out the rooms with green distemper as they came empty. Always the same colour. Grass green he called it, showing me my room, which had just had the treatment. I could smell it from the landing, dank, chemical.

'Fresh, en it,' he gobbled, swung his head round to admire his handiwork and then turned on me the kind of mirthless grimace that made you shiver. He was short, ferrety, bilious under the eyes; he gave me a resentful glare I couldn't comprehend when I asked for a front door key.

'You can have one if I got one. An' a rent book. I'll have a look.'

And shot out on the landing and down the stairs in a rickety scuttling movement, like a hunted man.

I followed him down. In his room on the ground floor facing out on the street he attacked the debris of clothes piled in heaps on the sideboard, muttering about the chaos and who's shifted his rent books, until his wife loomed out from the kitchen, hot-faced and suspicious, a big menacing figure.

She seemed a little confused by my presence and let the man rattle on, otherwise I don't think he'd have dared. He knew he was safe. 'How many times have I asked you not to move them books?' he moaned, still turning over socks and underpants, working himself up into a frenzy.

'Look on the mantelpiece,' the woman said flatly.

He turned on her, exasperated, mouth open, but the sourness and malevolence of the look she gave him was enough. He kept quiet until she'd left the room.

'Why don't you leave my bloody stuff alone, where I can find it,' he swore under his breath, darting about.

He gave me a rent book, and a key, and told me to watch out for the woman across the hall, whose husband was in the navy. 'Everybody who comes here seems to think she's a good grind, well I ent avin' it. This is a decent house.'

Then after a few days I heard about the job at the depot: he worked there himself. The first morning I went in with him. He had a small attaché case for his snack and thermos, and no sooner had we stepped inside the big gates past the police box than he shot forward, leaning forwards from the waist in a racing walk, then scurried off to the left up one of the side avenues. I remember how his chest suddenly stuck out and he nearly burst his collar with self-importance. Seven years he'd been there and I suppose he wanted to show it was his domain, his little kingdom. He was some sort of chargeman at one of the store counters: he had his morsel of power to give him that extra puff and strut.

It was an incredible place, a town, roads and intersections of its own, great hump-backed sheds crouched alongside railway tracks, some of them heaped to the roof girders with packing cases, others full of tanks and armoured cars, snub-nosed bulgy olive-green tin cans on wheels. For nearly a week I kept getting lost, then I located the barracks over to the north, in the upper field against the wire fence—I could get my bearings from that. You'd hear the 'come to the cook-house' ta-ra on the bugle, and quite a bit of parading up and down. Later on I went wandering up closer and peered in at the paymaster's office—more clerks—and the guardroom, and once I saw a little posse of ramrods marching some poor sod in between the flowerbeds on a charge. 'Left . . . whee-al!' Ever since the war a recurring nightmare of mine has been the call-up, finding myself in a suit as thick as sacks, deep-sea diver boots and a number as long as the envelope on all my letters, wheeling and gasping with a swollen kitbag, at the mercy of these spit-and-polish bastards. So at first I crept about warily and kept my distance, afraid I might be sucked in even now: after all conscription was still going strong and I was young enough. Each time I found myself nearby I'd creep a little nearer, goggling at them, their town-in-a-town, kids of the young generation dwelling in that incredible comic opera land, playing goodies and baddies with real guns, bullets, bayonets . . . it was archaic, so funny, they kept spitting and polishing and frog-marching because they'd always done it: somebody had mislaid the order to halt. Still, it was frightening, it was still nightmarish when I saw those red necks and shaved skulls, that health, the mild English freshness of the National Service boys as they blundered about so willingly, so resigned. I found that it was the thrill of fear I got, coming up a bit closer and closer each time, which gave the pleasure. Then one Monday, in the corner of the big office where I sat keeping records of officers, the files stamped 'Private and Confidential', amending their details on the card index and the chart so we had an accurate personal record of each officer, his posting, rank, home address, etc, etc—up marched these two big-booted boys from Liverpool. They were National Service lads, drafted in for a spell of clerical work, though there was bugger-all to give them. They sat at the tables and nodded at me, and one gave me a huge wink.

'Cushy number, this,' he said. He was Curly, he explained, and his mate was called Jacko.

I carried on working and kept sizing him up, this Curly, the one who impressed me. I was slightly elated at the idea of some new company, and I liked the glint of devilment in his eye. He had a gamin quality, I could imagine him dodging through a warren of decrepit back streets, giving orders, a gang leader. The army hadn't got him; nothing had. He knew how to slip under fences, gazes, from tight corners. And get a kick out of doing it.

My boss was a fierce lip-biting ex-serviceman with an artificial leg and a medal, quick as a terrier, very proud of the efficiency of his tiny section. We ran it between the two of us and had time to spare, he'd go limping all over the building poking his nose into other people's affairs, I'd hear his thin yelping laugh and glance across and there he was, jabbing somebody in the chest, waving his arms about. Back stiff, collar and tie immaculate, ready for inspection, not a hair out of place. His colleagues admired him for his energy, courage, high spirits. Now he saw the two young soldiers arrive, spotted them from a distance and came stumping over, rubbing his hands briskly: he was delighted to have a little squad of his own again, like old times.

'Alright, lads, let's be having you—now this is the drill,' he barked, and they stopped slouching in their chairs and sat up stiff, startled for a minute or two, till they got his number. No work to give them, so he set them busy repairing the most tatty-looking files, replacing the covers of the worst ones. He could never stay still: in five minutes he was away again, off to the far side of the vast room. But if an officer breezed up with some query or other, or to register his arrival, you could bet Maurice would be on the spot before he left again, breathing down the man's neck: 'Everything satisfactory, sir? Any further information you may require, sir, let us know and we'll soon have it chased up—okay, sir?' He threw in plenty of sirs but looked them straight in the eye and never sucked up to them. More than once I saw one of the young, rather languid subalterns flinch and go pink, backing away from his head-on attacks.

Curly was a heavy hulking lad, ginger; when he sat down he planted his elbows on the table the way his boots were on the floor. He existed, he was a fact, like his meaty hands. When he said something funny he opened his eyes wide and kept his face deadpan: his humour was pure Scouse. Maurice took to him, I could see how it was going to be. He liked his independence, he recognised a kindred spirit. The other lad, Jacko, was too shadowy to bother anybody or be noticed hardly, a dark scrannel with a pasty pimply face and a red mouth which struck you as shocking, it was so lurid, and swollen and sore like a blister. He had nothing to say; he lived in the shadow of the other one.

Soon it was full summer and I still stuck there, mainly from inertia. I was in a trance, what with the strange city, knowing nobody, my affair with Leila stagnant. She'd gone to Norfolk with her family and some friends, nothing to do with me. I'd met Lou but hadn't been to his place or got thick with him. At the depot there was even less work to do, long yawning afternoons when I stepped out for a breather on the tarmac runways and found myself drifting between the sheds, a haze of heat on the turf and flowers over towards the barracks. Then I'd go back inside and sit down in the corner and nobody had missed me: I was like the invisible man. The warehouse job all over again, I thought, except that here you didn't have to pretend, if you weren't busy you cleared off outside. It didn't matter, as long as someone was there holding the fort for any officer who shot in with his case history. But the supply of officers seemed to dry up with the coming of the hot weather. Maurice dodged out of sight more often, and once I was wandering round a corner near the sidings and bumped into Curly and Jacko, both of them strolling along nice and easy but purposeful, as if they were really going somewhere.

'Eh, I thought you was holding the fort, wack,' Curly said, stopping dead in his tracks like a cowboy and giving me his look. The blue-eyed boy.

'I thought *you* were,' I said.

We stood having a quiet laugh and Jacko's eyes kept slithering about warily, keeping a lookout. They were in uniform, conspicuous. Curly seemed indifferent, but he was nobody's fool: you could never tell what he was thinking.

'Good ole Maurice,' Curly said. 'Hope he ain't too lonely.'

'If he's there,' I said.

'See you then, me ole fruit,' Curly said, moving off.

'Where you going?' I called.

'Nowhere,' he said, 'same as you. See who gets there first.'

'See how far it is.'

'Tarra,' he said, waving.

13

A LETTER from Ray caught me by surprise, struck into me fiercely: walking around the streets of this city had bitten through the cord of our closeness and I thought we were lost to each other. There was his gabby scrawl and I loved to see it. I tore open the envelope joyfully, unsuspecting, and the letter overwhelmed me with the force of its longing, too vivid, too much. It struck at me, sharp and soft at once, his real tongue, the dedicated desperation I knew better than my own, it slid down my throat and made my eyes smart, burst deep inside me with a warm explosion. And left me stranded in a heap of darkness, a kind of thick vapour of loneliness, my heart thawed to no purpose. It wasn't letters I wanted, it was him in the room, standing there before me: timid and ineffectual in the eyes of the world, bold and decisive to me. Now more than ever I wanted him in the flesh, to feast my eyes on, now his presence haunted the grubby room.

'I'm in the park, Thursday, it's my dinner hour. In the park with the phoenix, who sits beside me consummated with a cheese sandwich. A few yards away there's a cat with a gleeful expression. I have to report many clouds, they hove in sight from all directions. The sun still sweeps through them. It's not really a park here but just a grove with a lot of trees, off the Parade, remember? In the heart of the town with sounds of traffic rumbling all around I always think of those parks in London with their strange sanctuary quiet and the city roar tucked away, hidden. Or even of the churchyard in the middle of Brum. Bell chimes—half past one. You know this dance routine upside down! A young chap on this bench has just told me it's his first day at work. He's in his Sunday best, poor bugger. An office. Getting used to it now, he says. A businessman in a brown summer suit has perched between us. Polishes his specs, the paper is unfurled. REDS REPLY: LET'S TALK. I sneak another squint: "Last woman left tells her story." He's moved now. The kid gets up and goes as well. Businessman on the grass in the shade, the sun's too strong for him. It's nearly as strong as I am— stop shoving, sun.

'Evening now, the prison gates opened with a clang and I went streaking off down Union Street like a mad horse just escaped from the circus. Tonight the horizon is more naked than I've ever seen it, the sea a very deep dark blue, and to look at the horizon pushes your eyes back into your head, snap, it's so close, it's all there is and you can tell there's a hell of a drop beyond it where the sea's pouring over in a vast silent waterfall. The horizon moves in even closer—comes to have a look at us all: the far headland seems beyond the horizon, clear and shining in the setting sun . . .

'I wonder if you remember how the evening sun lights up this cottage room? Our paintings are still up on the walls, the salt air rusts the drawing pins. The wireless is hidden in the corner by the window, the heather is still in the vase, the sea still outside the door.

'Whenever I look ahead into the future—and it must be the same for you—I can't reach forward more than a few months without wondering where I'll be. What a state of affairs! While I live this treadmill routine it's a twisted sort of consolation to know that *some* change is inevitable at short notice, yet how I dream of a time, a place, which all the weathers nourish, and each day grows out of the one before in a natural ritual, and me part of it, in it, instead of gnawing away at the skirting boards like dry rot, like a rat on the fringes, wishing my bloody life away . . . Like you when you worked here, I dive down to the office lav for some privacy now and then. My hermit's cell. It stinks too, this one. The green mould on the window ledge is growing luxuriant, looks like a lush meadow a long way off. The smashed window with the wire netting outside, the council flats, the black grimed windows that won't open. Enough, I've had enough. Can't go on like this any longer, hanging on the brink. For months I've been stoked with this feeling, of being on the point of making a great break. Every day my veins choke with rage, the storms pour through me. My guts are sown with dynamite, one day I'll go off with an almighty bang. I seem to be walking about half the time with my eyes closed and a great light sizzling through my eyelids. What's happening to me? How long can it last like this?

'Another day, Friday: this is a continuous performance. I'm sitting in a stationary train at the station, en route to a creek near Saltash—we've heard of this motor torpedo boat and we might rent it. It's been moored up permanently and converted to a houseboat, 32/6 a week including barnacles. I remember how I used to look at the station here at North Road with such tenderness, go and stand near it, because when I was doing my National Service it meant freedom to me. This very station would bring a lump in my throat, just thinking of it. Once I was wandering round the town all evening with a book in my hand—Fyodor—and found myself outside the station. Dark and drizzling. Went into the wooden waiting room and there were some old folk in there wheezing with age and some kids shouting. It was dimly lit, raining outside and Prince Myshkin had just thrown a fit, a fit of such beatitude that I was spellbound, I wanted to foam at the mouth and be as blessed . . . Train's moving, here we go, first stop Paradise—no it ain't, it's the dockyard halt. The dockyardies pile in, dozens of men, grim stone-faced bastards some of 'em, they fill the train like a tide and we go clanking off again, groaning and work-weary . . .

'Imagine us living on a boat, eh Colin? Twas on the good ship Venus—by God you should have seen us! Sail at daybreak, cast off at sunrise for the promised land, the Virgin

Isles, Cape of Good Hope, the Easter Islands, Samoa, Golden Bay, the Aegean, Land of Heart's Desire. Only one thing wrong, matey: what are all these ugly mugs I'm surrounded with?

'Those were the days be Jesus when we were mad comrades laughing fit to bust, making the roof ring, the gates of doom crack open—nothing mattered, we'd be staggering drunk with laughter on neat nothing. Let's have another binge old friend, I'm badly in need of some more of that intoxicating juice we distilled and shared. All I've done by way of affirmation since you left is one hand-sized watercolour, also put brake blocks on the bike and had a bath. Connie's thoroughly down in the mouth and who can blame her—I've been in the salt mines so long I've forgotten what my name is. Yes Colin if you do hitch down here for a few days this summer, that would be great. If we had one I'd put the red carpet out—the sea's already soaping itself all over, getting clean and ready. I'll have the laugh-drink brewed and bottled and be pacing up and down on the corner like a hoodlum waiting for his best cracked pal, long-lost twin, of the cracked order of champion chokers. So take care and be happy, never forget those times of ours.'

14

BEFORE I moved into the bedsitter I lived in a family house out at Sneinton, a grim district near the public baths. Once a week there was a market in the streets nearby, pushcarts appeared loaded with junk, old clothes, bedsteads, one or two lorries heaped with gaudy fabrics, lino, glassware, a man on the tailboard talking nonstop, a lump of wood in his fist for thumping on the rolls of lino. As a kid I was fascinated by their spiel and the way it ran out of their mouths seamless like the yards of flaming orange ribbon and lassoed us, bunched us into a captive crowd. One sharpie at Sneinton would give away free ball-pens with every purchase, he'd hand down a paper bag to his assistant after dropping in the article and then the pen very fastidiously from his finger and thumb: 'One, two for the price of one, it's ridiculous . . . another over there, and another, another!'

I was a lodger in a house with students, a bus driver, a young ex-miner. The Y.M. had given me the woman's address, and the day I tapped on the door she was getting a room ready for the students, she said. Really she was full up, she explained, but if I'd like to sit down a minute and excuse the mess she'd have another think, see if she could fit me in.

I took it that she had already decided, but liked to give the impression she was bestowing favours: a peculiarity of land-ladies.

We were at the rear of the house. Through the window I could see a narrow yard with a shed at the end. She saw me looking and said yes, she had another folding bed in there, that wasn't the problem, it was space she was stuck for. She was middle-aged, a tall floppy woman in a grey dress and slippers, wearing glasses. The glasses made her look shrewd and capable, then she took them off and I saw she was ignorant and cunning, her eyes a bit scatty and bloodshot.

'Don't let me put you to any trouble,' I said.

In those days I was perfectly willing to let a situation decide things for me. It wasn't fatalism, it was a kind of suspension of the will. If a thing pushed me in a certain direction, I went. At the back of it was I think the old nagging desire for something to happen. Perhaps this was the direction, now, so I went.

'It's a funny old life, don't you think?' the woman said, not even listening. Or so I thought. In fact she chose to ignore anything she didn't want to hear, but she didn't miss a thing.

'Now let's see what we can do about you, young man,' she said archly.

She was smirking and showing her dentures. Her voice was honeyed and crude and genteel, she slid from one to the other in the course of a single sentence. I shifted my feet uneasily as she gave me a hard unwavering look.

'What did you say your name was?'

I blushed because she wanted to know much more than that. I began to hate her. She had a queer nervous gobbling curiosity.

I told her.

'May I call you Colin?' she said, and now her eyes were ingratiating, she waited almost breathlessly and it was clear that a lot depended on how I answered.

'Certainly,' I said.

This had the effect of jerking her into action: from being a slovenly torpid creature she changed immediately, leapt up and bustled me out through the kitchen to help her bring in another bed.

'If you don't mind helping, that is,' she panted, dragging open the shed door and standing a moment in pretended horror: 'My son's been here again, I've told him a hundred times not to play here. Did you ever see anything like it?'

I stared in at the chaos, the cheap wardrobe, burst mattress, cobwebby pushbike with inner tube dangling, dark green cast-iron mangle, brass fenders, it was like market day all over again. But you're a liar to act surprised, I thought. The room I'd been sitting in was in absolute disorder and so was the kitchen: if I'd had to cook a meal in that mess I'd have been sick before I got to eating it. Funny, I wrinkled up my nose at the mingled gas and fried onion smells, the congealed fat on the cooker, sink jammed with dirty crocks, hurried through with my guts cringing in revulsion and yet it never occurred to me that I was contemplating living here, being fed from this filthy hole.

It turned out that the bed I was helping her carry was for the second student she'd taken on. It was an attic room at the back, with a view of the yards, sheds, wash-houses.

'Michael he's called. He's ever so nice, black curly hair like a golliwog, only small he is but full of cheek, in a pleasant way I mean, nothing offensive at all. And he's so cuddly, I'll have to be careful not to mother him. Still, some like to be mothered, don't they?'

I ended up that first night sharing a bed with Len, the ex-miner, a temporary arrangement while she retrieved more sheets from the laundry—'I'm sure that's where they are.' It was a three-quarter bed, stuck under the sloping ceiling in an even smaller attic room next-door to the students: I could hear them horsing around in there, cries of mock pain, snatches of false contralto. The radio came on, a news bulletin. Someone sliced off the voice in the middle of a flood disaster.

I got into bed and Len was already in, turned to the wall, his bare white arms looking big and significant on top of the blanket. Getting in I saw more of him. His singlet was too large; there was hair round his nipples. He was a young

Yorkshireman, disabled, so the landlady said, though he looked alright to me. Round baby face, moony white, his hair dank and pale, and his voice came out thick, slow, heavy and puzzled. Len Bolton.

It was the first time I'd slept with a complete stranger and it was curious how easy it was. We had no option, but all the same it could have been nasty. I didn't mind his stale, old-iron body smell. After all it was his bed, I was the intruder. We managed not to touch. To strike up some sort of aquaintanceship I asked him a few things and he answered shyly, obediently, like a timid kid replying to his teacher. I felt a fool, and guilty, as if I was probing. He was content to just lie there, stranger or not; it was all one to him.

'You say you haven't been in the Midlands long?' I said.

'About three yeer. Summat like that.'

'At Nottingham?'

'Ay, outside like. Moreton Wood pit, mostly. That was where I copped it.'

'Like it there, did you? Until the accident, I mean.'

'After a bit it weren't bad. Funny lot they are. I mean they're all right but they kept to themselves. Moreton gang wouldn't mix with them that cum from town, not at any price.'

'How about you, from Yorkshire?'

'Oh, they both gev it me, they did. I got ragged be both lots.'

'You got used to it, I suppose.'

'Oh ah.'

It wasn't quite dark, the man's breath came loud and regular beside me, the night thickening and moving in a respiration of its own and we sank slowly into it together. What light there was came from a street lamp outside.

I ought to have left him alone and it was clear I would have to, soon: he wasn't going to sleep but his silence was growing

400

implacable. One thing kept nagging at me and I wanted his reaction.

'How d'you get on with the Mrs here?' I said.

Once again the response was immediate. He swung his body over to lie on his back and then waited inert like a discarded sack, cleared his throat portentously and I thought, Here we go—expecting a speech. But all he said was, 'She ent bad when she likes.'

Coming from him, the touch of animation was like a little explosion.

'When she likes?' I coaxed him.

'Ar, that's it.'

I laughed softly into the dark.

'What about when she doesn't?'

I thought he wasn't going to answer, that he was finished, but he gave one final burst before rolling over to face the wall again: 'Her, she's a bloody nuisance! Won't let yer alone . . . pesters yer to death . . .'

I had to sleep on that, but in the next few days I began to see what he meant. She blew hot and cold, blustery and coy by turns, hanging round the table when Michael the new student was having his breakfast. He was the present favourite. She'd done a stint with the bus driver, so I heard, going out drinking with him at night. I don't know what had gone wrong but he made himself scarce now, and when he did appear for a bit of tea some evenings she gave him the cold shoulder, spoke curtly, made her eyes anonymous, shoving across the pot of jam or whatever it was with a jab like a rebuff. I was intimidated as much as him. He took it without a word, stuffing his mouth and keeping his head down, especially if the husband was at the table. It was a queer atmosphere at that place: something was always going on. I soon learnt to mind my own business like the others. You had to keep your eyes to yourself, and make sure the friendliness was out of them if you looked: she was a great one for seizing on crumbs of encouragement. Sid, the husband, was a seething, acrid, thickset little man. If he did squeeze you out a smile it was sickly and measured like an undertaker's, and he had the face to go with it, cadaverous, droopy-nosed. He was a Derby man, with their flat working-day accent, and had the knack of repeating your question so that it sounded sarcastic, though it was probably habit.

Once on an impulse of pity I said, 'How are you?' and he snapped back as if it was red-hot, 'How am I? I'm as you see me, lad.' You're no great shakes then, I thought, and gave up even pretending to like him. He came in from his Co-op counter job each night and stalked through to the kitchen to inspect the squalor, which never altered all the time I was there. Back into the dining-room with his little-man strut. The yellow-faced glare he wore would be a picture, and completely lost on his wife. Tom, the other student, who seemed more or less a fixture amid the comings and goings of lodgers, could hit off Sid's tired whiney voice perfectly. 'Doris, can't you please get that kitchen a bit straight?' he'd mimic, up in his room.

They had two boys still at school, and because nobody cared what they did and their parents were always missing in the evenings, they ran riot whenever they were left alone. So the lodgers pushed off into town or the nearest pub for a bit of peace, the students likewise, if they weren't barricaded in their room and supposed to be studying, with the radio on full blast. Meeting them on the stairs they'd con me with dazzling smiles; they were as bland as the cream surfaces of the doors.

I'd have the evening meal to get my money's worth and then turn out with the others into the streets, waiting for the trolley bus or walking, all going in our different directions. It was like living at the Salvation Army. You'd munch up your grub mechanically and escape, quick, no idea where you were heading.

402

15

I CAN'T remember how I came to get hold of the address of the International Friendship League, the secretary, but it must have been while I was at Doris's. One evening I stood ringing at the door of a tall house in Elm Drive, close to the base of the Castle. The last thing I am is a joiner, but nothing was happening with Leila, I was well and truly lost in the void, and now I came on this ravishing word friendship. In the state I was in, weak with self-pity, it was irresistible. The very thought of it made my eyes prickle. I would have joined a bible class if someone had asked me nicely. Friendship: the sound it made in my head was like the password of a secret society. It would unlock the orchards, fields, the secret fruits. Open the cage. I wasn't bothered about the international part, it could be universal, provincial, spatial for all I cared. And I was on the track of it, I found myself in Elm Drive. I rang the bell. No answer. Rang. I could hear the ringing in the depths of the house. Someone came down the stairs.

The secretary was a Scotsman, a thin thoughtful fellow in his thirties, sucking a pipe. He looked too ordinary to be a dispenser of friendship. Up we went to his flat, a large high-ceilinged room with thick plaster mouldings and huge skirting boards, cream woodwork and olive green walls. I gazed in wonder at the shelves of books while he sat me down against the window and sat with crossed legs in a carved chair yards away, giving times of meetings, particulars of activities and so on. I listened to him vaguely, he was a teacher, telling me precisely but remotely what he thought I wanted to know, as if he had a whole group of people in front of him. His platitudinous nature rejected me of its own accord, without him even being aware of it. There was the urge to say: 'Go on talking if you like, but we're wasting our time.' The bell rang again and some friends came up, I sat for an hour or more on the fringe of things, content to absorb the air of leisure, the secretary's accent, which sounded exotic and fascinating. I enjoyed watching the working of his jaw.

'Would you care for a coffee?'

He smiled in an effort to include me.

'Thanks a lot,' I said, 'but I'd better be going.'

'Oh and if you're ever at a loose end at weekends,' he said rapidly, 'why don't you call on Mrs Collis, she keeps a sort of open house—I'm sure she'd be pleased to see you. Hang on, I'll write down the address. You know the Mansfield Road? It's out in that direction, past the Forest . . .'

Mrs Collis was the treasurer, another official. I called one summer evening, much later, after going to one session of the club and not having the stomach for another try. Still, I had the address and it was a private house, after all. It might be worth a visit, I said doubtfully in my mind.

The house was bigger than the one the secretary lived in: up a wide deserted side road with old-established chestnut trees growing out of the pavements. No voices: the kids of the district were either locked up or exterminated, I thought, forgetting that they were probably at boarding schools. All I could hear were wood pigeons cooing, a motor mower chugging in the depths behind one of the high keep-out walls. The one I wanted was called Beechwood, with a thick scratchy beech hedge sprouting out of a stone earth-filled wall at the front. I crunched over the gravel in the shade of wistaria and the coiled springs of a monkey-puzzle tree, the biggest I'd seen. Stone urns, roses, herringbone brick pathways, rings of turf crammed with begonias, the walls covered in ivy: everything was mellow and ordered. You felt constrained to walk sedately, appreciatively. It was a Saturday afternoon, dry and still. Two steps inside the gate and the city was cunningly spirited away. Not for a miniature landscaped country, no, it was a cloistered, monkish world the seclusion created. The door was at the side. It was what my mother would have called without resentment a posh house, simply meaning that the people who lived in such places were incomprehensible to her. To live surrounded by space, unused rooms and gardens laid out in a kind of pomp like a park was inhuman, even frightening. Such people must be terribly different, coldly so: she heard their loud confident voices and knew she was right. The money had made them hard, icy. Their big unfriendly houses were the same, they had to be. Beautiful, yes, but stately, stiffly beautiful. A cold beauty. She preferred small buildings, like cottages. They were human, they fitted you, snug and warm like a glove, stiflingly close so you were never alone and nothing echoed. In the posh houses of the wealthy she imagined Gothic horrors, cobwebs out of reach in high draughty corners, mad blazing cats and gloomy panelling, with peremptory voices everywhere, the voices of doctors, schoolmasters, solicitors, all the professional voices she dreaded.

They must have seen me approaching. As I reached the door it opened and a pretty girl with a pale high forehead, hurt mouth and thick long Alice-in-Wonderland hair stood waiting to welcome me. Unprepared, I began to stutter who I was.

'Do come in,' the girl said, cutting me short, and moving to one side she stood there, smiling. She seemed delighted to see me and I walked in gladly but I thought, How can she be, she's never set eyes on me before. Of course it was manners.

From behind she directed me like someone important into a large gracious room that was cool and restful, softly seductive with its velvet cushions and footstools, gold damask curtains in still waterfalls from ceiling to floor, brown embossed wallpaper in a Florentine design. Over by the French windows sat her mother, smoking a cigarette, examining a piece of embroidery; against her a sewing basket on legs. She nodded pleasantly to me and put her cigarette in an ash tray, but held on to the embroidery while she foraged in the sewing basket with her free hand.

'I'm Mrs Collis,' she said. 'Won't you sit down, Mr Patten?'

'Thanks very much,' I said. I glanced round for the girl but she'd slid away.

'That was Amanda,' Mrs Collis said, moving her legs. A long skinny woman, beaky, hair drawn back severely, flat on her head like a black shiny cap, parted exactly in the middle. 'She's the youngest. I have another daughter at university, Sarah, and a son, Quentin, who's married and lives in Kenya.'

'And a dog,' I said, seizing my chance. A silky fawn Peke, no bigger than a cat, had jumped down from a stool and come prancing up, jaunty and comical on its short bandy legs, to put its flat nose-holes against the toe of my shoe. It stayed there, eating the scent. I put my hand down to it and it collapsed sideways against my leg, eyes bulbous, showing the whites, and there was its tender studded belly on show, abandoned, soft and pinkish like a piglet's.

'Oh yes, that's Ching,' said Mrs Collis, her mouth lifted at one side in a crimped smile of appreciation. 'There's another one somewhere.'

'Smallest I've seen,' I said.

'She is tiny, isn't she? I think they call them sleeve pigs.'

'I haven't heard of that.'

'Oh yes. They're a Chinese dog, you know; Imperial China, of course. A court dog.'

I nodded, though I hadn't known. The long string of pearls hanging down into her lap struck me as incongruous. I was half listening to her and also absorbing the room, its untidiness, which had to do with leisure and money and carelessness, a cool attitude to living, asking nobody's approval. With the poor, tidiness was a necessity. Her domain was impressive, yet I didn't believe in any of it, or the liberal values that went with it. In my mind I took it like a toy and twirled it by the corners: I bristled with dissent. This room, the civilised woman being kind to me—it was a package licked all over with the safe, sheltered life these folk sucked in at their mother's breasts. Or was that done any more? Surely as a breed they managed to get their kids weaned without suffering the humiliation of that disgusting part? Even the welcome I was getting was suspect, somehow cancelled at the outset by the cool air of disengagement. My mother would have been strained and peculiar, anxious and flustered if she had to entertain someone she didn't like, bustling and eager if she liked them. Either way you'd soon know, there'd be no doubt. Here it was all manners, principles, nothing registered on the feelings. This left you free to be yourself, respected your thoughts, opinions, an ear listening most cordially to anything you might say, but emotions ran thin and you had a sneaking feeling they were unmentionable; at the very least they were messy, avoidable. Just as sex was unacknowledged in my mother's world, a nasty fact you could skate around by ignoring, hoping it would go away. Except at night, you could let it out then, under the sheets and private where it belonged. But feelings, she was lapped around with them in her family and all her activities. Thoughts were of no account, just words. Feelings were inescapable, hot waves of exchange between people, pressing away, pulling in. Her breast ached with the rich emotional charge, her memory a dark turgid compost. They wore her out, and it was impossible to bypass them in her mind, stand outside herself in a thought, an idea, even for a moment's respite. Work and feelings went pouring like a warm snake through the days of her life, filling her world completely, right to the corners.

And as long as I lived with her I was the same: not pawed over, hugged and kissed, we were an undemonstrative, reticent family, but swaddled by her constant loving devotion, nevertheless. She couldn't help herself. As a boy I exploited her love shamelessly, took and took and gave nothing in return. She asked nothing, never once complained, the joy for her was all in the giving. It was when I grew restless, itched to be off, started shutting myself away in my room—that made her bite her lip and want to cry out. I can think of some utterly contented mother-and-son times which must have been the happiest days of her life, wandering through the market with her on school holidays when we had little shared jokes, say a woman bearing down on us placidly with vast shaking bosom and I'd whisper from the side of my mouth, 'Jelly on a plate'. She pretended to be shocked, said, 'Colin!' and then blushed and laughed like a girl. The man on the stall where they sold sheets, plaid tablecloths, napkins, thick yellowish working men's vests and long pants, he sang out loud and guttural whenever the searching women delved too freely, 'Nah then ladies, if yer don't want the goods don't maul 'em!' and this was a war cry we mimicked and were always repeating, to amuse each other. 'Don't maul 'em, don't maul 'em!'

In those market forays I made a beeline for the magazine counter, we brought a pile of comics from the house for my mother to trade in: I forget how much he allowed us but it was useful and I came away with a fresh batch, *Hotspurs* and *Rovers* and *Skippers*, never the *Magnet* or *Gem* or *Boys' Own*. They were secondhand, dog-eared, but to me they were glowing with unread adventures. My mother paid the man carefully from her purse, the black purse she gripped like a lifeline, and rearranged her shopping basket to make room for the wad of magazines. From that moment the basket had an effulgence. She said, 'There, that'll keep you out of mischief for an hour or two' and we were on our way home, arms linked like old lovers. Passing near the fish counters she'd say, 'Do you fancy some haddock for tea? Would you like that?' and I answered off-hand, grudgingly, 'Don't mind.'

Or more than likely I said, fussy as an old maid, 'If it's not too salty.' She knew how I finicked over my food and she liked to pander to me, asking me to try this or that but often spoiling me, giving in to my whims and fancies. Not my father. The waste on my plate would disgust him, he'd snarl, 'Make him eat it,' and 'If he can't finish that dinner, don't give him any pudding, he's not hungry.' But where meals were concerned my mother ruled, on came the pudding, steaming with newness, and I got a helping like the others. My father tucked into his with relish and forgot me, rattling away with his spoon vigorously, chasing the last gobbet of custard.

16

'WOULD YOU like to go through to the garden?' Mrs Collis was saying, honeyed and vague, receding further each time she opened her mouth.

She was a good sort, I suppose. All the same I didn't need any encouragement to leave. The unreality was becoming a strain: the blue grass of the carpet was sapping my energy. The grit and grind of the streets were beginning to seem very desirable.

Out in the garden Amanda was sitting in a deck chair reading, and on one of those suspended garden seats with striped upholstery and an awning sat a youth, he could have been her boy friend, idly pushing himself to and fro with his foot. Seeing me approach he put the brake on at once and smiled, perfectly friendly and in charge of himself, a friendliness very much aware of the vulgarity of overflowing. I lowered my backside into the carnival upholstery, feeling stupid to be posed there on the gay colours like an advertisement. It was comfortable alright. I sank back discreetly in the corner.

'This is nice,' I said, for something to say.

'Isn't it,' the brown-haired youth said.

Half an hour dozed by and I couldn't see the point, I was about to get up and say cheerio when Mrs Collis appeared with a wicker tray, glasses of orange squash. It was getting on for five before I decided to make a break for it.

'Call in again whenever you're passing, won't you,' Mrs Collis droned out absently, and her daughter glanced up from her book and gave me such a warm smile, exactly like the one she'd doled out at the door, clapping eyes on me for the first time. Out in the street and making for the main road into the

410

centre, the jubilation and rumpus of a city Saturday night, I let out a huge sigh of relief, relaxing. My blood ran free, I was alone and glad in my skin. Being lonely wasn't so bad after all. I strode along loose and irresponsible like a vagabond, whistling like a blackbird, cheerfulness spurting out of me at every step. I knew I wouldn't be back there again.

But I did land up at a house not far from there, later. I'd gone once with Aline because the woman was a friend of hers and she wanted me to meet her: this friend had a strange niece who was a bit mad and might have a touch of genius, Aline thought. She wrote poems on a blackboard and they got rubbed off in the course of time and lost forever. Her aunt encouraged her, let her do whatever came into her head within limits, even though she was baffled by the girl's behaviour.

'What about her parents, what do they think?' I asked.

'She hasn't got any,' Aline said. 'They were killed in the war.'

The girl wasn't in when we called, but we sat having tea and scones in the drawing-room, and bang in the middle of the carpet, before the window, was an easel and blackboard, half the size of a school one, and three verses of a poem scrawled over it, untitled, filling up all the space. I couldn't decipher many of the words, but Marion, the aunt, didn't seem concerned about the content, it was the activity, the phenomenon, she found extraordinary. She was a short puggy intense woman; crisp greying hair and a bright, happy voice, and I tried to imagine what her niece was like. Marion kept talking, referring to her niece in an attitude of complete acceptance, passing no judgements. Only in her eyes could you detect the mother signs, the lurking apprehension. She had no children of her own. 'She's a remarkable woman,' Aline had said. 'Betty's lucky to have an aunt like her.' She was unusual, certainly, but I didn't know where I was with her. It struck me as a funny set-up and I began to feel sorry for the girl, whatever she was like. Maybe she would have been better off with a demanding mother, I thought.

The blackboard stood and stared at us from the middle of the room, so bloody significant you had to look back at it and comment on it.

'Did she write that long ago?' I said.

'Oh no, only yesterday.'

'She doesn't just write poems, does she?' Aline said, prompting, wanting me to have the full story.

'No she doesn't, she often does drawings.'

'What of?' I said.

'Trees, always trees.'

I decided to shut up, it was somehow ridiculous, we were sitting around all solemn and ponderous like a bunch of trick cyclists.

The next time I was there alone, a spasm of curiosity had got me there and this time the girl was at home. No resemblance to her aunt: a tall thin gawk, cloud of long black hair tied with a red ribbon, straight bony nose that gave her a puritanical look. She was dressed wrong for her age. She wore white ankle socks and a drab pleated skirt, a queer mixture of too young and too old. She stared at me haughtily and refused to speak, gliding soundlessly out of the room as soon as she could. Her timidity was hard and lacquered, it wore a shell of arrogance, something I knew all about. In the drawing-room the first thing I noticed was the blackboard, it was wiped clean.

To my amazement Marion started talking to me in a detached yet curiously urgent manner, questioning me about my relationship with Aline. Finally she said quietly, smiling and steady, 'You know she's married, don't you?'

Resistance stiffening at once, I said, 'Separated.'

412

'Yes but Francis is hoping they'll come together again, he wants it very much.'

I blurted out stupidly, 'Who's Francis?' and could have bitten my tongue off. Now she had the whip hand.

She maintained her neutral role with her lips, smiling calmly, while her eyes said clearly: Now why don't you run along and stop being a nuisance, like a good little boy.

'Does *she* want it?' I said, stubborn, slipping down the slope and digging in my fingers, demoralised and cornered by the swift attack. The treachery of it dazed me, I felt sick and guilty. The woman saw my defencelessness and pressed in, triumphant.

'Oh I'm sure she does in her heart of hearts,' she said, superbly confident and knowing, and her voice expressed the deep concern of a friend. I sensed that its resonance was meant to shame me. 'You don't know her, she has such tremendous pride—that's the whole crux of the problem.' She paused, showed at last the cold steel of her hostility, her face shutting me out for good. 'If you care for her, I shouldn't keep on seeing her. You're making things worse for her, I'm sure you can see that. We musn't be selfish, must we?' And the mask was back, she was actually laughing, showing me to the door.

'Will you think about what I've said?' she purred smoothly.

'Sorry,' I said, walking off stiff-legged with hate for her, the advice gathering inside me like a poison, seething. Sorry, sorry, I was yelling inside, furious at the deception, the sprung trap, the oiled ease and unruffled calm of it. Everything in the garden was always lovely for these well-layered bastards, they never dirtied the air with foul language, screamed blue murder, came at you with a broken bottle, they just smiled like a dear friend as they slid the knife in and said ta-ta. Well she could take a running jump, I wasn't even listening, I was a thousand miles away, I was as deaf as my grandfather. Sorry, you rotten bitch, sorry and get stuffed,

413

sorry for nothing you smirking shit. I was afraid now, I imagined enemies everywhere. Worse still, I had the worm of doubt wriggling through me, those words she'd dropped into my ear so sweetly had taken on a life of their own. And perhaps she was right. Who was telling the truth, who could I trust? I even doubted her, Aline. I pushed along in a fury of hurt pride and fear, squirming again and again in that boxed-in corner, turning my head to avoid the advice like a betrayer, like a man trying to ward off the truth, the slap in the face. What I was most scared of was the sudden terrifying challenge without warning to my own powers. I wouldn't admit this to myself but it was true: I just didn't know how strong I was. That was what was being tested, the strength or weakness of my desire. In a wild instinct of self-preservation I kept laying into the woman, the advice-giver, all the way into town.

17

FOR NEARLY a week I had Lou's address and did nothing about it, though my instinct was to go straight there and knock on his door. I stored him up, kept him for a rainy day, tasted the pleasures of denial. He was a contact, a friendly face. The instant I got back to the bedsitter, climbed the stairs past the navy man's wife screaming at one of her kids behind the door, unlocked the padlock on my own door and went in, I thought of Lou Coltman. His address was burning a hole in my pocket but I still hung back, unwilling to risk a rebuff. He'd come round to see me, he'd sought me out, that was true, but I'd taken the initiative, hadn't I? Written the note etc—and he hadn't given me his address until I asked for it. Even as I weighed up the pros and cons I knew very well I was only postponing it, I'd go anyway, in spite of all fears, shrinkings. It's not timidity, it's excess pride that makes you fear rejection.

The couple in the room next to mine were at it, I could hear them. Once I'd heard their voices, coming in, but they were faceless; I didn't know what their names were. All I was familiar with was the sound of their bed. It made a regular rhythm. I was so naïve that I heard it several nights running before realising what it was.

I made love to myself, stretched out full length on the monk's bed. The evening was stifling, a dull heat surged at the roof and I imitated it, threw off the sheets and let the soft slopes of my thighs entice each other. They were a couple, they clung to each other stickily, broke apart with a sucking sound. But it wasn't enough, I wanted them to burst into blossom. I got a towel and knotted my legs together, hid my sex, achieved the constriction of an embrace. My body writhed slowly like a woman, I looked down at the floor through the glistening hairs of my armpit, let out low moans like a prostitute struggling to earn her money. I shut my eyes so that my hands could go over me like lovers. The couple strained, swelled against the knot and it parted, my erection rammed the door and shook the wall, it was gigantic. Sperm shot up to the ceiling and cascaded, spattered my chest, smeared my groin. I decayed, lay stagnant, held my breath.

Somebody was banging on the door along the landing, where the couple lived. That was the noise I'd heard. They hammered again, once, then I heard the footsteps move off stealthily and go down the stairs.

One night I opened my door and it was too much, ugly beyond words, an empty hole fit for crawling into and going to bed and that's all: nobody in their right mind would dream of sitting in it, not even to eat. I had to get out, it was either the streets or Lou Coltman. I knew I'd be sweating it out during the last few yards, plagued by all kinds of idiotic ifs and buts: well, that would come later. I sprang about with new zest, eager to leave, escape, giving my face a rinse, hair a quick comb through. I had a destination, a purpose, I was alive with expectation. Gave the room a rapid going-over, straightened the bed, washed out the bowl for cornflakes in the morning, emptied the slush of tea-leaves in the pot. Jacket on and I was ready, going. It was good to be going, great to have a reason for leaving, instead of having to flee as I usually did, pursued by furies, no directions. Went dropping down the stairs lightly and eagerly, feeling the jacket on my shoulders like a benediction, straightening my back inside it with a strange mixture of luxury and gratitude. Out in the street I patted my pockets to hear money and went prowling off for Slab Square, where the buses gathered.

416

It was Thursday, a warm sunless evening, the kind of summer evening you take absolutely for granted in a city in England; a heavy grey sky waiting in dejection over the Council House roof, and if there was any smoke rising it would be the same lifeless sky colour. The air warm and thick. On the bus trundling through the crowds—the open space of the square full and moving, a man in a dark suit up on the wall making a speech, his face congested, one or two on the benches listening, lots just walking past without giving him a glance—men were digging thick fingers into their collars and saying 'sticky'. A couple of hours earlier there had been a cool breeze blowing, so I'd pulled on a red cotton polo-neck sweatshirt over my shirt and now I realised my mistake. No wind now, I was too hot. I took off my jacket and nursed it, then dragged the bus window open. We roared over the canal by the Midland Station and I got up for the next stop. Still two stops away from where I wanted, but I'd walk from here. The conductor had given me rough directions. I was getting off too soon because I needed air, I told myself. I was sweating, but the fact was I needed time to calm down inside. This always happened: I gave myself time and I became worse instead of better. I blamed the red polo-neck, felt like a jockey in it. The street was grim, broken pavements, gaunt terraced houses stuck together, back-to-back and more facing, exactly alike and dwindling off in rows like railway lines. Windows bodged up with cardboard, a mongrel on a table in one front window scrabbling at the glass and going frantic with barking, mad bulging eyes following me as I went past.

Giving me the address Lou had said, 'Coming from town you'll see a cinema, the *Astoria*—we're not far past there on the left.' 'Who's we?' I'd thought vaguely. Now here it was, a scabby peeling little fleapit, two long cracked steps and then the paydesk, painted maroon and cream when it was built and never again by the state of it; more scars than paint. A crumbling temple, swallowed by the brick jungle.

417

A girl of fourteen or so with bared white face sat on the top step, keeled over sideways but awake, watching, gobbling me up with her eyes, with her whole face as I passed. Kid opposite mending the entrails of a motorbike in the gutter, spanner poised while he watched me by. It was like entering a village, the curiosity was intense.

All the houses had garden walls at the front, low humped barriers with a gap for a gateway, but no gardens: the tiny patch was scummy greenish concrete, a sump in the corner for the downpipe. I was nearly there, watching the numbers and more and more tense in my chest. An acrid smell from somewhere, perhaps a factory.

The air was motionless, nothing in the street stirred: it was so abandoned I could hear the youth tinkering with his motorbike, right back there by the picture house. I banged on the brown door and heard my blood beating. The houses seemed to press in, I felt watched.

No answer. Banged again, then heard feet clattering down bare stairs inside. Next thing, a fellow I'd never seen before stood in the doorway.

'Lou Coltman live here?'

'That's right.'

'First time I've been here . . .' I began to grin.

'Oh yeh.'

'Is Lou in?'

'No, afraid not. He might be back later, I dunno. He just went out.'

'Oh—well . . .'

We stood staring at each other, it was funny; a young bloke with a few days' stubble, washed-out, crumpled face, and very steady grey eyes, long-lashed. Suddenly I remembered something Lou had said that night in the pub—'You ought to meet Ron Cousins, painter. I'll fix it up one day.' I said: 'Are you Ron Cousins by any chance?'

'That's right,' he said, still not even the ghost of a smile, but his voice more interested, his face less blank. 'How d'you know that, mate?'

'Lou told me.'

'Go on?'

'He said I ought to meet you sometime.' I told him my name but it meant nothing.

'Better come in, yeh,' he said. 'If you want to, that is. Lou might be back—he sometimes comes in early. Sometimes not at all. All depends how the money is, all depends. Christ knows where he gets to. . . . This is his place, you know.'

'I know.'

I followed him in.

'I'm just staying here for a while. He lets me use his back room.'

'Oh.'

We tramped up to the first floor, the stairs painted blood red at the side and then bare white wood where there had once been stair carpet. Neat, narrow, industrial cottage stairs, not an inch wasted. There were doors opening off the landing, old panelled matchwood doors made flush with hardboard and painted yellow, with chrome numbers screwed on amateurishly. Instructions were pinned up on each door, a list of don'ts. No tea leaves down the sinks, no scum in the bath, no girls in the beds and so on.

Ron led me into number four and jerked his thumb at the notice. 'Look at that shit.'

'Friendly,' I said.

'Shitbags.'

My place didn't go in for those written litanies, you got it verbally at the beginning.

'Makes you feel at home,' I said.

'Yeh, well, it's cheaper than a welcome mat.'

'Suppose so.'

The room was small, with bare floorboards, old and shrunken, gappy wood, stained black so crudely that the stain was in daubs here and there all along the bright yellow skirting boards. The walls were white, painted over a pink stripey wallpaper, and again the job was slapdash, the stripes barely covered in places. The grate was blocked up with a piece of hardboard decorated by hand in a gay zigzag design like an African shield, black and white, the fireplace slopped over ineffectually with the same white stuff they'd used on the walls. Originally it was one of those modern brown tile abortions that squat like toads, millions of them there must be, spawned up and down the country in towns and villages alike. One wall, opposite the window, was pasted all over with newspaper cuttings: only it wasn't a wall, it was a partition, you just walked round the end and that was the sink and cooker. A kitchenette.

I don't know where it came from, it might have been curled up asleep under the rickety coffee table—up jumped a young, very virile Alsatian, wagging, ferocious wolfish teeth on show and great red tongue lolling out, planting its forefeet on my chest.

'Down, Sailor—down, yer great daft bugger!' Ron Cousins shouted, grabbed it by the collar and hauled it off me, then pointed to a chair in the corner and it slunk away under it obediently, a beautiful, powerful animal.

'Who's it belong to?' I said.

The dog was watching me, measuring and setting me like a bone, its soft melting gaze fixed on my face.

The fellow shrugged. 'Lou's I suppose—well it sort of goes with the place,' and he disappeared behind the partition.

'Want owt to eat?' he bawled, out of sight.

'Not me, thanks.'

'Tea?'

'Okay, thanks.'

I sat on a bed which was pushed against one wall and looked vacantly at a biggish painting hung above the fireplace, greys and blacks in subtle tones, a scrabble of lines as if inscribed in the paint with a pointed fingernail, nervy, fine like fusewire, some kind of dim bulky bowed figure emerging from the apparent mess of stains, blobs, bleedings. It was glum and looked drearily undefined, like something seen through a net curtain, but a certain gravity and struggling purposefulness saved it from mere sophistication, it glowered through to me, a bit aggressive and lonely. I found it disturbing, and began to wonder, to wake up.

'This your picture hanging up?' I called. Apart from the news cuttings, nothing else adorned the room.

'One on 'em,' he shouted back shortly.

He came out with a pot of tea and two mugs, let them thump down on the table, callous, and went back to fetch his food, a two-decker sandwich, pilchards smothered in mayonnaise in one layer, tomatoes in the other. It was huge, it looked as if half a brown loaf had gone into the making of it.

'How many sugars?' he said, and before I could answer, said, 'Help yourself.' I dug into the paper bag while he tipped the teapot over my thick green beaker and poured, letting the tea spout forth while he transferred his aim to his own mug. Tea ran steaming over the table, dripped on to his knees, scalding him, and he jerked back violently: 'You bastard!'

He sat on the other side of the table on a wobbly folding chair, facing me, frankly staring into my face and waiting, non-committal, as if he only had to sit there long enough and it would happen, he'd get the hang of me, find out what my game was. He wasn't bothered, but he suspected my motives. He had nothing to say but when he spoke he articulated very clearly, unlike Lou, who was inclined to mumble. This man liked to be what he was: he didn't see the necessity for hiding. I admired this, but it was so unlike my own nature that I withdrew into myself.

He lifted his tea like a tankard of beer. 'Cheers.'

'Cheers.'

He was still watchful and unwavering as he drank, then when it came to his sandwich he had to switch off from me, give it his full attention. He got it between his fists almost grimly, tomato slithering out from one edge. I laughed and said, 'You'll never make it, you'll get lockjaw.'

'Watch me,' he said, stretched his mouth violently and got a mouthful, filling up his cheeks. For a while he was unable to speak, so I sucked up the hot tea and waited. I felt curiously contented to be there, even though I wasn't exactly welcome. The man didn't pretend friendship, he watched and waited like the Alsatian, he was indifferent but he might be interested later. That was good enough. Secretly I was going to work on him, softening him. I began to like him, his resistance, and I was here, this was Lou's place. I was in, anyway. Here was a port of call, something different. Things might even happen here. It looked hopeful, I liked the feel of its free-and-easy atmosphere. I hadn't been in a room quite like this before, though I'm damned if I could have said what made it special. It wasn't special, that was the point. It was a transit place, a passing-through room. A test room. I began to feel pleased with myself, as if I'd already achieved something.

Still chewing laboriously, Cousins sat eyeing me. It was getting funny, I felt the urge to giggle. He wore an ex-army khaki shirt with one of the shoulder buttons missing, so that the shoulder strap dangled loose. His long fingernails were ringed with dirt, the fingers pale and surprisingly womanish.

'Good?' I said, to break the silence.

He merely nodded, chewing and keeping the deadpan look on his face, then said something I wasn't expecting at all, as if he'd suddenly made up his mind about me: 'You'll have to excuse me if I don't say much—I don't have much to do with folks. Keep out of the way. So I don't have a lot of practice.'

I nodded sympathetically. 'I'm not much better,' I said.

'Better?' he said, very quick, and again I was floundering. He was like he was for reasons of his own, aggressively. I hadn't meant to imply he was some sort of lame dog, or expect him to be touchy about it. So he wasn't completely out in the open, he could be stung. What the hell, I thought, he can be what he likes. But I quickly corrected myself with 'No, not better—I mean I'm similar.'

For reasons of my own I was out to please him. He seemed satisfied, but a little depressed, thoughtful.

'Good,' he said, nodding his head solemnly.

He startled me by beginning to whistle tunelessly between his teeth. It was aimless, like someone rattling coins in a pocket.

'Doesn't Lou have much company then?' I asked him.

'Christ yes, I'll say. Too bloody much. I push off out, or go into my own hovel and lock the door . . . thank Christ it's got a lock. He needs a lot of folk round him, Lou does, they come in bloody droves when it suits 'em. Drives you nuts.'

Suddenly it dawned on me how lucky I was, not having Lou here in the room. I nearly closed my eyes with pleasure of anticipation, visualising myself tapping secret sources of information, drawing close to the enigma. I hadn't understood either how much the enigma fascinated me. Lou the melter into crowds, Lou the charmer, the elusive seeker of others. Lou being friendly, Lou looking into the distance, through the wall, round the corner. I saw him once in a pub, helping a blind man to the door, steering him through the customers with great tenderness, with complete absorption, obliterating himself. Lou the saintly man. The nomad, diving into the streets to feel alone, to feel free. Lou who knew what was going on, the power, who had his finger on things.

'You say he likes people?'

'Christ knows if he does or not. He don't mind any road, he lets 'em all come. I can't complain, can I? That's what I'm doing here. He's a queer bloke, Lou is. I've got my own

423

ideas on this coming and going he indulges in. Mind you, it's only my idea, I know fuck all about the bloke really.'

'Have you known him long?'

'Let's see, how long have I known him—two months? Not much more. Any road, he won't let on what he's up to, but my theory is that he's trying to get to know all kinds of people—as many types as possible. Know what I mean?'

I nodded, eager to keep him going.

'And not only types, he's out to collect experiences, anything at all. He wants to sit down in the middle of things and let it happen. That's what I reckon. I like old Lou but he's a funny close bugger, you won't get to the bottom of him in a hurry.'

'You're right there,' I said: thought of endless space, bottomless eyes, streets going on for ever.

'Ah, you think so, do you?' Cousins said, really alert and lively at last. He sat back and reached for the teapot. 'More splosh?'

I shook my head.

'What's he doing it for then?' I asked.

Cousins was filling up his beaker, he shrugged, the subject seemed without interest, beyond him suddenly. 'To find out . . . .' he said tonelessly.

'Yes, but when he finds out, what then?' I persisted.

'I think he might be on with a book or summat . . . I dunno. Ask him,' he said, rigid, unco-operative again, 'he won't tell you,' and he narrowed his eyes suspiciously, fishing a loose cigarette out of his shirt pocket and lighting it. Drawing on the cigarette he relaxed, the tension eased. 'You say Lou wanted you to meet me?' he said, brightening up, though puzzled.

'Yes he did.'

'An' now you 'ave,' he said heavily, mocking.

I grinned at him and he just sat there, stolid, not giving an inch. We had another period of complete silence, with him draining the dregs of his tea and banging down the beaker. Bump. The end of something. He was no longer my accomplice: the source had dried up. No vindictiveness in him: I guessed he was alone a lot and enjoyed making a clatter, maybe found it reassuring. Like his whistling.

'How's life with you then?' he said unexpectedly, and I took the hint. I'd been at the receiving end long enough, sponging it up, now it was my turn to flow. So I told him a bit about myself, glad of the chance to restore the balance. I was beginning to feel like some kind of snooper. He sat nodding, interested to know I was a stranger to the town like himself, who came from Leeds, then as soon as I stopped talking he jumped up, said, 'I'll have to leave you, I gotta meet this woman at the Ring o' Bells.' He made straight for the door, going just as he was. 'Come if you like,' he added, with a brusque movement of the head.

'I can come that direction anyway,' I said, wanting to hang on to my new contact for as long as possible. I felt obscurely dissatisfied, as if I'd made a poor impression. This was my last chance to impress myself on his memory.

Jolting into town on the bus I told him I was sure to run into him again before long, when I came out to see Lou.

He gave me a hard look. He had a flat spreading nose: from the side he reminded you of an eagle that was half monkey.

'Don't bank on it,' he said flatly. 'I live from day to day, me.'

We swung into the square and he dropped off the platform neatly as we swished round the corner, gave me the thumbs-up sign and was gone. It was only nine-thirty, plenty of people were strolling up and down, standing on corners. I stood where I was, fizzing pleasantly with my new impressions, not at bay or lonely for once. I felt alright, almost a stray citizen out on the town instead of a drifting, homeless wanderer. I stood leaning against the plate glass of a store, let my head go back and saw the night settling flat on the city like a slate, a grey-blue enormous cloud darkening while I watched, at the skyline some long ribbons and channels of amazing greenish light still running afire over the roofs as the sun died, killed by buildings. I stood wondering quietly what to do next: a new experience for me. Usually I went, my legs took me, I was driven.

18

DAVEY IN the street or from the vantage of a car was restlessly, voraciously on the look-out, eyes skinned for anything female; yet I wouldn't have called him a womaniser by any means. Let's say, not a philanderer. That conveys a cynicism, a calculating cold eye, a detachment and a readiness to exploit, to use as an object and then toss away. Pleasure object. Davey was innocent of all that. He wasn't guilty or innocent, he was simply unaware of the existence of that sly world. He gave blood, he gave heart, he tore at the innards of himself. Davey was consumed with hunger: he'd frequently say insulting things about women but he had to have them, his metabolism demanded it. His need for their response and sympathy was desperate and he could never satisfy this need: one woman was never enough. But with each one he'd be full of eagerness to give utterly, unconditionally, to the limit. This generosity was his great gift: I loved him when he turned it on me.

When I saw him in action for the first time, in the street, the market, shops, anywhere, and realised he was the most gregarious person I'd ever known, I wasn't so pleased. I grudged him his capacity to project his joy, his energy, flood his face with feelings, I was irritated again and again by his ceaseless sniffing for skirt, not so much indifferent to my reactions as unaware of them. But he wore no masks, no disguises, if he gave a girl the eye and she cut him dead, if he didn't even squeeze a self-conscious little smirk out of her, he'd mutter under his breath, 'Fuck you then, don't be friendly,' and on his face would be a genuinely puzzled expression: he'd frown and go quiet for a minute or two, really put off his stroke, hurt even. It sounds stupid and his face would look stupid, uncomprehending. How could people be like that? Wasn't he offering himself like a flower, like a fountain of charm, couldn't they see how he appreciated them, made them beautiful, snapped them up in a wink and loved every sweet morsel in his swinging glance, right to the curve of their instep? What was wrong with the world, what were they so suspicious about? He recovered in a few strides, in time for the next encounter. He was what he was, you had to accept him.

He professed love for me, more than once, his eyes soft and shining, and while he was saying it I know he believed it absolutely. It wasn't his insincerity I squirmed under, it was the knowledge I had of him by then, that I wished I didn't have. Of how indiscriminate he was in his friendships, how sinuous, how striding. Even then I drew back from judging him, preferring to take him as he was. I had that much wisdom. Who was I to say how many people he could love without it being a lie? If it came so easy to him, professing love, was it any less genuine than my painful, intensely given, one-at-a-time kind? I envied him his spontaneity, the free generous gush of him, while another part of me held back and distrusted it, always wanting to know what it was worth. I had to have relationships which meant something, but did that put mean limits on your life, your everyday impulses? It did for Davey: he was quite a theoriser when he got going, he took pleasure in spinning it out in words, the path he was taking. Politics, sex, society, it was all grist to his mill when the mood was on him. All you had to do to start him off was mention the word 'Tory'. 'Oh what shits they are, what mean little bastards . . . Can't they ever stop measuring life out in columns, profit and loss . . . the cunts! What did old Bevan call them, what was it? Vermin. That's it, he was dead right an' all. Keep the garden parties flying, keep quacking away with that stiff upper lip, and they will, oh my Christ yes, they'll rustle up funds in thousands of ways while those silly sods in the Labour Party sit round squabbling . . . and what the fucking hell, they're half Tory themselves. Don't get shut of the public schools, not yet, my Johnny ain't had a chance yet. Don't it make you spew. You know what, I reckon this whole fucking country is basically Tory if they tell the truth, scratch the working man today and there's a little shitbag Tory grovelling under his skin, itching for a mini-stately home, for clubs, privileges, superiority . . .'

He'd rant on and gradually shift gear and the vituperative yawp eased off into something less energetic, much more ambiguous and at the same time more vital to him, a definition of values, directions. Meanwhile I was using him to define myself, usually to my own dissatisfaction. I was tall as him but thinner, nervy, warier altogether: a bloody worrier. Davey would abandon himself to a black mood, bare his breast to it with a wild despair I found shocking. I ran upstairs once to his place and he was sitting on the floor of the kitchen, crying, a mess of eggs was spattered over one wall, dripping down in awful warning, like a diagram of fragmentation. Judy and he had had a fight, his boot had caught her in the side and now she'd gone: he'd go mad, stick his head in the bloody gas oven, he couldn't bear the pain of misery. He sat bunched on the floor tugging at his hair and rocking to and fro, sobbing.

'Let me get you a cup of tea, Davey, come on,' I said, coaxing him into a chair. I was horrified by his transformation, he seemed completely broken, finished.

'Oh God,' he moaned, 'what a thing to do . . . How did it happen?'

'She'll be back,' I said. 'It's happened before, hasn't it? Didn't you say it's happened before?'

'Oh Christ no, not like this, it was terrible. She ran out screaming, she was going to fetch a copper, she thought I was going to do her in. She needled me about this other girl, Linda, kept on digging and digging . . . I couldn't stand it, I grabbed a chair and ran at her, wanted to smash her to bits, anything to shut her up . . . The poor kid, you should have seen her face . . .'

'She'll be back, you'll see.'

He closed his eyes and his head fell forward.

'I'm a bloody madman,' he said.

He was in such a state I was scared to leave him, went off haunted by the scene, by his broken state. Next dinnertime I dived in to see if there were any developments and he met me on the stairs, smiling from ear to ear.

'Okay?' I said, baffled by the recovery, beginning to feel like an idiot.

'Eh?' he said. The question on his face was sincere. 'Oh that, oh yeah, we made it up. Come up here and have a dekko at these binoculars I sent away for, week's free trial and fifty years to pay, summat like that. Here y'are, me boy, peep through them lovely goggles at that view over the chimney pots. Bet you didn't think chimney pots looked like that, did yer?'

And Judy was there smiling secretly, unchanged, unmarked.

He was brought low by rows, tormented by ugly atmospheres, but he was never one to anticipate trouble. He lived from day to day, had no defences, but recovered rapidly if the woman was willing.

Gradually I saw that the differences between us were striking, and that what I was doing, as usual in my friendships, was effacing myself and playing to the other man, encouraging his dramatic flights, his flamboyant gestures, his wild speeches and comic turns. He was so fluid, changeable, furious, and I saw myself as static, stoically existing. He was impulsive, often disastrously so. Unless I was driven, I always knew what I was going to do, well before I did it. Davey was either brimming over with self-confidence, full of bounce and resolution, his impetus taking him headlong over obstacles I would have baulked at, or he was absurdly

bashful and blushing. My trouble was shyness, a very different disease. It meant I was continually unsure of myself,
unable to assert myself, bitterly uncertain of other people's
opinions of me. Half the time I was too withdrawn to be
noticed, I felt. Friends tended to dominate, call the tune,
because of my initial self-effacing trait, and a streak of cowardice in me made me avoid rows whenever possible. If I got sick
of the domineering side of someone, if it didn't suit me to
agree, I could call on some stubbornness and very rarely I'd
let fly, stand my ground and insist on doing what *I* wanted
for a change. But if it meant a scene I preferred to compromise, even though I'd accuse myself afterwards of being
gutless. Having a row always boomeranged on me: I'd brood
on it for days, re-enact it, reopen all the wounds. In short, we
were both emotional flounderers, we lived emotionally, yet
looking at Davey I despised myself for being secretive instead
of suicidally in the open and hand-to-mouth like him.

The point was, he took no account of others. He was sensitive, yet curiously unaware, oblivious. If he was grief-stricken
he howled, whether there was company in the room or not;
and flowing over with joy he had to share it, no matter how
little it mattered to the sharer. He ignored all the evidence. I
could never be like that, but I admired him. And loved his
power to seize on moments of happiness, suck the marrow of
a moment just as a child does, without the slightest self-consciousness.

'I tell you what,' he said once, jogging along beside me
in the street one dinner hour—I was on the way back to work
and he'd taken it into his head to come and look at the dump
I spent my days in. There it was facing us, four storeys of the
usual box, concrete and glass and forlorn coloured plastic
panels, around the base a litter of cars, vans, Land-Rovers.
Davey forgot what he was going to tell me; his mouth fell
open.

'So long then,' I said, suddenly embarrassed by his

431

presence, resenting him there as a gawping witness to my incarceration. I wanted to scuttle inside anonymously with the other work slaves. But he was standing still with his head back and his mouth open as if he'd seen a vision.

'Oh Colin you poor fucker,' he said, really aghast.

Instead of being angry I was touched, and I laughed, it was so funny. I came back to him and said, 'Look, I'm not the only one, am I? There's hundreds of us altogether.'

He was sighing, shaking his head as he turned away; then he remembered something important and his face lit up.

'I tell you what,' he said happily. 'Tomorrow's Saturday, what about us going up Dovedale way and sleeping out? We'll take a tent but if it's dry we'll just kip on the ground, lie on our backs and count stars like sheep. Ever slept in the open, have you?'

'No, never.'

'That's what we'll do then!' His face shone, he looked astounded, as if the idea had hit him with the force of a wave, washing him into paradise. 'Bugger me, I'm so looking forward to it—get us purged of all this shit. Won't it be great, eh? You know, you can lie there in the middle of it and forget clean about the traffic knifing across from one city to the next, racing each other's knackers off as if the gate's going to clang shut on 'em and they'll be locked out of all them lovely shitty streets . . . You lie on your back scratching your balls and right overhead is a lark bubbling away and that's all, splintering out its song fit to bust, faint and strong and steady. It's virgin out there, Colin, honest, the purity is fantastic. And silent! Yet you know it's teeming with life. I lay out there once all day on me belly, hid meself away and watched. You won't believe this, but thirty foxes crossed over the tiny patch of the field I was watching. In one day, man!'

'See you tomorrow,' I said, edging away. 'I'm late, they're winding me in.'

432

'Ta-ra!' he shouted, broke into a run and went off round the corner like an athlete, like a thief.

Lou was urban in all his instincts, not against nature but unable to see its relevance. You got on a train and sat against the window with your paper, smoked your fags, went for a slash, found the buffet and bought a can of beer and if you noticed the country at all it was green, dun-coloured, farms and animals and old crumbly moss-covered walls and churches were part of it, stuck in the mud, stuck in the past. We'd gone on from that. It was there still, nobody had cleared it away, a few people pottered around there or went for visits at weekends, holidays, like they sat in their gardens or trimmed the grass on the graves at the cemetery. It was there but oh Christ it was boring, and full of nothing when they opened things up with some really new motorways. Granted it could be nice and peaceful and pretty but the point was, nothing was going on there any more. A void. In the cities was where it was happening, now and in the future: that's where the clues were to be found, in the streets. 'The Industrial Revolution happened here, in England, we were the first. Spread out from here, but you'd never think it. We still go round like yokels, we don't know how to act urban. That's why our cities are such bloody awful places: the people haven't moved into them yet. Anyway they're not fit. They're nineteenth century, we haven't got any twentieth-century cities. We've got a few new towns but they were born on drawing boards and can't you tell it when you step into one, what abortions.'

Whatever his visions of the new city were, the city he lived in he used like a vending machine. And the pub was his element; that was the place for human contact, his plaza. Davey, surprisingly for such a gregarious man, wasn't much for pubs at all. At night he wouldn't go near one, said he could smell the violence. He had a dread of the city at night altogether, the streets: he had a nose for hatred, for violence, perhaps because his own was never far below the surface. It was easy to enrage him, topple him into violence, especially if you were a woman and wanted to humiliate him. All you had to do was shut him out, cut off his supply of affection: he couldn't bear that. I was there once when Judy did it—I'd missed the previous instalment and came in when she was refusing to speak to him. I didn't know how long it had been going on, but Davey's face was white, tortured: I hadn't seen him like this before and he frightened me. The war of nerves went on as if I wasn't there, that was the horrible thing. She sat twisted away from him on the settee, sewing, mending a sock or something. Each time he bent over her shoulder to speak she snatched herself clear, turning her face away in a gesture of loathing.

'Judy, love . . .' he begged, croaking it, in a strangled little voice, his face drawn tight with the strain of struggling with his temper. But he was also in terror of being cut off, isolated, and the rage and fear mixed on his face. 'Don't be silly now love, listen, don't make a scene out of nothing . . .'

His voice crawled to be conciliatory, so abject I wanted to get up and kick him. All at once he grabbed her head in his long hands from behind and held it while he tried to kiss her.

'Get off me, you pig!' she hissed, breaking free and lashing out at him viciously with her arm. 'Don't come near me, keep off!'

She hurled her sewing at him and rushed into the kitchen, slammed the door.

Davey looked helplessly at me and tried to smile, but it crumbled. He let out a huge despairing sigh and sagged into a chair.

'I'm sorry, Col,' he mumbled by way of apology. 'She's so bloody stubborn when she gets an idea into her head . . . then I go mad and thump her one . . .'

'Perhaps I'd better shove off.'

434

'No, don't do that—hang on for Christ's sake,' and he gave me a wan smile, still sprawled exhaustedly in the armchair, legs splayed out. 'Things generally get more peaceful when you're around . . . we have to behave ourselves a bit. Though it didn't look much like it a couple of minutes ago, did it?'

He laughed shakily, a convalescent receiving a visitor, already on the mend. I couldn't help marvelling at him: in his shoes I'd have been laid low for the rest of the week after a scene like that.

We sat there. I kept him company for a few minutes. No words. The silence from the kitchen was hostile. I got up.

'I'll be going anyway, I think,' I said.

'Can't say I blame you,' he said.

'No, I've got to go,' I told him.

'Cup o' tea?' he said, without hope or enthusiasm.

'Tomorrow,' I said. 'Okay tomorrow?'

'You don't need to ask. You're always welcome, you know that,' he said. 'You're my best mate.'

19

SEE LOU again, he's important to me. See him before he disappears from view, before life swallows him up.

I was back again at Lou's place after a decent interval had elapsed. The street looked as mucky and forsaken as ever, yet less unfriendly. The door too seemed a trifle more inviting. Banged lustily, it opened at once and a nifty-looking youngster in cord jacket, a Paisley cravat, blue and emerald green in his red aertex sports shirt, stood looking mildly startled. He gleamed at the throat like a dragonfly. He smiled.

'Is Lou in?'

'Afraid he isn't,' the boy murmured.

'Ron Cousins?'

'Sorry, no.'

I scatched my head, baffled, was about to turn away and he added, 'I think Lou's only nipped in town for half an hour. Would you like to come up and wait?'

What manners, I thought, impressed in spite of myself. 'Alright,' I said, glad to be saved from defeat. On the stairs the boy said, 'I'm Steve, by the way.'

In the room I almost go to sit on the bed where I parked last time, then see it's occupied, a tousled blond head on the pillow, face buried. Longish hair, so for a moment I'm not sure if it's male or female. Hearing us come in he twists over, throws the sheets off to his waist and blinks up at us sleepily, raking over his bare hairless chest with one hand. He's older than Steve, my age perhaps.

'Hallo there,' he says, yawning. 'What time is it, Stevie?'

'Nearly eight,' says Steve, leafing through a magazine.

I can hear noises behind the partition, water pouring, crockery sounds.

436

'My God, isn't it dreadful,' says the young man in the bed, Graham, and to me he says coyly, 'We had a party last night, well an American poet visited us, friend of Lou's you see, and we celebrated with bottles of red wine, foul stuff, Spanish Burgundy wasn't it, Steve?'

'Don't ask me,' Steve says, 'I wasn't here.'

Graham laughs, gay fluttering charm of eyes and lips. 'No of course you weren't, aren't I stupid. Honestly I don't know who *was* here. Where on earth did they all come from?'

He throws back the sheets, he's in his trousers, his bare feet are narrow, elegant, sun-tanned. For a moment he sits admiring them, moving his toes, then swings his legs off the bed and stands, stretches his arms. I can count his ribs, he's a greyhound.

'Morning, Josephine!' he calls to the partition. 'Lovely evening! What are you doing?'

No answer. The washing-up sounds continue.

'Josephine?'

No answer.

He looks at Steve and shrugs. Tries once more.

'Josephine,' he appeals plaintively, like a girl, 'please tell me.'

'What's it sound like?' comes a woman's voice.

'Let me guess,' Graham says, cooing and malicious, holding up a shirt and examining it carefully around the collar, then suddenly turning on me the most charming smile, dazzling me with it deliberately. I've never seen charm used so flagrantly, with such deliberate intent.

The woman with the rough croaky voice comes out and I'm amazed, she's no more than a kid, white-faced and dopey-eyed, hair dyed a harsh copper colour. She's lifeless: she heads for the door without looking at any of us, and Graham says to her, 'Thanks for doing all that awful washing-up, love, you're a darling.'

He can't seem to open his mouth without sounding ironic.

'I didn't do it for you, I did it for Lou,' the girl says sullenly, not exactly resentful; just blank and sullen. 'Say ta-ra to him for me.'

'Why, where you off to, ducky?'

'Manchester.'

'Alright love. Take care of yourself.'

When she's gone I ask again when Lou is expected and Graham says without hesitation, contradicting his friend: 'You won't see him tonight.'

He takes a mirror from his hip pocket and props it on the mantelpiece, goes down on his haunches like a miner against a pub wall and combs his hair fastidiously.

'Steve, isn't it ghastly, I'm getting old,' he moans falsely, and a hard edge creeps into his voice. He glances over his shoulder at me. 'That girl who's just gone out, she's a pro,' he says coolly. 'I suppose you guessed, did you?'

'No I didn't.'

'Lou's been putting her up for a couple of nights. She's just had an abortion, she was in a bad way, poor kid.'

He's laying it on too thick, I think to myself, the coolness is exaggerated. Maybe it's my imagination but it seems that he wants to impress me, the newcomer, with their exciting goings-on. And it's true, as I find out later, that he is very proud of Lou. More than once he draws my attention to Lou's tolerance: even refers to it rather self-consciously as his 'humility'. His manner generally is inclined to be ikey, like a girl who isn't going to be had cheap a second time; he's a working-class lad and the genteel, mealy-mouthed accents are to elevate him in his own eyes. He doesn't despise crude men, he's no stranger to their backgrounds, but he fears their stolid living-rooms: he has to escape their uncompromising black-and-white realm. Ambiguity is his natural element. He adores Lou, emulates his touch of culture, and like any uneducated man talking posh he comes out with stiff, pompous phrases when he has something significant to say.

438

So he says, 'I can give you several instances of Lou's humility.'

Back to the present: I sit idle while Graham gets himself dressed to kill, flouncing to and fro looking for a tie, for socks, shoes. They're going across the city to Steve's house. Once again I'm stranded. All at once I remember the Alsatian, realise it's missing.

'Where's the dog?'

'Sailor? Lou must have taken him.'

'Is it his?'

Graham shrugged. 'Somebody left it here.' He glanced across at me. 'He's scared of that dog, you know.'

'That so?'

'Isn't he, Steve?'

But Steve is immersed in his magazine. 'Hmm?'

Graham laughs gaily. 'You should have been here the other night,' he cries to me. 'Sailor suddenly gets frisky, throws back his head and bays, doesn't he, Steve—charging up and down like a pony. Lou goes red in the face shouting at the thing, "Under the chair!"—"Down dog!"—"Sit!"—and pointing like this'—he twirls on heels like a bullfighter, to demonstrate.

Steve lowers the magazine to watch, amused. 'What does that prove?' he smiles.

'It doesn't prove anything, it was funny that's all. But Lou's scared of that animal. He is, you know.'

'Think so?'

'Yes and I'll tell you another thing,' Graham says. Not exactly excited, that would ruffle his composure, but speaking now with a certain authority, firmness: it seems out of character and I look harder at him. 'He likes being scared. Enjoys it. You watch him next time. That's why he's got the lolloping great hairy thing.'

'You mean instead of a smaller dog?' Steve says, a bit stupidly.

'That's what I think.'

Steve may look elegant, I think, but he finds it heavy going when he has to think. He is gazing fixedly at his friend in some perplexity, his expression a mixture of bewilderment and irritation. Really he doesn't want to be disturbed, he'd rather flick through his film star mag with his mind vacant, but now he's troubled. He frowns, he shifts on his chair, uneasy.

'I don't get you.'

Graham opens his mouth to answer, then remembers and swings on me, courteous in a mocking sort of way: 'I'm sure we must be boring you to death. I'm sorry, it's my fault, I go on so when I start, don't I, Steve——'

'No no,' I protest, laughing, 'if I can't manage to meet Lou, at least I can hear about him from somebody else. If you don't mind, that is,' I add needlessly.

'Oh nobody cares who hears what around here,' Graham says, flopping on the bed and picking a thread off his jacket. He's his superior self again. 'We love taking each other to pieces, it goes on all the time,' and he is using his normal, slightly satirical tone.

I begin to lose interest. But he hasn't quite finished being serious, he switches back to the subject of Lou's cowardice, which intrigues him, and he can see he's got me hooked and that delights him. He loves an audience. I try to make my face well and truly agog, to encourage him to pour revelations over me. Steve laughs out, 'Speak for yourself!' and I think, that's done it, but Graham has his story to tell, he's primed, nothing can throw him off his stroke. It flows out. Apparently Lou brings in one of his lame dogs one day—the expression 'lame dogs' means something important to Graham, he curls his tongue round it with deliberate emphasis—and the man is a real yob, a menace. 'He's destitute, Irish, he drools charm and he has this heartrending story to tell about his mother fished out of the canal all horrible, yellow and bloated. He looks the picture of misery, and Lou of course says he can doss with us. Well, he wanders off and I breathe again—how he stank! I've got a nasty feeling about this one somehow, but not Lou, oh no, he won't hear a word against him. Around midnight in he comes, blazing drunk, and starts smashing the place up. In the end I'm screaming at Lou to do something but he just sits there in the corner, dead white, trembling all over. The yob gets bored with breaking things and ripping up my shirts with a knife and makes for me, I rush out yelling blue murder, come back with a buddy, Big Jim, and by then he'd done over Lou, there he was with blood on his mouth and one eye closed up. He had an enormous shiner for weeks after, remember, Steve? But you know, do you think you could get him to kick this maniac out? Not Lou. "No, give him another week to find his feet," he said. "You must be mad, Lou," I said to him, "that mick's going to do you in, do us both in, if he stays here." He just shakes his head, that stubborn look on his face. And I can see he's terrified, yet he's made up his mind about something and he's got to go through with it. He's terrified, and at the same time he's getting a terrific kick out of the situation.'

Steve has been listening intently, leaning out of his chair. He pouts thoughtfully, working things out. He's thinking. Finally he settles back, opens his mag and flicks the pages as before: gives it up as a bad job. Graham sits where he is on the bed and muses, hands flat, fingers wriggling restlessly. In an entirely different voice he says, 'Steve, do I look respectable enough to meet your mother?'

And as if he's had an order, Steve jumps up. 'You know you look beautiful, you horrible man you.'

'Respectable I said, respectable!'

'Just right,' Steve says. 'Perfect.'

Graham is on his feet too, lounging in the doorway. 'You sure?' he says, and looks at me: 'I can't tell if he's joking or not.'

441

'Of course I'm sure,' Steve says. 'Come on.'

I go trailing down with them to their bus stop, unwilling to be on my own again so soon. Streets empty, blurring with the dusk of a soporific summer evening. We turn down a cobbled Lowry-like street of charred brick terraces mixed in with nineteenth-century lace factories, both sides, pitched steep on a hill, in front of each house a broken plinth of cement within a picket fence no more than a foot high, orange-box wood painted chocolate or bottle green or baby-shit yellow, uprights splintered or hanging loose like rotten teeth or ripped off for firewood, stains of rust from the nails weeping down. I don't know where I am, but it makes no odds, there's an endless supply of these mean streets. At the bottom of the hill we are on one of the big boulevards, traffic barging by in a steady procession. The bus stop is round the corner, opposite a modern pub throbbing all over with red neon, car park full at the side.

'Want to come with us?' Graham asks as we wait.

Naturally he assumes I'd like to, or I wouldn't be there. In a sense I would, but I mutter some excuse, standing between them both pointlessly, waiting impatiently now for them to depart: a queer tension has built up. A woman joins us at the stop, the bus roars up and then an extraordinary thing happens. Graham takes my hand softly, murmurs good-bye and before I know what's happening he bends his head in a graceful, feline movement and tenderly brushes my cheek with his lips. The next thing is comical but I'm stunned and too moved to laugh: the bus storms past, full up. I sneak a glance at the woman, who hasn't batted an eyelid, maybe hasn't even noticed, it happened so swiftly. Now we stand facing the empty road in silence, gazing blankly at the bloodily glowing pub. Without appearing to rake the distance I've spotted another bus coming, I don't want to get rid of them but simply put an end to the tension, which is much worse now—the crazy incident has given it an extra screw. The bus is stopping, I wait utterly passive now for whatever is going to happen, and sure enough he takes my hand again, I squeeze it to show he hasn't shocked me and encouraged he makes the same swift feline gesture as before, kissing my cheek. Steve smiles tenderly down, getting on, the bus gathers speed with a roar of triumph and I go drifting off full of strange sensations, deaths and births, touching my cheek with my fingers. Whatever I think of it later, when it happened the first time and astonished me I was suffused with pleasure, it broke down my isolation with beautiful simplicity, at one stroke, it seemed the most natural thing in the world. I walk in the vague direction of the town, a happy zombie, get lost several times, laugh aloud, going towards my grubby room because that's the direction my feet know, there's nowhere else they take me of their own accord. And for the first time in this city I don't feel alone.

20

I SEND Ray a report, making it sound more hectic than things are, putting plenty of swagger into it, as I always did when I wrote to him from afar. Off it would go and I imagined him opening it, his growing excitement, admiration, envy even at the thought of the life I was living, so untrammelled, and these new contacts, strange enigmatic characters I was getting to know. Opening his reply only confirmed my success: I'd be uneasy, guilty at once. Why couldn't I write him the plain facts? Nothing much was happening to me, was it? Not really. Yes and no.

What's going on up there, Colin?

Lots of things.

Such as?

If I told you, you'd never believe me.

Give me a clue.

How can I? That's the very thing that's missing.

I don't get you.

There's a key, but I keep losing it.

What?

Never mind—nothing.

If anything was happening I couldn't put my finger on it, the events I described were too nebulous to be interesting, so to avoid boring him I dramatised, seasoned things with significance. What I did catch was the busy roar of the city, such a difference to that timeless washing and pounding of the sea we heard day and night at the cottage, unfamiliar and maddening, insanely active I thought at first, until it sank away beyond my eardrums and I heard the steady pulse beat, old as creation, infinitely reassuring if you were in the right mood. Otherwise the most cruelly indifferent music in the world, worse than the squalling of babies. Life going on, howling, hammering at the doors. Reality roaring, in a fury of endless activity. Round the corner death waiting, eyes closed and its mouth open. But the thing I found truly frightening was the sight of that ocean coming at you in winter like a great grey toppling wall. I used to lie in bed in the dark and I could see it, it kept coming, if I didn't move quick it was going to bury me. I moved, I lived.

The curious unreality of my letters to Ray, except for the roaring sound and the feverish restlessness, both accidental effects, was I suppose matched by the vacancy of most of my days: I could almost say caused by them. The highlights were all I lived for in this city. Nothing in between was of the slightest consequence, I swooped down for the scraps, ardent, they weren't flung in my path very often and they had to mean something. I made them nourish me. If they quivered with light for Ray, it was me who gilded them. I was the morning sun, it was my moon that provided the madness. I couldn't distinguish any longer between the Lou Coltman I wanted and the one who existed in his own right. The same happened with Davey, he offered no resistance, he was made over in accordance with my need for kinship. I was threadbare, he clothed me. Both of them were unseeing, uncaring, deeply absorbed in themselves: my motives went unchallenged. Their needs were being met elsewhere. Aline was different—straight away she began to detach me from my image of her, I had to take account of her as a human being, separate from me. In my letters to Ray I said little about her because it was no good, she refused to fit into the dramas I liked to enact for him in writing. She resisted, simply by being herself, by making demands—and detached me too from the Lou and Davey I thought I knew. I began to see them in a new light.

A letter burning with impossible journeys came from Ray: 'If the lad would go off to sleep for four or five hours I'd have a go at a mammoth drawing, but he won't rest for long. So I dip into the sea off Sardinia till I can't stand it any longer. Every time I read it (Sea and Sardinia) this book makes me burn with envy and shiver with desire for those golden towns thrust up at the sky as the boat comes in off the sea, for the islands, the flower-opening sunsets and the brand of the sun above Africa. I grit my teeth and sweat a sea fever, an opalescent jewel melts in my mouth. I've had a taste of this fresh-created vivid world where the sea breathes in the cosmos and the land abideth for ever. I can never still the longing in my blood for what I drank in when I was a sailor-lad: not in voyage or ship but in the times of freedom between watches, on leaves. I'm no Vasco da Gama or even a potential Bilbo— one day I'm going to start a pilgrimage that will last as long as I live, an adventure in the living world amongst the things that fill the soul with strength and liberation. Now I dream of a voyage I made hundreds of years ago in a many-sailed schooner. There was no scurvy, no Captain Bligh, no purpose of cargo. I sailed with a knot of men who dreamed great dreams and lifted veils off the horizon every day. And for a long time we voyaged together and set foot in many new lands. We were full of simple joy. We knew the voyage would go on for as long as the earth lasted . . .

'I'm reading old newspapers to keep off the verdigris. There's a heap of them in a damp cupboard here. What I want is a really old one, say 10,000 B.C. Then I'd know who I am.

'Remind me to tell you of my nightmares one fine day. I am guilt personified. Sometimes I am struck with a club as I try to grasp where my old life, my relationships, my home life with brothers and mother and father all vanished to. The cut was utterly severe and I suffer for it, yet because what I want is so different from their way it couldn't be otherwise. It happened too soon, before I ever got to know my family. I struck out of the street and it's there behind me always like something I'm linked with forever and love and suffer for. If I'd deliberately planned to strike in the most vital places I couldn't have been more devastating.

'Outline of my life. Full stop. Now here's some curses, vows. I must have Change. Sod the stupid sheep, the imbecile docile cows, the scratching old hen. The way animals' lives are absolutely unchangeable makes me rage and quail. I demand it—CHANGE. Change, you silly bloody sheep, change into a ten-headed monstrosity but for Christ's sake change!

'I can smell the winter coming. I want like hell for us to get away and out of the rat-trap before much longer. England is a wonderful place, all it wants is a chance to die a natural death.'

21

IT WAS bound to be Lou of course who put me in touch with Davey. He was always the shy fixer: when he put two characters like Davey and me in touch he liked to fade away discreetly. It used to mystify me, how he could possibly get a kick out of such an introduction when he wasn't there himself to witness it, but I suppose it was the outcome he was more interested in. The grape-vine kept him in touch with that.

I never once saw them together. Davey was living out at Ilkeston when I first met him. He had three or four addresses in as many months after that, in and out of the city, and from what I could make out he'd lost touch with Lou altogether. Which didn't seem to bother him. Once or twice I tried to get him going on the subject of Lou, and immediately he'd be evasive, sullen, curiously resentful. Most ominous of all, he referred to him by his surname. 'He's a cagey bugger, Coltman,' he blurted out angrily one day when he was down in the mouth: he couldn't see where life was leading him except up the garden path, it had him by the balls (meaning Judy had) but by Christ he'd do something soon to change the pattern. 'I'm divided, that's my bastard trouble,' he said with soft bitterness, and thinking he was in the mood for self-examination I asked him what he thought of Lou—I seemed to go round asking everybody's opinion, trying to fit a picture together, intrigued—hoping it would lead on to the quarrel or whatever had brought about his present attitude. But that was his only comment. Whereas Lou had said of Davey, 'He's nice, you'll like him,' and I could tell he meant it. 'Don't be put off by what you might hear about him,' he added mysteriously. 'He's his own worst enemy, Davey is.' And it was working out the other way round: the one I kept hearing about from others was Lou.

They didn't have very much in common that I could see, only negatively. Neither of them had any time for the values most people accepted unthinkingly—and saying that immediately brought you up hard against their differences. Alright, so they belonged to a new post-war, post-Bomb breed: then you were in difficulties if you tried to embrace them both from where you were standing. Lou would never have used the word 'values'—there was a revolution going on, self-evident but we were all unaware of it, we needed to get tuned in. They faced different directions: if you thought of a bag of crisps ripped open in a city pub, the fingers heedless, the eyes elsewhere, that was Lou, and Davey slicing lovingly into a block of cheese and licking his chops appreciatively would be rural, harking back. Yet both children of the age, rubbed out and reborn on Hiroshima Day, fundamentally rootless, indifferent to tradition, no respect, no hope and no despair. Society was a load of lies round our necks. A breed free at last of the age-old cant—but there's your mam and dad still living, so unless you can be brutal you're only half born, half free, half out. Free and nowhere to go, nothing to do with it. Free to kick a tin can, free to piss your freedom up against the wall. What could you do on your own? Plenty, inferred Lou, the glint in his eye sent you wild to know, you hung on to him, he was on to something. Davey's bashing bitterness of his bad days was at least out in the open, naked, but unless you lived in Lou's pocket you wouldn't know how he was faring, good or bad. He was nocturnal like an alley cat, if he blazed or shrieked it would be at midnight. He was of the night, the city night.

A few weeks later this was literally true, his electricity was cut off for non-payment. The room was light enough while I was there but he had a candle stuck on a saucer on the coffee table, which had one leg falling off every time the dog rubbed against it. Ron Cousins had come in, grunted at me and sat on a cushion on the floor, leaning back against the wall with one leg doubled under him, morose and silent.

'All you need is a capful of money, you'd look like a pavement artist,' I said, to poke a spark of life from him.

'Oh ah,' he said tonelessly, shrugged, stared at the floor and that was that. I squatted on the bed nearby, looking down on the top of his head, the sight of his soft feathery hair correcting my first impression of him as a bristly uncouth lump of a bloke. I remembered his pale feminine hands from last time, looked again and saw I wasn't mistaken. But he had a hard, bitter rind to him.

Lou was looking distinctly twitchy; as soon as it began to get dark he wanted to be off, he needed the conviviality of a pub: but he was in good form, saying things like, 'It always amazes me how nice the English are.'

'They are?' I said, sounding dubious, yet in fact feeling pleased by such a preposterous statement. A good sign. Ron didn't even lift his head.

'I'm thinking of the electricity man coming the other day, eight in the morning, there he was with his bag of tools to cut off the supply. I was still in bed, I opened the door all bleary and this little ginger chap is gaping at me like he's seen a ghost. What a time to come banging on folk's doors, disgusting isn't it, he says, so apologetic, so friendly. And cutting off me electricity he keeps yapping away, nice weather we're having, live here long have you, he had a week at Skeg with the missus and kids in June and it never stopped raining . . . on he goes, while I bumble around pulling my pants on, and he apologises another five or six times before he's done.'

'I know what you mean,' I say, warming to him, grinning.

'Smashing, I thought. Worth getting cut off for that.'

'You'd recommend it then,' laughing.

'Ah, I would, any day.'

A bit later we adjourned to *The Iron Man*, leaving Ron

stubbornly miserable on the floor, had some good talk and I went off rejuvenated. Nothing had been said that amounted to much, but I felt in a current of life instead of stagnant and veering as I'd been before. So much so that I was totally unprepared for the next little development, swinging up the slope by St Peter's one Saturday afternoon, the town bustling with shoppers. Suddenly I had an urge to mooch about in the gloomy abandoned streets of the old Lace Market, obsolete towering buildings barricaded and empty at weekends. I went under the vast blocks of silence, it was like prowling through a museum. No traffic, you could walk on the cobbles in the middle of the road, peer up alleys, read the notices announcing the vacancies for machinists, stocking hands. At a high point a flight of steps leads down giddily towards the railway and a scabby black iron bridge, then more girder steps and a maze of little streets and a tea stall below your feet, just off the main road out to the Midland Station. I started down the first flight and met Ron Cousins, clumping up like a farm labourer in a field of mud.

'Seen Lou?' he said, and when I said no, I was thinking of going out tonight, he looked strangely crafty and triumphant.

'Out where?' he said.

'To the flat. Why?'

Then he comes out with it; the flat is no more, Lou's been evicted by his landlord.

'You mean the rent?' I asked, beginning to feel irritated by this character who insists on giving me the story in driblets, meanly. I can't understand either what's making him grin from ear to ear: he looks more cheerful than I've ever seen him. Has he got it in for Lou too, for some obscure reason of his own? And surely he's out on the street as well? What's so funny about that, for Christ's sake?

No, it's not the rent, he tells me. Lou always took care to keep that paid, bang up-to-date, whatever else went by the board. It was a rule with him.

451

'What was it then?' I burst out impatiently, more and more disliking the man's obvious elation, the air of furtive plotting, of secrets held back, traps being set.

At last I worm it out. Apparently the rot set in when the mad Irishman smashed up the room that night and did Lou over. The whole household was terrified, naturally, and when the rest of the tenants complained to the landlord they threw in everything else they could think of: weirdies coming and going at all hours, noise, pros, police visits——

'Police?' I said. This was a new one on me.

'That was my fault, an accident I had. They wanted details. All it was, I went up home and coming down again I climbed in the back of this lorry at a transport caff. Trouble was I nodded off, like, rolled out and hit the road, wham, travelling about fifty he was. Hell of a state I was in.'

'Where can I find Lou then?' I asked in a sudden panic.

Again the look of crafty pleasure flitted over his place. 'No idea, mate. He won't be gone far though. You'll knock into him, bound to.'

I did, and the upshot of it was that we decided to share a flat. We searched a few districts and found one on a hill, five minutes' walk from the hub of the city. Lou had to be near that hub. I couldn't believe the miraculous ease of it, or my luck. And with this golden opportunity to get to know Lou, fill in those missing details, came, almost immediately, the meeting with Aline, and so I was spending most of my free time with her. Everything happened at once.

22

IF ANYBODY had said I'd be having a bitter heart-searching row with Davey one day, all the more deadly for being half concealed, implied, conveyed by tone of voice rather than outright furious accusation, I'd have laughed in his face. We got on so well: there was nothing to quarrel about. We saw eye to eye on everything. Even now I can't imagine what it was about, can only think it was an explosion of resentments built up unawares over a long period, a steady accumulation of things we found irritating, disappointing, maddening in each other. That's the way a marriage backfires or a lovers' quarrel happens, so why not the row of two friends who think they know each other inside out and of course don't? It was a harrowing scene for me because the generosity between us was being smashed to pieces and we both had an urge to smash it; we sat motionless, festering, imprisoned in our cages of mean thoughts. Davey was talking a blinder, slowly working himself up into a frenzy and I couldn't understand him, the convoluted stuff poured out and it sounded pure gibberish, none of it made a grain of sense to me. All I knew, and I knew with absolute certainty, was that I was being got at in some unspeakably unjust fashion, and I trembled with hate for him. Both of us goaded to fury because we had nothing with which to accuse each other, yet the generosity we were jettisoning crackled and burned, reduced to ashes in seconds.

The memory of this scene weeks and months later would send me tracing back for signs, origins, like a man searching the ruins for some explanation of the disaster which brought his house down with such an incredible, inexplicable crash. Davey was living in a top flat, two rooms and a bit of a kitchen right under the roof at the rear, you had to ascend a twirl of steel steps to a platform hung in the open air, the door tucked under the eaves against the main chimney stack. He also had the use of the back garden, his steel staircase took root in one corner of it, among a clump of Michaelmas daisies.

I think it was while he was living there that I first woke up to the fact of how numerous his friends were. All kinds. Some real toughs, malingerers, students mad about jazz, like him, a photographer, young socialists and anarchists, an electrician's mate who was light-fingered—each time I dropped in there would be someone new. If he met a bloke hitch-hiking through the town with a bulging pack on his back, that was enough, a fatal attraction, he'd bring him in for a yarn and a night's kip, and more than likely he'd be hanging round up there a week later.

Frank Coggin was a good example: an art student on the loose from Newcastle, the spring term had started but not him. He wasn't going back. He stayed a month, would have been there for good if Davey hadn't winkled him out. He took root. 'He sat in that chair nursing a sketchbook, singing folk songs, wearing out my records, which was alright, fine, till he started getting demanding. "When are we going to eat?" he'd say, cool as you like. And never wash a pot, not a hand's turn with anything, the bugger. Would he, Judy?' But I knew how thick as thieves they both were when he first blew in; Davey delighted to have a real afficionado in the place, he dug out his records and they played them till one in the morning. They sat swopping yarns and singing songs and would have gone on all night. It was finally Judy who laid down the ultimatum, to Davey one night in bed. Either he goes or I do. He avoided decisions, there was no finality in his nature. Judy had found out long ago that decisions had to be imposed on him in such a way that his ancient cunning, his innocence, was helpless. He loathed scenes, his instinct was to turn his back and act sullen, boorish, if he actively disliked

454

anybody; but Judy would occasionally force him into a direct confrontation by calling him a coward. It wasn't cowardice: to act meanly with someone he didn't hate was just impossible for him, a violation. I was with him once in a caff, we waited patiently for the usual dish-wash tea and pallid cakes. My cake was sawdust, topped with that ersatz animal fat cream, but we were hungry and it was eatable. On his cake the cream blob had gone rancid, he took one bite and dragged down his mouth. 'Take it back, get them to give you another one,' I urged him, but he wouldn't. He pushed it away sheepishly: 'I'm not bothered.' Sat looking at me a little uneasily, in case I jumped up on his behalf, until he couldn't stand the suspense any longer. 'Let's go,' he said, the second I'd finished.

Traits like this might irritate but they belonged to the good, positive side, like his indifference to money; they could never aggravate and boil up into a row. Did I begrudge him his guileless friendships with all and sundry, the spongers who battened on him, the deadweights who contributed nothing, was I jealous of that lot? No, I didn't think so. Anyway, I was never conscious of it. The more people I met who were connected with him, the more I felt our friendship was being slowly whittled away, diminished, and I had to admit the picture I'd first formed of him was changing too. As he was changing, growing, his paradise still green but a little tainted, his need for purity as infectious as ever but less urgent, his heart naked and soft when he shows it but he's learning caution at last, he doesn't bare it to fools quite so often. When he reminisces in a hoarse loving voice, low with wonder on the subject of childhood sweethearts, rapturous first loves and the shame of touching them, the urgency and guilt and sweet grassy flesh, and looming above it, arching over, his mother's steadfast heart, her tears, his father's clumsy, harsh word, shy pride, you understand how exactly his happiness is measured from his early days, a falling curve . . .

455

I used to see his motorbike parked outside at the front and that told me he was in. I nipped up the clanging steps and banged on the dirty window which looked into the galley-kitchen. The kitchen door was always open, I could press my nose on the glass and peer in to the living-room, right through to the street at the front. I'd make out a figure waving, either him or Judy, and let myself in. In those days he did a lot of swimming, going to the public baths every day when he finished work, ramping up and down for twenty, thirty lengths nonstop. He wasn't in a team or entering a competition, he swam for the sheer joy of it. He loved to try and explain in detail what it meant to him. 'I'm going to write songs about it one day, when I'm ready. I want to swim a few more years yet, then I might be able to. Colin, everything about it's great, there ain't nothing like it in this world, honest. I remember as a kid how exciting it was, getting your cosser and a towel from your mam, then paying your money, going in with butterflies in your belly and hearing the yells and echoes, that bloody awful chlorine smell getting nearer, marching round the edge gingerly and feeling such a nit in your clothes and boots. In the booth, that was great too, stripping off all nervous and butterflies again, like stage fright, that oilcloth curtain on rings you pulled across, the sweaty hairy bollocky man-smell the booth had, Christ it used to make me shake more than anything, that man-stink. Oh but the water washing over you, it gurgles past and you can plough away all day if you want to your heart's content, you're alone like a fish and nothing matters; I tell you you can't beat it . . .'

One night he'd just come in from his swim when I arrived, his hair damp and sleek, he was in the kitchen frying a couple of eggs and some bacon, a few left-over potatoes and beans for himself. He was happy, glistening with well-being: he had cracked his own record and lapped up forty lengths. 'What d'you think of that then, me ole sport?'

'You must be dead beat.'

'Shagged I am, fair shagged. Going up and down, though, it seemed so easy, I could have done a hundred, I reckon. It was only when I stopped I felt buggered. Funny, that. Climbing up the steps I was wobbling at the knees, then I caved in; had to sit down on my arse where I was for five minutes or I'd have fallen over backwards.'

I walked into the main room and a middle-aged, grey-haired man sat on a hard chair by the fireplace, a widower from down the street who came in sometimes. 'He's got interesting tales to tell, old Mac,' Davey had told me. 'Been to America, Australia, all over the place,' but whenever I was there he was utterly silent, sitting in his green pullover and collarless shirt, needing a shave usually, smiling his seraphic caved-in smile and observing the company slyly.

'Sit yourself down, boyo,' Davey called out in mock Irish. 'I'll be right widja!'

He sounded in fine fettle, I thought, settling on a stool on the other side of the grate. The evenings had turned chilly; I put my hands out to the fire, which had lumps of painted wood smouldering on it, giving off more stink than heat. Judy opened the door of the other room, poked her glossy, pert head in and said in the direction of the kitchen, ignoring me and Mac, 'I'm tired, I'm going to bed.'

Before Davey could answer she'd slammed the door. He came in holding the loaded frying pan, said, angry and defensive, to the blank door, 'You are, are you love? Good-o.'

He went back to the kitchen. I was used to these flurries, sat tight and maintained a stupid sort of neutrality, waiting for things to blow over, though I knew the chance of a gay evening was pretty remote when this happened so early. I I glanced over curiously at Mac to see his reaction. He was impassive, smiling thinly to himself and his eyes fixed tight on the smoke drifting up the chimney. I waited on edge to see what Davey would do, either try to placate her or plunge us deep into the gloom of his angry moodiness. This time it was neither. I heard a roar, something went smash in the kitchen, he yelled out, 'End of a perfect bleedin' day!' and charged through to the other room, the bedroom, eyes gleaming, murderous.

If he emerged again after a session like that and I was alone there, things went to a pattern. He'd have reached some kind of reconciliation, achieved a patched-up truce and want to talk wistfully, confide in someone, an ally, so that a warm intimacy would grow between us. I did my usual passive act, nodding and listening, dropping in the odd sympathetic remark—not calculatingly but because I couldn't help myself. And from this childishly injured mood of his would flow his confidences, then tender memories, hankerings and yearnings, the whole room awash with his happy sadness and I'd sit on the shore, dabbling my feet, uninvolved as ever yet drowsily enchanted by the gentle music. That's what he was, a musician, at such times he didn't need the record player, all he needed to do was play on the instrument of himself and reality dissolved. That was what was dangerous: he hadn't found a way to incorporate the reality behind the door; the clashing dissonances faded out and he'd have you almost believing they didn't exist, you'd dreamed it up, you'd imagined what was snarling and snapping nastily in front of your eyes. Everything was marvellous and blissful if you only shut your eyes and listened. 'If that silly cow would only let you,' he moaned. And another time, if you ventured to take sides, he'd cancel it all with some fanatical, unarguable statement such as, 'Judy means everything to me, if she ever left me for good I'd go raving mad, I would—I'd chuck myself under a bus.'

I suppose the deterioration between us set in during those visits to the roof flat, that rookery where they all congregated and he flapped his wings more and more impersonally. I became conscious anyway of something wrong, for a long time I couldn't put my finger on it. It was to do with the atmosphere, that was it. The kettle went on just the same, the welcome ritual, but I felt they were much closer now, in accord, and because of this closeness they were ganging up on me. I'd bang on the window, call out, get the answering wave and step into that kind of atmosphere which has voices hanging in it. I had the feeling they'd been talking about me, something derogatory. There was an air of insincerity, no more than a hint, but painful, hurtful. I was sure I wasn't mistaken—I have a nose for such things—but how can you ever be sure? And I wanted to be wrong. I must have wanted to, because when the storm broke, before I felt the surge of exultation which always heralds a release of home truths for me, I remember being astounded by the antagonism between us. I couldn't believe my ears. The sound of my own voice horrified me.

23

THE DAY comes, a Sunday, when I have to write Aline a note, simply asking if I can call and see her. We have had the little innocent tea-party, no arrangements made on parting, but somehow there isn't any need. Already, at one bound, we have reached an understanding. She's a book lover, an art lover; apart from that I know little about her, likes or dislikes, why her marriage is on the rocks, if it is, or anything. She knows even less about me. Strangers! It is that wonderful lack of knowledge I find so attractive, exciting, someone utterly devoid of credentials, brimming with a past and you're ignorant of it, but it has brought them in slow stages to your door, or you to theirs. So either you take them on trust as they are, just exactly as you see and sense them, that instant, or you don't, you reject, dislike, recoil. Either a spark leaps across the gulf or you're left stranded and unchanged; simple as that. So the spark jumps, we're connected, the separate boats we've been sailing untouched and so woebegone swirl together all at once with a life of their own. I descend behind her to the street, reach for the Yale lock and open it, swing back the door proudly, a master of life, like opening a casket, then move aside chaste as a priest with my head ducked while she passes through and out. And before the door closes we have exchanged rapt smiles and glances of absolute quiet willingness in the surge of the street.

'Can you come this Thursday afternoon, around three?' she writes by return. 'If you can, don't bother to reply—I'll expect you!'

Thursday's a work day but that's easy, I'll just be missing. I walk around at the depot with the measured policeman tread I've developed for killing time, spinning out the afternoon rambles, every so often pulling out the tiny note to read it again, though I'd committed it to heart hours ago. Afterwards I think how fateful are these first written words of hers, but taken in sequence it has the inevitability which things happening naturally always have, and you aren't in the least surprised or even impressed, it strikes you as being right; the only thing possible. We have arranged it all before, wordlessly, on the doorstep that evening. If the reply hadn't come —never mind the hosts of possibilities, the snags, chances of illness, sudden callers, acts of God, accidents, house on fire— that would have been incredible. It has to come.

I don't know how many unknown doors I've knocked on since I've been in this city. Lost count: all that matters, I say to myself, is that they've been leading me to this one—and the fits and starts of friendships have been priming me for this one desire. That's how it seems as the bus snores up and I read the words over the cabin, University Boulevard, climb in and ask for Queen Street, and now I do quiver like the bus window in my guts with fateful flutters, getting nearer, the engine driving me forward with the same grim grinding relentlessness it uses for delivering me at the gates of factories, offices; my heart pounds and goes sick and I think, Christ, is it all one process, isn't there any escape? Do all roads lead to the black rubber-tyred slugs carting you off to the cemetery, same deathly chugging beat, same blankly cunning attendants disguised as passengers? I glare, queerly scared, at the conductor wading up the gangway vague and unquestioning as a child. Jump off at Queen Street and begin to feel better at once, making my own way at my own pace to my own chosen destination, uncharted. With each step I shake free of the rigid engine-paced system, my trepidation is more human and natural, normal human-sized fears I can at least cope with. What does she think of me? Does she like me or have I imagined it, am I dreaming? Following the directions in her note I push on past the blackened brick terraces, dumpy and flush to the street. In the country they'd have been called cottages, straggling out and the dark hedges and flat fields starting: here they are all stuck together in a long dingy chain under one black slate roof, every now and then a sweet shop, newsagent, murky greengrocer's window no bigger than a house window, the sill mouldy with damp, falling to bits. Inside, skips of carrots, heaps of weary-looking cabbages, flopping cauliflowers, a woman standing at the counter with big forearms folded belligerently, pallid legs in ugly knots of varicose veins. I go by and she stops talking to the shopkeeper and takes note of me, granite-faced, arms knotted in a tight brawl over the frilly flowered pinafore. I can see a level crossing ahead and the hump of a brick bridge, then a great flat desert of ash and lorry ruts and rusty railway tracks running up to the beetling black fort of the power station plumed with white steam. I'm on the right road: march on grey and gritty inside, hanging on to meagre shreds of ragged belief in myself.

The disused, bomb-blasted look of the streets, the shattered landscape dominated by the power station block and its grid towers spanning the mounds of rubble, littered iron, battered car wrecks rusted out, gaping with jagged wounds all over, the smoking pits and black blotches of water, sinister as acid—my spirits sink at the sight of it and I have to stop myself running. What a plague-infested country. Like a fugitive I slink round the corner, the Godforsaken view mercifully blotted out and this is it, Chapel Terrace, a cleaner straggle of reddish brick houses, broken by an open space halfway down sprouting weedy coarse grass and defiant bushes, with unkempt branches snapped off by kids who have worn paths across the patch of green like cattle tracks, left a litter of toffee wrappers, ice cream papers, lollipop sticks.

Her house is next to this playground, a gate at the side into the back yard, since it's accessible, and the back entry to the rest of the terrace comes out here, the cindery mouth of it behind some bushes. No answer at the front, and I spot a face squinting down at me from the bedroom window of next door, over the entry arch. Being spied on unnerves me, so I decide I'll try the back way.

Before I can move, the door flies open.

'I was in the kitchen,' she says, glowingly beautiful in her summer dress, iridescent peacock colours, a scooped-out simple neck baring her throat, the skin faintly tawny from the summer sun on her throat and fresh cheeks and ripe round arms. In I tread, already bemused by her rich female gleam and glow, and this is the front room, her sanctuary as she tells me later. No hallway, opening straight on the street.

'All the houses in the street are like this, nothing between you and the pavement,' she explains, too happy to be bitter. 'I'm used to it, I don't care now. I hated it though at first.'

'Where I lived as a boy was like this, just the same,' I said quickly.

'Really?'

'Except for the contents—the decor.'

'Ah.'

And she glances round with pride, nodding, while I try again to take it all in, confused by this amazing room and the shock of coming into it from outside, the inferno view round the corner, one course of bricks keeping it at bay. It's late September. In cities I'm hardly aware of seasons, only time and temperatures, hot or cold, and whether it's raining or not: but this woman is. Because she is so aware, and I am her guest, I partake of her awareness. She is in touch with nature through the parks, her excursions, trips to the sea—within the last few weeks she's been to Skegness, to Ingolmells, and she speaks longingly of it and the cruel deprivation she feels in the city. Yet it is her city, she has favourite spots, Friar Lane, the Arboretum, the Forest, the Ropewalk, the limes of Wollaton: with her associations and her receptivity she gets

more out of it than I ever could. And October, autumn—
we're nearly there—is her favourite time, when the trees
flame and the berries burn. 'What trees?' I want to say,
ashamed, I feel exactly like a blind man, listening willingly
but not intently, hearing the song she sings rather than the
names, details of things.

The walls in the small jewel-box of a room are intense flat
white, the skirtings and doors and window wood matt black;
there's a long low studio couch in tasteful sooty grey, with
other quiet touches of grey in hangings, cushions, bookshelves. Dove grey, silver stone. In a corner a standard lamp,
heavy gold encrusted carvings on the pillar and big balancing
lilac shade, the woman shimmering against the grey in her
bold peacock colours.

Over the fireplace, in narrow gilt frames, two paintings:
they are fantasies of decay and death in woods livid with
tree trunks, clusters of spongy fungus, crimson and bitter
yellow, nets of cobwebs hanging, festooning everything.
They are rivers of dissolution. Then I notice a curious thing:
the two pictures are complementary, the serpent writhe of
them is like one circuit, it runs from wall to wall. Yes, they
are her work but she's too modest to call herself an artist. So
is her room her creation, and telling me in the low unsure
melancholy voice she uses for involved explanations, her
exuberant body such a contradiction, I can only think audaciously that she needs reassurance, I would love to reassure
her. She is lost in spite of herself.

'They're a bit mad,' she says of the pictures, laughing, her
eyes flaring in a kind of astonishment at herself, as if the things
she does are always surprising her. Her delicately sensual lips
smile at her own impulsiveness.

'There's mad and mad,' I murmur incoherently, inner eye
still haunted by the vision of rape and pollution, clanking
chains, the iron and sulphur progress-stink, presided over
by that smoking fortress of power and its louring sky.

'Oh yes,' she says at once, warmly, gratefully.

I have the feeling she is replying to something personal I've said with my voice—by the sound, quite apart from the words.

She has a small cheery fire snapping—'It gets so damp in here'—and we consider the merits of the bluish tiled fireplace. 'I loathe the thing. If it was left to me I'd have it ripped out. A friend said he could build us a beauty, by hand, a stone one, but the landlord won't let us. Stupid man.'

I stand nodding foolishly in sympathy, saying at least it's bluish grey, not bad in the scheme of her room, thinking simultaneously that she said 'us'. Is she still living with her husband—was Marion right?

And I'm aware that although she is probably my age or only a year or two older, she is compared to me so poised, mature, dynamic in her body. Whenever she speaks I can hear the morbid sighing of her loneliness, the buried life that mourns in her, the bleakly sensitive mouth that her records unfreeze momentarily. These unshed tears are so poignant, they break something in me. But her melancholy is also sensuous, it slides dangerously like a snake, suave, self-destructive, or it can tread delicate and fluting and exquisite like a rain in the heart. She's a Debussy lover.

My laugh brightens her, joins forces with the lapping fire.

'I'm so glad you came,' she says.

'So am I.'

'Let me take your raincoat. We'll have something to drink soon. What would you like?'

'I don't mind. Anything liquid.'

She laughs.

'Aren't you easy to please!'

'Very.'

She is looking at me so steadfastly I have to lower my eyes.

'I forgot to offer you a cigarette—do you smoke?' she says.

And I shake my head.

'I do. Too many.'

'It's a matter of what you like.'

'Or can't help.'

She likes to express herself in innuendoes, but this doesn't satisfy for long. Sooner or later she has to be direct. She wants immediate answers. That's what her way of looking tells me.

'Come and look at these . . . but I'm afraid of boring you.'

'You won't do that.'

Out come her treasures for my eyes, and this is more than appreciation, I am being offered a whole interior life on trust. I don't know what to say: it's like one of her beautiful Japanese silk scroll paintings, you unroll it slowly, open little by little a world of ephemeral bamboo groves, a mere brushed-on suggestion of slender stalks, flicks and tints to convey the dry scratchy papery stems and leaves, swimming in a pale mist of moonlight at the side of the road; among the milky meadows parting stalks with their noses are the blurry foxes' heads, more and more distinct as the scroll unfolds. Bristling and still, pointed touches of ears and smudged skulls in the moonstruck bamboo groves like soft thistles everywhere: a crop of foxes.

Now at last I can contribute, air my knowledge. I gabble away about Hokusai, his life, the old man mad about drawing who lived with his daughter in absolute filth, had over ninety different addresses because each time the squalor overwhelmed them he simply moved, rented another hut. Utterly indifferent to money, he'd be paid for his prolific work and leave the packets of money scattered over his table. Tradesmen howling in with unpaid bills would be handed one of the packets: if they came back still complaining they'd be given an extra one. All he wanted was to be left in peace, if you could call it that, thousands of things clamouring in his eye to be drawn. I suddenly dry up, feel absurd.

'Go on,' she urges. 'Sounds fascinating.'

'That's all . . . I don't know any more.'

She is tearing open a fresh packet of cigarettes, Gauloises.

'You seem to know about painters.'

'No, not really.'

'Have you ever done any yourself?'

'I've tried, but I can't express myself properly.'

I look at her, overcome by an acute sensation of my clumsiness and ineptitude, my reddish hot hands, awkward stance. The fixed, porcelain beauty of her room confounds me, I swell red-hot, bubbling with a fierce lava of things I want to do, say. The room won't let me, disposing its elegant objects in a bland ripple of pride. The fire snaps, sends swift puffs up the chimney. I stand on the turkey carpet, glance down at my clumsy shoes, Aline in a deep chair by the bookshelves, drawing out a sumptuous art book with her slim connoissuer fingers.

She opens the pages, the heavy book sags over her thighs, I bend lower to bask in the alluring spread of a Van Gogh sunbaked land, smallholdings, woven fences, red carts with the shafts pointing into the sky. She is speaking and her voice breaks, a cry like a moan breaks from her; in awful clutching love we reach out and find each other, reaching across the fathomless gulf between strangers, her arm pulls me down wildly to her mouth and I drown there in the melting softness of her, tasting her sweet softness, filling my mouth with her hot breath, her frenzy, then the billowing soft sea of her body, warm and luscious and willing as it rises to her mouth and I taste it, my hand stroking down her side and over her thighs of its own accord.

Somehow she has got rid of the book in a sliding urgent movement. I take its place on her lap, we rock together in soft eruptions, closer and closer, rocking into each other as if we don't know what else to do, hugging ever tighter and closer with shuddering bear-hug convulsions. Literally I think I'm trying to frantically press myself through her skin to her heart, I want her heart beating inside me. How could I have ever been alone, how can I ever be alone again? In a sudden comical lull we draw back a fraction and become aware of our childish postures and it's alright, we rest on a pillow of peace and slow lust rising and the ripening concern of bodies, even our laughter sinks away, juicy and thick on our tongues, our eyes glossy and large with desire.

'Come down here,' she whispers, slips from the chair and we take to the carpet noiselessly like conspirators.

'Draw the curtains,' she tells me.

I jump up and make a false dusk, a dim dusty light. We roll into each other innocently for a moment, like campers, then freeze and lie still as stones, letting the firelight lap us, footsteps clumping by a few feet from us on the pavement outside.

'I thought they were walking straight in,' I mutter thickly.

At first she doesn't answer; she has her eyes closed, she is intent on her body's sensations.

'Yes, it sounds like that,' comes her voice, far off.

My heart beats in my throat, my tongue.

'You want me,' I whisper, iron-hard against her, prodding at her with a force that is totally beyond me, that surges up from the ground, from the centre of the earth, molten from the fire. It can split rocks, I feel, trembling, she'll be split in two, and to calm her I stroke her hair again and again, my mouth buried in her throat. I want to scald her, tear into her, and I long to comfort and heal, my chest aches with the intensity of my tenderness for her.

She clings to me powerfully; I go drowning down in her open flesh.

'Don't go away.'

She takes hold of me, opens her thighs, gives in and I swoop to and fro in a dream of unison with her, this unutterably soft bursten stranger wrapping me almost calmly, nursing me along comfortably in her big blossomy thighs.

468

We're weightless, the magic carpet wafts us clear out of the street.

'Darling,' she croons.

I want to laugh or giggle; it's so easy, life! Then the power begins to surge and take me, I lord it, I hear her hiss through her teeth and she bucks me, I go bearing down cruelly, burying the full shaft in her to the hilt. 'Farther in, I want it farther in,' she moans. That's what she wants, she snatches greedily, gobbling, she'd like to swallow me, balls and all, boots and all—for an instant I feel revulsion, I seem to hate her. Then her cries come, so pitiful, I am riven to the centre of my being, all my love comes spilling out in abandon for her.

'Take it!'

We lie on the shore of our passion, naked and shattered. The street still there, still outside, after all. The world eddying, circling; different. A sadness creeps over me for others, the loveless on the earth. I have sorrow for all kinds of poor devils; the sheer darkness of the planet oppresses me.

'Tell me what you're thinking,' she whispers, after what seems a very long time.

She is seeking reassurance, I think dimly.

'Thinking?' I echo.

It is a way of not answering. I begrudge having to speak, the crudity of it daunts me after the eloquence of the language of touch. I lag behind, regretful, I want to hibernate.

'You say so little,' she says softly, gently pleading.

Later she will say the same thing fiercely, challenging me to declare myself. But I have nothing to declare, can't understand her need. Being unfledged I think it's sufficient to be just blithely there. Words like 'Love', phrases like 'I love you' stick in my throat, I'll do anything to avoid saying them aloud.

'Do I?' I say, heart sinking.

The accusation has been made before, often, though admittedly in different circumstances. But it's the kind of remark that's liable to make me clam up completely. How do I explain that for me words are used, soiled, I grope in the void inside myself for words fresh and tender enough, and get lost. I want words that are like smells, where there can't be any mistake, like the smell of washed hair, the smell of newly-ironed clothes, the aroma of apples, pears, the swift wafting smell of flowers on the night air.

'Don't you like me?' she asks in a small timorous voice that's not really hers: I can't recognise her. She is at the mercy of her insecurity.

'No,' I say.

'I'm serious.'

'What a question!' I laugh, stupidly unaware of the danger I'm running.

I put my arms round her more tightly, hold her close, the fire gives a sudden sharp crack, a bit of coal exploding, and she jumps nervously; delightful. The slow hissing of the flames, the settling, shifting coals, sifting ash, we lie like babes in the wood listening. It's as if I've never really heard these sounds before: they've become part of our sensual happiness.

'Tell me about other women you've had.'

It sounds too ridiculous for words, I get a leering man-of-the-world picture of myself and I laugh. 'Had?'

'Well, you know . . .'

'No, I don't. Tell me.'

'I mean . . . made love to like this.'

'What makes you think there've been any?' I say, teasing gently, inwardly surprised and flattered. I begin to feel absurdly pleased with myself.

'Because you know what a woman likes. You know how to please a woman.'

'Oh.'

And her low appraising voice sends a shiver through me; like a hand curling round my balls. I begin to want her again.

'Won't you tell me who else?' she pleads pathetically.

'Let me think,' I say, laughing, enjoying myself.

Tempting, I think, to swagger out a story that sounds big, my path littered with abandoned wilting flowers: then it occurs to me that she's saying it to flatter, put confidence in me. Surely she can tell by my eagerness what a novice I am? As if to prove it, I do another perfectly naïve thing, trot out for her ears the whole story of Leila and what went wrong, why it could never have come right.

'Yes,' she murmurs from time to time, listening.

She listens with her wide clear eyes steady on my face, nodding and murmuring with perfect understanding, her longish, wide-apart breasts naked and vulnerable. A woman with bare breasts looks so defenceless, so at the mercy of a man. I finish, trail off into silence and she takes up another tale of frustration, an experience of her own, joining it to mine by way of illustration, as if it belonged there. These things are cyclical, she seems to be saying; I don't quite understand but her voice soothes and smoothes beautifully, even when she is describing pain and misery. I feel blissful, lulled on the sea of it. What I thought were bitter wounds begin to glow like medals.

Not a word though about her husband. I don't ask her, it doesn't seem to matter. Instead she says, 'I'll make you something to eat—something tasty!'

She jumps up and dresses quickly while I watch smiling, in the grey-toned room.

'Don't look, please,' she begs. 'Hide your eyes.'

'I want to look.'

'Well, don't.'

I study the fire, the slow smoke. The paintings.

'Now you can look.'

We both laugh.

'Dressing is a secret rite with me.'

'Why not?'

She looks at me, clothed, more sure of herself.

'What are you smiling at?' she asks.

'Just thoughts.'

'Tell me.'

'Oh . . .' I let it out slowly, in a long sigh of pleasure. 'Just that it's so barmy, so pathetic the way people go on, that's all.'

'Is it?'

'Don't you think so? I mean, everybody bunged up, constipated with problems, worries, anxieties . . . and there aren't any really, are there?'

'Not really,' she says, standing over me, shining. She doesn't agree or disagree, her smile is infinitely indulging.

'There bloody aren't any,' I repeat softly. The simplicity and naturalness of things suddenly comes home to me, astounding. What are we all struggling for, what are we bashing our brains out for, working and striving, trying to accumulate, to reach? It's here.

I stand before her, dressed, hands on her hips. She holds my waist lightly, there's a space between us.

'My ballerina,' she says, playfully. 'Sugar plum fairy.'

'With a wand.'

'Oh yes!' She becomes serious; she asks me calmly, her eyes full on me, 'You do like me, don't you?'

She doesn't flinch, she's hardened herself for the truth and intends to have it: she won't be put off. No compliments.

Arms around her, I say urgently, 'Can't you tell?'

She doesn't answer.

'Can't you?'

'I suppose I'm afraid of being hurt,' she said, with the faintest quiver of tears in her voice, 'I know it sounds silly . . .' and my nerves respond, shivering.

'No, no it doesn't.'

'I don't trust people very much. It's a bad habit of mine.

While I'm with them I do, then as soon as I'm alone again I start to doubt. That's horrible, isn't it?'

'I can understand it.'

'Can you?'

'You can trust me.'

'Yes, I think I can. I can't believe it, my trusting you.'

'Can't you?'

'I hope I don't stop trusting you when you've gone.'

'You won't. Anyway, I'm not going far. I can't, not now.'

'Oh I hope not. I want to love you terribly.' And she is clinging to me, kissing me. My heart breaks with love for her. It is going to be difficult after all, because of everything else. Painful, fighting in the teeth of all that's gone before. Of how things are.

I follow her into the narrow dark scullery, hovering near while she busies herself at the ugly blue-grey cooker, lighting the gas jets, working deftly, the blue rings of flame burning. Out through the narrow panes over the sink I can see the yard at the back, sunken, ground rising steeply behind, a shaggy bush on the handbreadth of waste ground to the side showing its head over the blackened run of brick wall. Path of bricks, sunk and broken, down to the dustbin, alongside the outdoor lavatory with its peeling green door, heavy downpipe painted the same standard green swelling down from the roof.

'Lovely view, isn't it?' comes her voice gaily, amused by my concentration. She detests her little prison-yard outlook, it sums up her isolation: she tells me this later. Now the ugliness can be skimmed off, skated over with child's eyes. Nothing penetrates the gaiety, the shabby world is created for pleasure.

'When I was a kid, there was a yard like this at the back,' I say. 'I was just trying to picture it. There must be thousands of backyards like this, all the same, yet every one different.'

'Now for some food,' she says, concentrating, scooping into her sizzling frying pan.

'Smells good.'

'Would you like to go in to the table?' she asks, oddly formal, and when I move to obey I take awkward steps. Sitting facing, plates before us, we're relaxed and happy again. I slice gratefully at the mushroom omelette, lightly cooked, browned on the outside. Lifting the cup of weak tea my hand shakes slightly, so I hold the cup cradled in both hands. I'm decrepit, I think, my excesses have aged me.

'Any good?' she says dubiously, watching me with the omelette.

'Good, very good. You're an expert.'

'You're distracting when I'm cooking. I want to look at you.'

'I'm a good influence.'

Her eyes narrow with laughter, and she contemplates, considers. 'Oh I hope so,' she says quietly.

24

NOVEMBER, gutters choked with gold leaves, red bonfires of leaves in the Arboretum: the autumn won't come to an end. I meet her outside the library, here she comes striding vigorously, pink-cheeked, opulent in furs; tucked under one arm her precious load of books, enough for a siege. Late November, winter sifting into the streets stealthily, in the night, under the cover of fog. Already there's been an icy flutter of sleet, like a chill brushing of wings.

She is comely in her shyness, offsetting this with the swinging arrogance of her walk.

'Now where?' I say.

We have a curious husband-and-wife familiarity. I seem to have known this woman all my life.

'Follow me!' she says brusquely, as a joke. But commands come natural to her. We hook hands and go off to the Arboretum, to inspect the Chinese ducks sailing the pond, near the cages where the peacocks live and the grotesque mina bird which makes human noises in a loud rasping voice when you least expect it. Then to a coffee shop just near the gates, a few yards from the convent school where she went as a girl.

'Are you angry?'

She shakes her head, she won't answer.

For half an hour we're the only customers: I can't believe it's a Saturday morning. At the small unsteady table she smokes Turkish cigarettes, grinding out the stubs in the ashtray obsessively, avoiding my eyes. Something is on her mind, I know the signs.

I am shut out, part of the tawdry everydayness.

'What's wrong?'

'Nothing at all,' she says in a bleak little voice. Usual answer. Lips thin with concentration, smiling unhappily at her own predicament. She sits back in a corner, a spider's stillness about her: a web of thoughts growing between her and me. I can't reach her, want to lash out at an enemy, I sit watching her bitter twisting movements as she grinds and grinds at her cigarette stub. I fight down an impulse to grab her wrist. She is pale, set, she knows she is being perverse. That's what her smile means. She torments me, but herself more. I clamp my teeth together, feel part of the city death, the hate simmering below the surface, I imagine cities with the lids torn off, bubbling with hatred underneath. The electric, grinding world bulges in, it's inside our blood. I want to spill blood, taste it. My eyes glare in my head, I feel yellow with venom.

She is smiling more naturally now, though still terribly tense.

'Don't worry,' she says, a little mockingly. 'I'm in a funny mood, that's all. I'm not nice today. It's nothing, really.'

She has changed, glazed and protected herself, moved away and hardened. She hides in a corner, smiling at me from a distance.

It comes out later that she distrusts me again, for no reason, nothing I've done. Afterwards she feels ashamed for doubting me. But I must say more, she tells me urgently, with real fear in her voice. I understand that my silences are making her suffer and it's a mystery to me why this should be. She has far too much pride to explain that she is plagued by an over-active imagination, undermined by a terrible insecurity. All she can bring herself to say is, 'Speak to me more often.'

Which brings her to Francis, her husband, a good, kind man horribly bound up in himself; a handsome, resourceful man whose only trouble is his Englishman's complaint. He'd rather fight a fire, enter a lion's cage than show some emotion in front of her, let alone talk about what goes on inside himself. If she makes any move that is likely to demand some emotional response he stiffens visibly: you can almost see him recoil, as if from something disgusting. He works at a firm manufacturing industrial chemicals, the new experimental wing out past the university—a great glass and concrete block, recently built and opened. She loves him but what can she do; their chronic lack of communication is killing the marriage. She blames herself as much as him.

'We're better apart,' she ends grimly. 'I feel I've got nobody, but he doesn't understand what I mean. I only make him unhappy, wanting him to be something he's not. That's it, really—he can't change. He'll never be any different.'

'Don't you see each other at all?'

'Oh yes, now and then. He doesn't want me to leave him, but I shall.'

'When do you meet?'

'At his mother's, every Sunday.'

'That must be jolly.'

'Don't be funny.'

'Well, I can imagine.'

'As a matter of fact, it's not that bad. Except that his mother blames me.'

'Naturally.'

'She doesn't say so. She doesn't need to.'

'Mothers don't, do they?'

And she laughs. Her sad laugh goes through me: all the forlornness of her predicament is in it.

'We seem to know about mothers,' she says.

477

25

'WHAT ARE you doing?' she said, stopping where she was on the other side of the room, half undressed, suspender belt dangling and her hands behind her back, high up, breasts pushed out as she undid the fastener of her bra.

'What d'you mean?' I said. I lay on the bed, watching.

'Nothing,' she said, and smiled her cat's smile.

I put my hands behind my head and lay there: I felt like yawning, but not my mouth; it was coming up from my knees, my legs, I opened my legs like a woman and the long yawn of desire came up from there, snaking through my blood lazily, circling up through my bones. I lay indolent and waiting with this weird endless yawn coiling through me. It was delicious, the soft moving lust. There was heat and grace and there was corruption in it, the flesh on my bones yielding as if it wanted to die.

'Don't watch me,' she said.

'Why not?'

'Don't, that's all,' she said sharply. 'You know I hate being looked at when I'm undressing.'

I closed my eyes, sighed, scratched my head. 'That's daft.'

'Never mind. Stop peeping.'

She came nearer, near enough and I pounced—'yaaarh!'—got her round her waist and bore down, toppling her on the bed. She gasped, laughed, starry and flushed. 'I knew, I knew you were going to do that.'

'When?'

'Oh, five minutes ago.'

'How did you?'

'I always do, it's just the way you start looking at me. I always know, I tell you.'

'I don't believe it,' I said softly, hoarsely, unwilling to grant her the knowledge of her power, though she had it and knew it and it was ridiculous to deny. Still, to say so aloud seemed too much, somehow it stuck in the throat. I held her and did nothing, moving my lips on her throat to speak, and without moving a muscle she absorbed me, my words, her enveloping softness drew me in.

'I can tell,' she said.

'No.'

'Yes. You have a peculiar expression on your face.'

Suddenly she clamped her legs together and caught me tight down there, like a naughty boy with his stick trapped. She kissed my mouth hard and her teeth bit down savagely on my bottom lip. Surprised, shocked by the pain I cried out into her mouth, muffled.

'Sorry.' She let me go. I drew my head away, bitten lip throbbing.

'What was that for?' I hissed, bitterly angry for the moment at her treachery, the betrayal. I lay inert beside her and felt the desire that had been short-circuited begin to run back, undulating. I lay still listening to my blood, its sing-song. Was that what she wanted? Was she out to punish?

'I'm sorry, darling,' she murmured, contrite and small-sounding.

'I don't get it,' I said sulkily, touching my bruised lip, wanting to draw out her remorse, force her into real guilt. I sucked in my breath between my teeth. 'Christ, it hurts.'

'I said I was sorry,' she said, the touch of impatience stinging me.

'Well, Christ, you're not playing the game.'

'Aren't I?' she said in a curious voice, sounding perverse.

479

I stroked her side, the long side curving to her back, I cupped my hand to the curve and stroked down the long soft warmth to the subtle swell of the hip, slipping behind, over the roll of buttock to the crack and down, behind the thigh to the shy knee-fold. She lay coldly, not stirring. I kept stroking, stroking, struggling not to hate.

It was dark now in the room and we lay in the bottom of the darkness hopelessly, as if in a pit. Outside the window the world pressed up, snouted, ugly, we were a replica of it.

'Men always have it over on you,' she said in a sour little voice.

'What men?'

'All the lot of you.'

'I'm the only one here, talk about me. What d'you mean, men? I wasn't stamped out on a men machine.'

'You don't understand.'

'Don't I?'

'Let's be quiet.'

'What's making you unhappy? Tell me.'

'Let's not talk about it. I'll get angry if you cross-examine me. It's not your fault . . .'

I turned my back on her. It was no good, a despair crept through my flesh. My face sank in the pillow: I had nothing for her.

'Now what?' she said loudly.

'Ask yourself.'

'Listen, Colin . . .'

'I'm listening. When are you going to say something?'

She moved away, avoiding me.

'Don't you want to?' she said, hard.

Into the pillow I said, 'I feel buggered.'

She came back, a mass of softness, tenderness, against my back, the backs of my legs.

'I know I'm a bitch,' she said softly.

480

She made love to my back, to melt me. She was intrigued, her arm sneaked around my waist, the slenderness excited her: like holding a girl, she liked to tell me.

'Aren't you smooth!' she crooned.

Her hand detached itself from the embrace, brushed down to where I was shrunken, wrinkled. The roll of flesh didn't unfurl under her dexterous fingers: she lost heart, fluttered briefly to my nipples.

'What a shame,' she mused. She was thinking aloud.

'What is? What are you on about?'

'That you haven't got breasts.'

I turned over flat on my belly on the bed.

She was fondling me, I must have fallen asleep. I was on my back.

'I want you, I want you . . .'

Then from lying there utterly congealed and dead it was changed to heat, to valleys unfolding, flesh in soft oyster clefts, in sticky furrows, and I didn't question a thing, let her sudden mad passion send me rocking into her hole. I filled her up slowly, vengefully, sank in hard to the root, quivering like an axe cleaving a log. Hearing her groan I began to lose control and worked helplessly, carried further and further down in the awful longing to unite, to marry, to decay and die, annihilate myself, burst out of the skin of myself. The flurry of cries unleashed a new violence and in the same instant melted the centre of me ineffably—that hard tight-lipped being who confronts the world crumbled into bliss, into tears. I was crying. I was a naked threshing weeping boy, the sobs torn one by one out of my chest and it was in the open, it was such a relief to be naked, stripped of vanity, frail as a shell. I'd forgotten how marvellous it could be. I lay like something foundered and lost forever, smashed to bits in the night, but it wasn't so, I mended, just waited on the waves of her breathing, swelling shape which took delight in nursing me back to health, and it came back slowly, a

481

mysterious creeping stealth putting the heart back in my chest, the manhood between my legs, the clean bowels, strangest of all the wavering candle-flamey desire to live, very delicate and weak but there, smoking in my veins. And during all this time of strange mending she waited, endlessly patient and satisfied.

26

WE MAKE plans to leave. No prospects, we'll get on a train and go south, have a quick look round. I'll aim at Ray and Connie, make them my destination, they'll help us. I have a little money saved up. All I need to do is give a week's notice: Aline wants to pack a few personal things. The day draws near, we hardly refer to it. I write hurried notes to Ray, ask for copies of the local papers, to look for accommodation and some kind of job, but my heart's not in it, I'm merely going through the motions. The day of departure is all we live for, to cut free—and in a sense we're dreading it, for different reasons. She of course is fighting down her remorse in advance, also recurring waves of doubt concerning me, the strange young man she now has to trust. I'm an unknown quantity, and so quiet: what am I thinking, feeling? Why don't I say more? When she's with me she isn't sure of me, often she doubts me bitterly. Only when she goes away from me is she sure. Then she feels desperately abandoned, lost, she needs me.

I break the news to Lou: a hard thing to do because we've both turned out to be so secretive in our affairs. Living together has made him more furtive, elusive than ever. Most nights he disappears without a word, and when I come crawling to bed say at two in the morning, back from Aline, he's lying silent in bed, the other side of the room. Once though he wasn't asleep. I get undressed in the dark and climb between the sheets, aching all over, my nocturnal walks through the streets take me three-quarters of an hour and I have to be up at seven—and Lou mutters under the sheets lugubriously, 'You'll never live to be old, mate.'

Because he's such a bloody mystery and all that, I don't

see why I should bother to confide in him. But now I've got to. The chance comes one evening, we end up having a meal at the Silver Star, a restaurant off Parliament Street where we've been a few times, filling in till next day with egg and chips, beans on toast, big clonking stoneware cups of strong tea. Neither of us like strong tea in the flat, we drink it weak as piss, cup after cup, like Russians, but in the restaurant we just drink it as it comes, indifferent.

The bomb's dropped. No reaction. Has it gone off or not? Yes, he's heard alright.

'When you pushing off then?' he says vaguely, munching away. I can't believe he's so unaffected.

'Monday morning.'

He nods, then lifts his head with sudden decision. 'I'm having some more tea,' and he waves at the waitress.

Curious in spite of myself, I dig at him: 'Think it'll work?'

The waitress brings his tea, he pretends to be absorbed in her. He shrugs, spoons in his three sugars, stirs away with a clattering noise, vigorous, as if he's mixing a pot of paint.

'If you can cope with the complications,' he says.

'We'll cope,' I say stoutly, a bit untruthfully, no idea how or what, stiffened in defence against his jibing tone.

He lifts his head and asks bluntly, 'Is it what you want?' And I like him again, he's alright.

We eye each other, give and take, we're in touch for an instant.

'It is,' I say, with all the authority I can muster.

'Good, good,' he jibes lightly again. If he could talk through a yawn, that would convey his attitude exactly. 'Can't go wrong then, can you. Got to do it, haven't you.' He's not asking questions. 'Don't sit round asking people's opinions. What d'you want, approval? If you want to do a thing, then do it. Do it a hundred per cent. Don't arse about. Me, I'm going to drink this cup of tea. Okay?'

'Okay.' I laugh.

484

I like what he trots out, lean and flinty: all the same it's clear that basically he disapproves. He expresses himself too dogmatically, and that's not his style. He's angry. His idea of me has been knocked sideways all of a sudden. Well, I can't help that.

Two days before we set off I have a dream. Lou says laconically next morning, 'You were in a right state last night.'

'Daresay. Had a nightmare.'

Sitting in the train with her, the dream clings at the edge of my consciousness, hooks its claws into the wire of the cage and hangs there, weaker but clinging horribly. I can't touch it, can't kill it off, I have to wait for it to shrivel and die in my blood.

I am in a room I don't recognise, a dreary sitting-room at the back of a house somewhere, and there's a man in it, sitting lumpishly by the table. Blank, I sit at the other side of the room waiting for the man to speak, declare himself, but he doesn't seem able to see me.

It dawns on me that this is Francis. I've never set eyes on him before, have no idea what he looks like, but it's obviously him, sitting in a spotlessly white starched chemist's coat. He pulls a book from one of the white pockets, opens it meticulously at a marker, reaches in an inside breast pocket and brings out a pair of glasses. Sits reading primly, from time to time pushing his glasses back on his nose with the forefinger of his right hand. That's his only sign of life.

I bear witness to his every movement but he deliberately ignores my existence. I am being punished. I burn with shame, waiting to have my crime revealed to me. I find myself listening intently for his breathing, watching his chest for some movement. Nothing. Regular as clockwork his forefinger comes up to the bridge of his nose, touches his glasses. I wait for him to turn the page: then Aline enters the room.

The scene freezes. My heart beating, I sit watching while Francis stares at his wife. He fixes her with his eyes.

'Stop staring at me like that!' she bursts out irrationally.

He blinks nervously.

More calmly, she tells him, 'Take that silly coat off, for goodness sake—you're not at work now. I'll make you a cup of coffee.'

'I've had some, thank you,' Francis says, very stiff and comical. He puts his hand to his mouth, coughs discreetly, says in the same colourless voice, glaring blindly at her, 'in that café down by the market where we used to go, if we were shopping on Saturdays, remember?'

'Oh I don't know. Yes, I think so.'

'The old woman's still around, still there, hobbling in and out with those huge boots she wears. You know, the tramp. I didn't realise there were women tramps. Suppose there must be. Not much of a life, is it? Are they men's boots she wears, d'you think?'

'How should I know?' Aline almost shouts. She sounds on the brink of tears. She fears what he is going to say, to remember: I feel pain at her anxiety.

'Remember how she used to dress, that black shawl, and those great lace-up boots. My grandfather used to wear boots like that—when we were kids he took us with him to the cemetery, and he wore those kind of boots, with a loop hanging out at the back, to pull them on. They always remind me of cemeteries, boots like that, isn't it funny? That woman does . . .'

'I don't want to listen,' Aline says, almost imploring.

'Trudging along with her chin down on her chest—how could she see where she was going, d'you think?'

'I don't know!' Aline says, as if in pain. She holds her head.

'She used to drag an orange box over the pavement, on the end of a piece of rope. Bent right over, she'd be, dragging it, like those pictures of Chinese coolies on the banks of the Yangtse . . . Did she have her belongings in that box, would you say?'

486

'Oh shut up!' Aline yells, 'shut up, you damn fool, shut up!' And Francis closes his book with a snap, the noise resounds in the room like a gunshot. Aline looks very pale, drained, she wears no make-up. He stares into her face without speaking, ridiculously solemn, until I glance away in sheer embarrassment.

'I'd be grateful if you'd sit down a moment,' he says at last, his voice utterly flat.

Aline closes her eyes, then opens them.

'Why?' she says, surprised.

But she comes to the table obediently and sits facing him. Then comes a long pause of suspense. She waits with obvious nervousness, tensely expectant while he struggles blankly to speak.

'Go on then,' she says, gently now, her voice like a hand over his hair.

His face goes blank with inner effort, his throat working painfully. She gazes at him now with helpless pity, says, 'And take your coat off, you're at home now.'

Without glancing in my direction or raising his voice, he says, 'We can't talk with him there.'

'Talk about what?' Aline says. 'There's nothing to say.'

He refers to me in the third person: 'Can't he go somewhere else? I'll do something violent, I know I will, I can't stand the sight of him,' and his fists clench, he pleads with her like a child.

I choke to speak, heart pounding up into my mouth, I sit bound and gagged in the dream desperate to speak and can't force my jaws open. Aline puts her hands to her head in anguish, shouts madly, 'Leave me alone, I wish I'd never seen either of you!' and rushes out of the room.

For the first time Francis turns and looks at me, and speaking now with a queer shyness he says, in simple bewilderment, 'Where's she gone?'

I shake my head helplessly.

Forgetting myself, I go forward and sit in Aline's chair at the table, facing him: grip my hands together convulsively and lean closer, without any fear or animosity, to hear him whisper, 'Women take some understanding, don't they . . .'

The carriage rocked us, rushed us south faster and faster, the wheels howled joyfully over the points, we flew past the wayside halts and the whole land was in motion: cuttings rose and fell on either side of the train like brown waves. We dived into the sandstone hill, burrowed noisily in the dark, an onslaught of noise and fumes, hissing and hammering and frantic as though we were lost, emergency lights glowing weakly. We burst out against the sea and the light struck at us, the sky a faded December blue, lifeless above the seething thin shine of the salt water. The harsh smell came in at the window, the opera of gull cries lifted us clean out of our bodies. We smiled madly at each other, sea-mad glittering smiles pinned on our cheekbones. Nobody else in the compartment: we sat perched face to face, knees touching, holding hands, our faces reflections of each other.

Strange listening looks we have on our faces. I sit transfixed by hers and know mine is the same.

'Happy?' she says.

I nod dumbly, eloquent beyond words.

'Kiss me,' she says.

Kissing, my hand rests on her knee, slips between, caressing. She shuts her knees suddenly, tight as an oyster.

'I love you,' she says.

I kiss her, trembling, hoping she won't force me to speak. I don't want to say anything trite. Footsteps in the corridor, door slides.

'Ticket collector,' I tell her, tugging to get free.

'No!'

Just in time she lets go.

We hover along feebly at the edge of the sea, the water, light and air a free world of no dimensions. The train races with whirring dry wheels like a toy and gets nowhere. A soldier sways down the corridor, broad shoulders filling the space with coarse cloth.

Restored by the sea, the train plunges inland, lifting the fields and farms level with our heads. Now it has power, now it strides.

'Change at Newton Abbot,' says the ticket collector, a black bear of a man, confronting us. He backs out.

I pocket the punched tickets. 'What shall we change into?'

'Dragons,' she says.

We hold hands, the world of the sea releases us slowly, the train scents the town on the horizon, sends itself streaming into the curves. Hedges, fences, stone walls, the rubble of a high cutting stream past us. The world is flowing. The train masters us as it masters the landscape, includes us in its destiny. It can do it, it can do it, the wheels chant. Eyes of joy kindling, intoxicated, I lean forward into the adventure: anything is possible. My back is to the north but she faces it, blocked by me, my body. One day I'll wake up to the significance of that. Ray and Connie are ahead somewhere, not far, already living the new life with the odds against them.

December, end of the old year. The wheels abandon it: everything looks ready for a fresh start. You can smell change, something in the air. Green pastures scudding by, green, green. Sudden raspberry-red earth, Devon soil.

'There it is, look. Red.'

We sit like blades of sunlight, shining.

YOURS
Philip Callow

"It is Philip Callow's sensitivity, imagination and precision as a writer which makes the book a *succès d'estime*. . .a masterful refutation of the old cliché that only a woman can write about what it's like to be a woman"– Barry Cole, *New Statesman*

"Philip Callow writes of the underside of human experience, and of its hidden centre in the human heart"– Isabel Quigly, *Financial Times*

"The absolute veracity and the sheer interest this author manages to give to the stuff of mere ordinary living. . .his delicate and economical manner of writing. The prose is quite consciously poetic, yet never sentimental"–*Times Literary Supplement*

"Flowing spontaneously, throwing up vivid and illuminating phrases"– Elizabeth Berridge, *Daily Telegraph*

"Philip Callow at his best. . . . His style is lean and violent"– Dervla Murphy, *Irish Times*

"The writing is beautiful; muted, precise, poetic in the best sense of the word"– *Hibernia*

"He is one of the few contemporary novelists who after flowering at the first reading, bear fruit at the second"– Ray Gosling

THE WINNERS
Julio Cortázar

The winners of a mystery cruise in a special state lottery could not be more different. And not long after they have left the jubilant dockside café in Buenos Aires the tensions emerge. For, quarantined from a certain part of the ship, served by a silent and forbidding crew, and treated more like prisoners than winners, they split into two groups; those who want to know what's really going on, and those who prefer to let sleeping dogs lie. . . .

With this brilliant and entertaining novel – part surreal thriller, part political fable – the acclaimed Argentinian writer, Julio Cortázar (1916–84), made his international reputation.

"Anyone who doesn't read Cortázar is doomed. Not to read him is a grave invisible disease which in time can have terrible consequences. Something similar to a man who has never tasted peaches. He would quietly become sadder, noticeably paler, and probably, little by little, he would lose his hair" – **Pablo Neruda**

"No less than García Marquéz, Cortázar writes out of a cornu-copia of imagery, an outpouring and a richness of language that has become the signature of Latin American fiction" – *New York Times Book Review*

"Cortázar's ability to present common objects from strange perspectives, as if he had just invented them, makes him a writer whose work stimulates a rare sense of expectation" – *Time Magazine*

"One of the century's most gifted writers" – *The New York Review of Books*

THE DISENCHANTED
Budd Schulberg

The Disenchanted is a great American novel which captures both the dazzling spirit and the bitter disappointment of the pre-war decades.

It is the story of Manley Halliday, a fabulously successful writer of the 1920s, a golden figure in a golden age. Halliday had everything – physical beauty, artistic brilliance, success and wealth, and the love of a strikingly beautiful wife. But he squandered his strength and his talent in folly and extravagance, in perpetual parties and perpetual drinking, riding the crest of the golden wave until it crashed, leaving him a diabetic and an alcoholic, cast up on the inhospitable shores of Hollywood.

"*The Disenchanted* is based, not too closely, on what happened to the author of *The Great Gatsby* and *The Last Tycoon* . . . Schulberg has not yet told us about the last days of Scott Fitzgerald as seen from his own youthful angle, and it is doubtful if he ever will need to. The fictional end of Manley Halliday in *The Disenchanted* is too fine a myth to be unscrambled into what is known as historical truth . . . Halliday is a three-dimensional creation who will haunt the imagination of all who have the good fortune to be coming, for the first time, to this remarkable novel" – **Anthony Burgess**

THE PIER
Rayner Heppenstall

The Pier is the last major novel by "the master eccentric of English letters" – **C. P. Snow**

It is a murder story – unusual and literary – told by an elderly writer who lives in a small English seaside town where his private peace of mind is shattered by the arrival of new and noisy neighbours. As he drafts his latest book and nurses his aching teeth, he begins to formulate the plan for a new novel about someone much like himself who sets out to murder his neighbours. And as the noise mounts next door, and his fantasy plot begins to look better and better, so it becomes more and more appealing to turn his fiction into fact. . . .

Rayner Heppenstall died in 1981. He "made a notable contribution to the history of the modern novel in England" – *The Times*. He "is a writer who has given us so much that is beautiful, so much that is funny, so much that is true" – *Observer*. He "is as inquisitive as Anthony Powell, as odd as Firbank, as minute as Sterne" – *Times Literary Supplement*. He "has an eye so sharp that it dazzles and almost hurts" – *Guardian*.

THREE LONDON NOVELS
Colin MacInnes
Absolute Beginners, City of Spades and Mr Love and Justice

"London is the real hero of these books with its capacity to nurture and absorb all species of humanity, from bent coppers to bus conductors, delinquents to debs, bigots to libertines. None of MacInnes' characters, often comically drawn, could have existed elsewhere; and it's London that shapes (and as often as not thwarts) each of their schemes, large and small" – *New Musical Express*

"Insofar that they lift the lid from aspects of London that had hitherto been unobserved or undiscovered, they can stand comparison with Dickens or Zola. . . . Brilliantly written, eminently readable" – *Times Educational Supplement*

"Although written in the late '50s/ early '60s, all three books have quite enough charm and energy to leap the decades unaided by nostalgia" – *Time Out*

"Brilliant social documentation" – *The Times*

"Strongly individual novels" – *Sunday Times*

Colin MacInnes's three London Novels are available as individual volumes or together in *The Colin MacInnes Omnibus*

THE KATHARINE MOORE OMNIBUS

Katharine Moore's first novel, *Summer at the Haven*, was published on her 85th birthday and won the Authors' Club award for the most promising first novel of the year. She followed that remarkable debut with two more novels, *The Lotus House* and *Moving House*. They have earned her an enviable reputation with the critics and have been warmly welcomed by a wide range of readers – and are here collected together in one volume.

SUMMER AT THE HAVEN

"Mrs Gaskell wrote *Cranford* in her early forties. Without in any way imitating that shrewd and gentle minor classic, Katharine Moore has, at the surprising age of 85, published a first novel which can stand comparison" – *The Observer*

THE LOTUS HOUSE

"Poignant writing and perceptive insights into human nature abound in this heartwarming book. Its bittersweet, wholly credible conclusion will haunt readers" – *Los Angeles Times Book Review*

MOVING HOUSE

"*Moving House* presents a lyrical rather than elegiac portrait of English country life throughout the century" – *The Times*